HASHTAG: DANGER™

PANIC ON DINOSAUR MOUNTAIN!

TOM PEYER

CHRIS GIARRUSSO

RANDY ELLIOTT

ANDY TROY

ROB STEEN

AHOY
COMICS

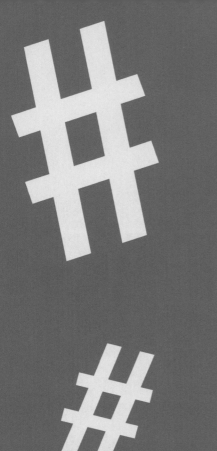

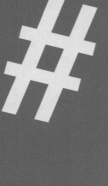

COMICSAHOY.COM

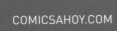

@ AHOYCOMICMAGS

HART SEELY - PUBLISHER
TOM PEYER - EDITOR-IN-CHIEF
FRANK CAMMUSO - CHIEF CREATIVE OFFICER
STUART MOORE - OPS
SARAH LITT - EDITOR-AT-LARGE

DAVID HYDE - PUBLICITY
DERON BENNETT - PRODUCTION COORDINATOR
KIT CAOAGAS - MARKETING ASSOCIATE
LILLIAN LASERSON - LEGAL
RUSSELL NATHERSON SR. - BUSINESS

HASHTAG: DANGER - PANIC ON DINOSAUR MOUNTAIN! Published by AHOY Comics LLC, 499 S. Warren St., Ste. 612, Syracuse, NY, 13202.

PRINTED IN THE U.S.A. FIRST PRINTING - NOVEMBER 2019 - ISBN: 978-0-9980442-6-2

HASHTAG: DANGER

PANIC ON DINOSAUR MOUNTAIN!

TOM PEYER	WRITER
CHRIS GIARRUSSO	ARTIST
RANDY ELLIOTT	ARTIST (MISSION 000006-000008)
ANDY TROY	COLOR (MISSION 000006-000008)
ROB STEEN	LETTERS (MISSION 000006-000008)
RICHARD WILLIAMS	COVER
TODD KLEIN	LOGO
JOHN J. HILL	DESIGN
DERON BENNETT	ASSISTANT EDITOR
TOM PEYER	EDITOR
CORY SEDLMEIER	COLLECTION EDITOR

CREATED BY **TOM PEYER** AND **CHRIS GIARRUSSO**

C O N T E N T S

HASHTAG: DANGER

HASHTAG: BACKSLASH!

Conventional wisdom says that you should 100% of the time judge a book by its cover. Far be it from me to disagree with "the popular opinion" and "those cool cats at Quotable Quotations," but I say you should judge a book by its foreword. And since this foreword is written by me, you know it's one badass bitch of a foreword and whatever book is lucky enough to have it is probably okay, too.

Just to be safe, if I were you, the unsuspecting reader, I'd read this foreword last. I'd recommend they put it in the back of the book but that would be confusing to the people who only bought this because they heard how good the foreword was. What's going to suck the readers in, if not this foreword? The story? Yeah, RIGHT.

Anyway, for a book this full of words and also art or whatever, I felt a mighty foreword was needed, and I went through several drafts of the opening sentence, each rejected (I've included my reasoning in a sort of "Foreworder's Commentary," you're welcome), and I thought you might enjoy reading them instead of a house ad for cranberry cigarettes.

REJECTED FIRST SENTENCES
TO THIS KICKASS FOREWORD

- THIS BOOK HAS WORDS AND PICTURES IN SEQUENCE
  Good, and factually correct. But need to dig DEEPER.

- I LAUGHED A LOT READING THIS BOOK
  True, but unrelated.

- THIS BOOK NEEDS A FOREWORD
  Too conundrum-y.

- DEPUTY DAWG IS A WHITE SUPREMICIST
  I'm just saying what we're all thinking.

- THE WRITING OF THIS BOOK IS REAL REAL GOOD AND WHATNOT.
  Too much spotlight taken away from the foreword? KEEP TRYING!

- *HASHTAG: DANGER* CURES GONORRHEA.
  Note to self: huge if true!

- ALSO THE ART IS CHARMING AND FUNNY.
  Note to self: Imagine a book that's all foreword! Oh, faptasmic day!

- GOOD LORD BUT I HAVE A FULL, LUSTROUS HEAD OF HAIR.
  Unrelated, but true. Give the people what they want.

- *HASHTAG: DANGER* IS MY NEW FAVORITE BOOK.
  It really is, though. Hashtag: It's dope.

Just as with any garden variety groin injury, eventually the fun stops and you have to get down to business. So here's my theory about *HASHTAG: DANGER*:

I think it's a Bizarro World Comic.

Hear me out.

Remember that comic where Batman was constipated and fought that serial killer who bit the heads off baby carolers at Christmas? What do you mean, "that's all of them?" You can keep your goddam bat-bashing to yourself.

The point is, most comics are grim. They have a fun factor of negative zero zero zero point five decimal zero machete to the face point one.

But in THIS book, whose name I forget, they seem to have gotten the formula exactly backwards. Or is that Zatanna? Damn you, Silver Age weirdo bastards. Talk normal, like Americans!

First, it's a fun set-up. It's like *Challengers of the Unknown* written for people who were born AFTER the dinosaurs died out. By issue somewhere around page one, I was hooked in. I love the characters, who are sometimes almost good people by accident, somehow. Like the best worst people you want to hang with.

Second, I've been a Tom Peyer fan for a long time, I was a fan even after that scandal with the nuns, and have always defended him (in public; in private, GROSS, TOM). I love how he fuses traditional adventure stories with often radical addition of the visual vocabulary and tactics of the best editorial cartoons. Each story is a joyful little nugget, complete in itself but part of a larger hole. I meant "whole." It'd be weird being part of a larger hole. Anyway, Tom Peyer is definitely part of a larger hole.

And the art is perfect. It's got the charisma of Jughead and the smarts of Jughead the Dracula or whatever thing they're doing with Jughead right now. I love the commitment to the bit, the entire Andy Kaufman-esque move of giving the sublime and the ridiculous the exact same level of verisimilitude. Chris Giarrusso is a wizard and I'm stealing him the first chance I get. EAT IT, AHOY.

Anyway, *HASHDUMP: DANISH* (or whatever, I don't "see" logos) is a great book and now you're looking at it, Mr. or Ms. Fancypants.

Gail Simone
September 2019

P.S. GODDAMN, this is a great foreword!

Gail Simone has written some things and some stuff that has sold bunches of copies. People like her work lots, but they seem to like Birds of Prey, Wonder Woman, Batgirl *and* Red Sonja *mostest.*

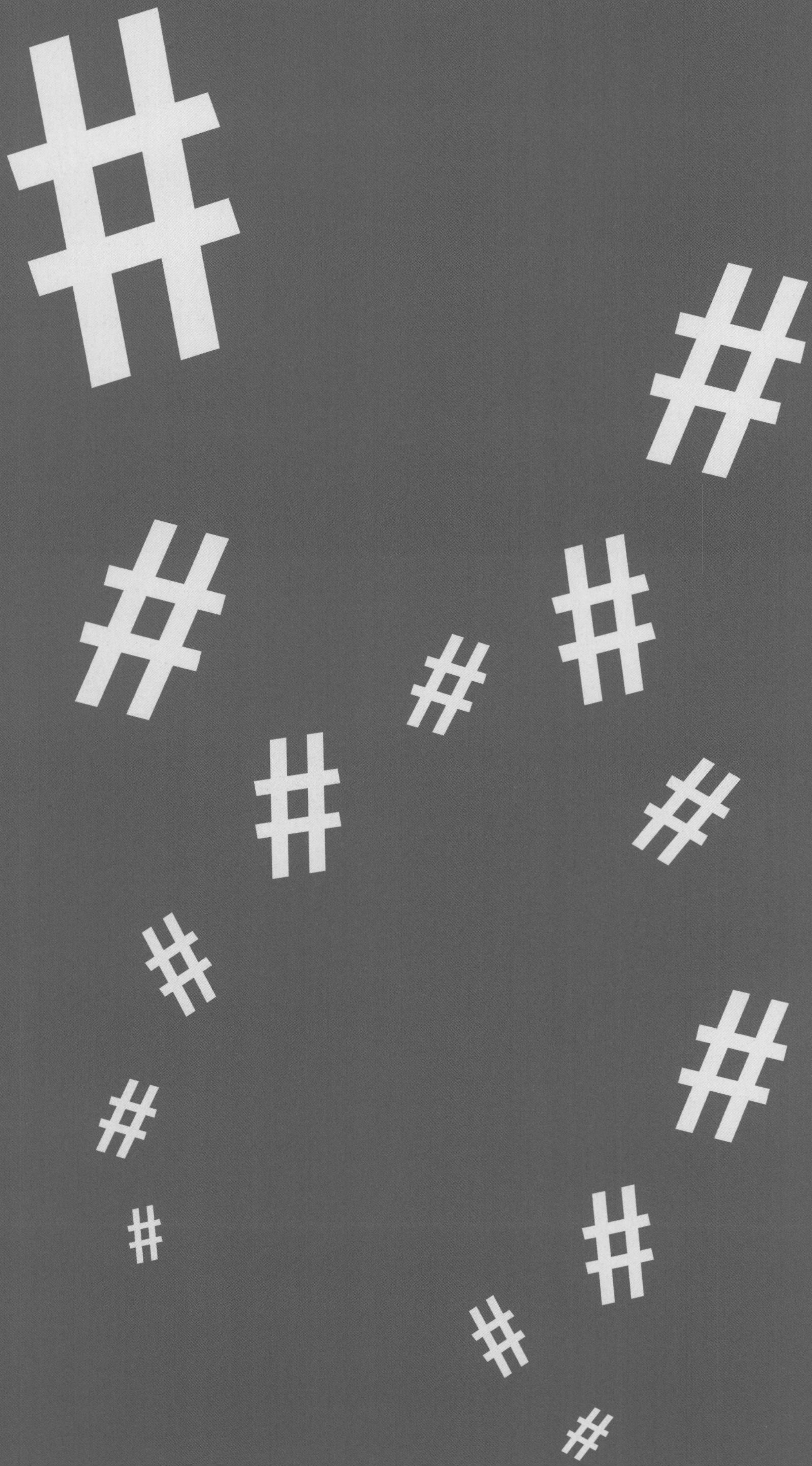

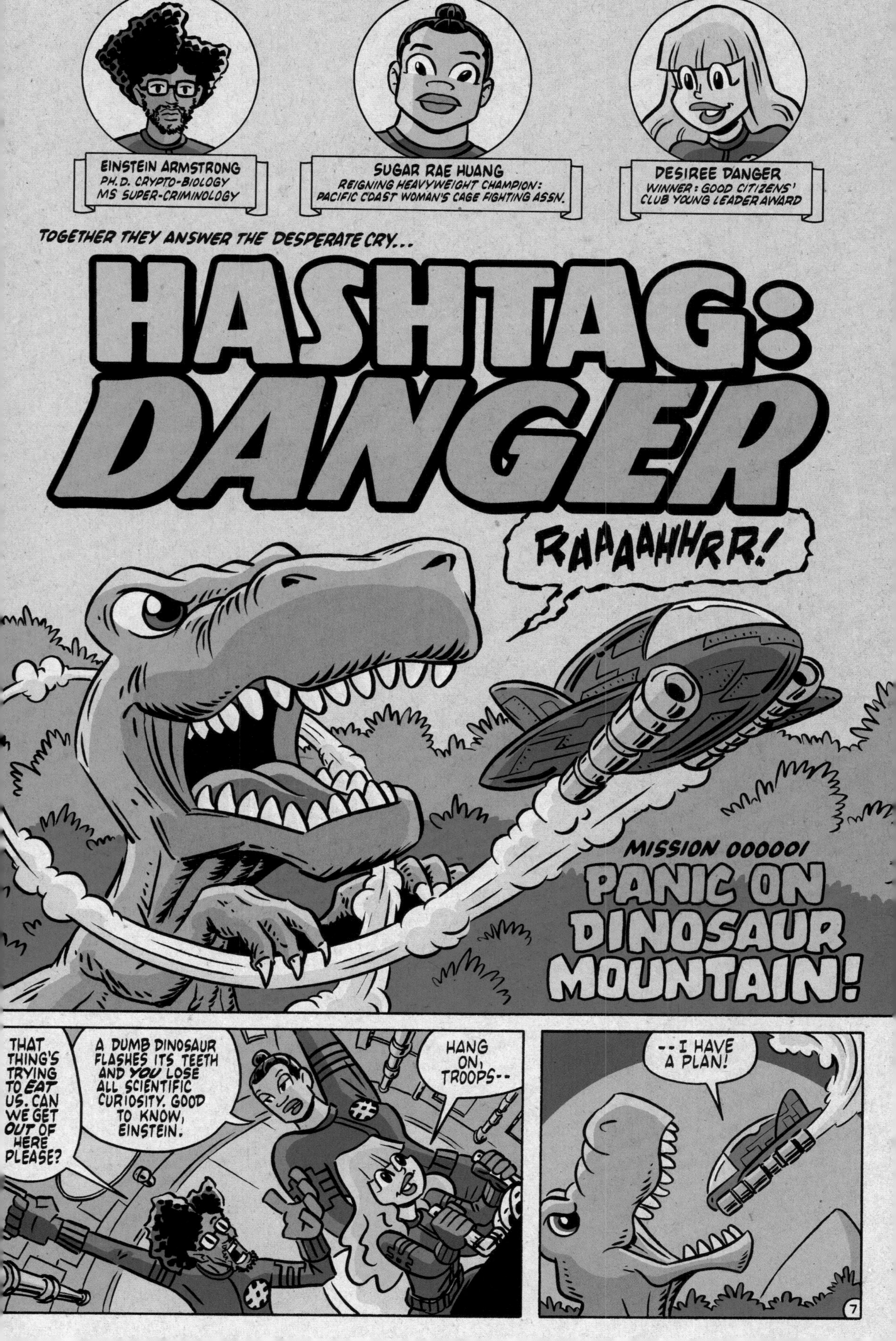
EINSTEIN ARMSTRONG
PH.D. CRYPTO-BIOLOGY
MS SUPER-CRIMINOLOGY
SUGAR RAE HUANG
REIGNING HEAVYWEIGHT CHAMPION:
PACIFIC COAST WOMAN'S CAGE FIGHTING ASSN.
DESIREE DANGER
WINNER: GOOD CITIZENS' CLUB YOUNG LEADER AWARD
TOGETHER THEY ANSWER THE DESPERATE CRY...
HASHTAG: DANGER
RAAAAHHRR!
MISSION 000001
PANIC ON DINOSAUR MOUNTAIN!
THAT THING'S TRYING TO EAT US. CAN WE GET OUT OF HERE PLEASE?
A DUMB DINOSAUR FLASHES ITS TEETH AND YOU LOSE ALL SCIENTIFIC CURIOSITY. GOOD TO KNOW, EINSTEIN.
HANG ON, TROOPS--
--I HAVE A PLAN!

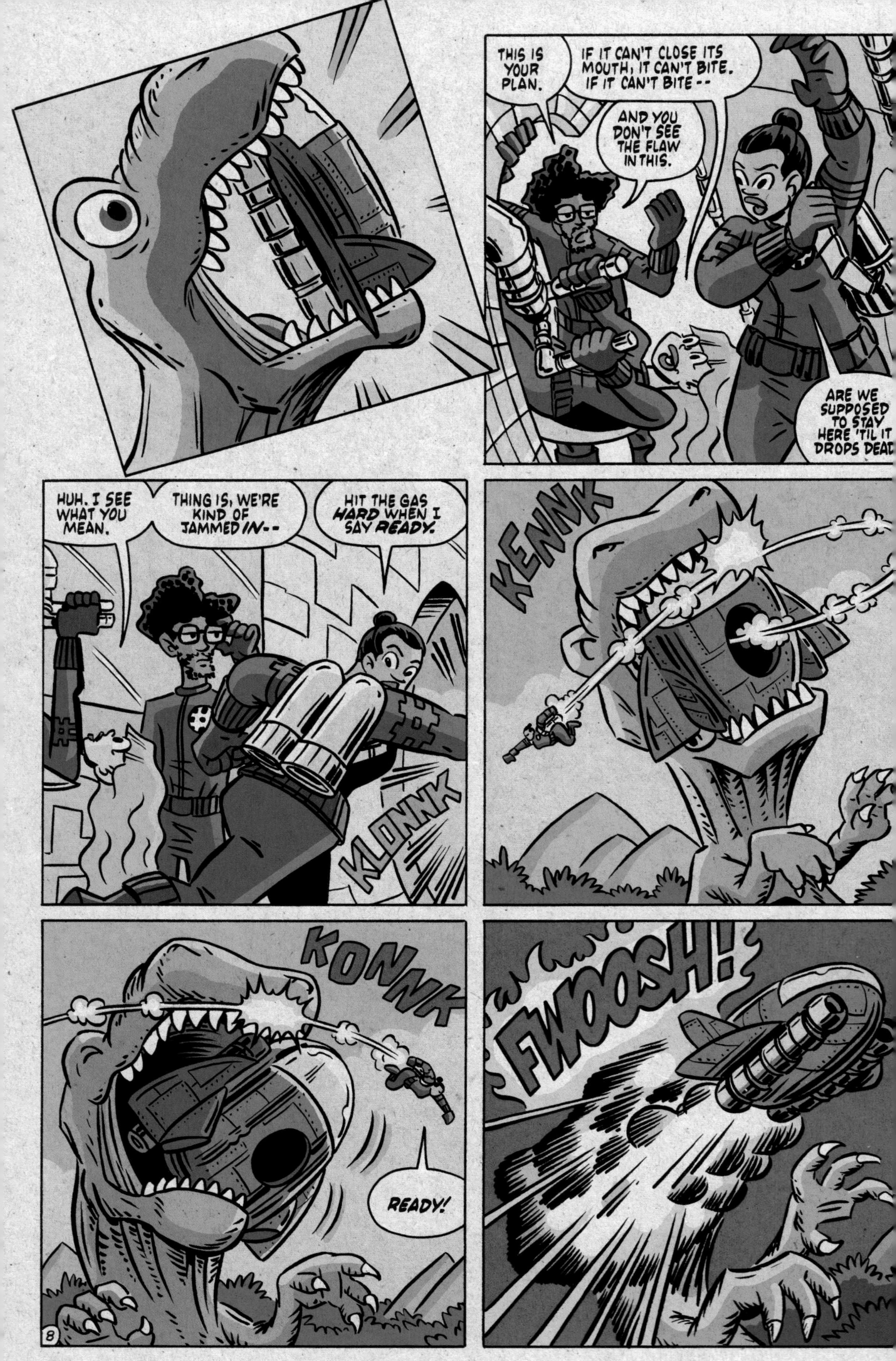
THIS IS YOUR PLAN.
IF IT CAN'T CLOSE ITS MOUTH, IT CAN'T BITE. IF IT CAN'T BITE --
AND YOU DON'T SEE THE FLAW IN THIS.
ARE WE SUPPOSED TO STAY HERE 'TIL IT DROPS DEAD
HUH. I SEE WHAT YOU MEAN.
THING IS, WE'RE KIND OF JAMMED IN--
HIT THE GAS HARD WHEN I SAY READY.
KLONNK
KENNK
KONNK
READY!
FWOOSH!

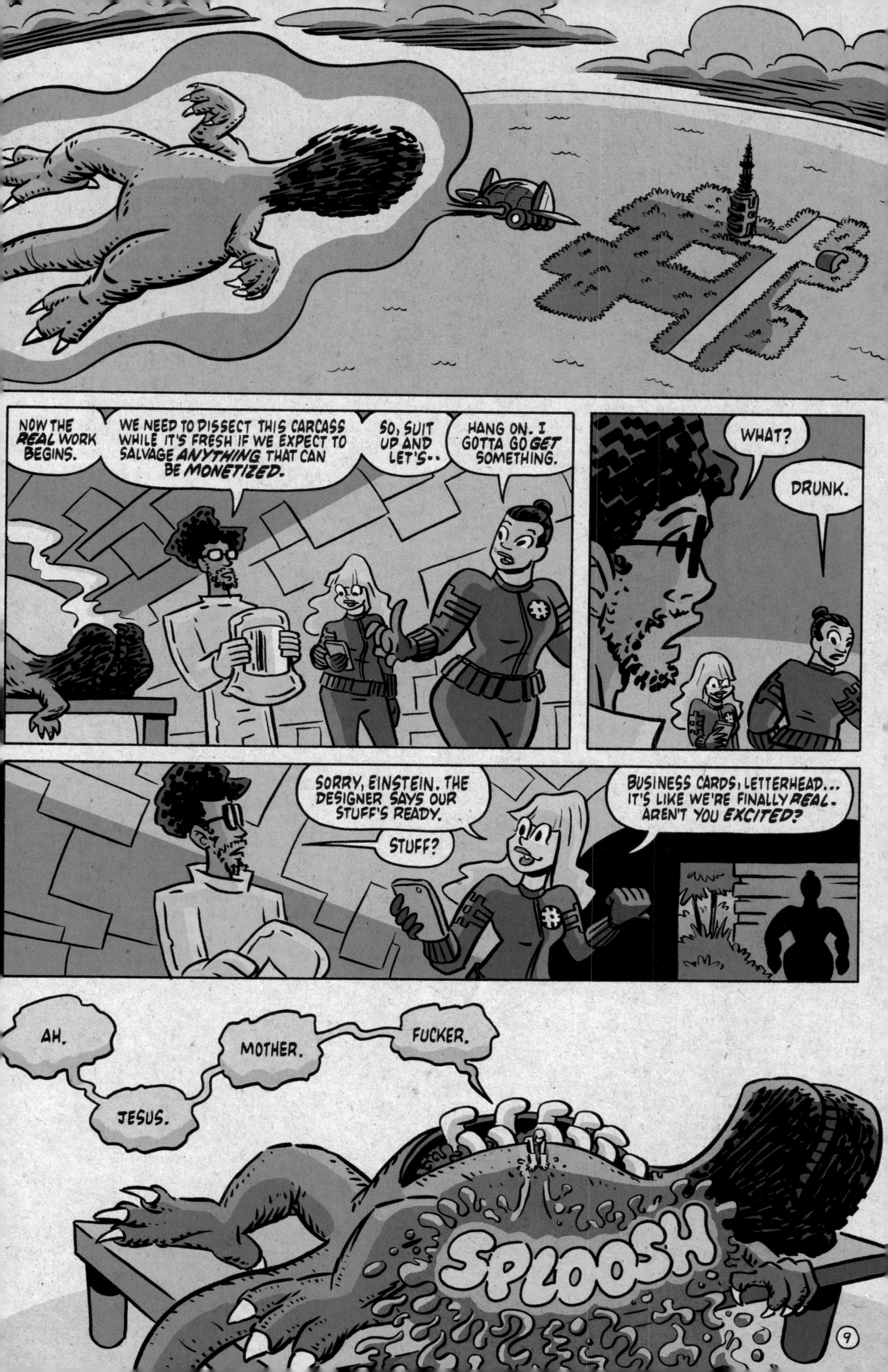
NOW THE REAL WORK BEGINS.
WE NEED TO DISSECT THIS CARCASS WHILE IT'S FRESH IF WE EXPECT TO SALVAGE ANYTHING THAT CAN BE MONETIZED.
SO, SUIT UP AND LET'S..
HANG ON. I GOTTA GO GET SOMETHING.
WHAT?
DRUNK.
SORRY, EINSTEIN. THE DESIGNER SAYS OUR STUFF'S READY.
STUFF?
BUSINESS CARDS, LETTERHEAD... IT'S LIKE WE'RE FINALLY REAL. AREN'T YOU EXCITED?
AH.
JESUS.
MOTHER.
FUCKER.
SPLOOSH

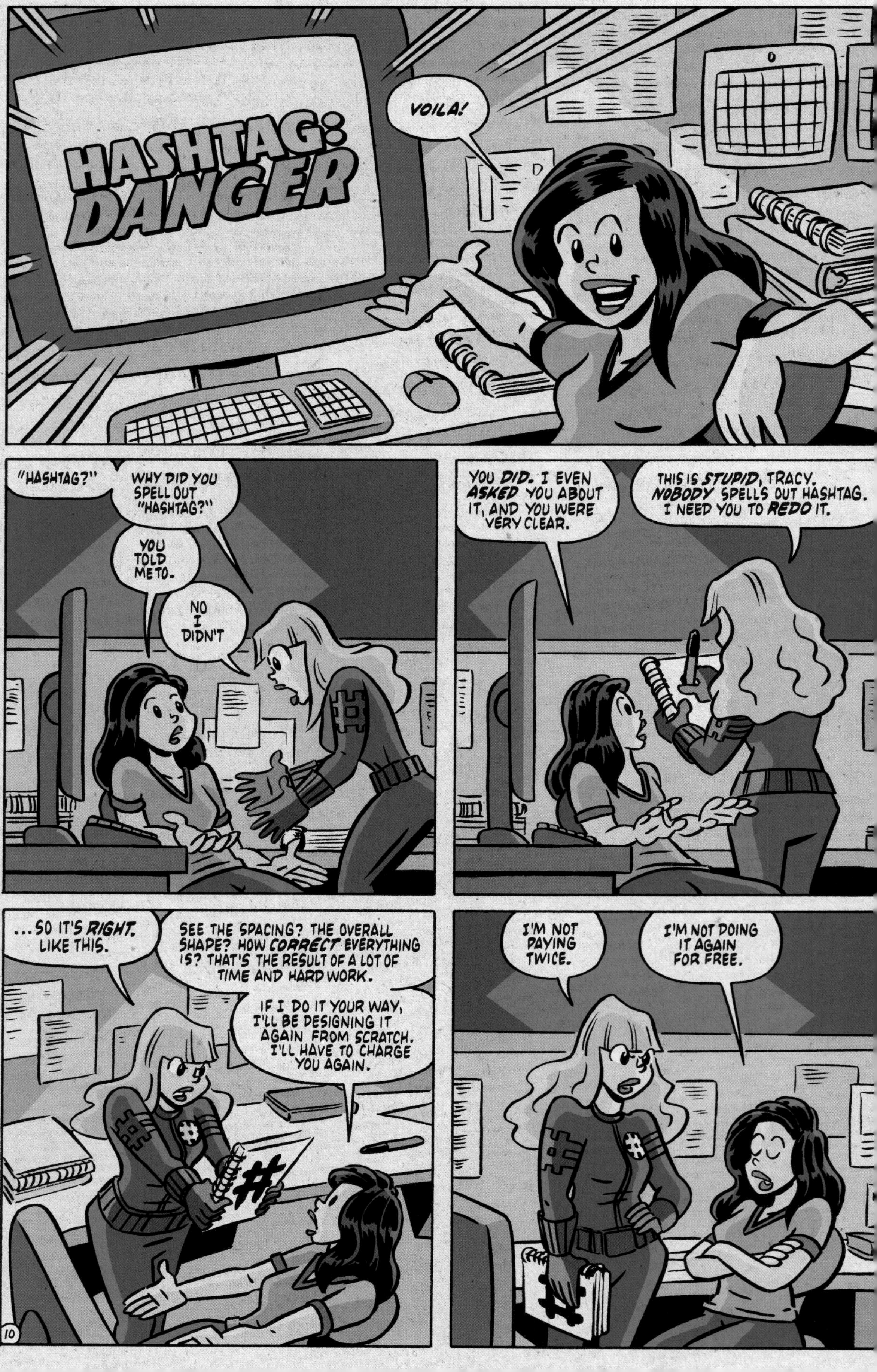
HASHTAG: DANGER
VOILA!
"HASHTAG?"
WHY DID YOU SPELL OUT "HASHTAG?"
YOU TOLD ME TO.
NO I DIDN'T
YOU DID. I EVEN ASKED YOU ABOUT IT, AND YOU WERE VERY CLEAR.
THIS IS STUPID, TRACY. NOBODY SPELLS OUT HASHTAG. I NEED YOU TO REDO IT.
...SO IT'S RIGHT. LIKE THIS.
SEE THE SPACING? THE OVERALL SHAPE? HOW CORRECT EVERYTHING IS? THAT'S THE RESULT OF A LOT OF TIME AND HARD WORK.
IF I DO IT YOUR WAY, I'LL BE DESIGNING IT AGAIN FROM SCRATCH. I'LL HAVE TO CHARGE YOU AGAIN.
I'M NOT PAYING TWICE.
I'M NOT DOING IT AGAIN FOR FREE.
10

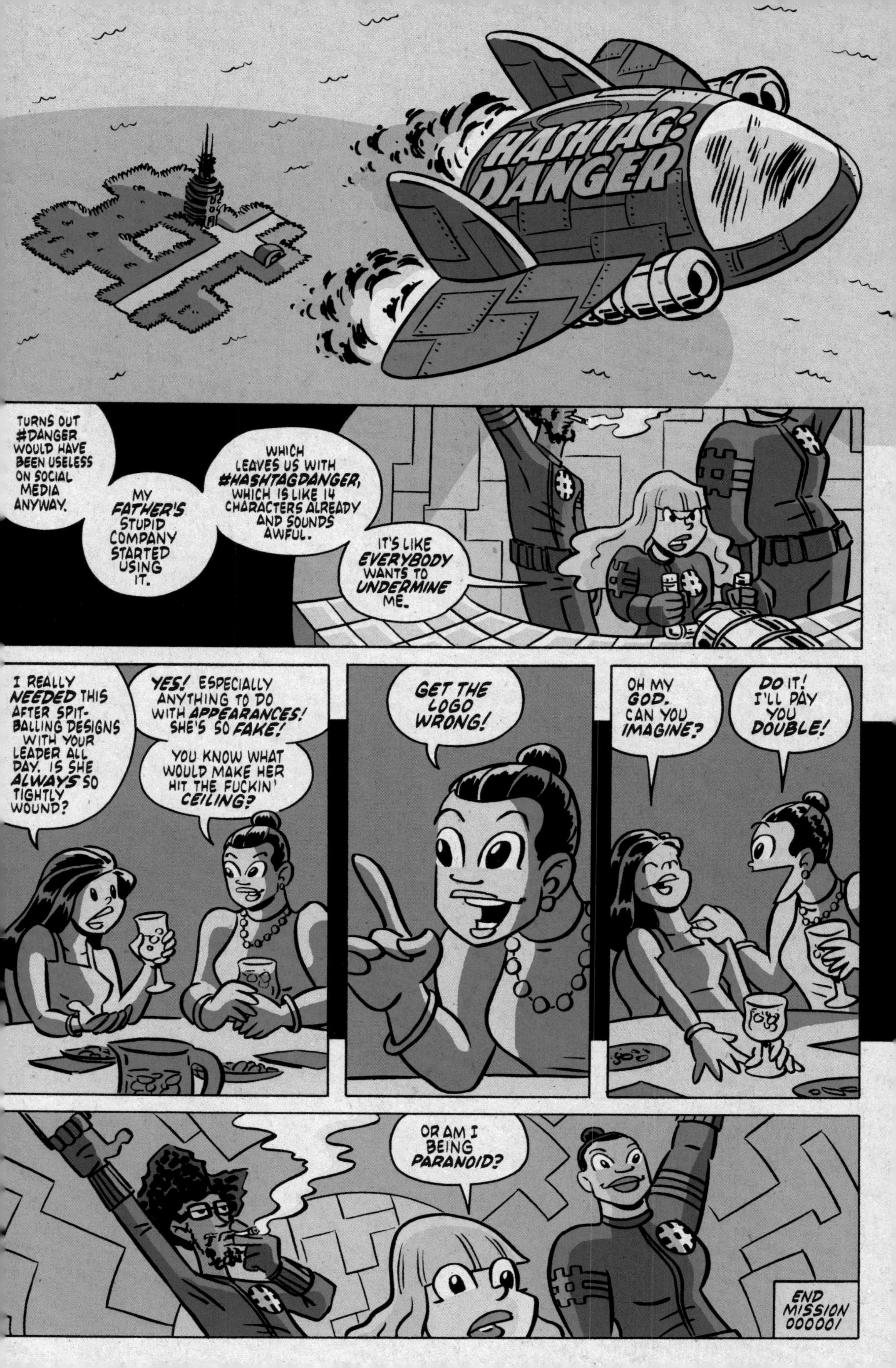
HASHTAG: DANGER
TURNS OUT #DANGER WOULD HAVE BEEN USELESS ON SOCIAL MEDIA ANYWAY.
MY FATHER'S STUPID COMPANY STARTED USING IT.
WHICH LEAVES US WITH #HASHTAGDANGER, WHICH IS LIKE 14 CHARACTERS ALREADY AND SOUNDS AWFUL.
IT'S LIKE EVERYBODY WANTS TO UNDERMINE ME.
I REALLY NEEDED THIS AFTER SPIT-BALLING DESIGNS WITH YOUR LEADER ALL DAY. IS SHE ALWAYS SO TIGHTLY WOUND?
YES! ESPECIALLY ANYTHING TO DO WITH APPEARANCES! SHE'S SO FAKE!
YOU KNOW WHAT WOULD MAKE HER HIT THE FUCKIN' CEILING?
GET THE LOGO WRONG!
OH MY GOD. CAN YOU IMAGINE?
DO IT! I'LL PAY YOU DOUBLE!
OR AM I BEING PARANOID?
END MISSION 00000!

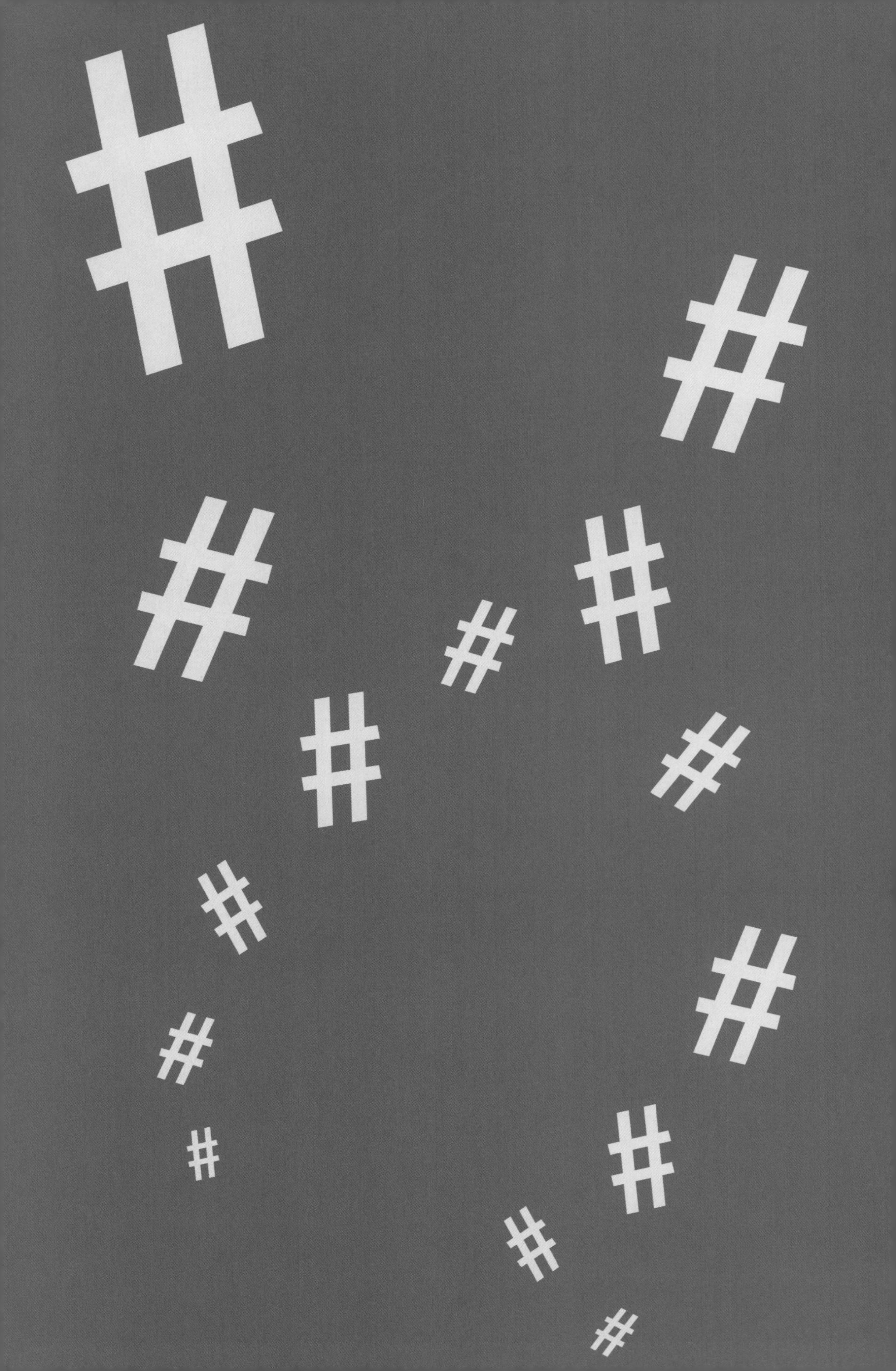

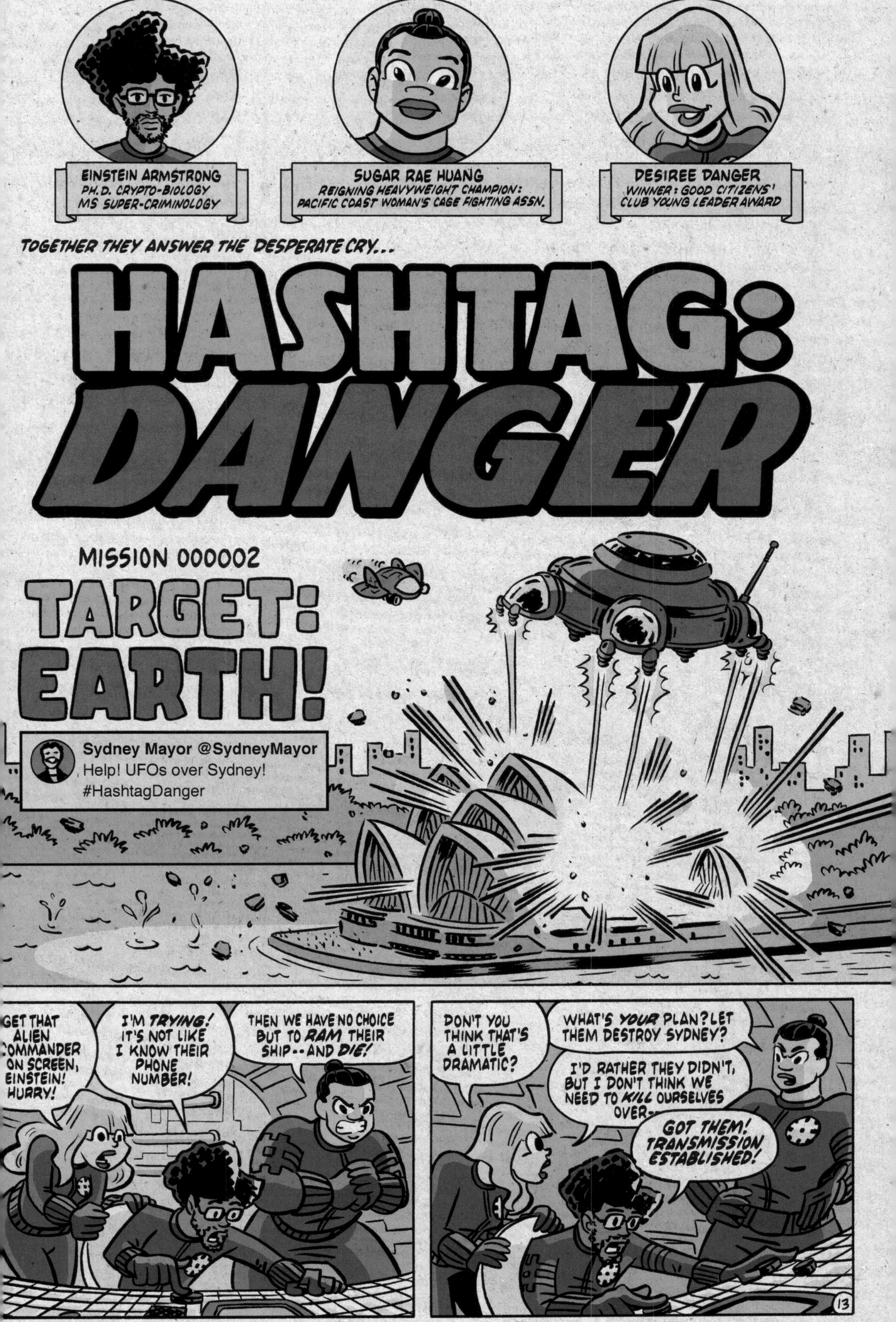
EINSTEIN ARMSTRONG
PH.D. CRYPTO-BIOLOGY
MS SUPER-CRIMINOLOGY
SUGAR RAE HUANG
REIGNING HEAVYWEIGHT CHAMPION:
PACIFIC COAST WOMAN'S CAGE FIGHTING ASSN.
DESIREE DANGER
WINNER: GOOD CITIZENS' CLUB YOUNG LEADER AWARD
TOGETHER THEY ANSWER THE DESPERATE CRY...
HASHTAG: DANGER
MISSION 000002
TARGET: EARTH!
Sydney Mayor @SydneyMayor
Help! UFOs over Sydney!
#HashtagDanger
GET THAT ALIEN COMMANDER ON SCREEN, EINSTEIN! HURRY!
I'M TRYING! IT'S NOT LIKE I KNOW THEIR PHONE NUMBER!
THEN WE HAVE NO CHOICE BUT TO RAM THEIR SHIP--AND DIE!
DON'T YOU THINK THAT'S A LITTLE DRAMATIC?
WHAT'S YOUR PLAN? LET THEM DESTROY SYDNEY?
I'D RATHER THEY DIDN'T, BUT I DON'T THINK WE NEED TO KILL OURSELVES OVER--
GOT THEM! TRANSMISSION ESTABLISHED!
13

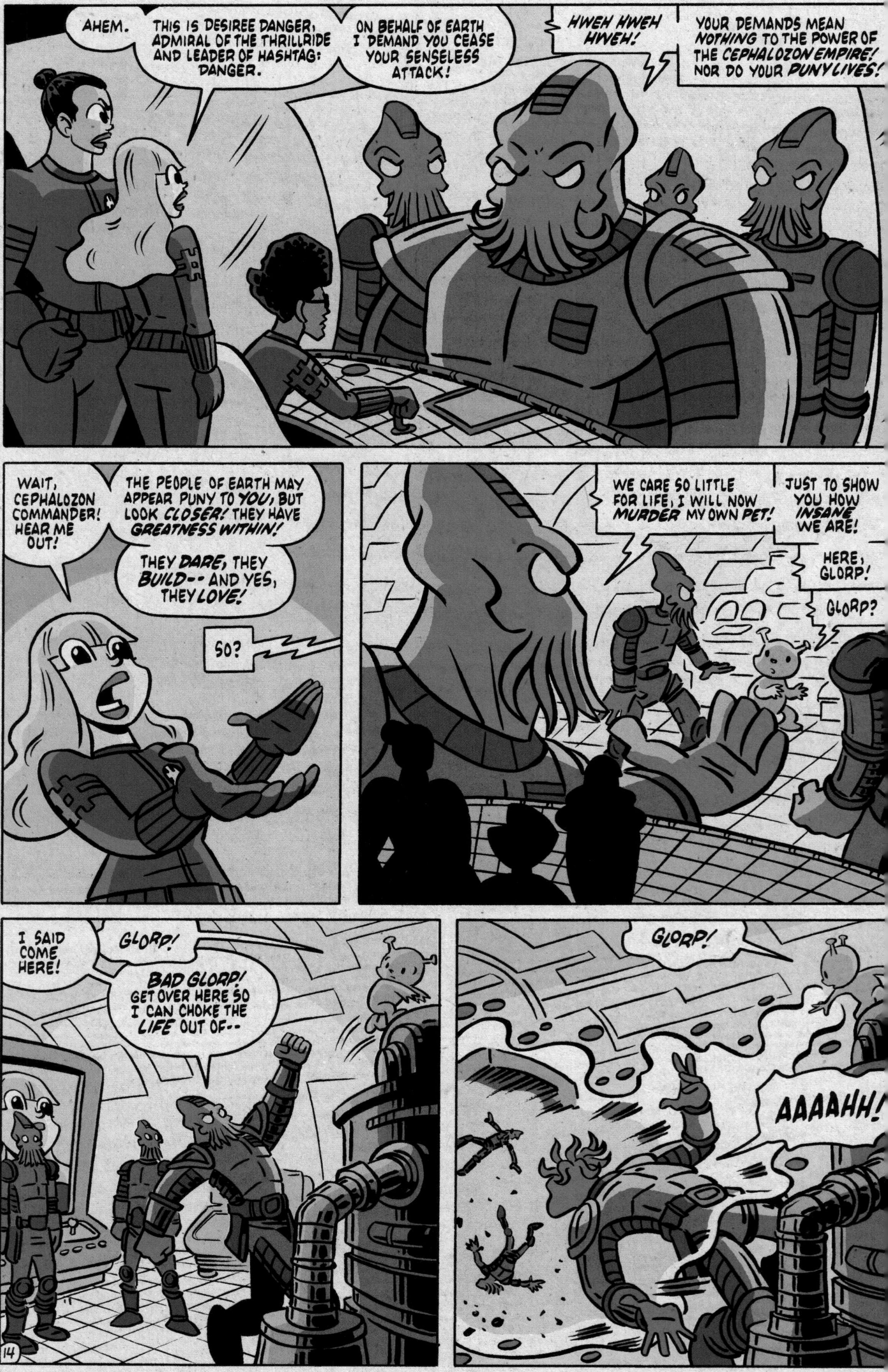
AHEM.
THIS IS DESIREE DANGER, ADMIRAL OF THE THRILLRIDE AND LEADER OF HASHTAG: DANGER.
ON BEHALF OF EARTH I DEMAND YOU CEASE YOUR SENSELESS ATTACK!
HWEH HWEH HWEH!
YOUR DEMANDS MEAN NOTHING TO THE POWER OF THE CEPHALOZON EMPIRE! NOR DO YOUR PUNY LIVES!
WAIT, CEPHALOZON COMMANDER! HEAR ME OUT!
THE PEOPLE OF EARTH MAY APPEAR PUNY TO YOU, BUT LOOK CLOSER! THEY HAVE GREATNESS WITHIN!
THEY DARE, THEY BUILD-- AND YES, THEY LOVE!
SO?
WE CARE SO LITTLE FOR LIFE, I WILL NOW MURDER MY OWN PET!
JUST TO SHOW YOU HOW INSANE WE ARE!
HERE, GLORP!
GLORP?
I SAID COME HERE!
GLORP!
BAD GLORP! GET OVER HERE SO I CAN CHOKE THE LIFE OUT OF--
GLORP!
AAAAHH!

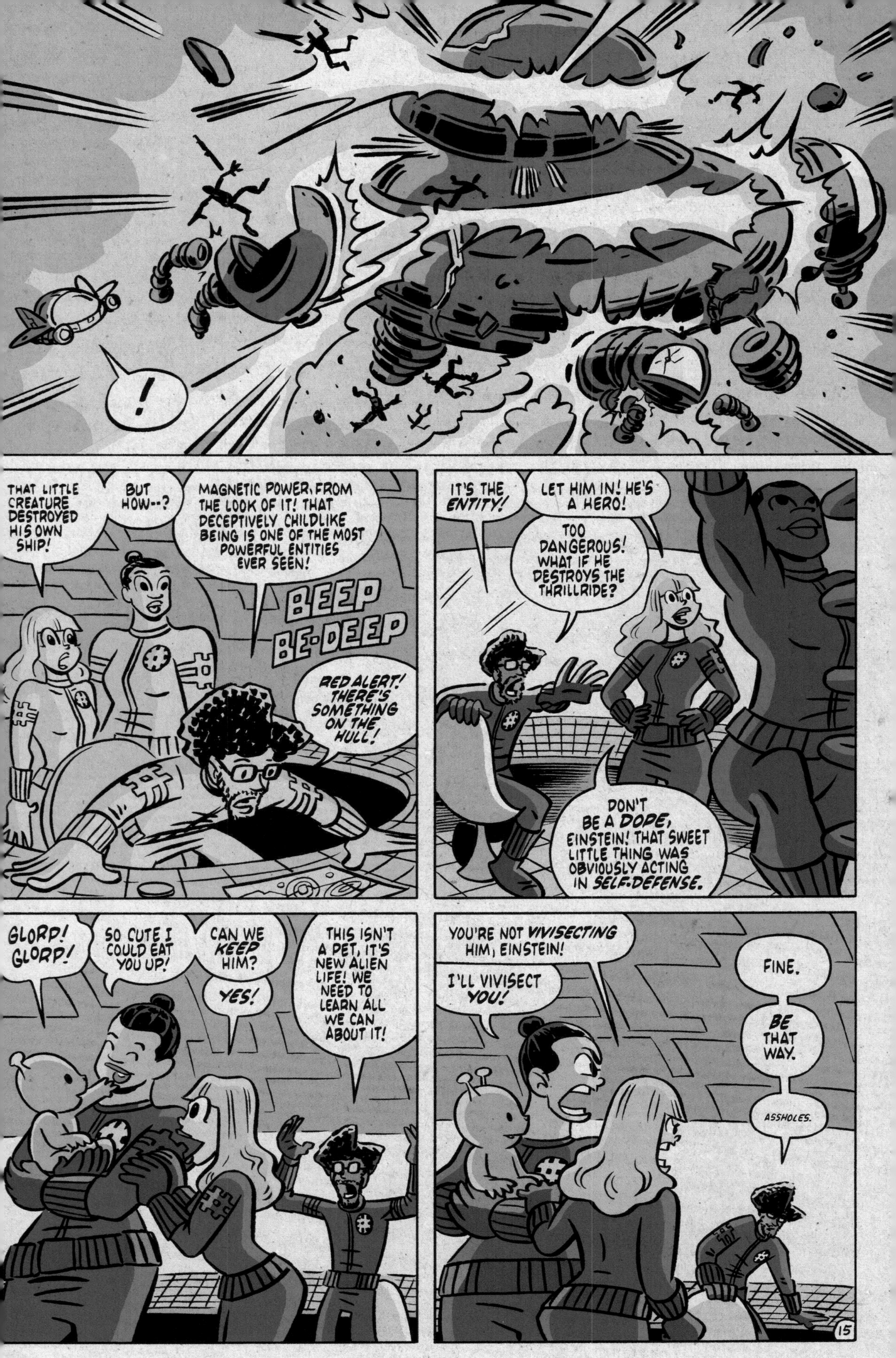
!
THAT LITTLE CREATURE DESTROYED HIS OWN SHIP!
BUT HOW--?
MAGNETIC POWER, FROM THE LOOK OF IT! THAT DECEPTIVELY CHILDLIKE BEING IS ONE OF THE MOST POWERFUL ENTITIES EVER SEEN!
BEEP BE-DEEP
RED ALERT! THERE'S SOMETHING ON THE HULL!
IT'S THE ENTITY!
LET HIM IN! HE'S A HERO!
TOO DANGEROUS! WHAT IF HE DESTROYS THE THRILLRIDE?
DON'T BE A DOPE, EINSTEIN! THAT SWEET LITTLE THING WAS OBVIOUSLY ACTING IN SELF-DEFENSE.
GLORP! GLORP!
SO CUTE I COULD EAT YOU UP!
CAN WE KEEP HIM?
YES!
THIS ISN'T A PET, IT'S NEW ALIEN LIFE! WE NEED TO LEARN ALL WE CAN ABOUT IT!
YOU'RE NOT VIVISECTING HIM, EINSTEIN!
I'LL VIVISECT YOU!
FINE.
BE THAT WAY.
ASSHOLES.

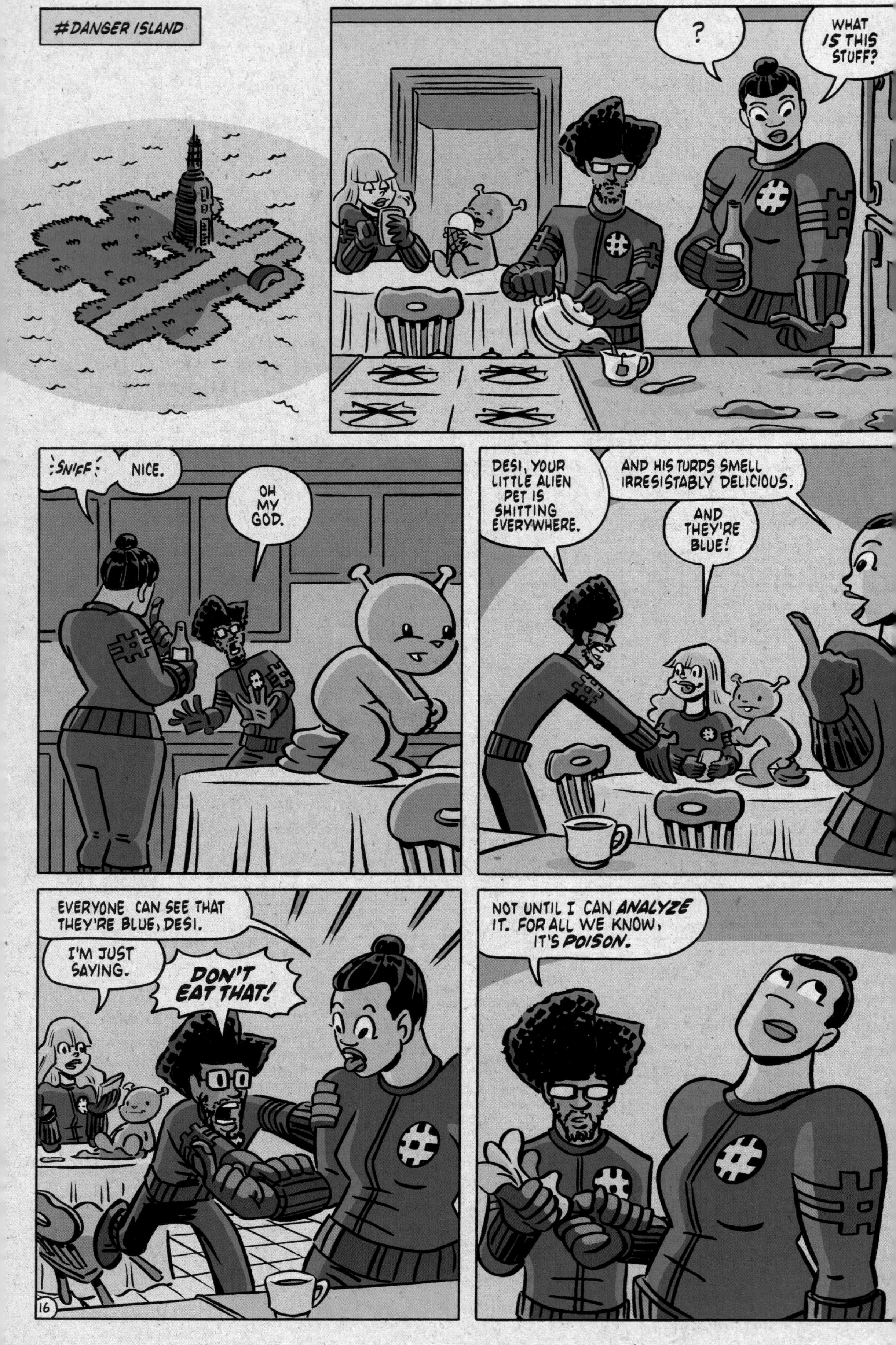
#DANGER ISLAND
?
WHAT IS THIS STUFF?
SNIFF
NICE.
OH MY GOD.
DESI, YOUR LITTLE ALIEN PET IS SHITTING EVERYWHERE.
AND HIS TURDS SMELL IRRESISTABLY DELICIOUS.
AND THEY'RE BLUE!
EVERYONE CAN SEE THAT THEY'RE BLUE, DESI.
I'M JUST SAYING.
DON'T EAT THAT!
NOT UNTIL I CAN ANALYZE IT. FOR ALL WE KNOW, IT'S POISON.

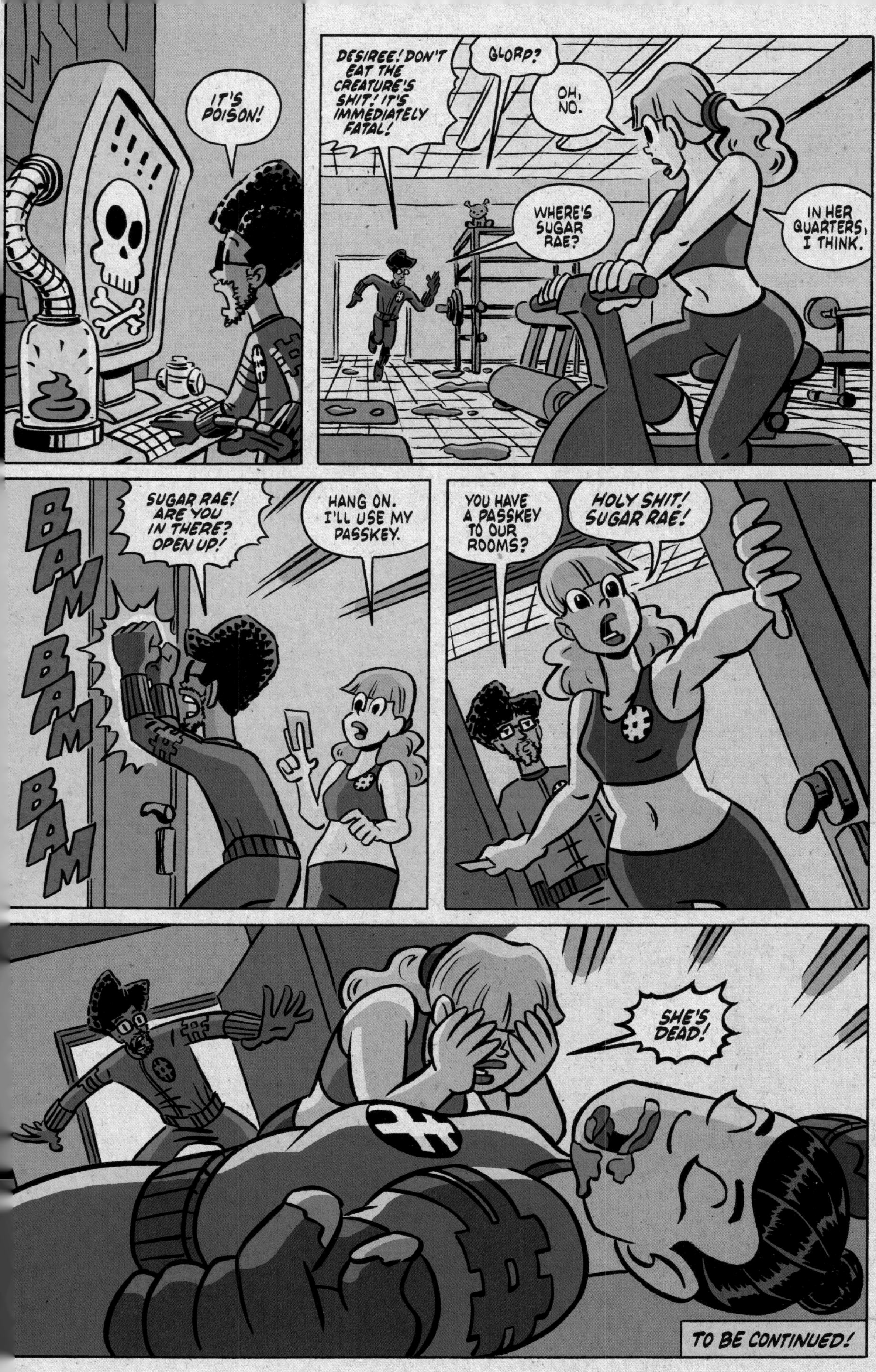
IT'S POISON!
DESIREE! DON'T EAT THE CREATURE'S SHIT! IT'S IMMEDIATELY FATAL!
GLORP?
OH, NO.
WHERE'S SUGAR RAE?
IN HER QUARTERS, I THINK.
BAM BAM BAM BAM
SUGAR RAE! ARE YOU IN THERE? OPEN UP!
HANG ON. I'LL USE MY PASSKEY.
YOU HAVE A PASSKEY TO OUR ROOMS?
HOLY SHIT! SUGAR RAE!
SHE'S DEAD!
TO BE CONTINUED!

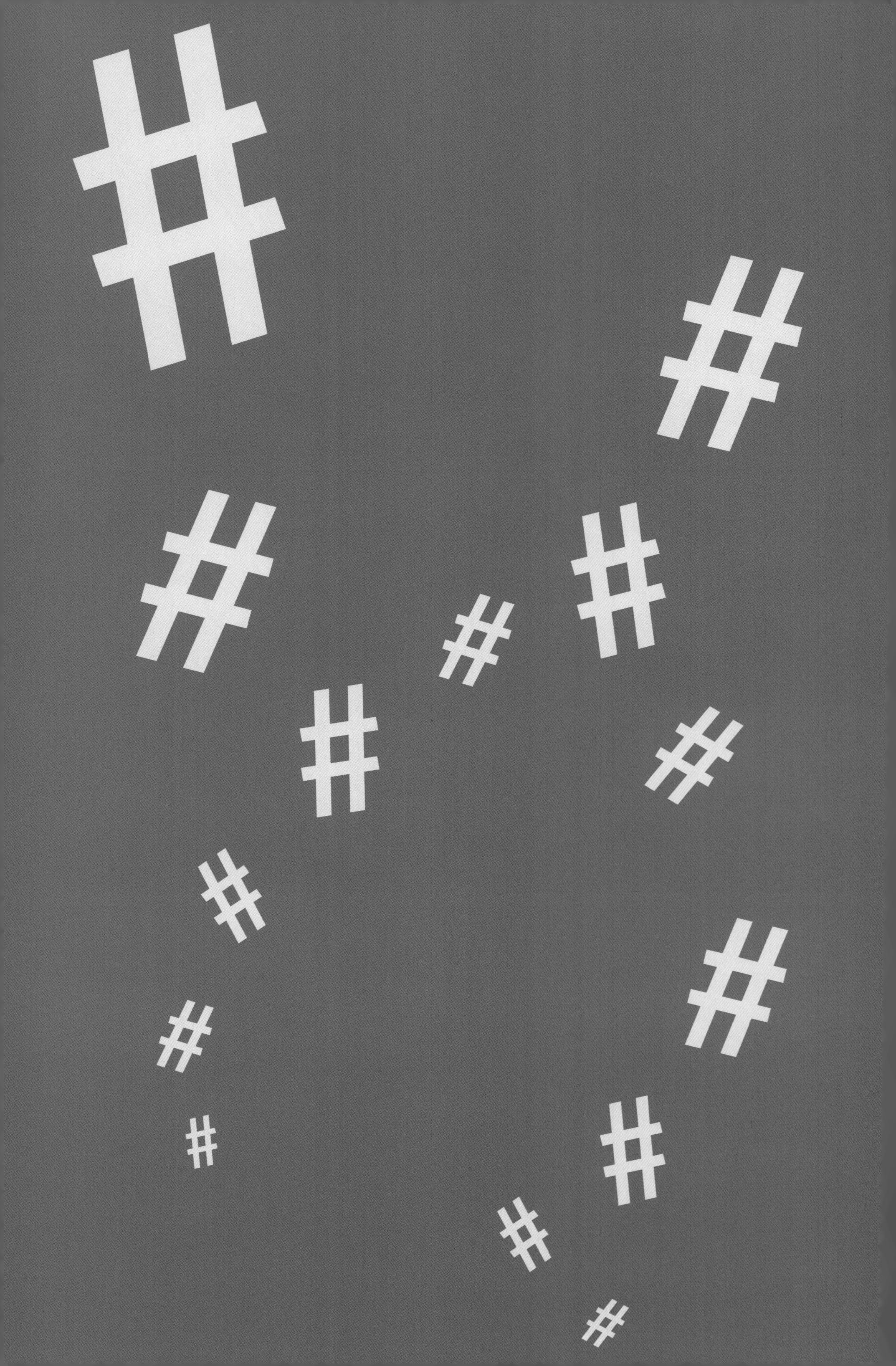

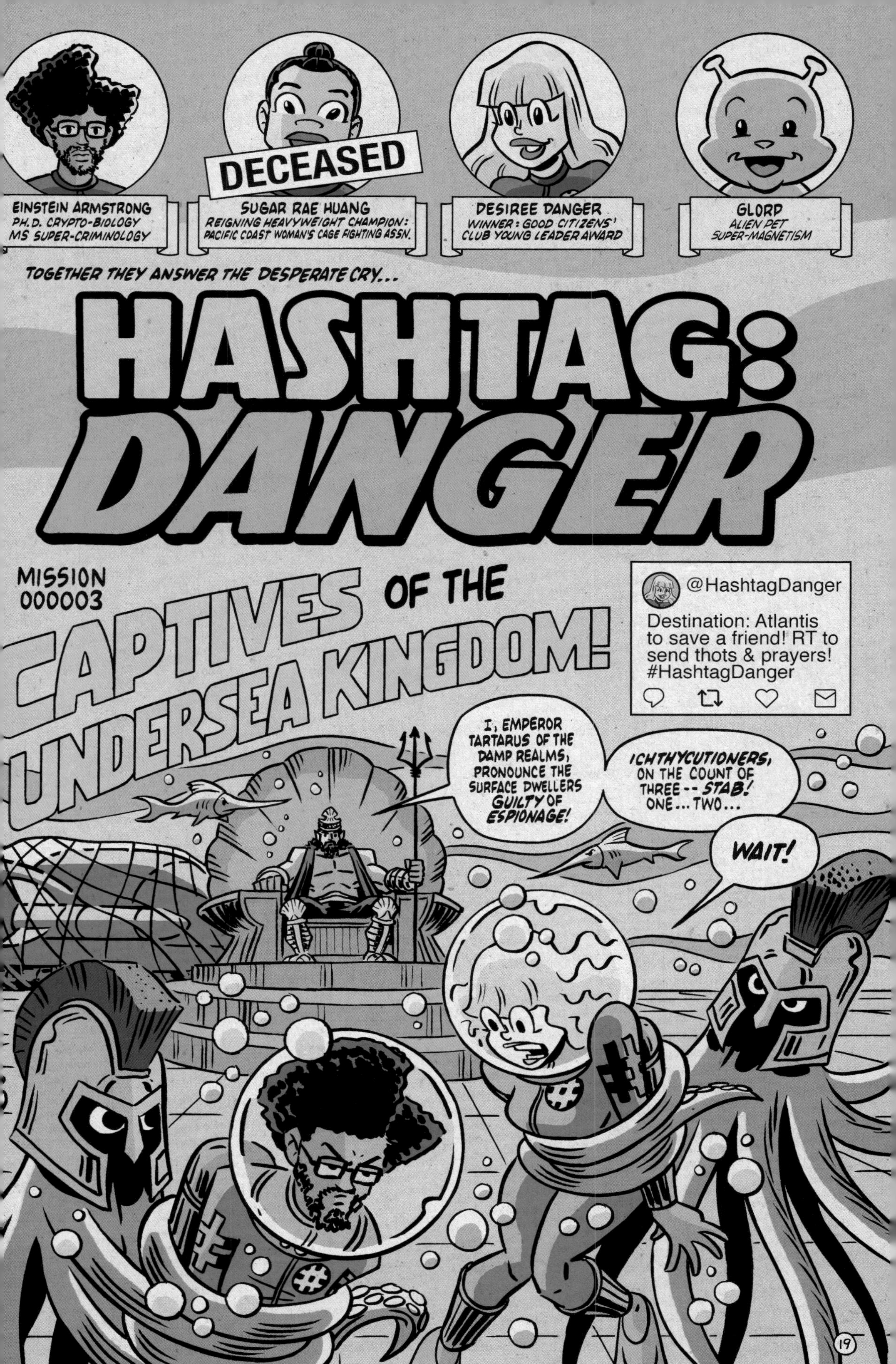
DECEASED
EINSTEIN ARMSTRONG
PH.D. CRYPTO-BIOLOGY
MS SUPER-CRIMINOLOGY
SUGAR RAE HUANG
REIGNING HEAVYWEIGHT CHAMPION:
PACIFIC COAST WOMAN'S CAGE FIGHTING ASSN.
DESIREE DANGER
WINNER: GOOD CITIZENS' CLUB YOUNG LEADER AWARD
GLORP
ALIEN PET
SUPER-MAGNETISM
TOGETHER THEY ANSWER THE DESPERATE CRY...
HASHTAG: DANGER
MISSION 000003
CAPTIVES OF THE UNDERSEA KINGDOM!
@HashtagDanger
Destination: Atlantis to save a friend! RT to send thots & prayers! #HashtagDanger
I, EMPEROR TARTARUS OF THE DAMP REALMS, PRONOUNCE THE SURFACE DWELLERS GUILTY OF ESPIONAGE!
ICHTHYCUTIONERS, ON THE COUNT OF THREE -- STAB! ONE... TWO...
WAIT!

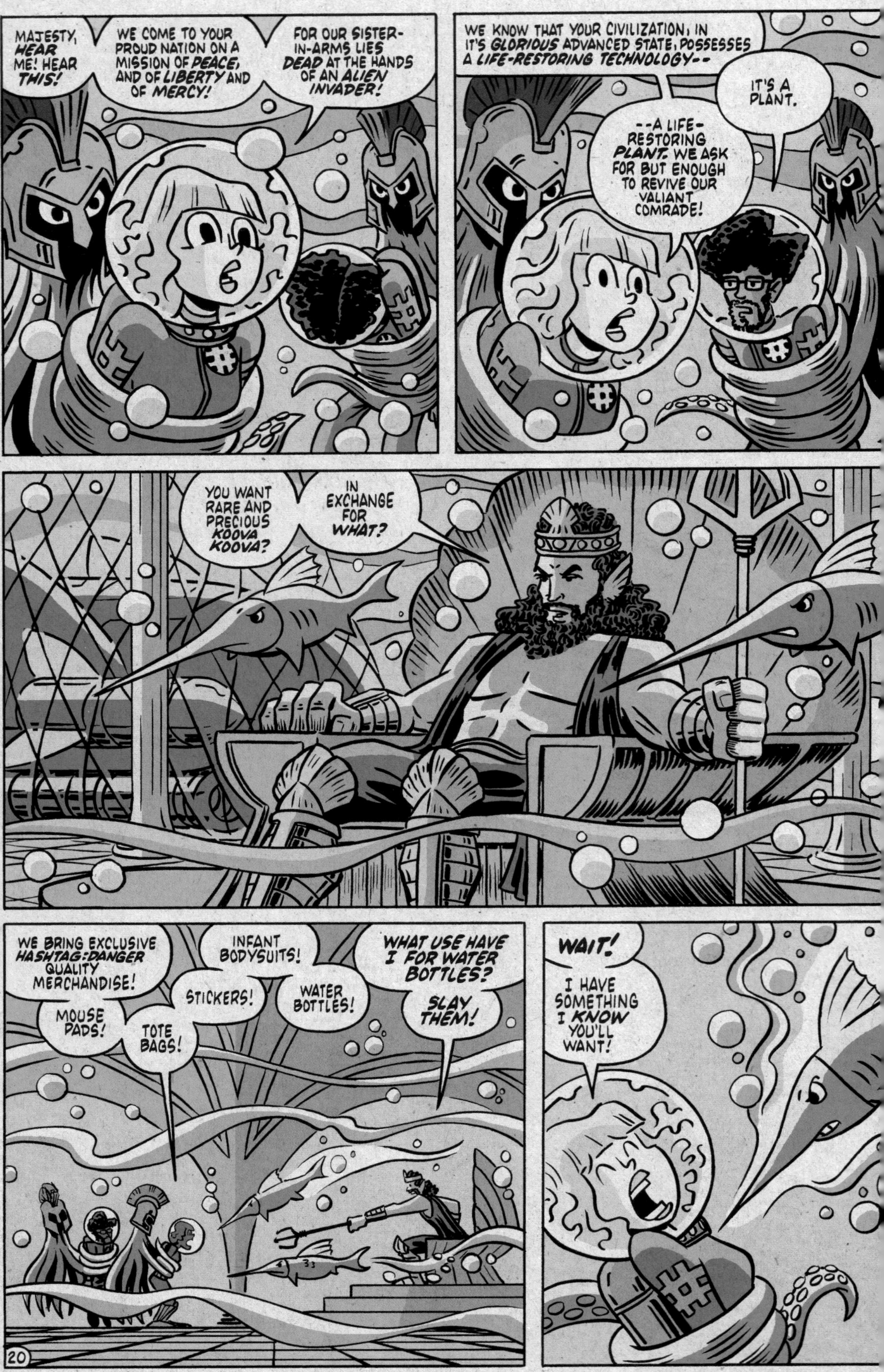
MAJESTY, *HEAR* ME! HEAR *THIS!*
WE COME TO YOUR PROUD NATION ON A MISSION OF *PEACE*, AND OF *LIBERTY* AND OF *MERCY!*
FOR OUR SISTER-IN-ARMS LIES *DEAD* AT THE HANDS OF AN *ALIEN INVADER!*
WE KNOW THAT YOUR CIVILIZATION, IN IT'S *GLORIOUS* ADVANCED STATE, POSSESSES A *LIFE-RESTORING TECHNOLOGY--*
IT'S A PLANT.
--A LIFE-RESTORING *PLANT.* WE ASK FOR BUT ENOUGH TO REVIVE OUR VALIANT COMRADE!
YOU WANT RARE AND PRECIOUS *KOOVA KOOVA?*
IN EXCHANGE FOR *WHAT?*
WE BRING EXCLUSIVE *HASHTAG:DANGER* QUALITY MERCHANDISE!
MOUSE PADS!
TOTE BAGS!
STICKERS!
INFANT BODYSUITS!
WATER BOTTLES!
WHAT USE HAVE I FOR WATER BOTTLES?
SLAY THEM!
WAIT!
I HAVE SOMETHING I *KNOW* YOU'LL WANT!

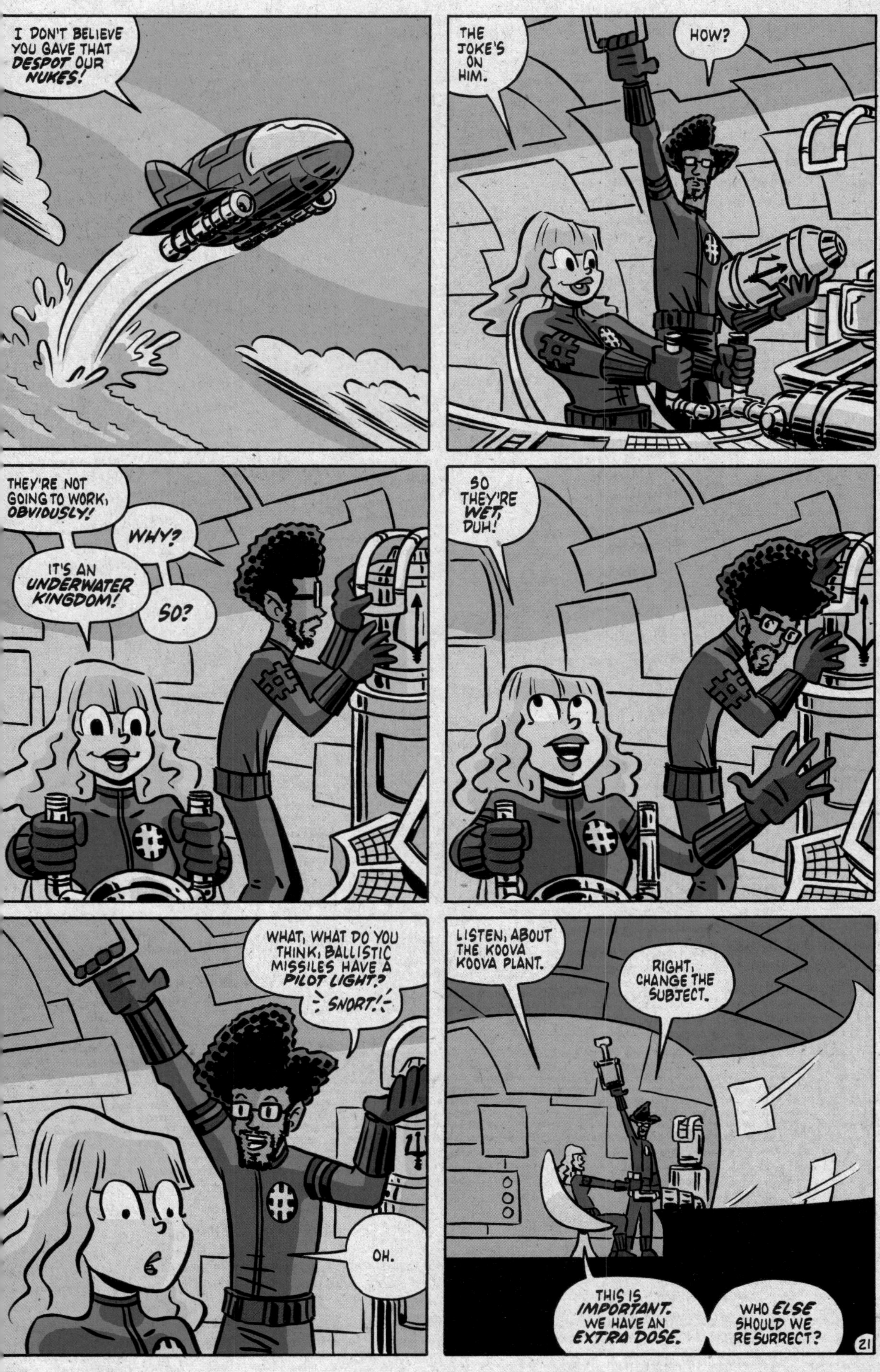
I DON'T BELIEVE YOU GAVE THAT DESPOT OUR NUKES!
THE JOKE'S ON HIM.
HOW?
THEY'RE NOT GOING TO WORK, OBVIOUSLY!
WHY?
IT'S AN UNDERWATER KINGDOM!
SO?
SO THEY'RE WET, DUH!
WHAT, WHAT DO YOU THINK, BALLISTIC MISSILES HAVE A PILOT LIGHT?
SNORT!
OH.
LISTEN, ABOUT THE KOOVA KOOVA PLANT.
RIGHT, CHANGE THE SUBJECT.
THIS IS IMPORTANT. WE HAVE AN EXTRA DOSE.
WHO ELSE SHOULD WE RESURRECT?

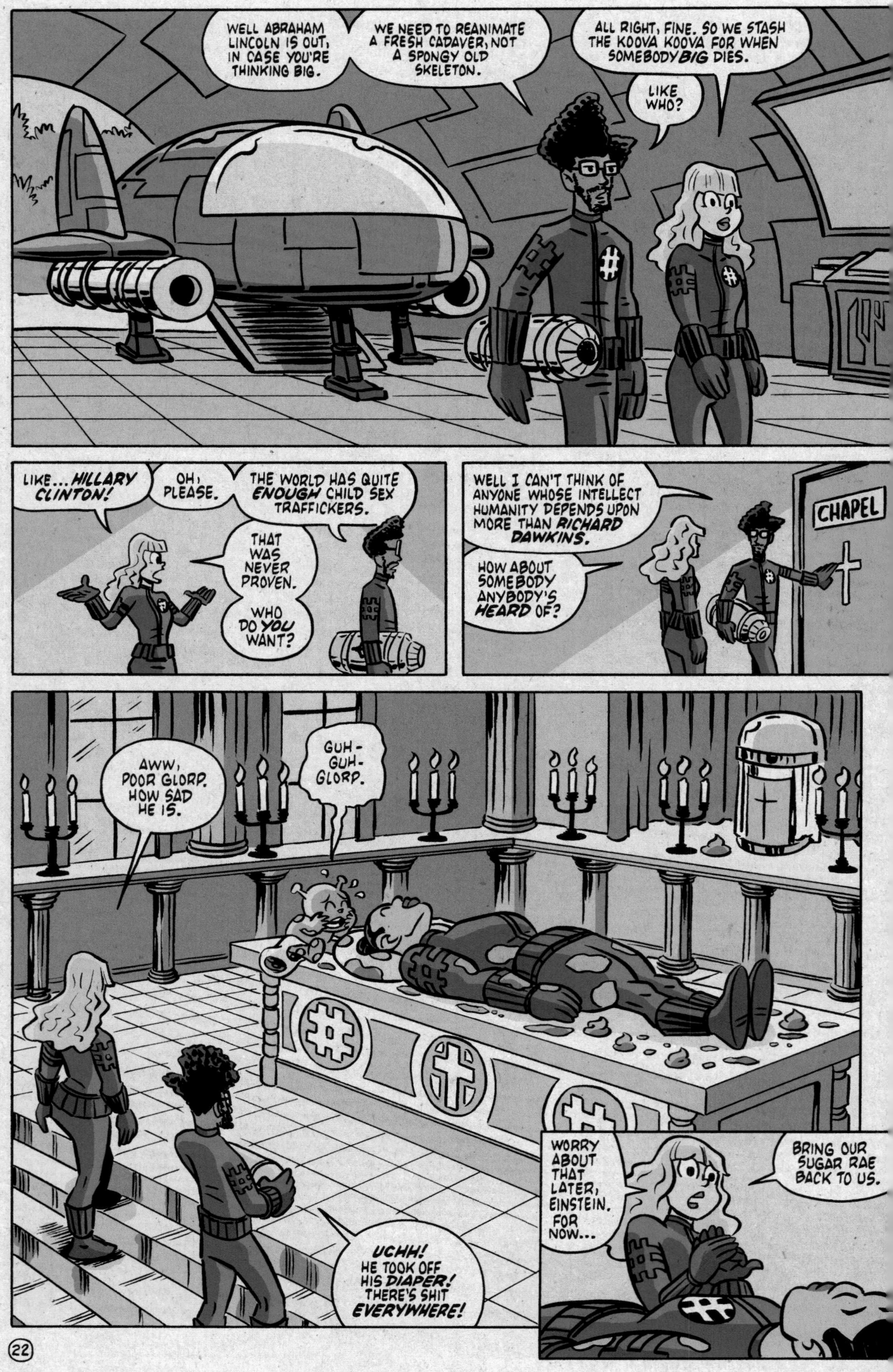
WELL ABRAHAM LINCOLN IS OUT, IN CASE YOU'RE THINKING BIG.
WE NEED TO REANIMATE A FRESH CADAVER, NOT A SPONGY OLD SKELETON.
ALL RIGHT, FINE. SO WE STASH THE KOOVA KOOVA FOR WHEN SOMEBODY BIG DIES.
LIKE WHO?
LIKE... HILLARY CLINTON!
OH, PLEASE.
THE WORLD HAS QUITE ENOUGH CHILD SEX TRAFFICKERS.
THAT WAS NEVER PROVEN.
WHO DO YOU WANT?
WELL I CAN'T THINK OF ANYONE WHOSE INTELLECT HUMANITY DEPENDS UPON MORE THAN RICHARD DAWKINS.
HOW ABOUT SOMEBODY ANYBODY'S HEARD OF?
CHAPEL
AWW, POOR GLORP. HOW SAD HE IS.
GUH-GUH-GLORP.
UCHH! HE TOOK OFF HIS DIAPER! THERE'S SHIT EVERYWHERE!
WORRY ABOUT THAT LATER, EINSTEIN. FOR NOW...
BRING OUR SUGAR RAE BACK TO US.

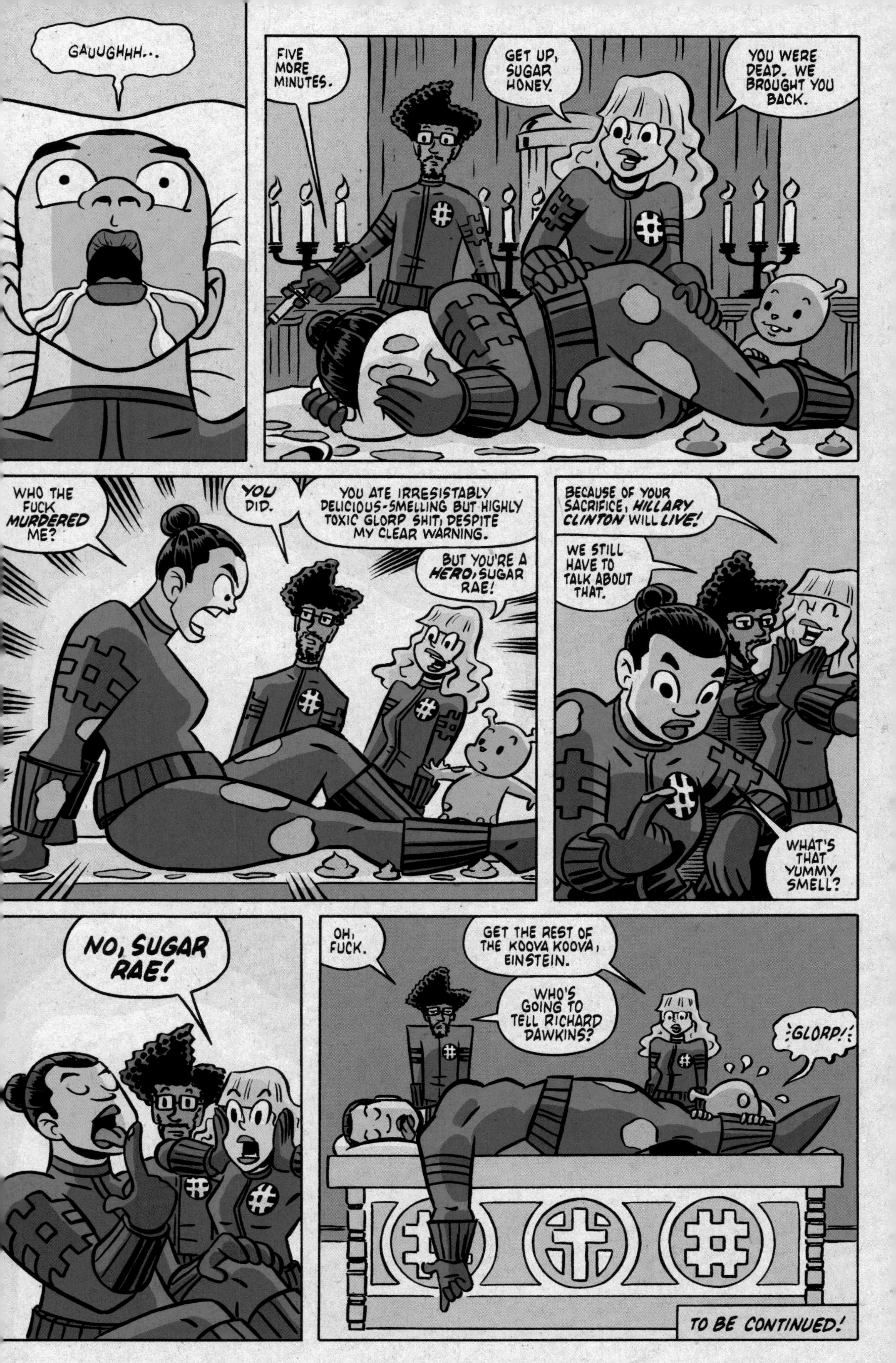
GAUUGHHH...
FIVE MORE MINUTES.
GET UP, SUGAR HONEY.
YOU WERE DEAD. WE BROUGHT YOU BACK.
WHO THE FUCK *MURDERED* ME?
YOU DID.
YOU ATE IRRESISTABLY DELICIOUS-SMELLING BUT HIGHLY TOXIC GLORP SHIT, DESPITE MY CLEAR WARNING.
BUT YOU'RE A *HERO*, SUGAR RAE!
BECAUSE OF YOUR SACRIFICE, *HILLARY CLINTON* WILL *LIVE!*
WE STILL HAVE TO TALK ABOUT THAT.
WHAT'S THAT YUMMY SMELL?
NO, SUGAR RAE!
OH, FUCK.
GET THE REST OF THE KOOVA KOOVA, EINSTEIN.
WHO'S GOING TO TELL RICHARD DAWKINS?
GLORP!
TO BE CONTINUED!

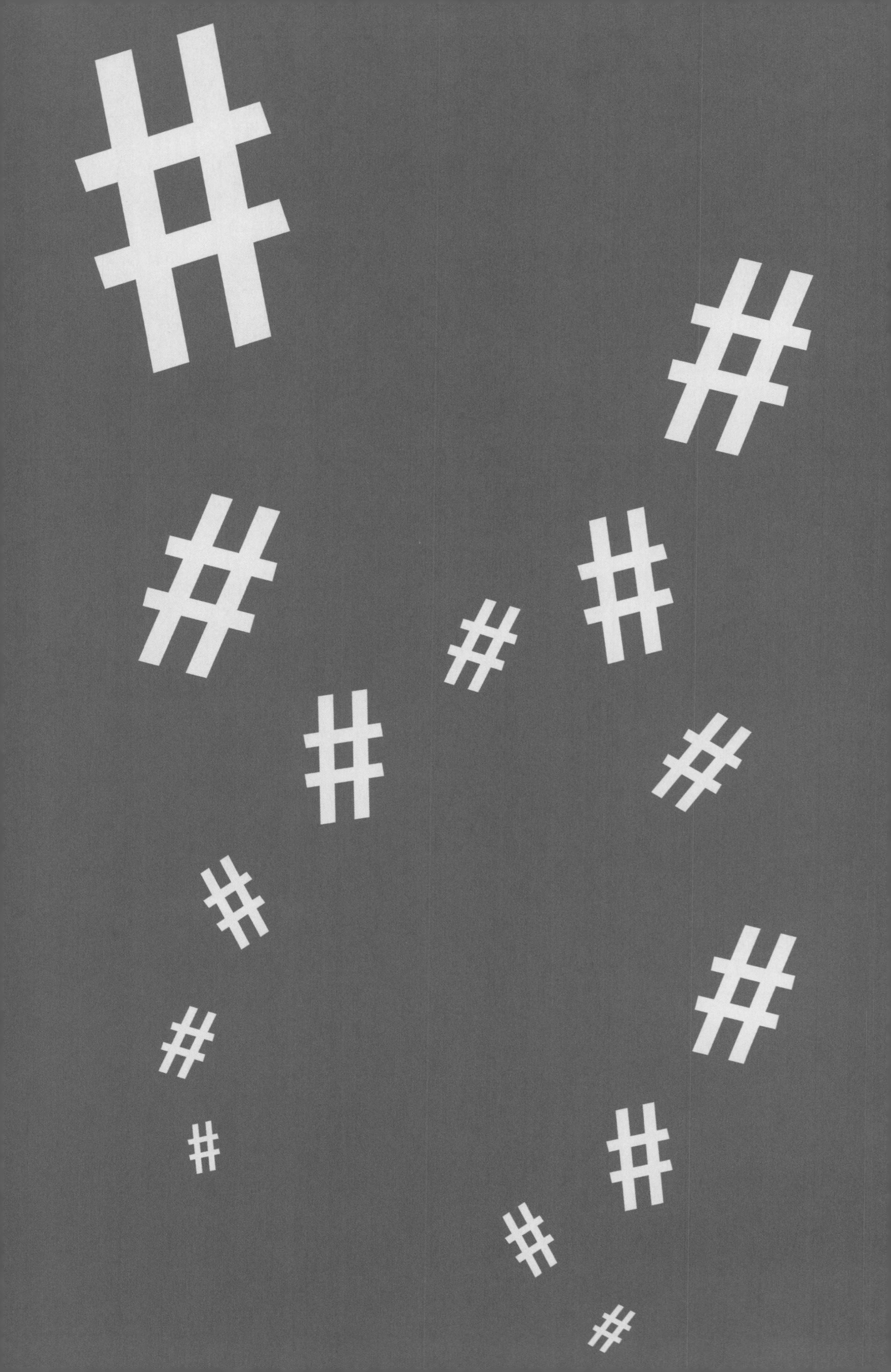

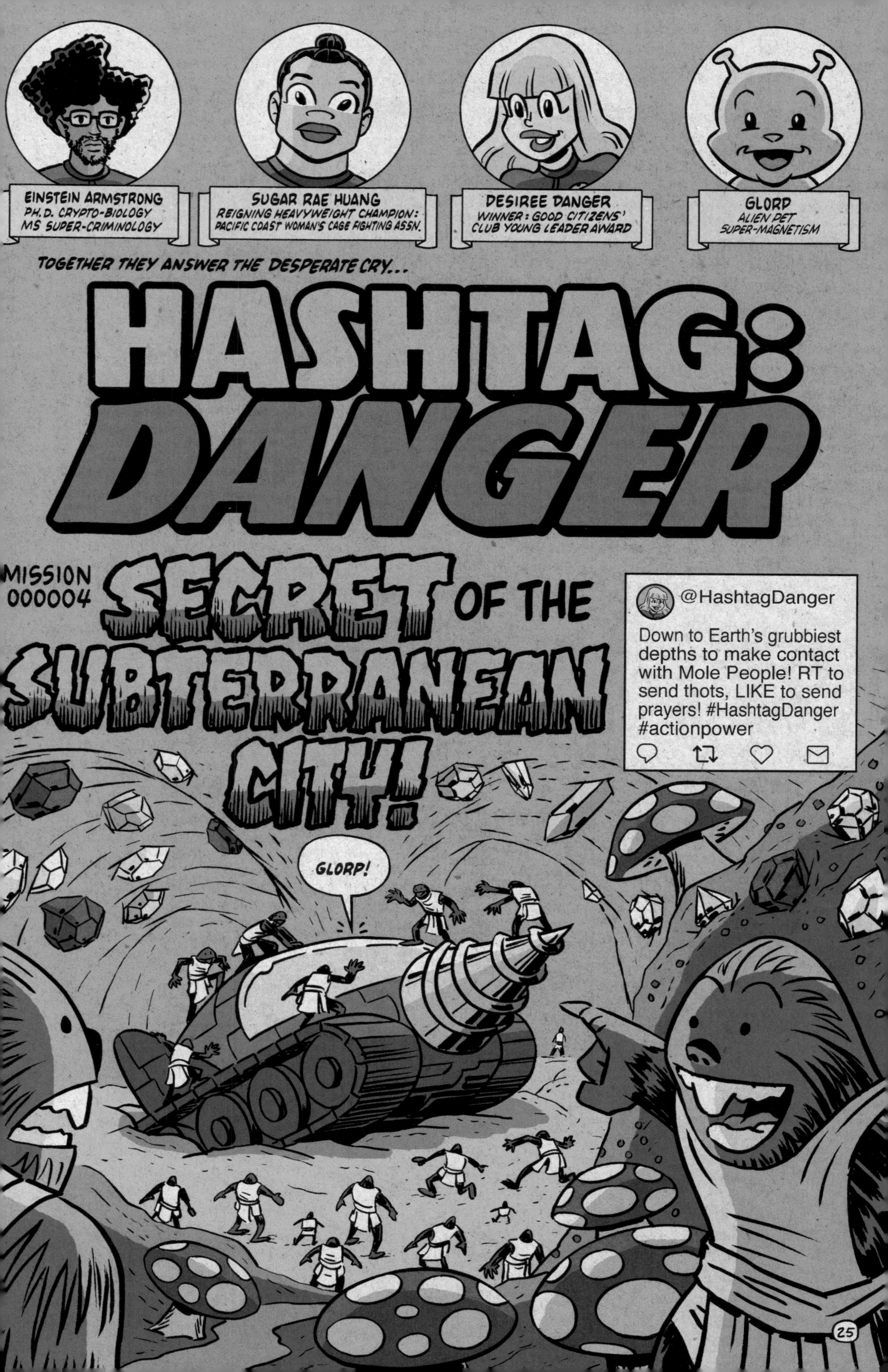
EINSTEIN ARMSTRONG
PH.D. CRYPTO-BIOLOGY
MS SUPER-CRIMINOLOGY
SUGAR RAE HUANG
REIGNING HEAVYWEIGHT CHAMPION:
PACIFIC COAST WOMAN'S CAGE FIGHTING ASSN.
DESIREE DANGER
WINNER: GOOD CITIZENS' CLUB YOUNG LEADER AWARD
GLORP
ALIEN PET
SUPER-MAGNETISM
TOGETHER THEY ANSWER THE DESPERATE CRY...
HASHTAG: DANGER
MISSION 000004
SECRET OF THE SUBTERRANEAN CITY!
@HashtagDanger
Down to Earth's grubbiest depths to make contact with Mole People! RT to send thots, LIKE to send prayers! #HashtagDanger #actionpower
GLORP!

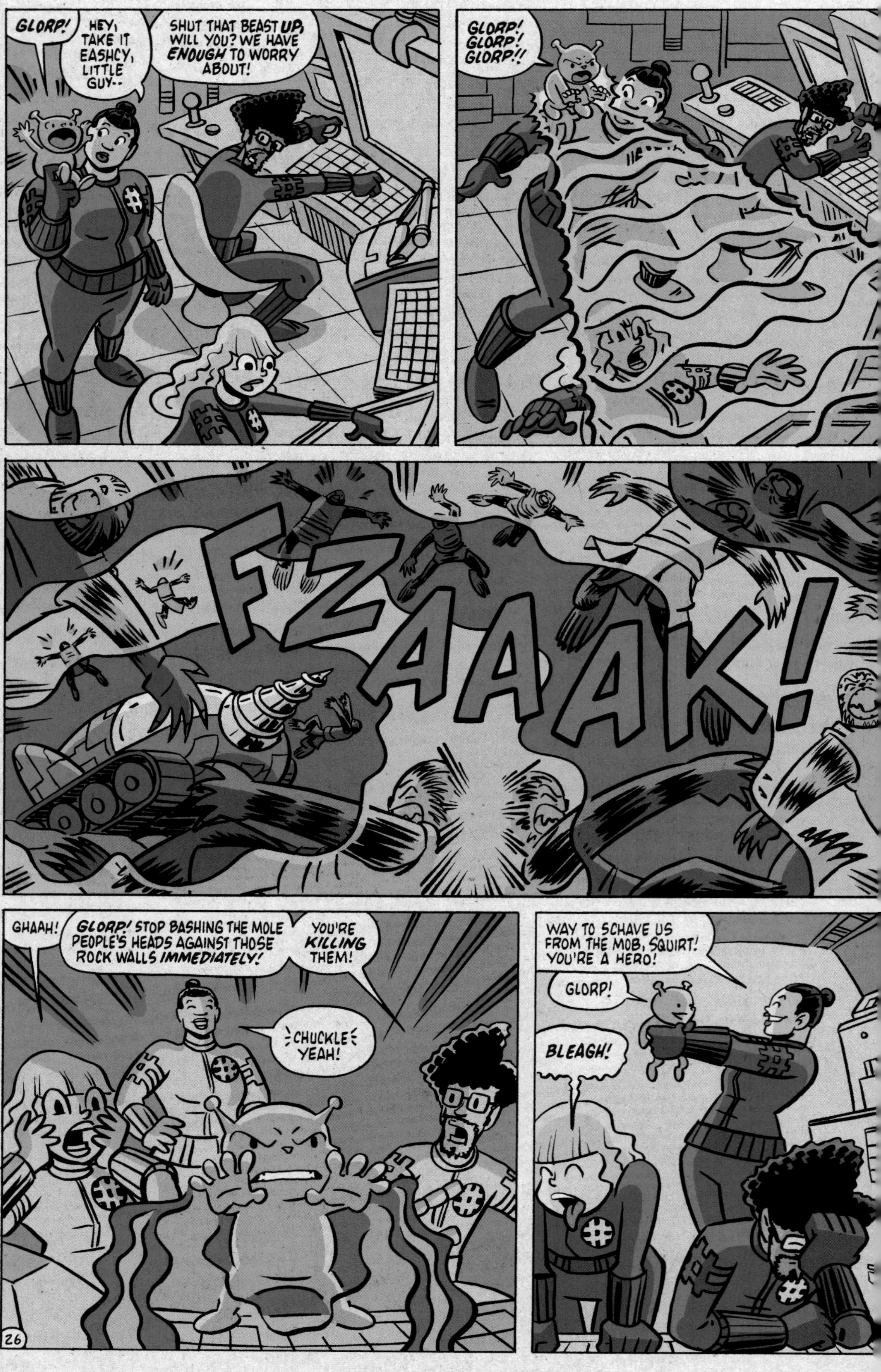
GLORP!
HEY, TAKE IT EASHCY, LITTLE GUY..
SHUT THAT BEAST UP, WILL YOU? WE HAVE ENOUGH TO WORRY ABOUT!
GLORP! GLORP! GLORP!!
FZAAAK!
GHAAH!
GLORP! STOP BASHING THE MOLE PEOPLE'S HEADS AGAINST THOSE ROCK WALLS IMMEDIATELY!
YOU'RE KILLING THEM!
CHUCKLE YEAH!
WAY TO SCHAVE US FROM THE MOB, SQUIRT! YOU'RE A HERO!
GLORP!
BLEAGH!

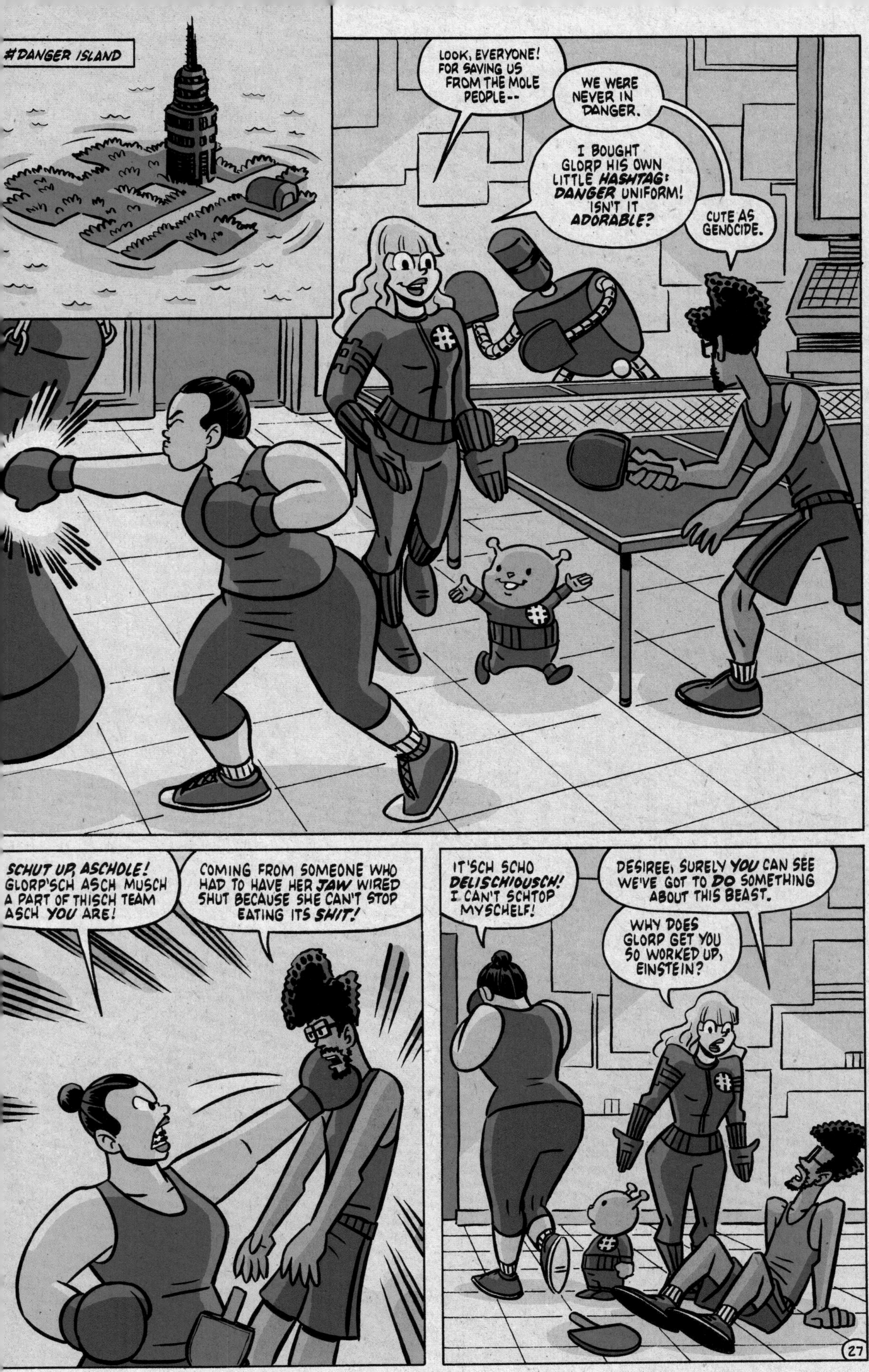
#DANGER ISLAND
LOOK, EVERYONE! FOR SAVING US FROM THE MOLE PEOPLE--
WE WERE NEVER IN DANGER.
I BOUGHT GLORP HIS OWN LITTLE HASHTAG: DANGER UNIFORM! ISN'T IT ADORABLE?
CUTE AS GENOCIDE.
SCHUT UP, ASCHOLE! GLORP'SCH ASCH MUSCH A PART OF THISCH TEAM ASCH YOU ARE!
COMING FROM SOMEONE WHO HAD TO HAVE HER JAW WIRED SHUT BECAUSE SHE CAN'T STOP EATING ITS SHIT!
IT'SCH SCHO DELISCHIOUSCH! I CAN'T SCHTOP MYSCHELF!
DESIREE, SURELY YOU CAN SEE WE'VE GOT TO DO SOMETHING ABOUT THIS BEAST.
WHY DOES GLORP GET YOU SO WORKED UP, EINSTEIN?

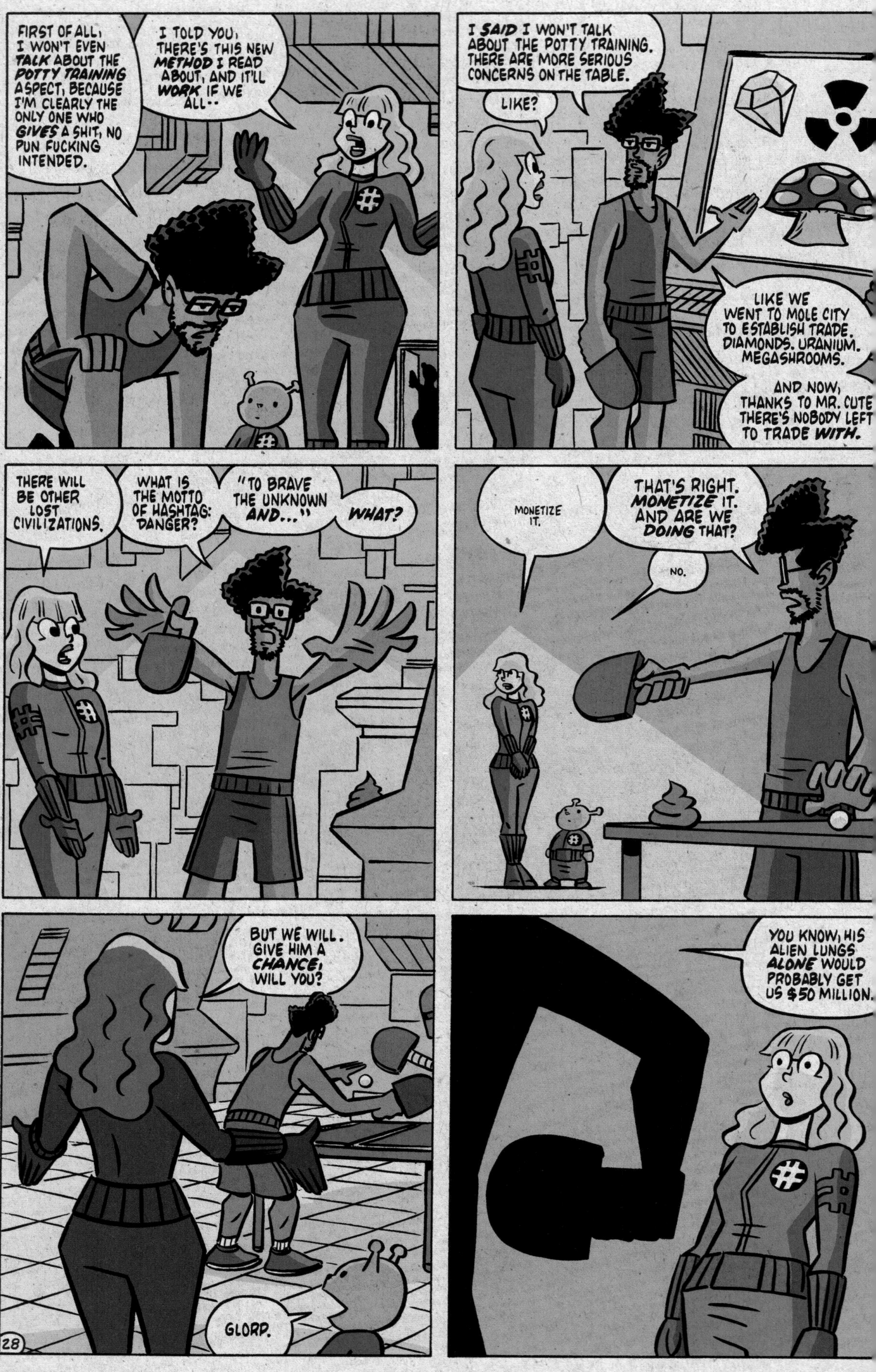
FIRST OF ALL, I WON'T EVEN TALK ABOUT THE POTTY TRAINING ASPECT, BECAUSE I'M CLEARLY THE ONLY ONE WHO GIVES A SHIT, NO PUN FUCKING INTENDED.
I TOLD YOU, THERE'S THIS NEW METHOD I READ ABOUT, AND IT'LL WORK IF WE ALL--
I SAID I WON'T TALK ABOUT THE POTTY TRAINING. THERE ARE MORE SERIOUS CONCERNS ON THE TABLE.
LIKE?
LIKE WE WENT TO MOLE CITY TO ESTABLISH TRADE. DIAMONDS. URANIUM. MEGASHROOMS.
AND NOW, THANKS TO MR. CUTE THERE'S NOBODY LEFT TO TRADE WITH.
THERE WILL BE OTHER LOST CIVILIZATIONS.
WHAT IS THE MOTTO OF HASHTAG: DANGER?
"TO BRAVE THE UNKNOWN AND..."
WHAT?
MONETIZE IT.
THAT'S RIGHT. MONETIZE IT. AND ARE WE DOING THAT?
NO.
BUT WE WILL. GIVE HIM A CHANCE, WILL YOU?
GLORP.
YOU KNOW, HIS ALIEN LUNGS ALONE WOULD PROBABLY GET US $50 MILLION.

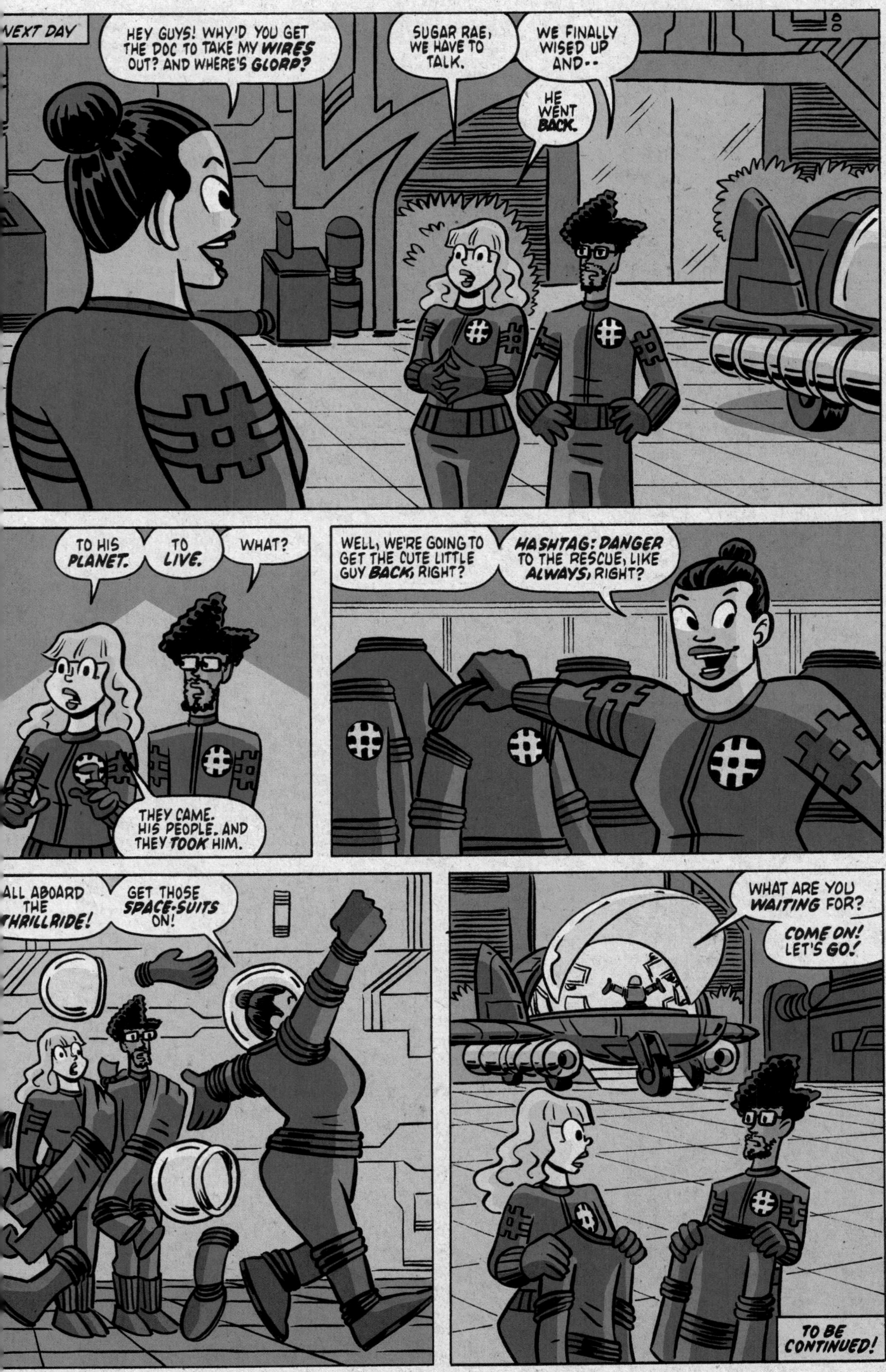

NEXT DAY
HEY GUYS! WHY'D YOU GET THE DOC TO TAKE MY WIRES OUT? AND WHERE'S GLORP?
SUGAR RAE, WE HAVE TO TALK.
WE FINALLY WISED UP AND--
HE WENT BACK.
TO HIS PLANET.
TO LIVE.
WHAT?
THEY CAME. HIS PEOPLE. AND THEY TOOK HIM.
WELL, WE'RE GOING TO GET THE CUTE LITTLE GUY BACK, RIGHT?
HASHTAG: DANGER TO THE RESCUE, LIKE ALWAYS, RIGHT?
ALL ABOARD THE THRILLRIDE!
GET THOSE SPACE-SUITS ON!
WHAT ARE YOU WAITING FOR?
COME ON! LET'S GO!
TO BE CONTINUED!

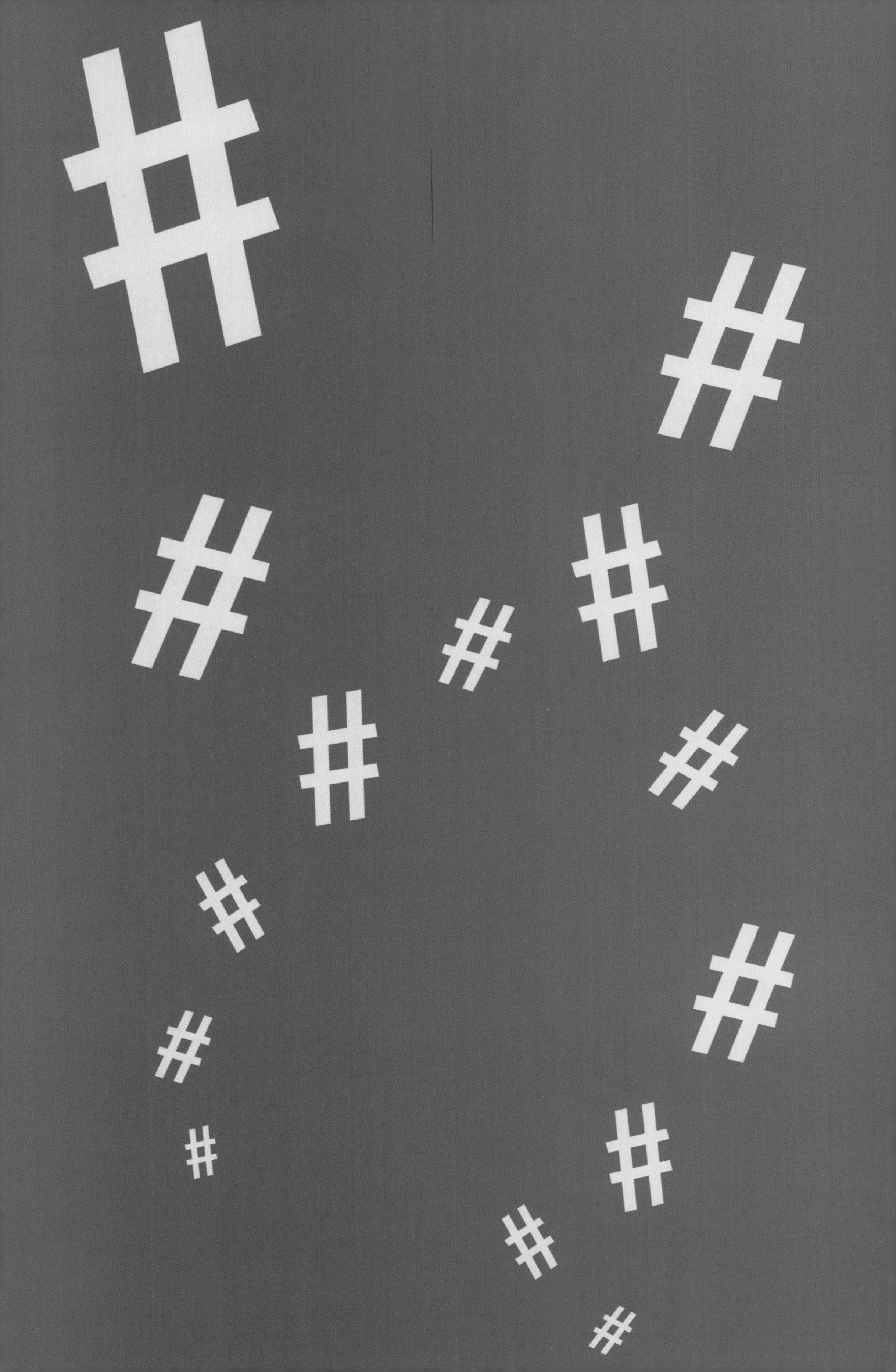

EINSTEIN ARMSTRONG
PH.D. CRYPTO-BIOLOGY
MS SUPER-CRIMINOLOGY

SUGAR RAE HUANG
REIGNING HEAVYWEIGHT CHAMPION:
PACIFIC COAST WOMAN'S CAGE FIGHTING ASSN.

DESIREE DANGER
WINNER: GOOD CITIZENS'
CLUB YOUNG LEADER AWARD

TOGETHER THEY ANSWER THE DESPERATE CRY...

HASHTAG: DANGER

MISSION 000005 RIDDLE OF THE ALIEN MOONBASE!

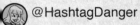

@HashtagDanger

Off to the moon! RT if you're rooting for us, LIKE if you're evil! #HashtagDanger #Pray4Glorp

EINSTEIN, OPEN A HAILING FREQUENCY! I WANT A WORD WITH THE *THING-IN-CHARGE!*

OPENING FREQUENCY.

BIP BAP BOOP

WHAT'S HAPPENING, YOU GUYS?

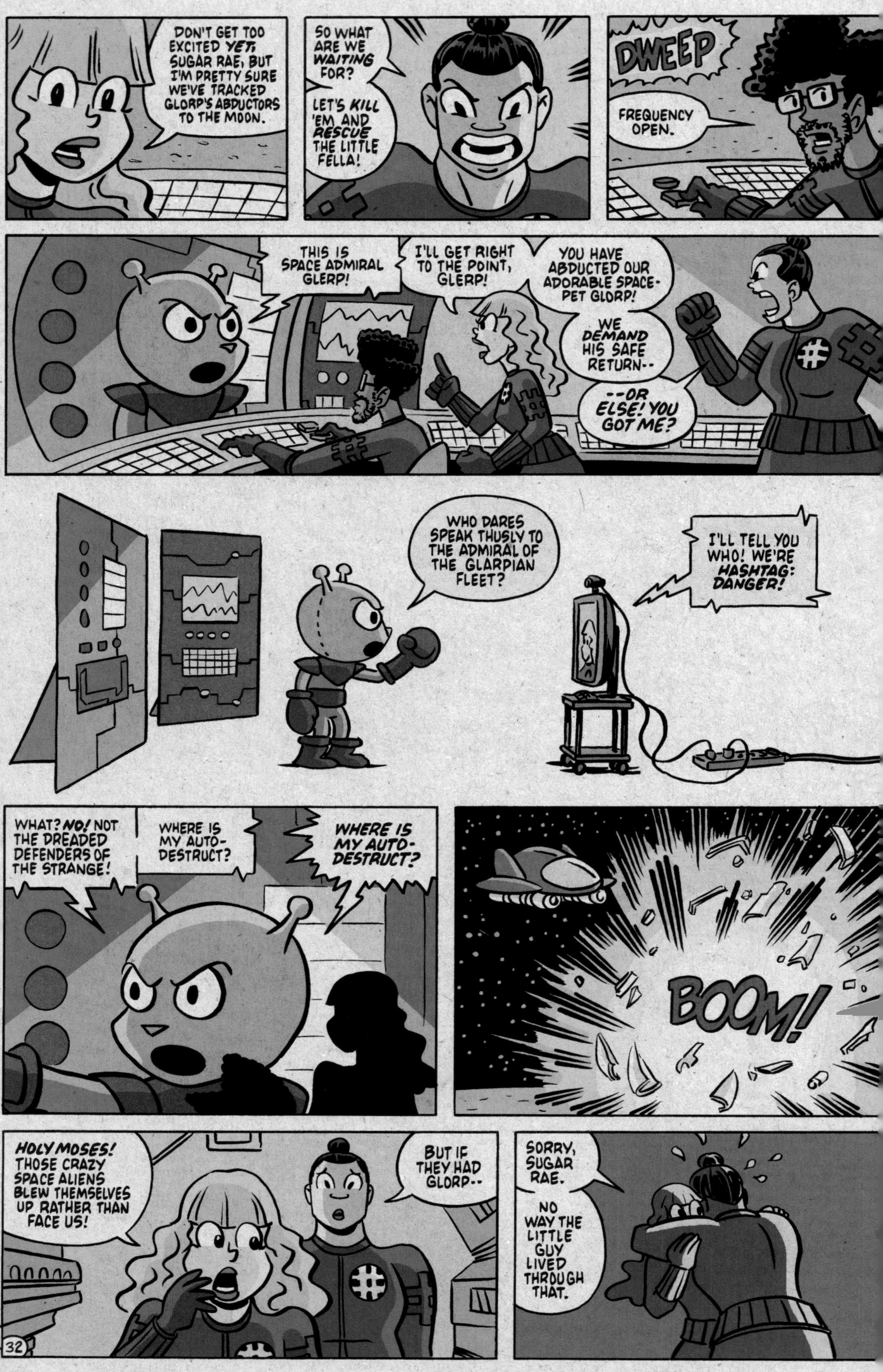
DON'T GET TOO EXCITED YET, SUGAR RAE, BUT I'M PRETTY SURE WE'VE TRACKED GLORP'S ABDUCTORS TO THE MOON.
SO WHAT ARE WE WAITING FOR?
LET'S KILL 'EM AND RESCUE THE LITTLE FELLA!
DWEEP
FREQUENCY OPEN.
THIS IS SPACE ADMIRAL GLERP!
I'LL GET RIGHT TO THE POINT, GLERP!
YOU HAVE ABDUCTED OUR ADORABLE SPACE-PET GLORP!
WE DEMAND HIS SAFE RETURN--
--OR ELSE! YOU GOT ME?
WHO DARES SPEAK THUSLY TO THE ADMIRAL OF THE GLARPIAN FLEET?
I'LL TELL YOU WHO! WE'RE HASHTAG: DANGER!
WHAT? NO! NOT THE DREADED DEFENDERS OF THE STRANGE!
WHERE IS MY AUTO-DESTRUCT?
WHERE IS MY AUTO-DESTRUCT?
BOOM!
HOLY MOSES! THOSE CRAZY SPACE ALIENS BLEW THEMSELVES UP RATHER THAN FACE US!
BUT IF THEY HAD GLORP--
SORRY, SUGAR RAE.
NO WAY THE LITTLE GUY LIVED THROUGH THAT.

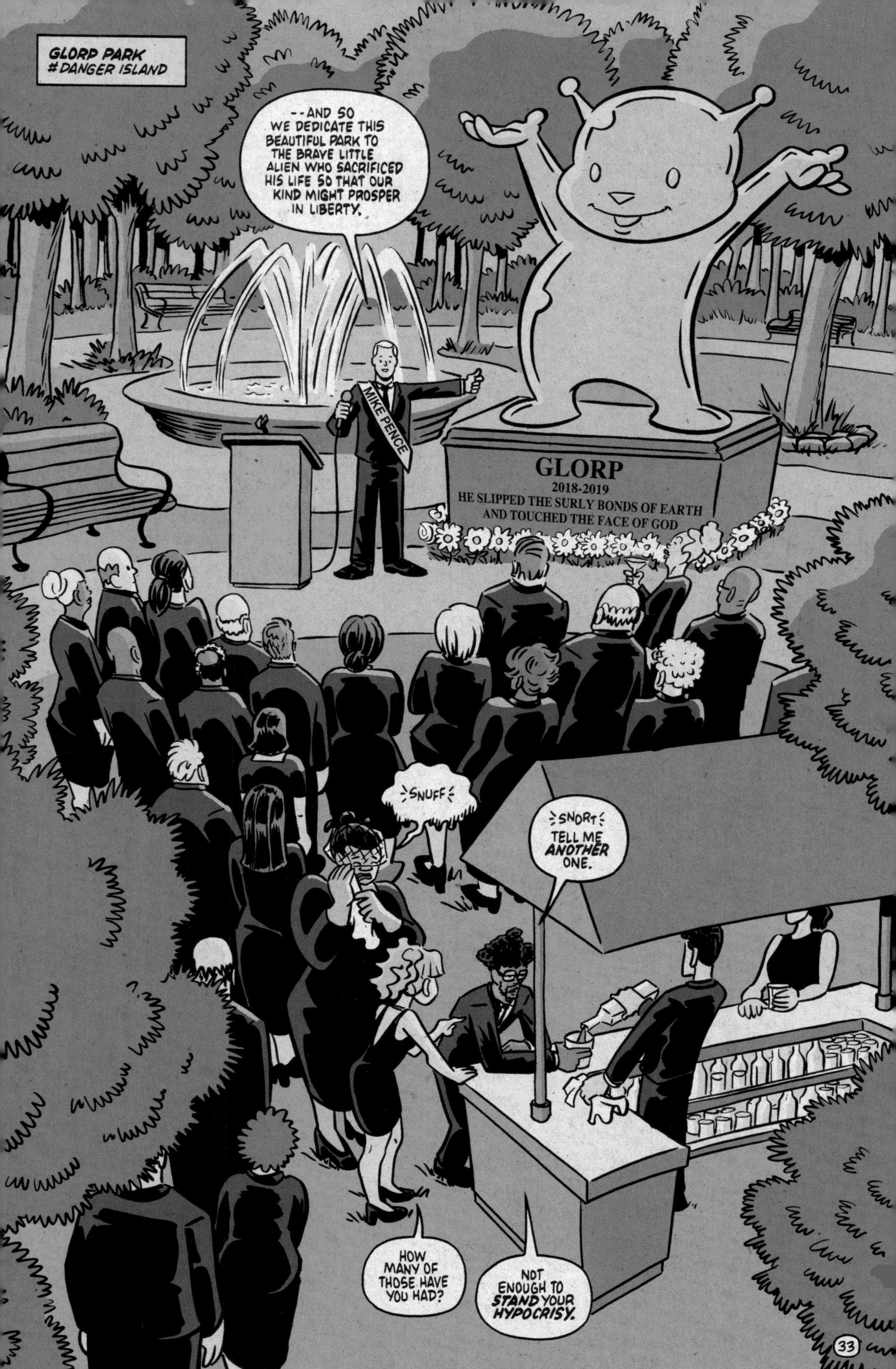
GLORP PARK
DANGER ISLAND
--AND SO WE DEDICATE THIS BEAUTIFUL PARK TO THE BRAVE LITTLE ALIEN WHO SACRIFICED HIS LIFE SO THAT OUR KIND MIGHT PROSPER IN LIBERTY.
MIKE PENCE
GLORP
2018-2019
HE SLIPPED THE SURLY BONDS OF EARTH
AND TOUCHED THE FACE OF GOD
SNUFF
SNORT TELL ME ANOTHER ONE.
HOW MANY OF THOSE HAVE YOU HAD?
NOT ENOUGH TO STAND YOUR HYPOCRISY.

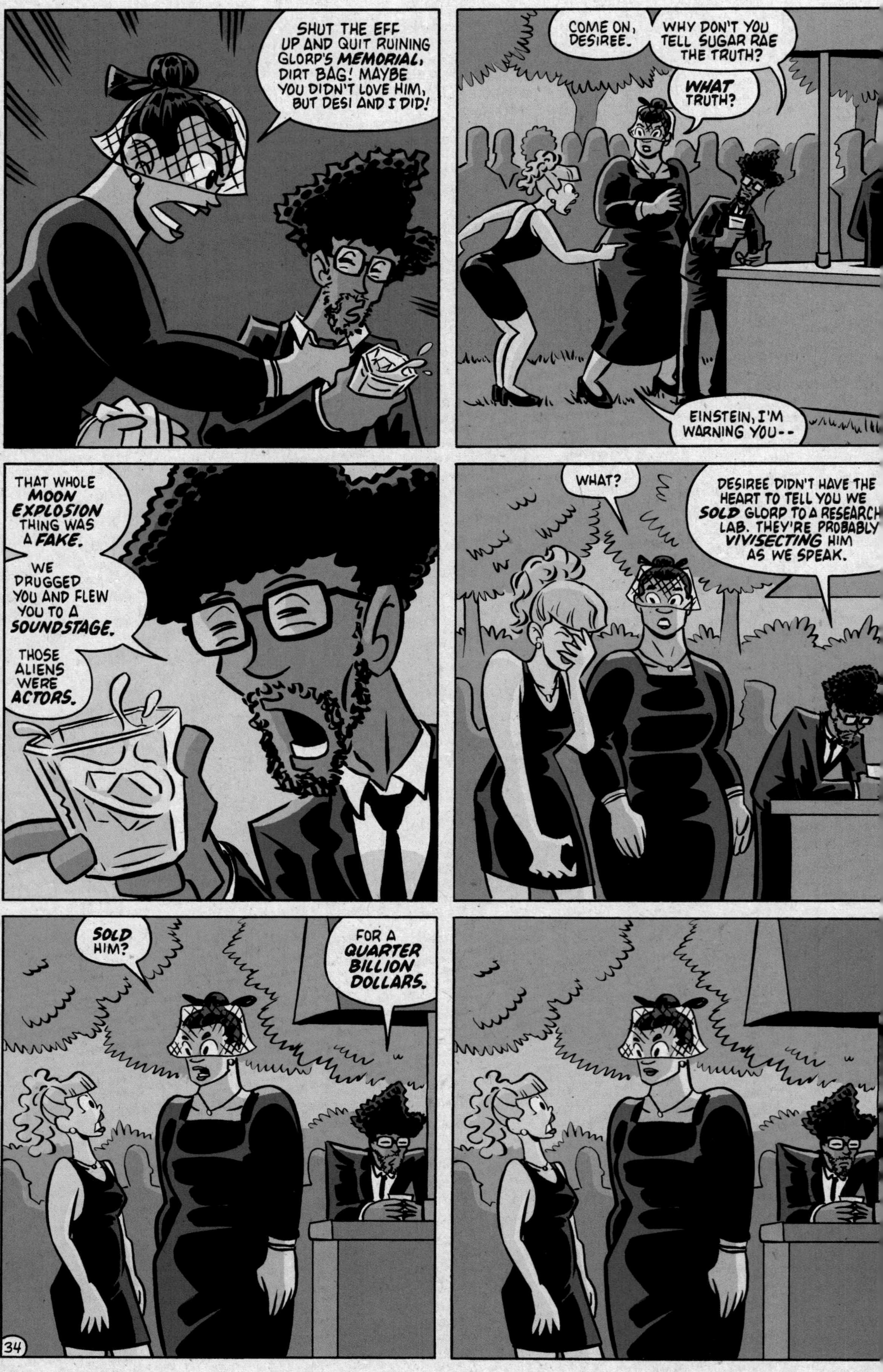
SHUT THE EFF UP AND QUIT RUINING GLORP'S MEMORIAL, DIRT BAG! MAYBE YOU DIDN'T LOVE HIM, BUT DESI AND I DID!
COME ON, DESIREE.
WHY DON'T YOU TELL SUGAR RAE THE TRUTH?
WHAT TRUTH?
EINSTEIN, I'M WARNING YOU--
THAT WHOLE MOON EXPLOSION THING WAS A FAKE.
WE DRUGGED YOU AND FLEW YOU TO A SOUNDSTAGE.
THOSE ALIENS WERE ACTORS.
WHAT?
DESIREE DIDN'T HAVE THE HEART TO TELL YOU WE SOLD GLORP TO A RESEARCH LAB. THEY'RE PROBABLY VIVISECTING HIM AS WE SPEAK.
SOLD HIM?
FOR A QUARTER BILLION DOLLARS.

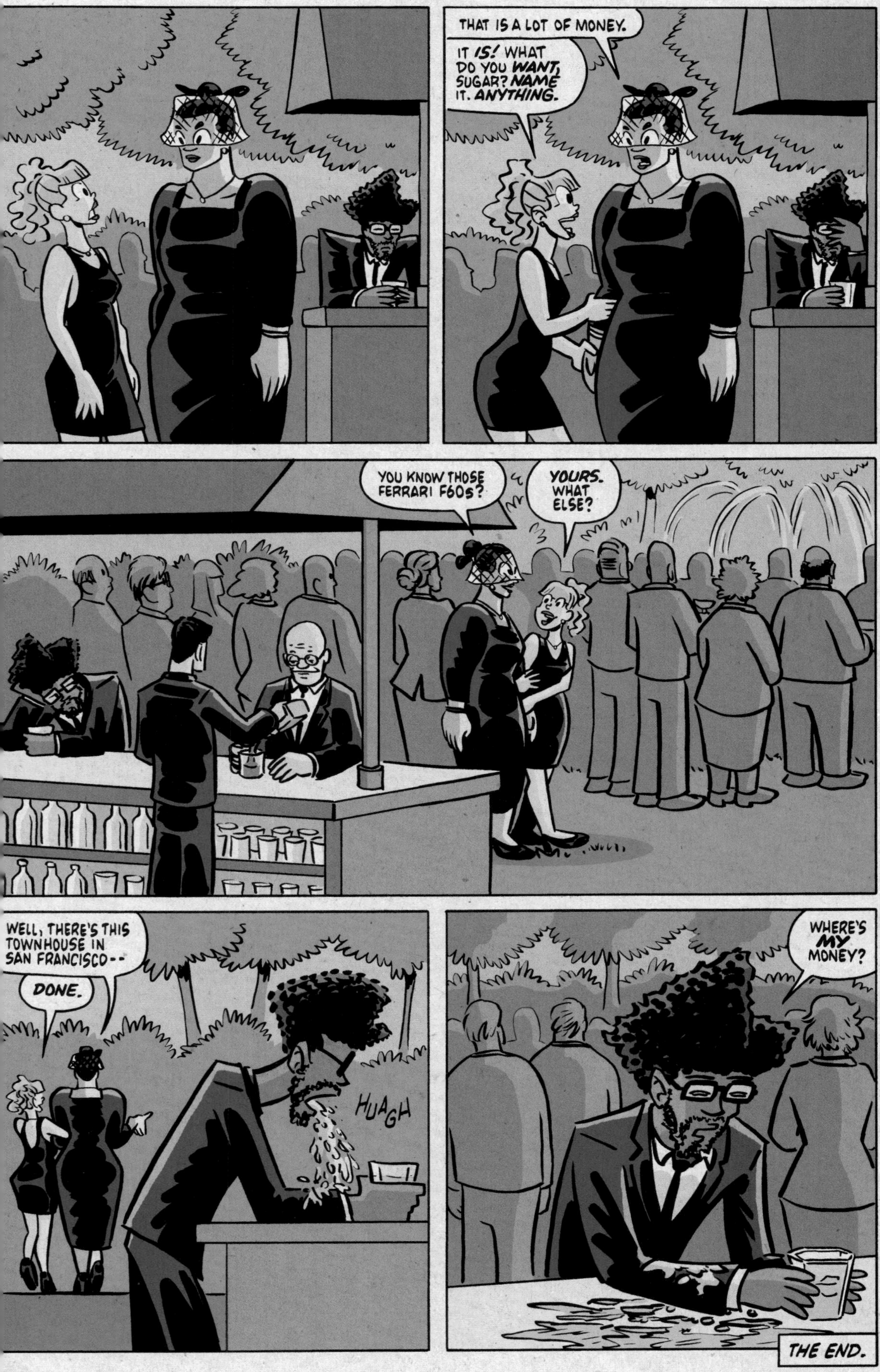
THAT IS A LOT OF MONEY.
IT IS! WHAT DO YOU WANT, SUGAR? NAME IT. ANYTHING.
YOU KNOW THOSE FERRARI F60s?
YOURS. WHAT ELSE?
WELL, THERE'S THIS TOWNHOUSE IN SAN FRANCISCO--
DONE.
HUAGH
WHERE'S MY MONEY?
THE END.

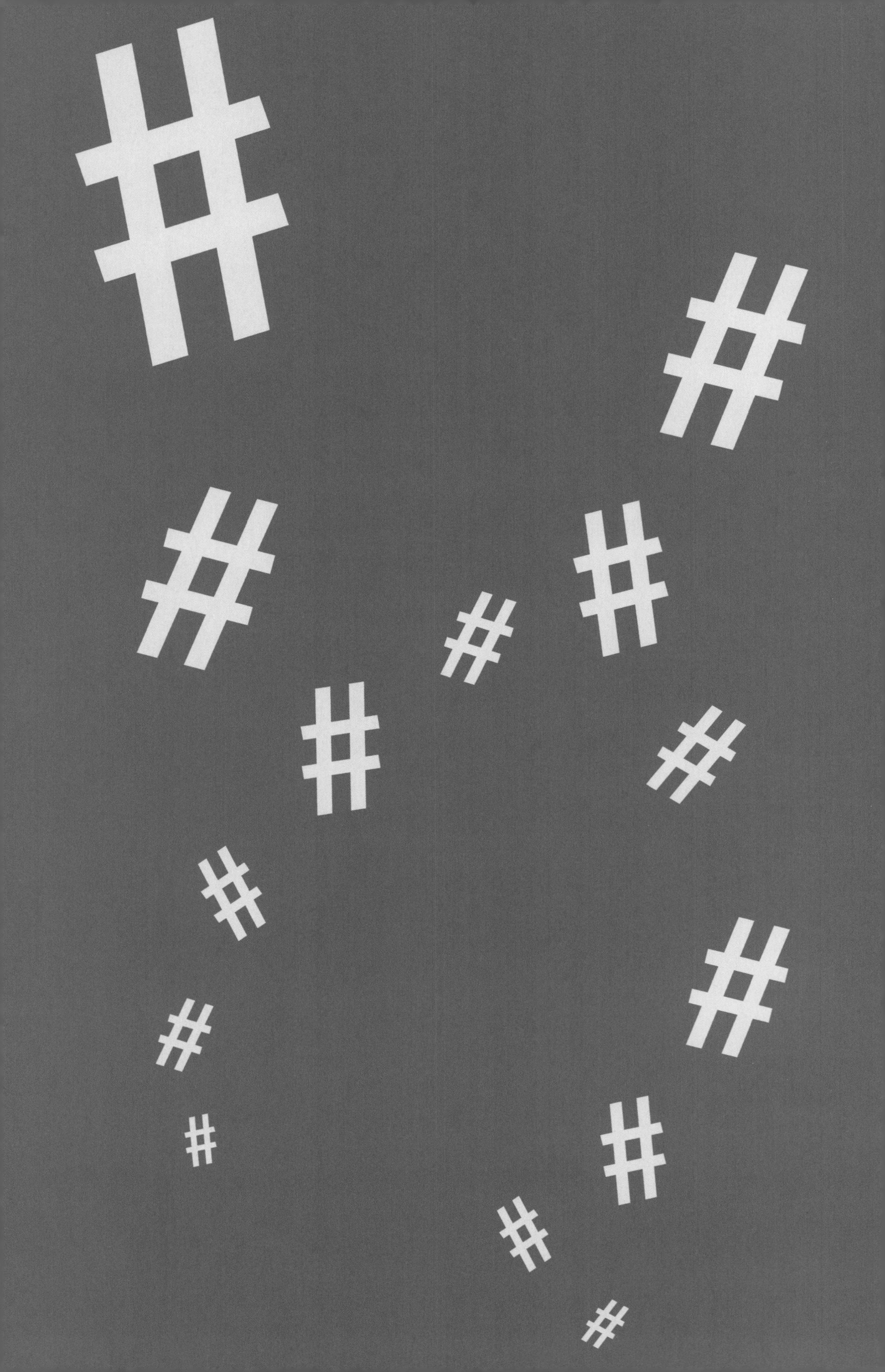

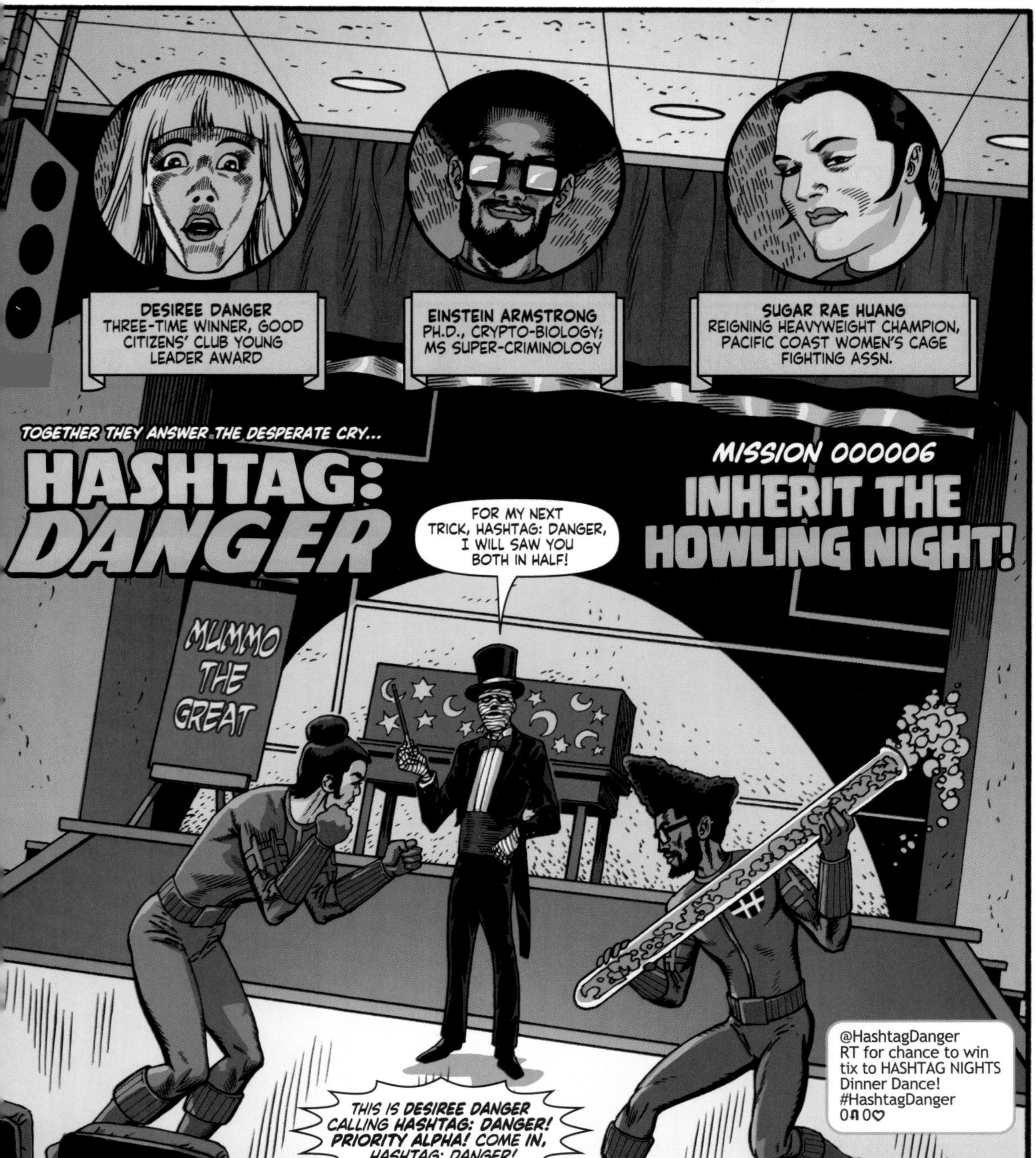
DESIREE DANGER
THREE-TIME WINNER, GOOD CITIZENS' CLUB YOUNG LEADER AWARD
EINSTEIN ARMSTRONG
PH.D., CRYPTO-BIOLOGY; MS SUPER-CRIMINOLOGY
SUGAR RAE HUANG
REIGNING HEAVYWEIGHT CHAMPION, PACIFIC COAST WOMEN'S CAGE FIGHTING ASSN.
TOGETHER THEY ANSWER THE DESPERATE CRY...
HASHTAG: DANGER
MISSION 000006
INHERIT THE HOWLING NIGHT!
FOR MY NEXT TRICK, HASHTAG: DANGER, I WILL SAW YOU BOTH IN HALF!
MUMMO THE GREAT
@HashtagDanger
RT for chance to win tix to HASHTAG NIGHTS Dinner Dance!
#HashtagDanger
0⇄0♡
THIS IS DESIREE DANGER CALLING HASHTAG: DANGER! PRIORITY ALPHA! COME IN, HASHTAG: DANGER!

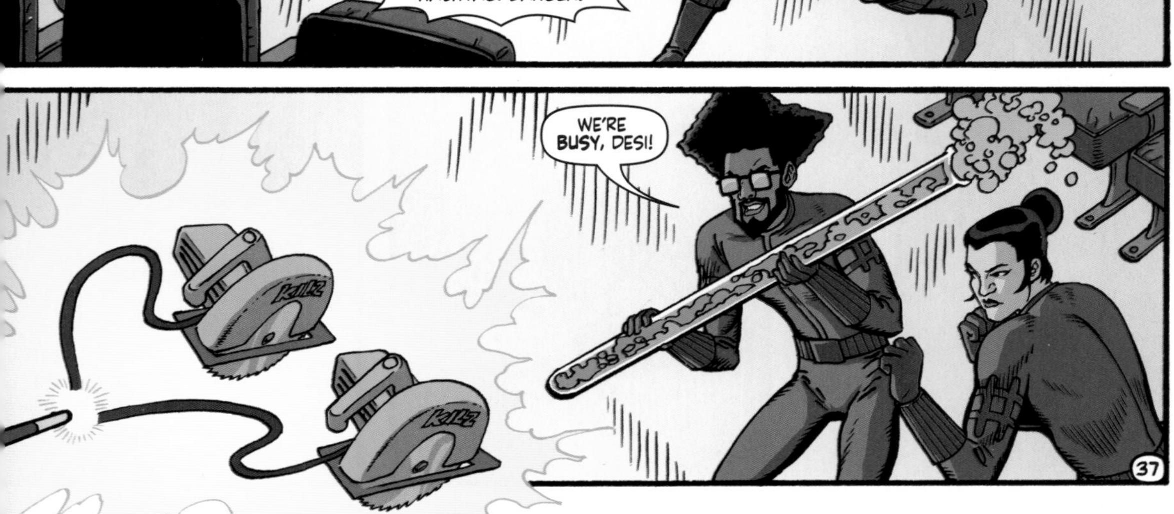
WE'RE BUSY, DESI!

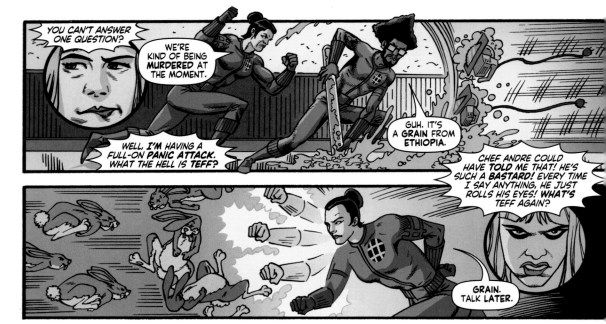

YOU CAN'T ANSWER ONE QUESTION?

WE'RE KIND OF BEING **MURDERED** AT THE MOMENT.

GUH. IT'S A **GRAIN** FROM ETHIOPIA.

WELL, **I'M** HAVING A FULL-ON **PANIC ATTACK.** WHAT THE HELL **IS TEFF?**

CHEF ANDRE COULD HAVE **TOLD** ME THAT! HE'S SUCH A **BASTARD!** EVERY TIME I SAY ANYTHING, HE JUST ROLLS HIS EYES! **WHAT'S** TEFF AGAIN?

GRAIN. TALK LATER.

WHEN? THE DINNER DANCE IS IN **FOUR DAYS** AND I'M THE ONLY ONE LIFTING A GODDAM **FINGER--**

HANGING UP NOW.

POW

GAD, I'D TRADE MY LEFT TESTIS FOR DESI TO BE LESS STUPID.

OWWW!

WHAT'S YOUR PROBLEM, BIG-BRAIN?

DON'T

SNAP

38

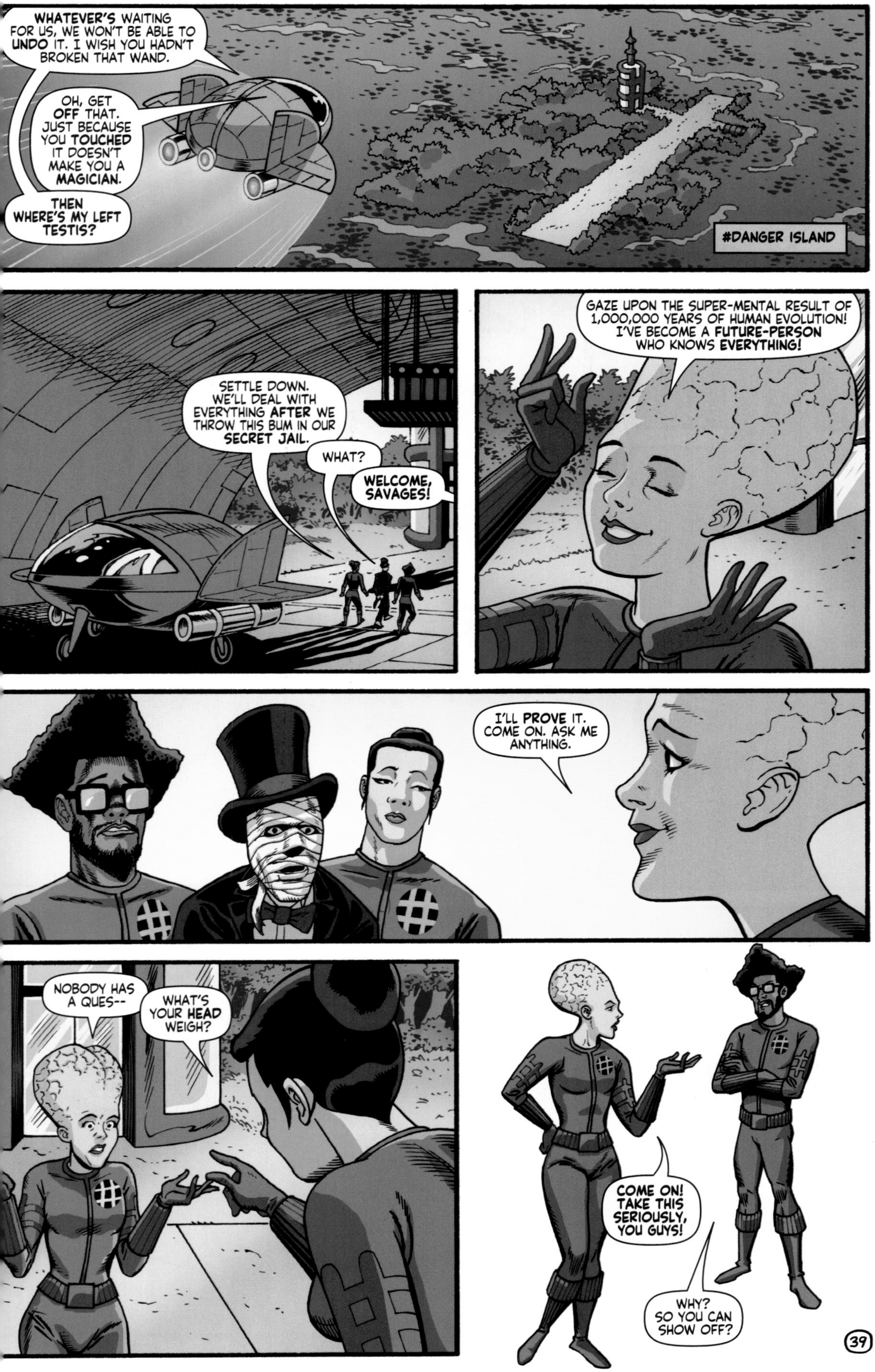
WHATEVER'S WAITING FOR US, WE WON'T BE ABLE TO UNDO IT. I WISH YOU HADN'T BROKEN THAT WAND.
OH, GET OFF THAT. JUST BECAUSE YOU TOUCHED IT DOESN'T MAKE YOU A MAGICIAN.
THEN WHERE'S MY LEFT TESTIS?
#DANGER ISLAND
SETTLE DOWN. WE'LL DEAL WITH EVERYTHING AFTER WE THROW THIS BUM IN OUR SECRET JAIL.
WHAT?
WELCOME, SAVAGES!
GAZE UPON THE SUPER-MENTAL RESULT OF 1,000,000 YEARS OF HUMAN EVOLUTION! I'VE BECOME A FUTURE-PERSON WHO KNOWS EVERYTHING!
I'LL PROVE IT. COME ON. ASK ME ANYTHING.
NOBODY HAS A QUES--
WHAT'S YOUR HEAD WEIGH?
COME ON! TAKE THIS SERIOUSLY, YOU GUYS!
WHY? SO YOU CAN SHOW OFF?

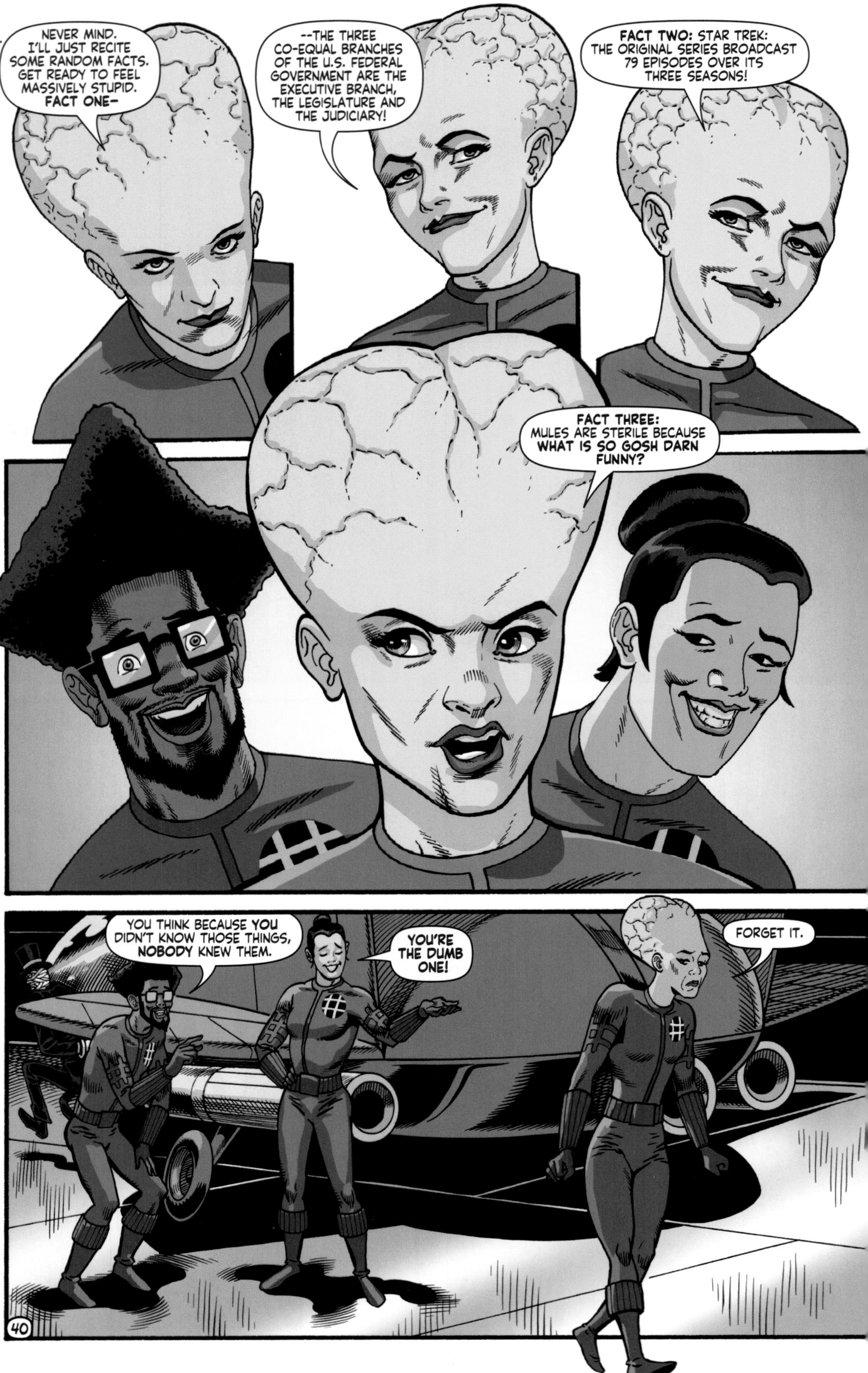
NEVER MIND. I'LL JUST RECITE SOME RANDOM FACTS. GET READY TO FEEL MASSIVELY STUPID. FACT ONE–
--THE THREE CO-EQUAL BRANCHES OF THE U.S. FEDERAL GOVERNMENT ARE THE EXECUTIVE BRANCH, THE LEGISLATURE AND THE JUDICIARY!
FACT TWO: STAR TREK: THE ORIGINAL SERIES BROADCAST 79 EPISODES OVER ITS THREE SEASONS!
FACT THREE: MULES ARE STERILE BECAUSE WHAT IS SO GOSH DARN FUNNY?
YOU THINK BECAUSE YOU DIDN'T KNOW THOSE THINGS, NOBODY KNEW THEM.
YOU'RE THE DUMB ONE!
FORGET IT.

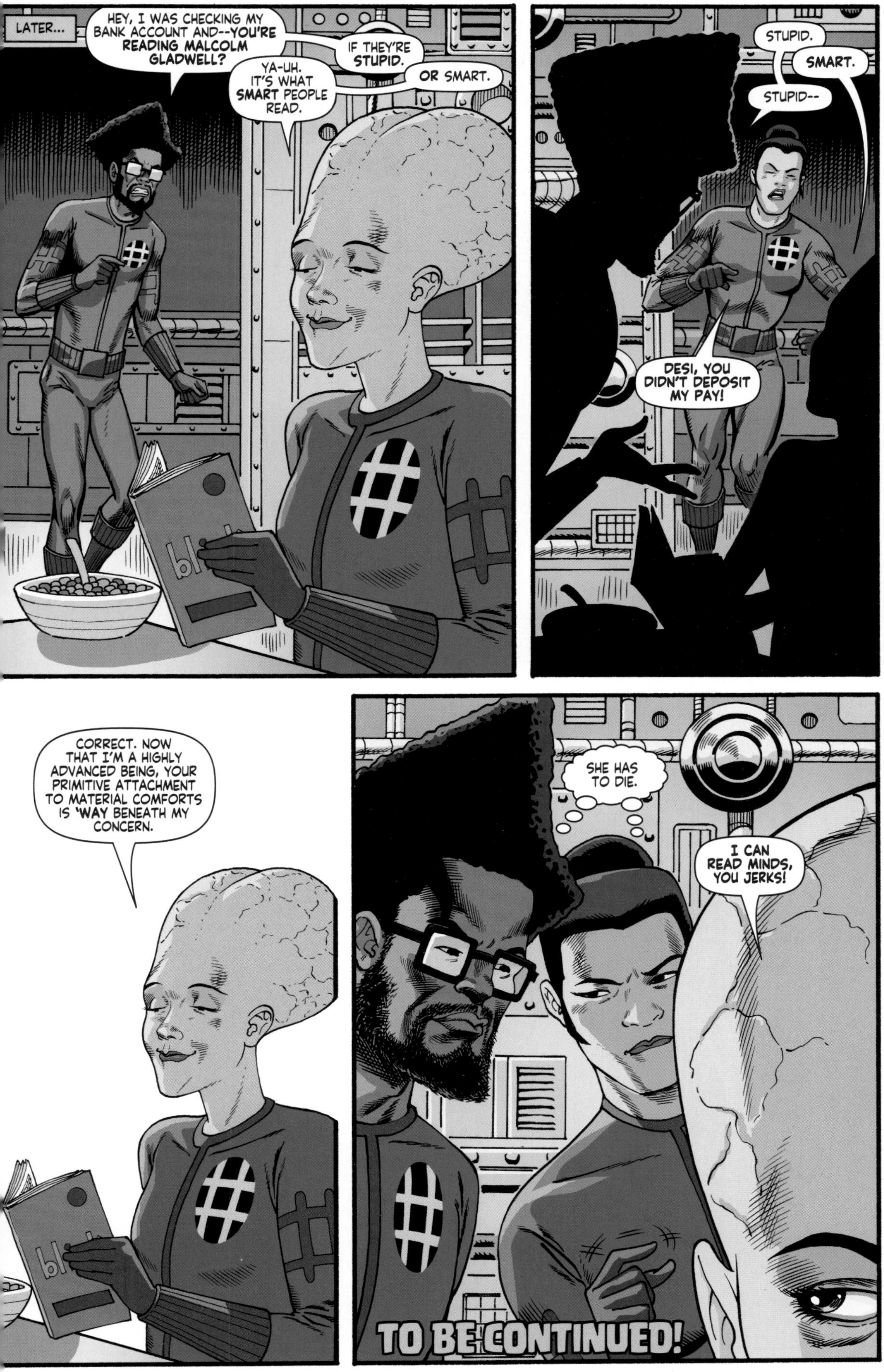
LATER...
HEY, I WAS CHECKING MY BANK ACCOUNT AND--YOU'RE READING MALCOLM GLADWELL?
YA-UH. IT'S WHAT SMART PEOPLE READ.
IF THEY'RE STUPID.
OR SMART.
STUPID.
SMART.
STUPID--
DESI, YOU DIDN'T DEPOSIT MY PAY!
CORRECT. NOW THAT I'M A HIGHLY ADVANCED BEING, YOUR PRIMITIVE ATTACHMENT TO MATERIAL COMFORTS IS 'WAY BENEATH MY CONCERN.
SHE HAS TO DIE.
I CAN READ MINDS, YOU JERKS!
TO BE CONTINUED!

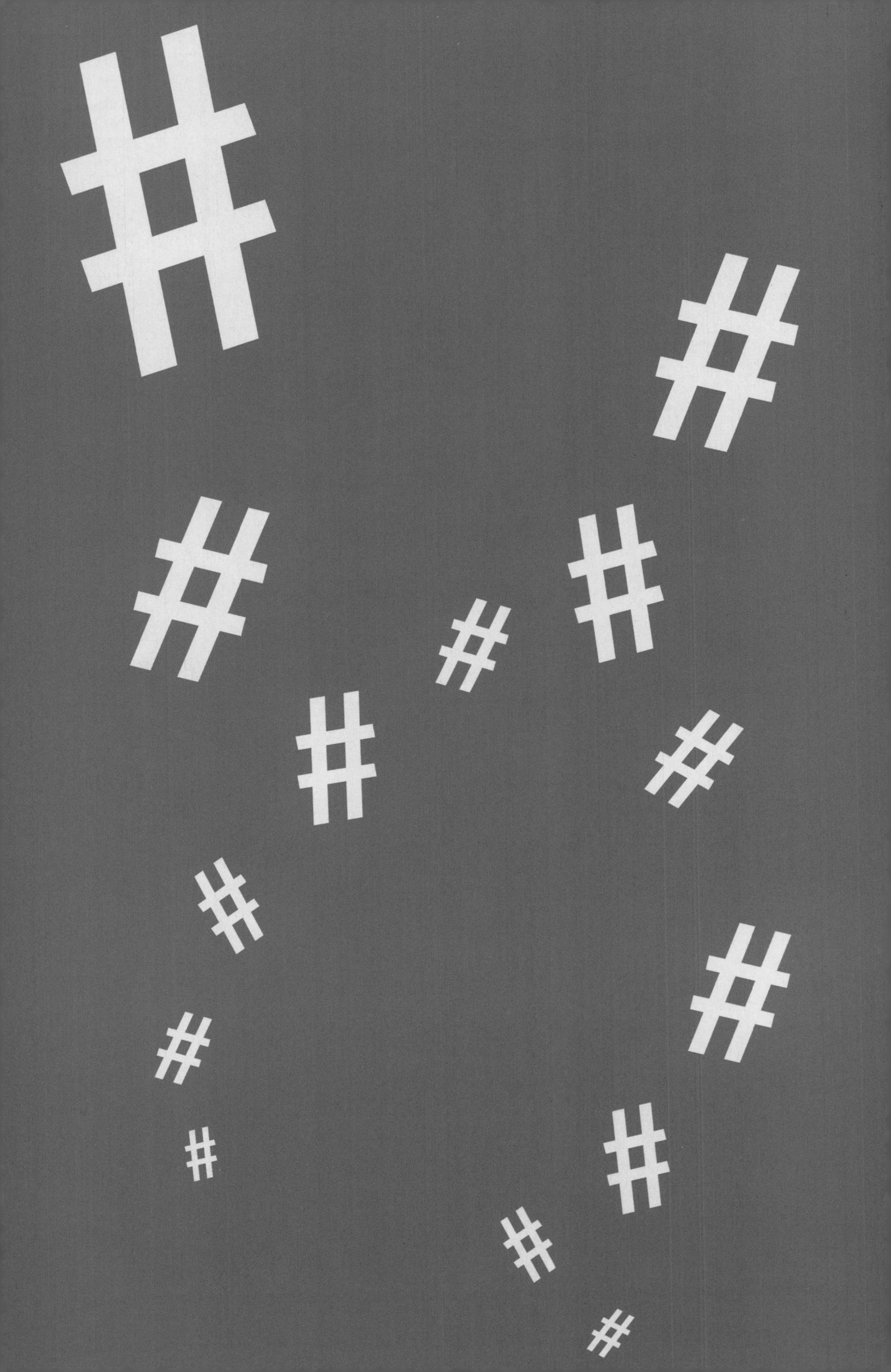

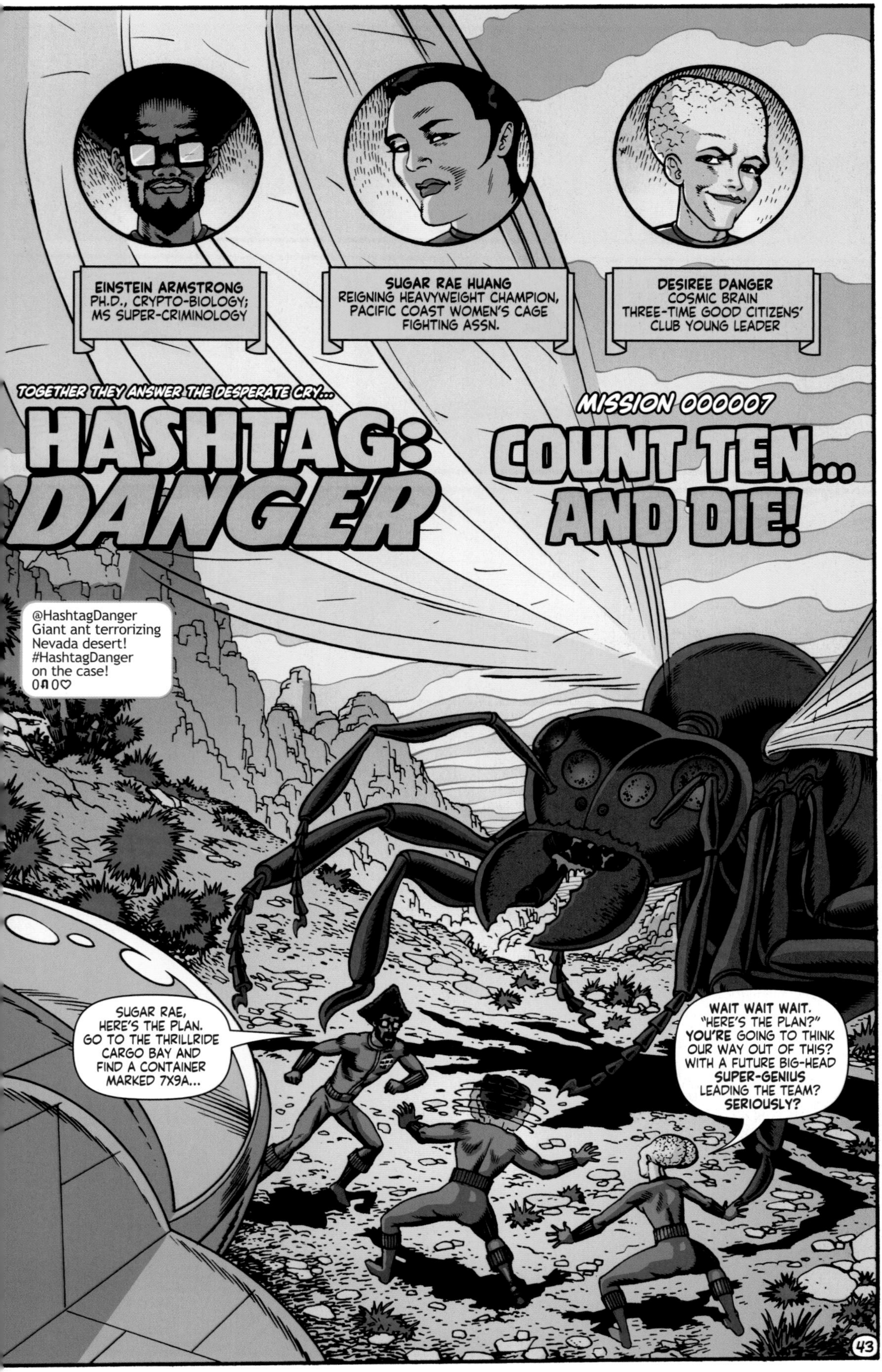
EINSTEIN ARMSTRONG PH.D., CRYPTO-BIOLOGY; MS SUPER-CRIMINOLOGY
SUGAR RAE HUANG REIGNING HEAVYWEIGHT CHAMPION, PACIFIC COAST WOMEN'S CAGE FIGHTING ASSN.
DESIREE DANGER COSMIC BRAIN THREE-TIME GOOD CITIZENS' CLUB YOUNG LEADER
TOGETHER THEY ANSWER THE DESPERATE CRY...
HASHTAG: DANGER
MISSION 000007
COUNT TEN... AND DIE!
@HashtagDanger Giant ant terrorizing Nevada desert! #HashtagDanger on the case!
SUGAR RAE, HERE'S THE PLAN. GO TO THE THRILLRIDE CARGO BAY AND FIND A CONTAINER MARKED 7X9A...
WAIT WAIT WAIT. "HERE'S THE PLAN?" YOU'RE GOING TO THINK OUR WAY OUT OF THIS? WITH A FUTURE BIG-HEAD SUPER-GENIUS LEADING THE TEAM? SERIOUSLY?

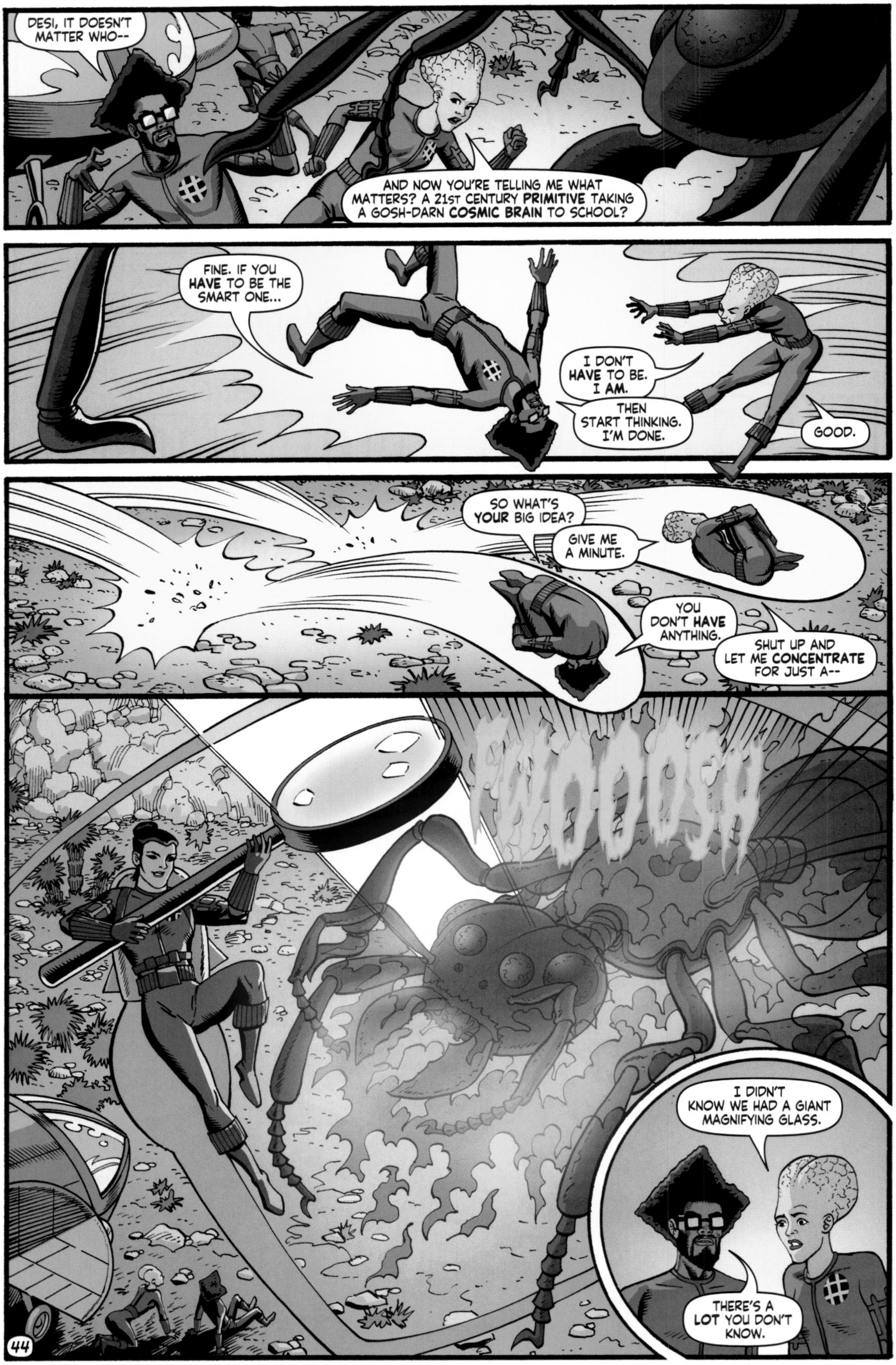
DESI, IT DOESN'T MATTER WHO--
AND NOW YOU'RE TELLING ME WHAT MATTERS? A 21ST CENTURY PRIMITIVE TAKING A GOSH-DARN COSMIC BRAIN TO SCHOOL?
FINE. IF YOU HAVE TO BE THE SMART ONE...
I DON'T HAVE TO BE. I AM.
THEN START THINKING. I'M DONE.
GOOD.
SO WHAT'S YOUR BIG IDEA?
GIVE ME A MINUTE.
YOU DON'T HAVE ANYTHING.
SHUT UP AND LET ME CONCENTRATE FOR JUST A--
FWOOOSH
I DIDN'T KNOW WE HAD A GIANT MAGNIFYING GLASS.
THERE'S A LOT YOU DON'T KNOW.

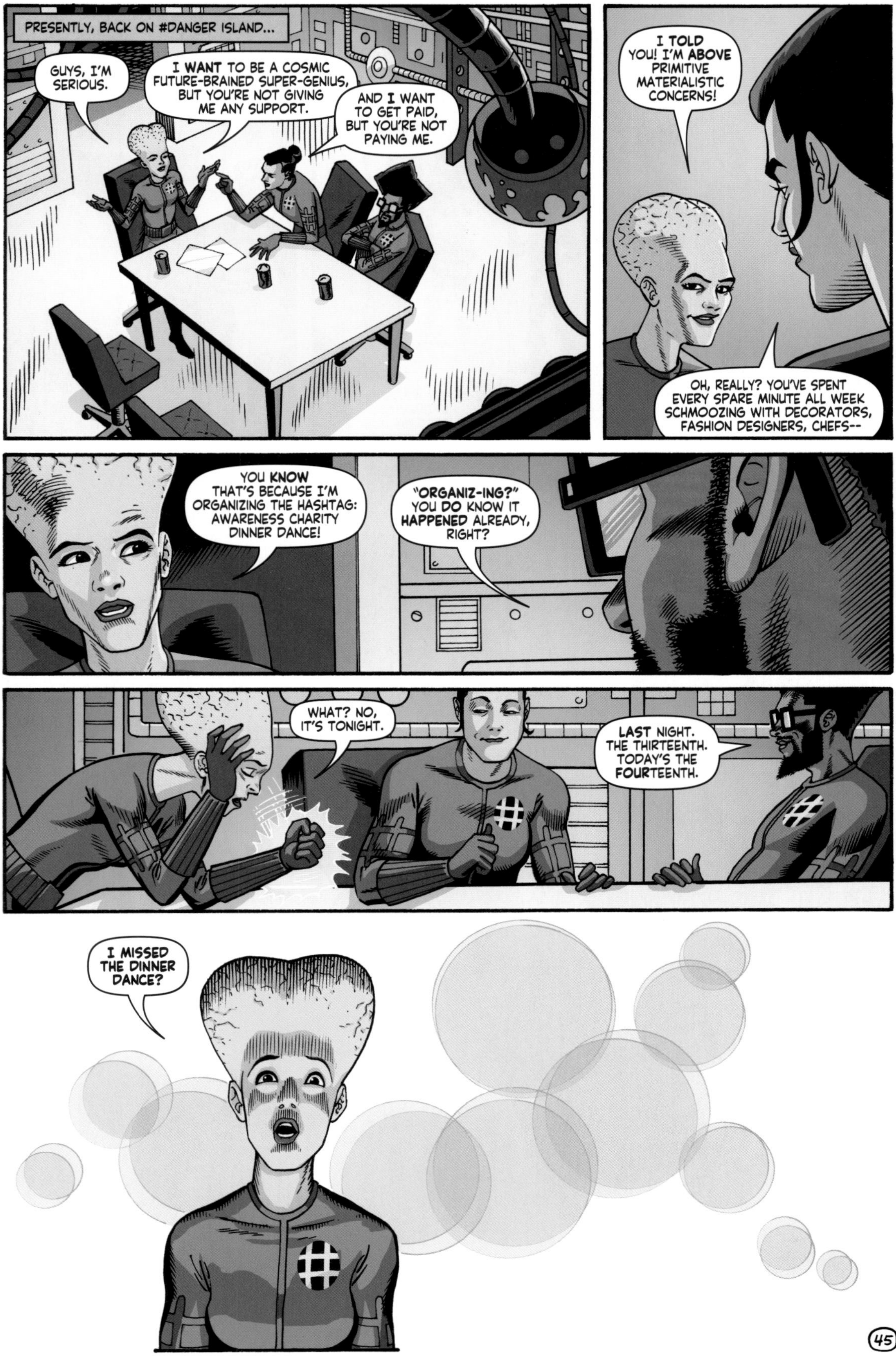
PRESENTLY, BACK ON #DANGER ISLAND...
GUYS, I'M SERIOUS.
I WANT TO BE A COSMIC FUTURE-BRAINED SUPER-GENIUS, BUT YOU'RE NOT GIVING ME ANY SUPPORT.
AND I WANT TO GET PAID, BUT YOU'RE NOT PAYING ME.
I TOLD YOU! I'M ABOVE PRIMITIVE MATERIALISTIC CONCERNS!
OH, REALLY? YOU'VE SPENT EVERY SPARE MINUTE ALL WEEK SCHMOOZING WITH DECORATORS, FASHION DESIGNERS, CHEFS--
YOU KNOW THAT'S BECAUSE I'M ORGANIZING THE HASHTAG: AWARENESS CHARITY DINNER DANCE!
"ORGANIZ-ING?" YOU DO KNOW IT HAPPENED ALREADY, RIGHT?
WHAT? NO, IT'S TONIGHT.
LAST NIGHT. THE THIRTEENTH. TODAY'S THE FOURTEENTH.
I MISSED THE DINNER DANCE?

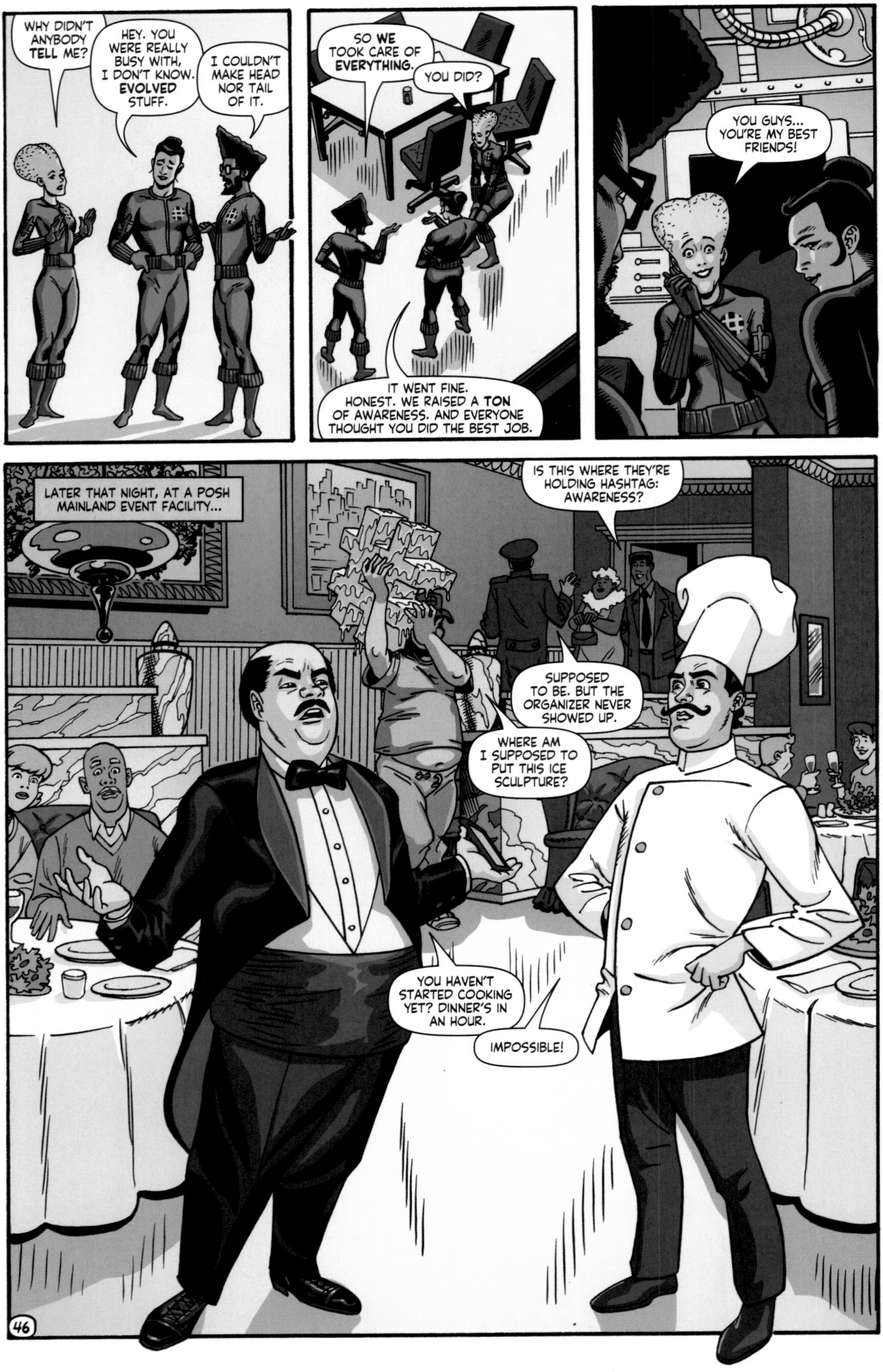
WHY DIDN'T ANYBODY TELL ME?
HEY. YOU WERE REALLY BUSY WITH, I DON'T KNOW. EVOLVED STUFF.
I COULDN'T MAKE HEAD NOR TAIL OF IT.
SO WE TOOK CARE OF EVERYTHING.
YOU DID?
IT WENT FINE. HONEST. WE RAISED A TON OF AWARENESS. AND EVERYONE THOUGHT YOU DID THE BEST JOB.
YOU GUYS... YOU'RE MY BEST FRIENDS!
LATER THAT NIGHT, AT A POSH MAINLAND EVENT FACILITY...
IS THIS WHERE THEY'RE HOLDING HASHTAG: AWARENESS?
SUPPOSED TO BE. BUT THE ORGANIZER NEVER SHOWED UP.
WHERE AM I SUPPOSED TO PUT THIS ICE SCULPTURE?
YOU HAVEN'T STARTED COOKING YET? DINNER'S IN AN HOUR.
IMPOSSIBLE!

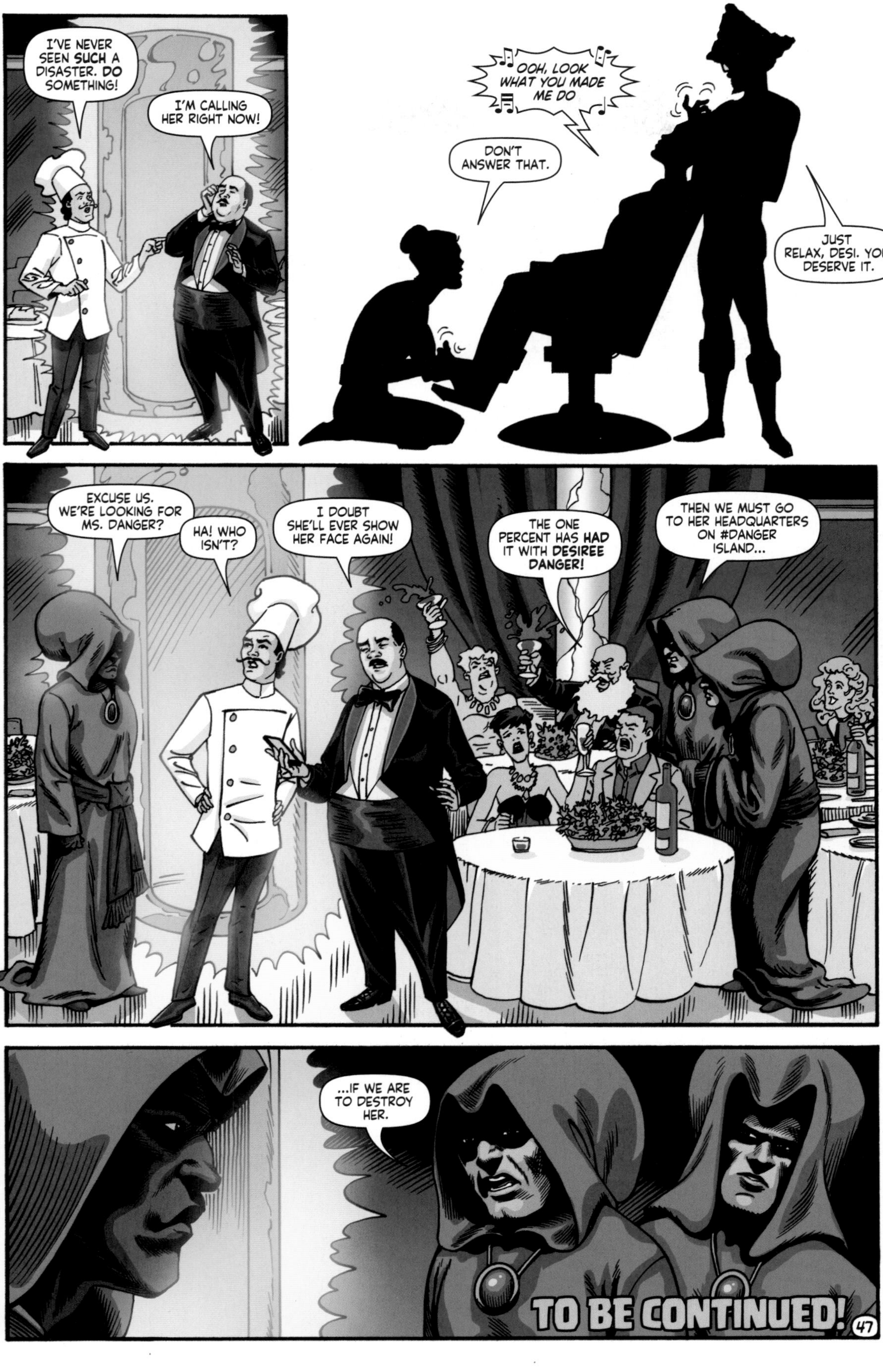
I'VE NEVER SEEN SUCH A DISASTER. DO SOMETHING!
I'M CALLING HER RIGHT NOW!
OOH, LOOK WHAT YOU MADE ME DO
DON'T ANSWER THAT.
JUST RELAX, DESI. YOU DESERVE IT.
EXCUSE US. WE'RE LOOKING FOR MS. DANGER?
HA! WHO ISN'T?
I DOUBT SHE'LL EVER SHOW HER FACE AGAIN!
THE ONE PERCENT HAS HAD IT WITH DESIREE DANGER!
THEN WE MUST GO TO HER HEADQUARTERS ON #DANGER ISLAND...
...IF WE ARE TO DESTROY HER.
TO BE CONTINUED!

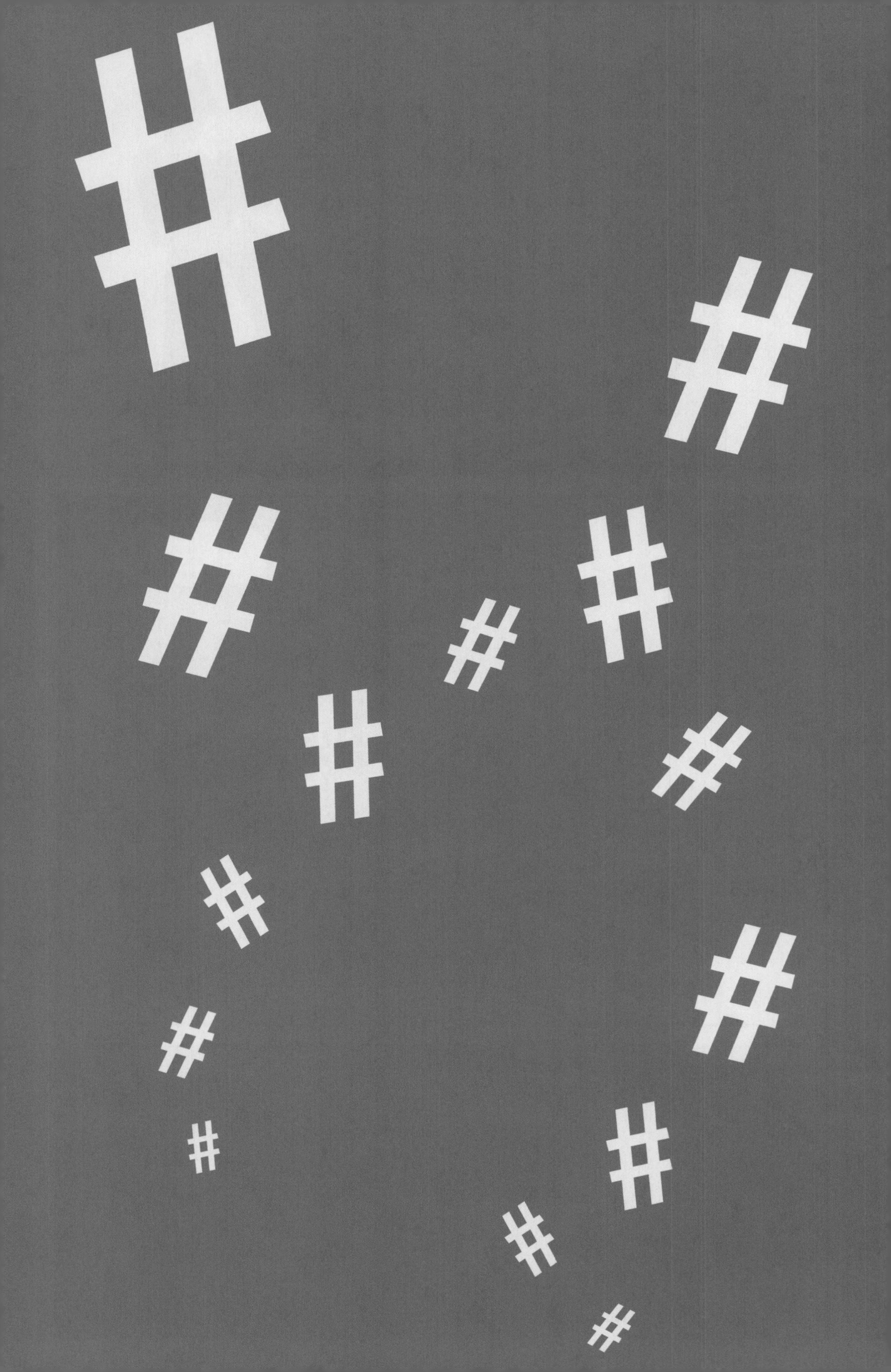

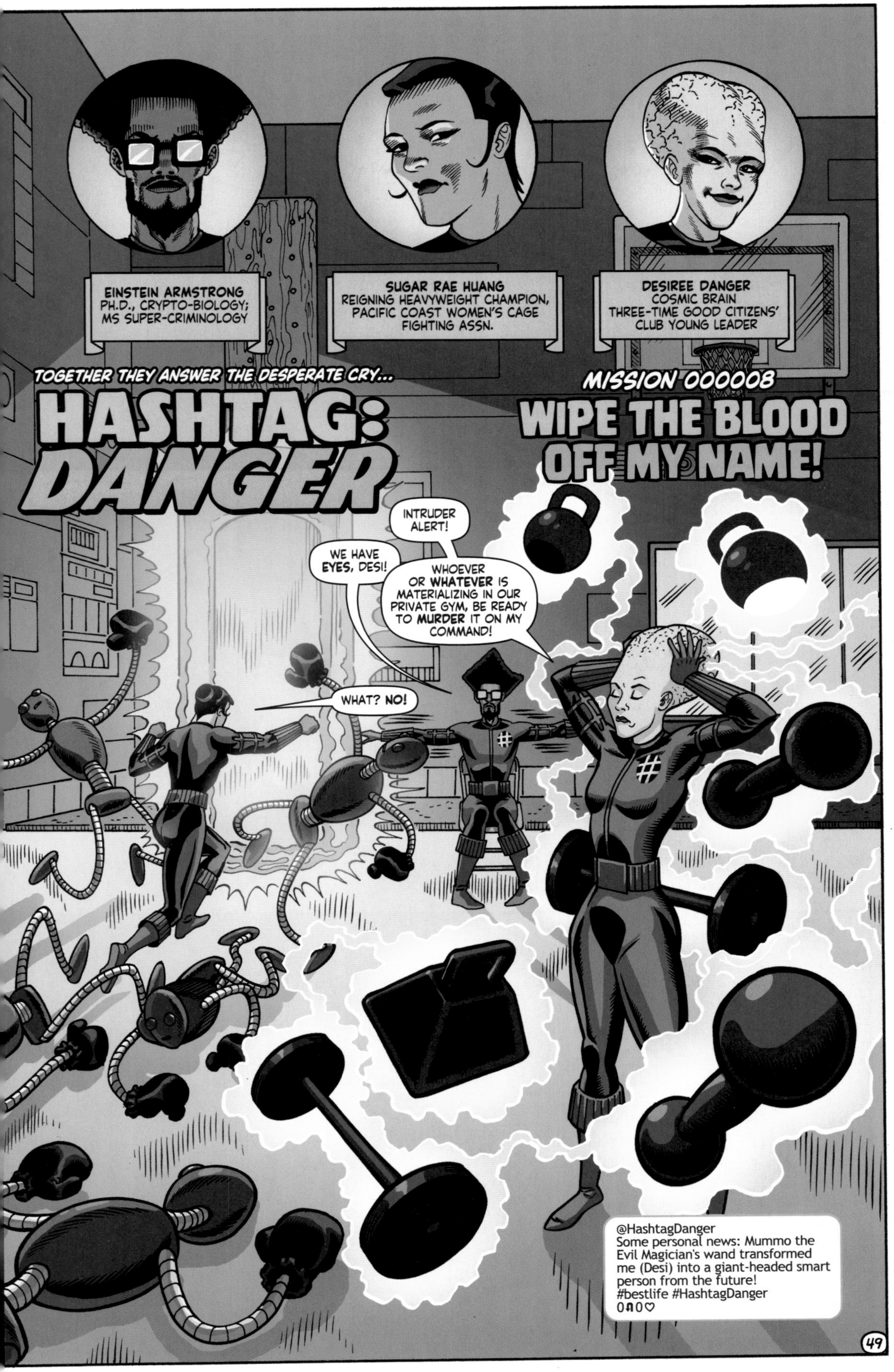
EINSTEIN ARMSTRONG
PH.D., CRYPTO-BIOLOGY; MS SUPER-CRIMINOLOGY
SUGAR RAE HUANG
REIGNING HEAVYWEIGHT CHAMPION, PACIFIC COAST WOMEN'S CAGE FIGHTING ASSN.
DESIREE DANGER
COSMIC BRAIN
THREE-TIME GOOD CITIZENS' CLUB YOUNG LEADER
TOGETHER THEY ANSWER THE DESPERATE CRY...
HASHTAG: DANGER
MISSION 000008
WIPE THE BLOOD OFF MY NAME!
INTRUDER ALERT!
WE HAVE EYES, DESI!
WHOEVER OR WHATEVER IS MATERIALIZING IN OUR PRIVATE GYM, BE READY TO MURDER IT ON MY COMMAND!
WHAT? NO!
@HashtagDanger
Some personal news: Mummo the Evil Magician's wand transformed me (Desi) into a giant-headed smart person from the future!
#bestlife #HashtagDanger

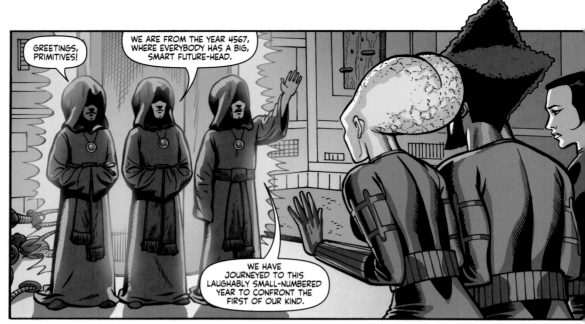

GREETINGS, PRIMITIVES!

WE ARE FROM THE YEAR 4567, WHERE EVERYBODY HAS A BIG, SMART FUTURE-HEAD.

WE HAVE JOURNEYED TO THIS LAUGHABLY SMALL-NUMBERED YEAR TO CONFRONT THE FIRST OF OUR KIND.

COMPUTING... BIG, SMART, FUTURE-HEAD, FIRST OF KIND...

ME?

YOU CAME ALL THIS WAY TO HONOR THE COSMIC BRAIN WHOSE LIMITLESS GENIUS LAID THE FOUNDATION OF YOUR HIGHLY ADVANCED UTOPIA?

BLEAH, NO. WE'RE HERE TO **PREVENT** ALL THAT.

YOU HAVE NO IDEA HOW NARROW-MINDED, NARCISSISTIC, AND **BORING** YOUR INFLUENCE MADE OUR CULTURE.

WE'RE **SICK** OF OURSELVES.

ONCE I RETURN YOUR MIND TO ITS PATHETICALLY LIMITED STATE, HUMAN EVOLUTION WILL RESUME ITS NATURAL COURSE.

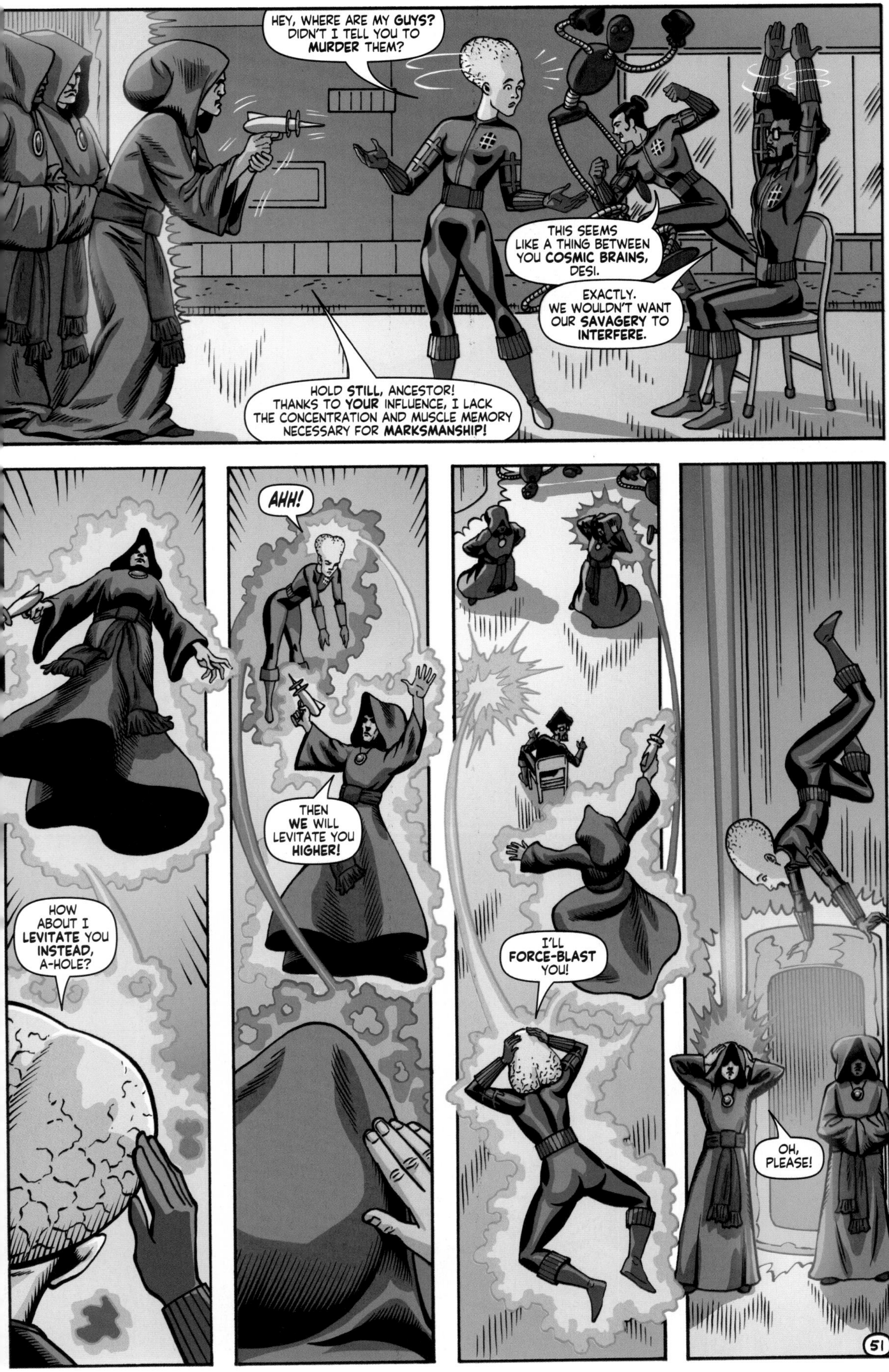
HEY, WHERE ARE MY GUYS? DIDN'T I TELL YOU TO MURDER THEM?
THIS SEEMS LIKE A THING BETWEEN YOU COSMIC BRAINS, DESI.
EXACTLY. WE WOULDN'T WANT OUR SAVAGERY TO INTERFERE.
HOLD STILL, ANCESTOR! THANKS TO YOUR INFLUENCE, I LACK THE CONCENTRATION AND MUSCLE MEMORY NECESSARY FOR MARKSMANSHIP!
HOW ABOUT I LEVITATE YOU INSTEAD, A-HOLE?
AHH!
THEN WE WILL LEVITATE YOU HIGHER!
I'LL FORCE-BLAST YOU!
OH, PLEASE!

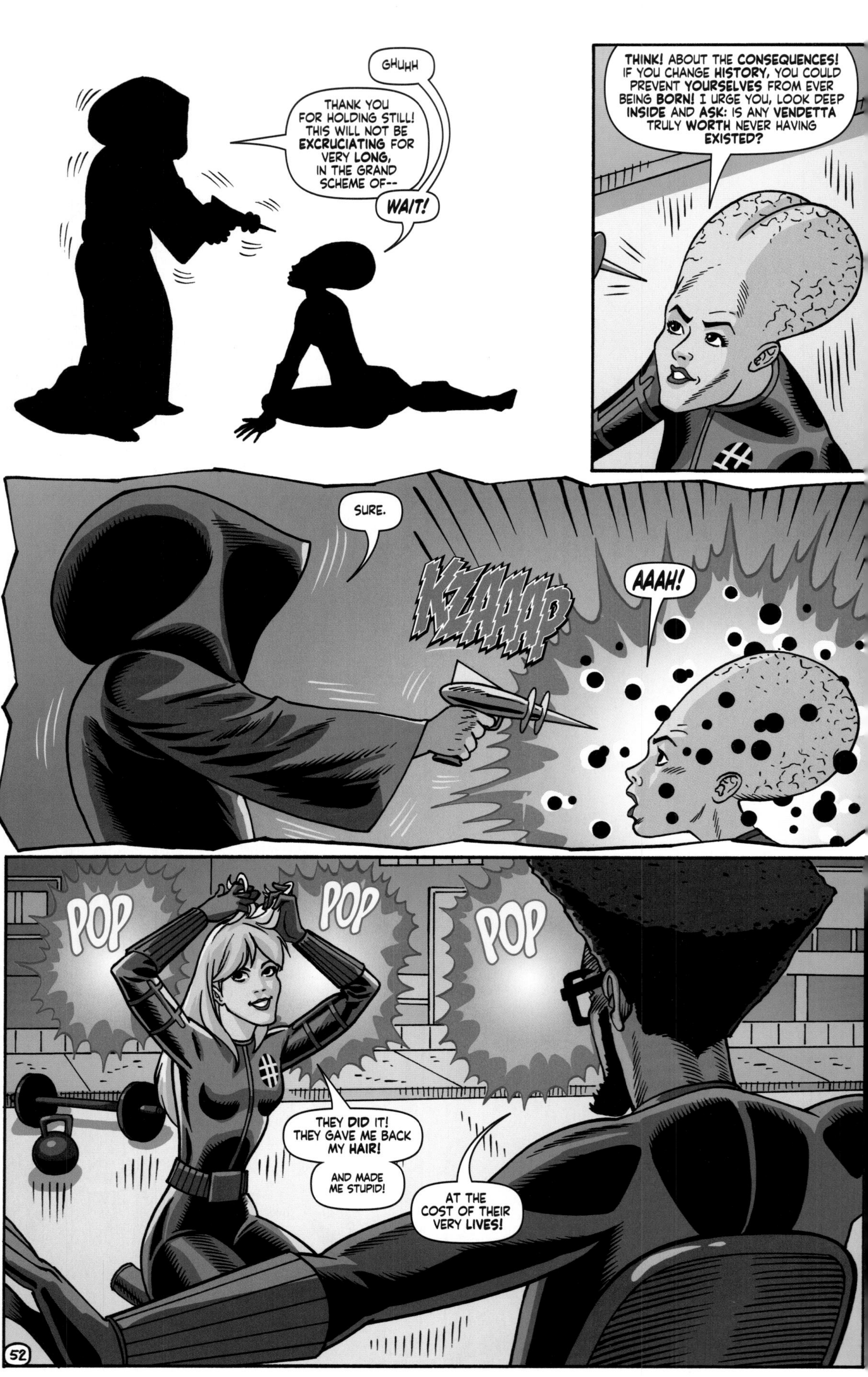
GHUHH
THANK YOU FOR HOLDING STILL! THIS WILL NOT BE EXCRUCIATING FOR VERY LONG, IN THE GRAND SCHEME OF--
WAIT!
THINK! ABOUT THE CONSEQUENCES! IF YOU CHANGE HISTORY, YOU COULD PREVENT YOURSELVES FROM EVER BEING BORN! I URGE YOU, LOOK DEEP INSIDE AND ASK: IS ANY VENDETTA TRULY WORTH NEVER HAVING EXISTED?
SURE.
KZAAAP
AAAH!
POP
POP
POP
THEY DID IT! THEY GAVE ME BACK MY HAIR!
AND MADE ME STUPID!
AT THE COST OF THEIR VERY LIVES!

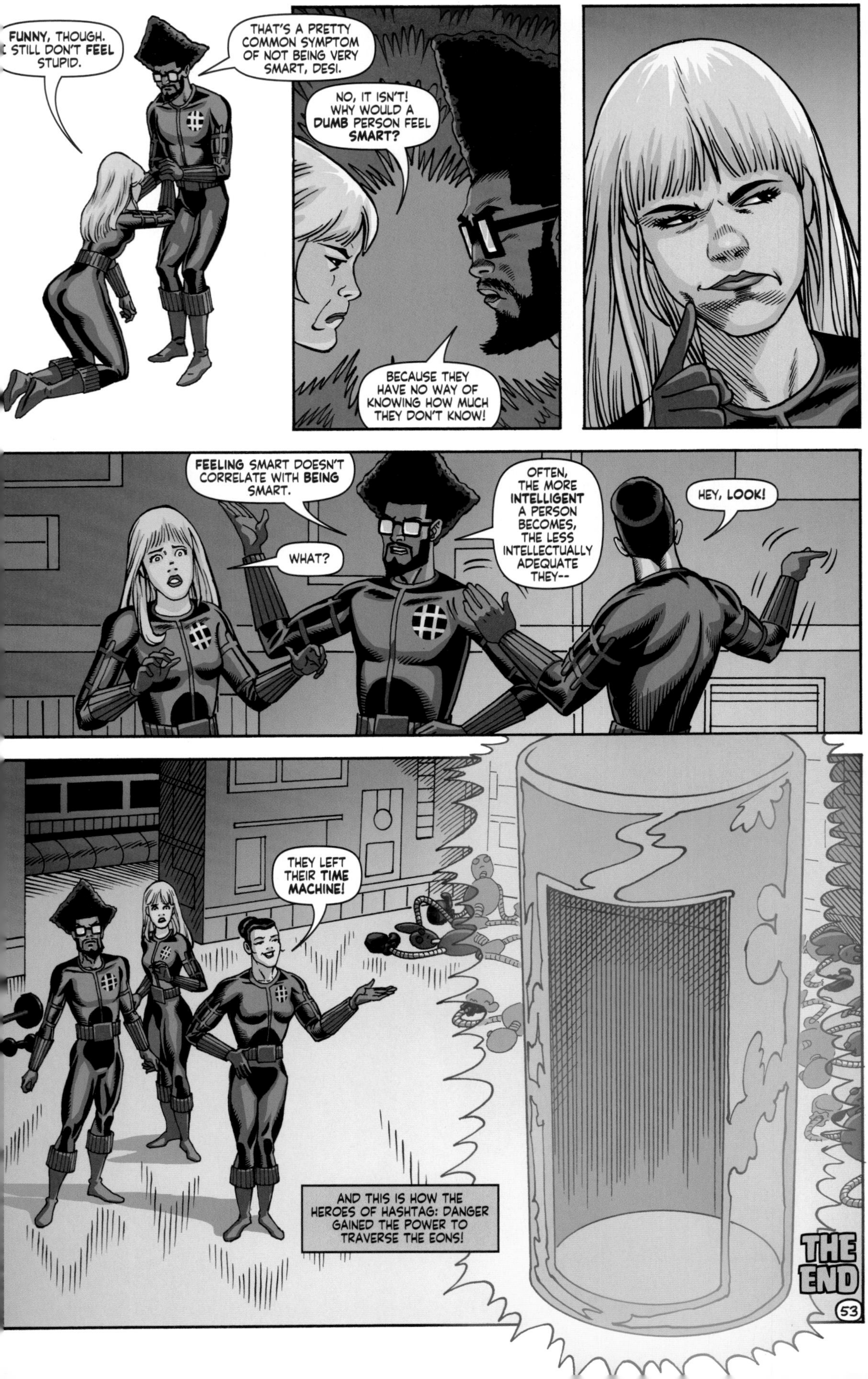
FUNNY, THOUGH. I STILL DON'T FEEL STUPID.
THAT'S A PRETTY COMMON SYMPTOM OF NOT BEING VERY SMART, DESI.
NO, IT ISN'T! WHY WOULD A DUMB PERSON FEEL SMART?
BECAUSE THEY HAVE NO WAY OF KNOWING HOW MUCH THEY DON'T KNOW!
FEELING SMART DOESN'T CORRELATE WITH BEING SMART.
WHAT?
OFTEN, THE MORE INTELLIGENT A PERSON BECOMES, THE LESS INTELLECTUALLY ADEQUATE THEY--
HEY, LOOK!
THEY LEFT THEIR TIME MACHINE!
AND THIS IS HOW THE HEROES OF HASHTAG: DANGER GAINED THE POWER TO TRAVERSE THE EONS!
THE END

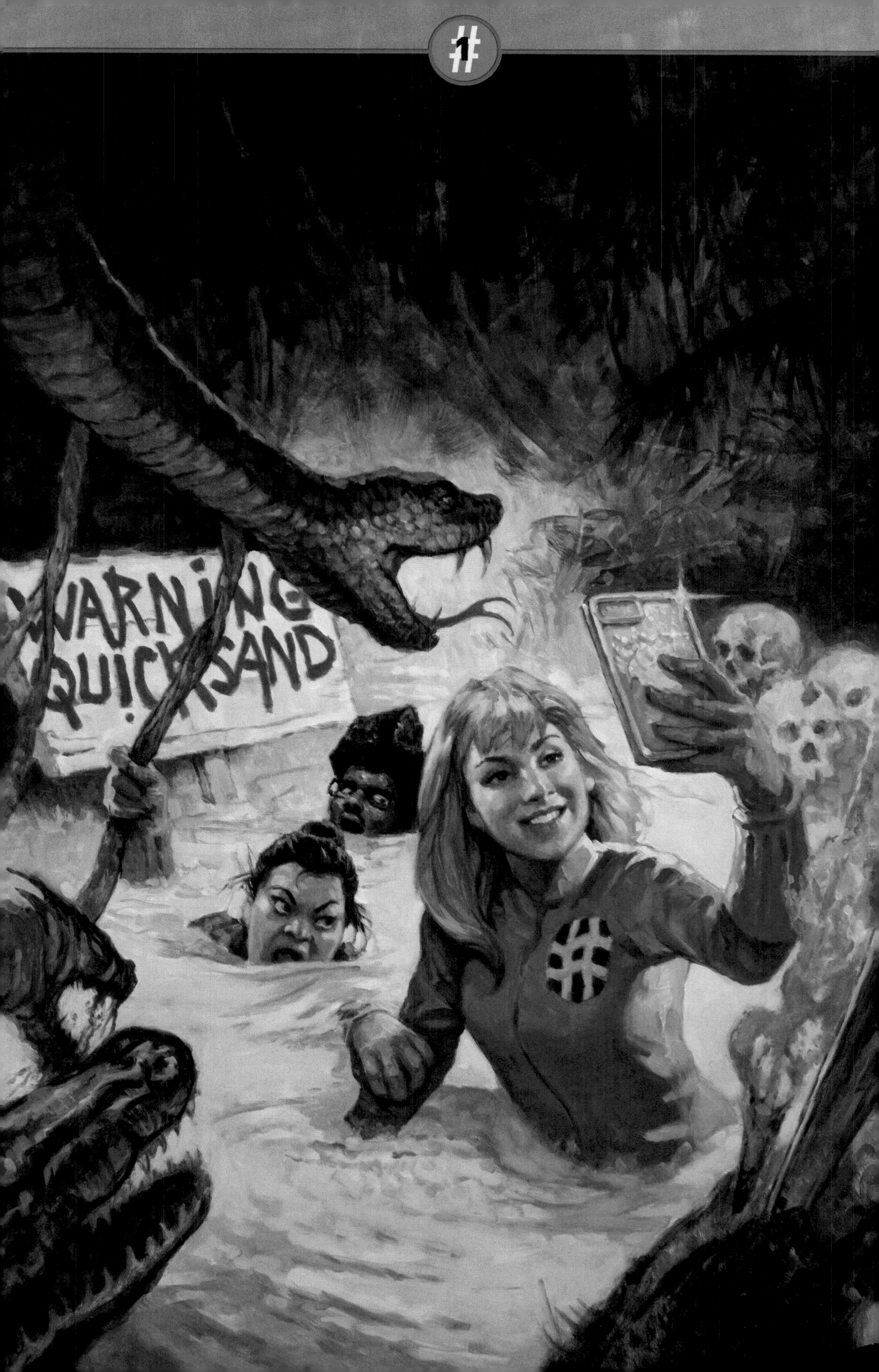
#1
WARNING
QUICKSAND

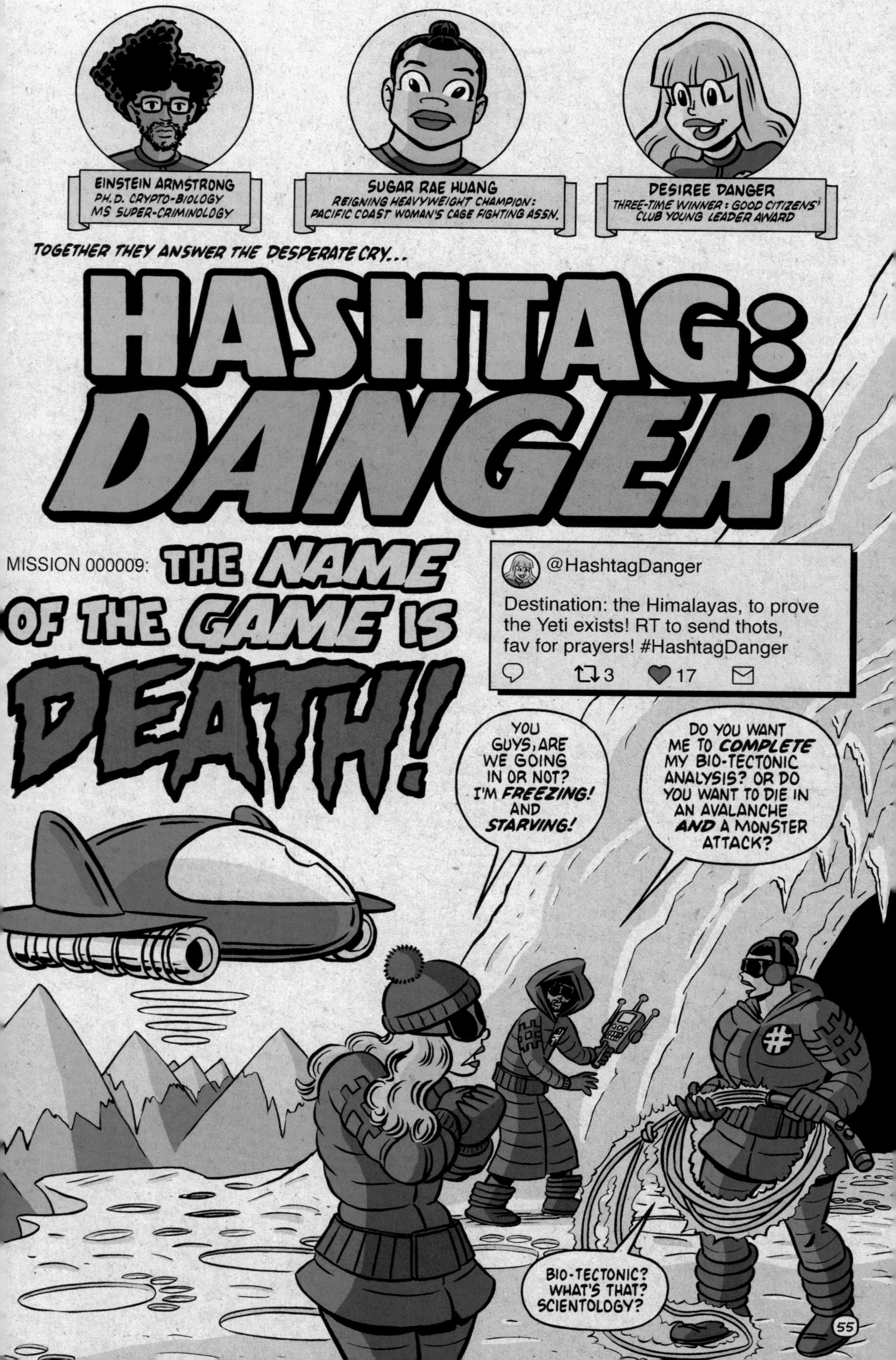
EINSTEIN ARMSTRONG
PH.D. CRYPTO-BIOLOGY
MS SUPER-CRIMINOLOGY
SUGAR RAE HUANG
REIGNING HEAVYWEIGHT CHAMPION: PACIFIC COAST WOMAN'S CAGE FIGHTING ASSN.
DESIREE DANGER
THREE-TIME WINNER: GOOD CITIZENS' CLUB YOUNG LEADER AWARD
TOGETHER THEY ANSWER THE DESPERATE CRY...
HASHTAG: DANGER
MISSION 000009: THE NAME OF THE GAME IS DEATH!
@HashtagDanger
Destination: the Himalayas, to prove the Yeti exists! RT to send thots, fav for prayers! #HashtagDanger
3
17
YOU GUYS, ARE WE GOING IN OR NOT? I'M FREEZING! AND STARVING!
DO YOU WANT ME TO COMPLETE MY BIO-TECTONIC ANALYSIS? OR DO YOU WANT TO DIE IN AN AVALANCHE AND A MONSTER ATTACK?
BIO-TECTONIC? WHAT'S THAT? SCIENTOLOGY?

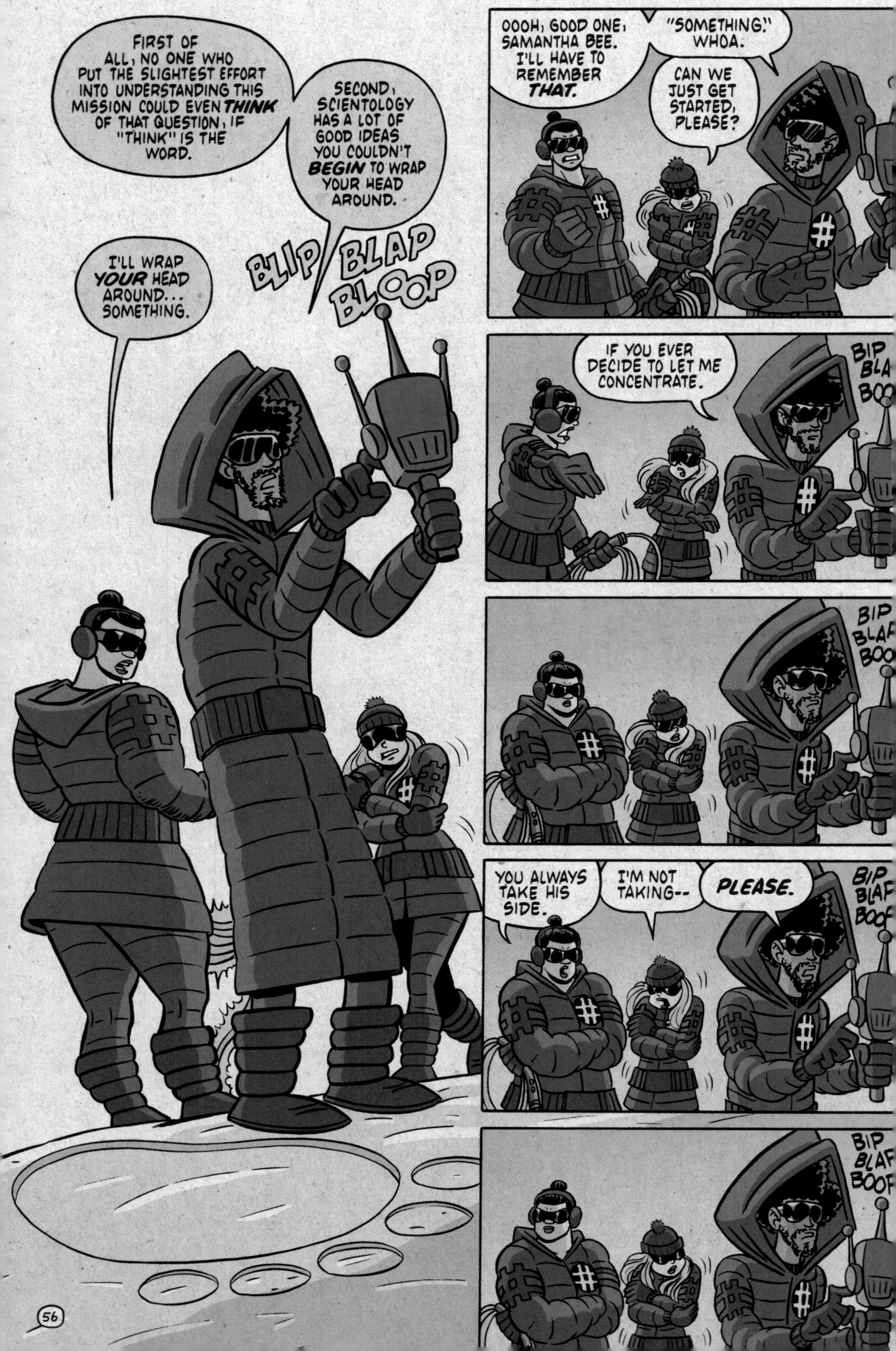
FIRST OF ALL, NO ONE WHO PUT THE SLIGHTEST EFFORT INTO UNDERSTANDING THIS MISSION COULD EVEN THINK OF THAT QUESTION, IF "THINK" IS THE WORD.
SECOND, SCIENTOLOGY HAS A LOT OF GOOD IDEAS YOU COULDN'T BEGIN TO WRAP YOUR HEAD AROUND.
BLIP BLAP BLOOP
I'LL WRAP YOUR HEAD AROUND... SOMETHING.
OOOH, GOOD ONE, SAMANTHA BEE. I'LL HAVE TO REMEMBER THAT.
"SOMETHING." WHOA.
CAN WE JUST GET STARTED, PLEASE?
IF YOU EVER DECIDE TO LET ME CONCENTRATE.
BIP BLA BOO
BIP BLAP BOO
YOU ALWAYS TAKE HIS SIDE.
I'M NOT TAKING--
PLEASE.
BIP BLAP BOOP
BIP BLAP BOOP

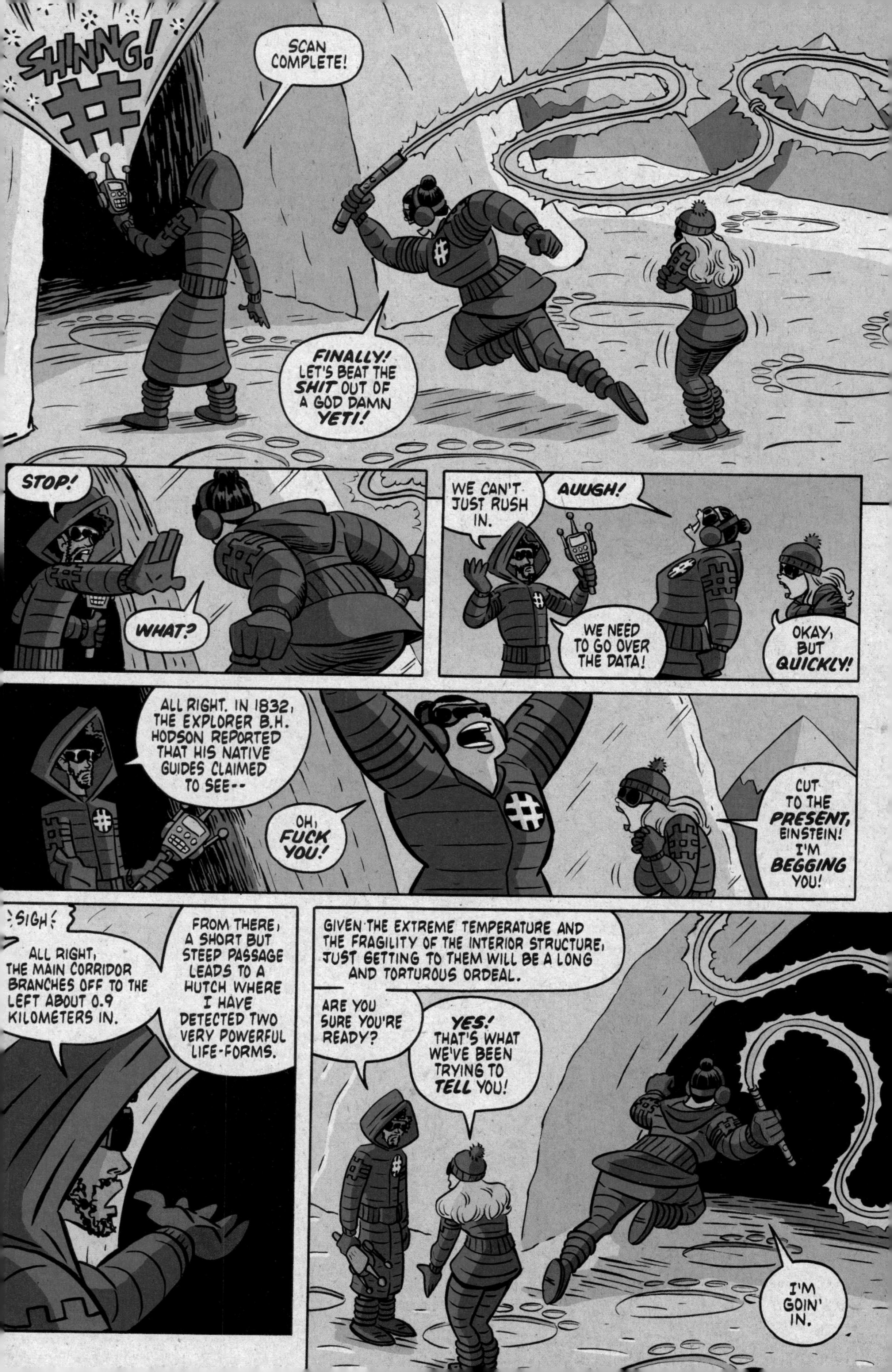
SHINNG!
SCAN COMPLETE!
FINALLY! LET'S BEAT THE SHIT OUT OF A GOD DAMN YETI!
STOP!
WHAT?
WE CAN'T JUST RUSH IN.
AUUGH!
WE NEED TO GO OVER THE DATA!
OKAY, BUT QUICKLY!
ALL RIGHT. IN 1832, THE EXPLORER B.H. HODSON REPORTED THAT HIS NATIVE GUIDES CLAIMED TO SEE--
OH, FUCK YOU!
CUT TO THE PRESENT, EINSTEIN! I'M BEGGING YOU!
SIGH
ALL RIGHT, THE MAIN CORRIDOR BRANCHES OFF TO THE LEFT ABOUT 0.9 KILOMETERS IN.
FROM THERE, A SHORT BUT STEEP PASSAGE LEADS TO A HUTCH WHERE I HAVE DETECTED TWO VERY POWERFUL LIFE-FORMS.
GIVEN THE EXTREME TEMPERATURE AND THE FRAGILITY OF THE INTERIOR STRUCTURE, JUST GETTING TO THEM WILL BE A LONG AND TORTUROUS ORDEAL.
ARE YOU SURE YOU'RE READY?
YES! THAT'S WHAT WE'VE BEEN TRYING TO TELL YOU!
I'M GOIN' IN.

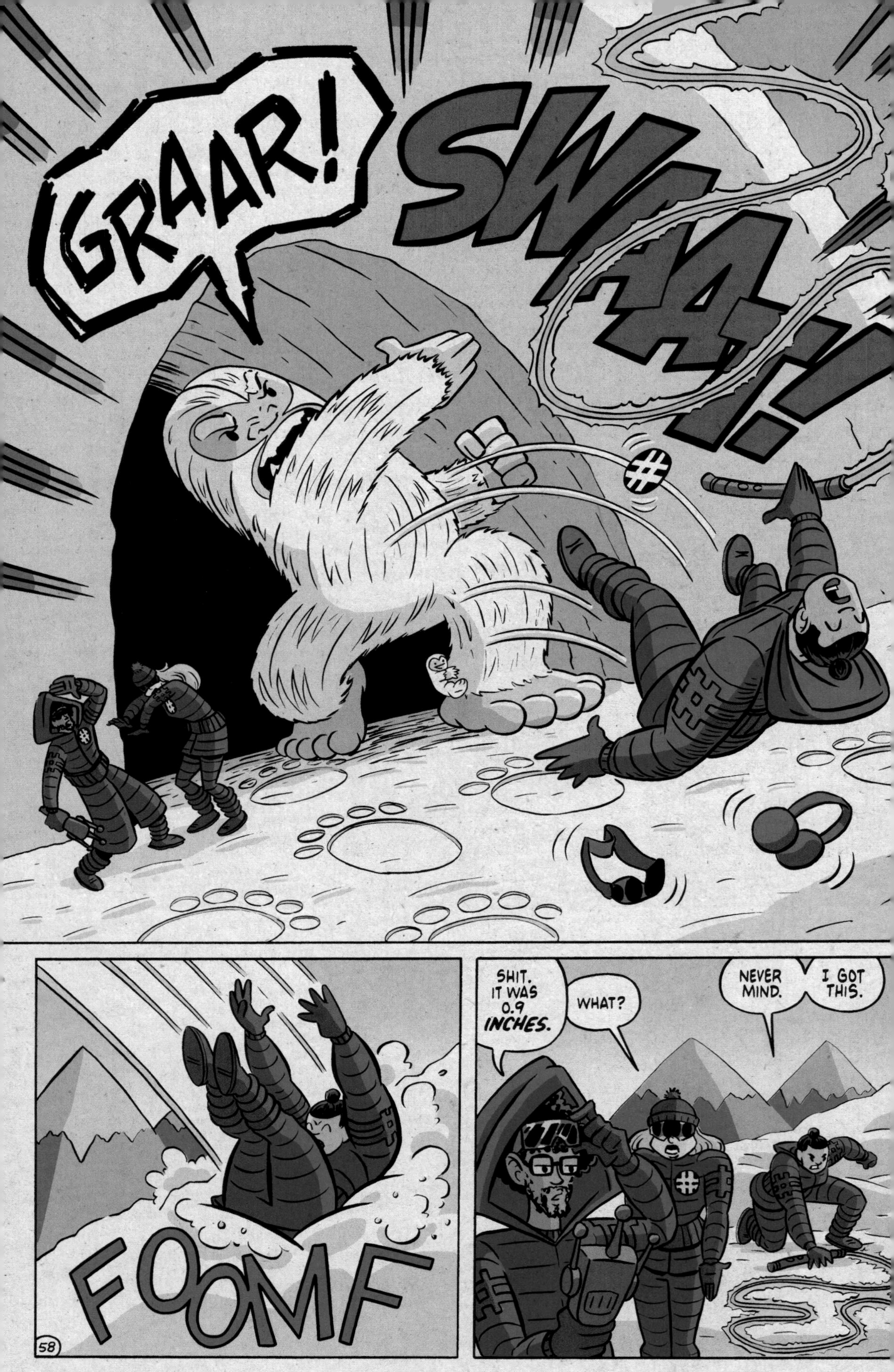
GRAAR!
SWAA!!
FOOMF
SHIT. IT WAS 0.9 *INCHES.*
WHAT?
NEVER MIND.
I GOT THIS.

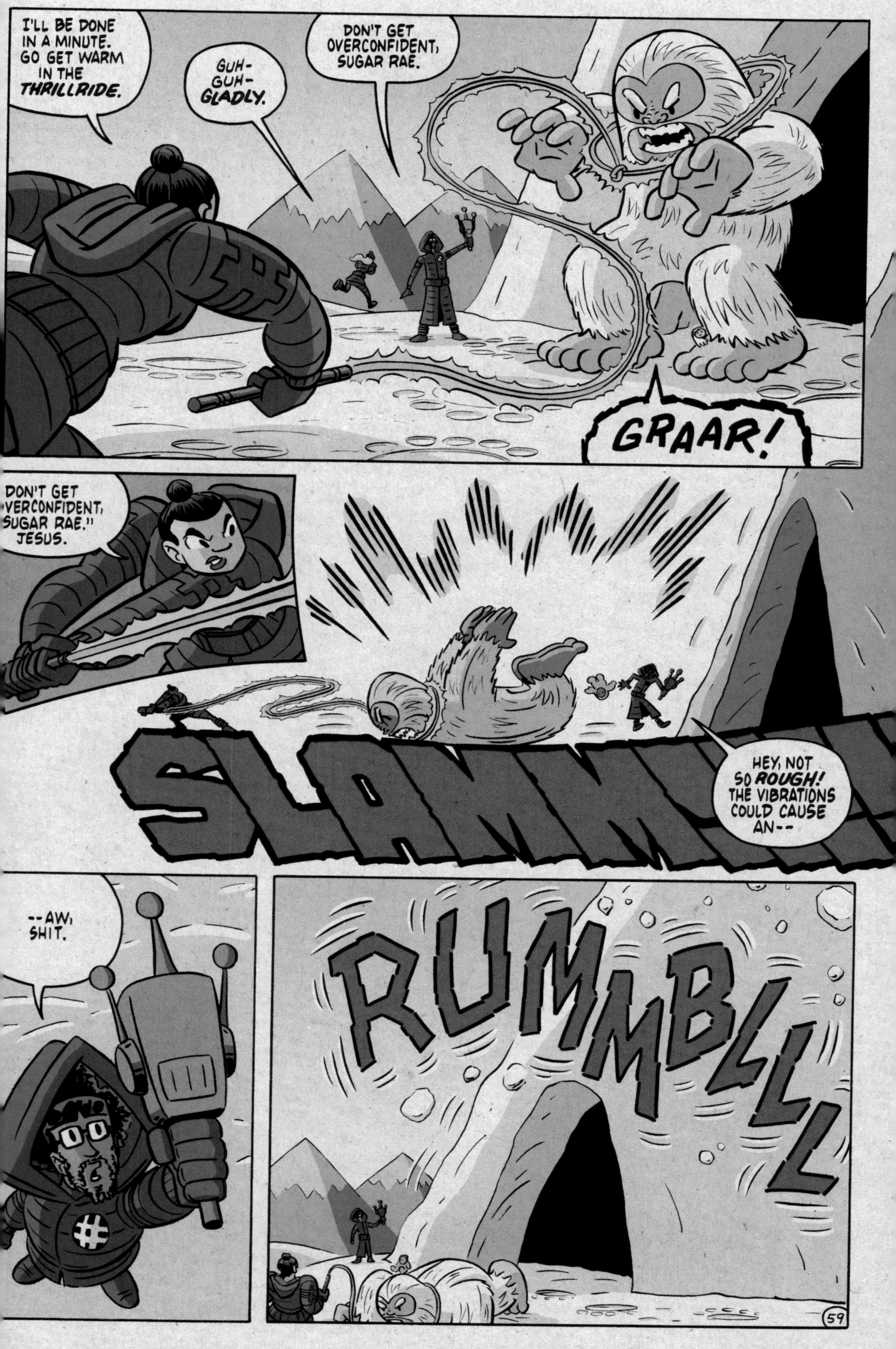

I'LL BE DONE IN A MINUTE. GO GET WARM IN THE THRILLRIDE.
GUH-GUH-GLADLY.
DON'T GET OVERCONFIDENT, SUGAR RAE.
GRAAR!
DON'T GET OVERCONFIDENT, SUGAR RAE." JESUS.
SLAMM
HEY, NOT SO ROUGH! THE VIBRATIONS COULD CAUSE AN--
--AW, SHIT.
RUMMBLLL

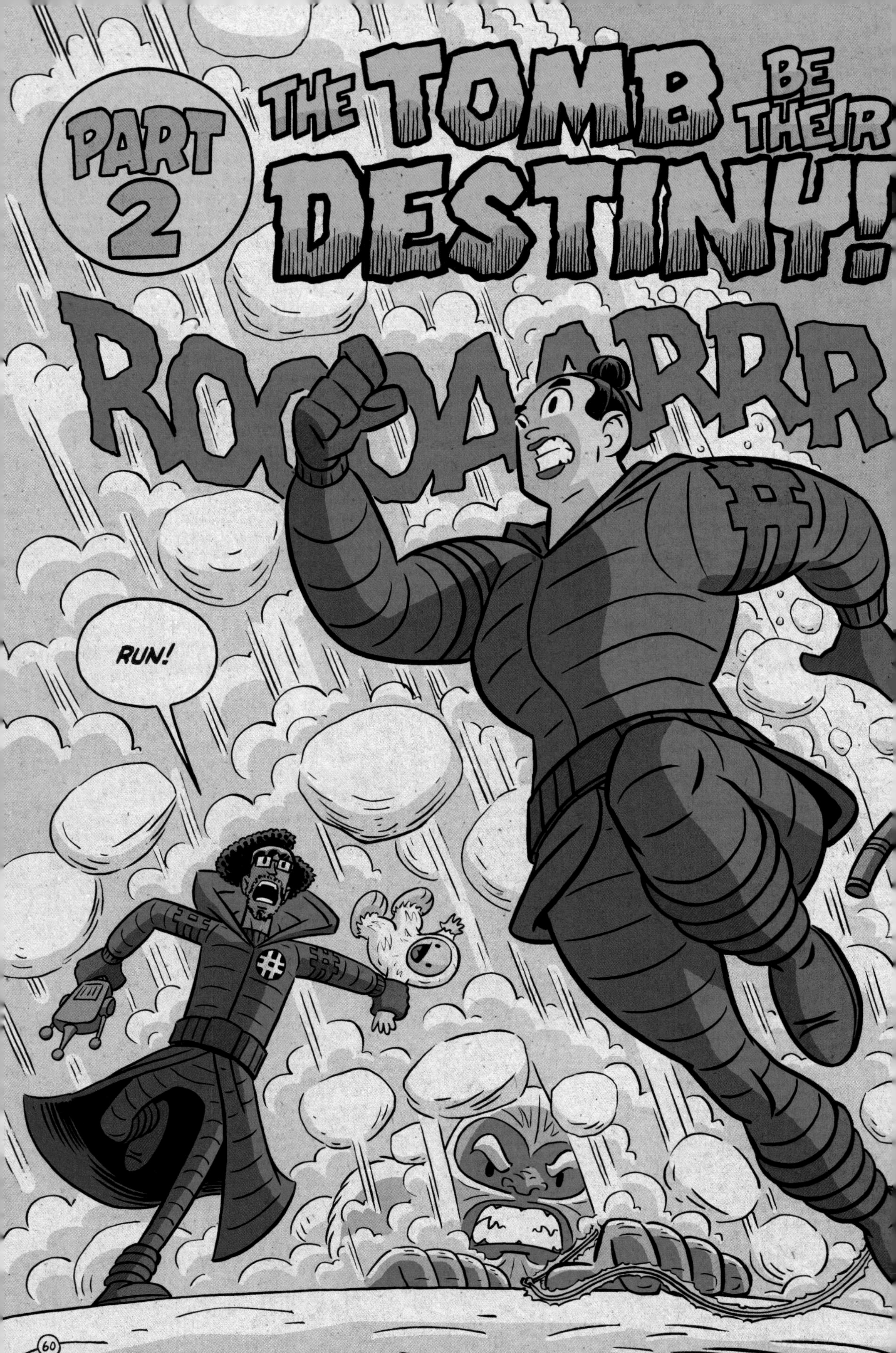
PART 2
THE TOMB BE THEIR DESTINY!
ROOOAARRR
RUN!

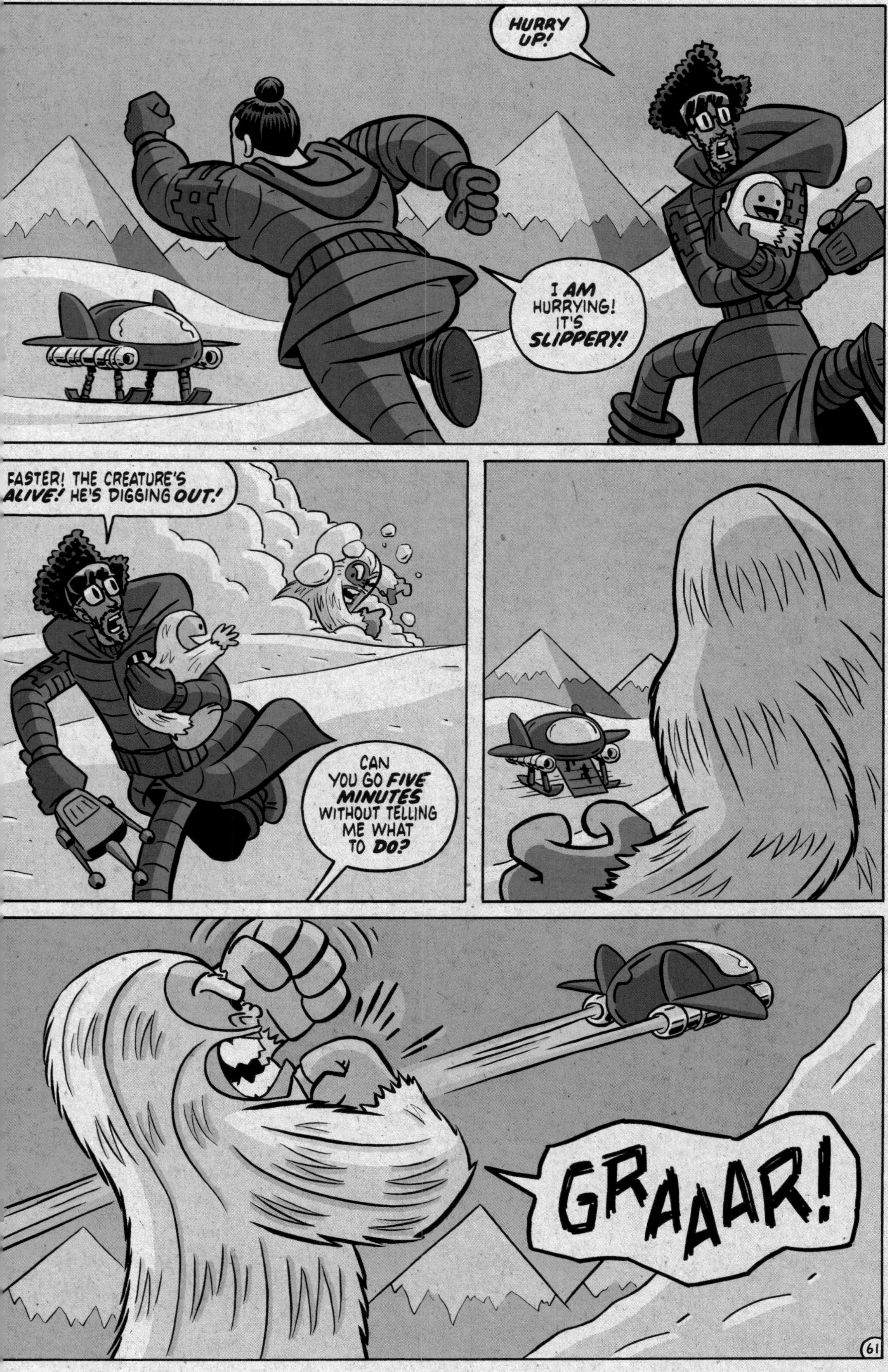
HURRY UP!
I AM HURRYING! IT'S SLIPPERY!
FASTER! THE CREATURE'S ALIVE! HE'S DIGGING OUT!
CAN YOU GO FIVE MINUTES WITHOUT TELLING ME WHAT TO DO?
GRAAAR!

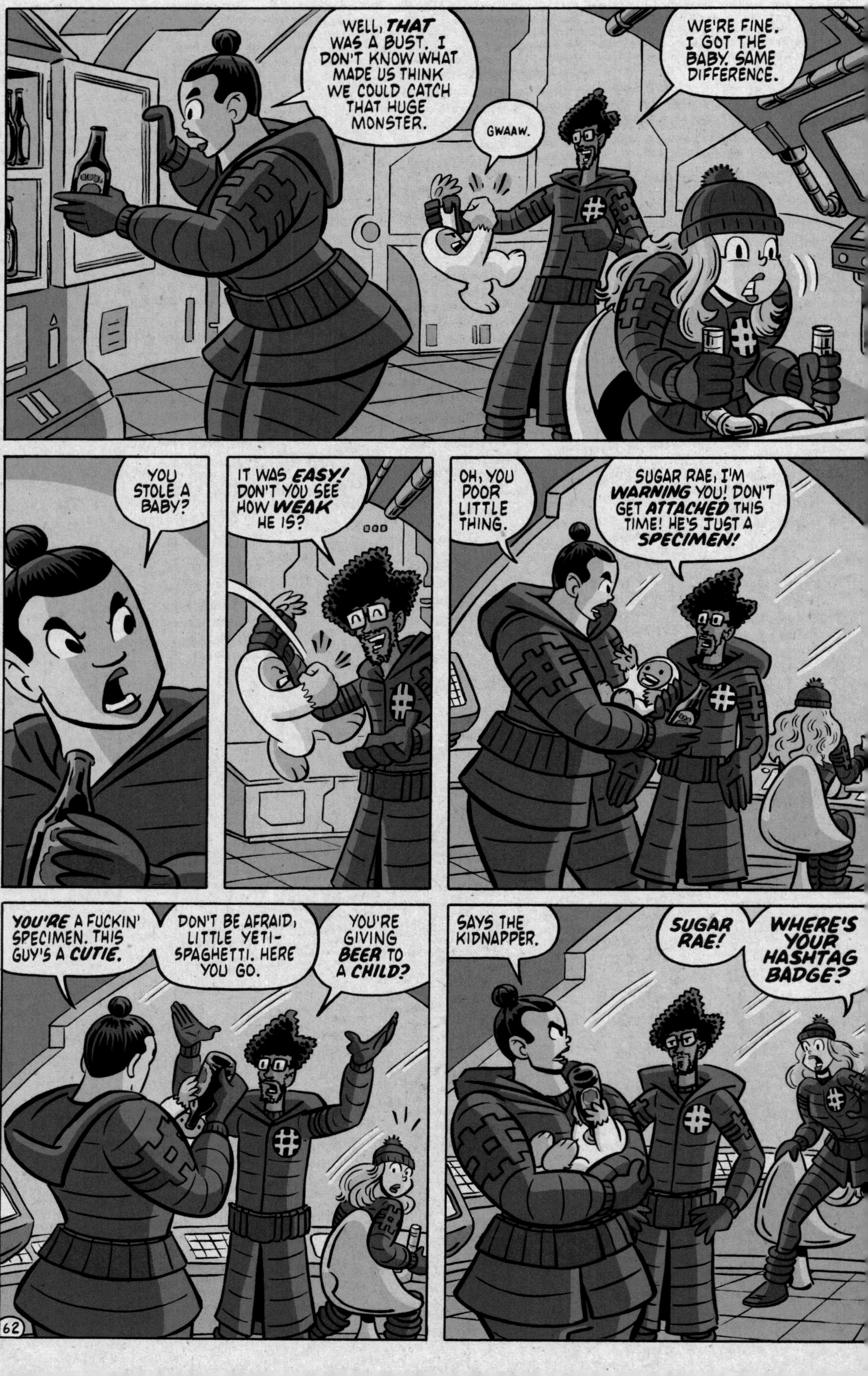
WELL, *THAT* WAS A BUST. I DON'T KNOW WHAT MADE US THINK WE COULD CATCH THAT HUGE MONSTER.
GWAAW.
WE'RE FINE. I GOT THE BABY. SAME DIFFERENCE.
YOU STOLE A BABY?
IT WAS *EASY!* DON'T YOU SEE HOW *WEAK* HE IS?
OH, YOU POOR LITTLE THING.
SUGAR RAE, I'M *WARNING* YOU! DON'T GET *ATTACHED* THIS TIME! HE'S JUST A *SPECIMEN!*
YOU'RE A FUCKIN' SPECIMEN. THIS GUY'S A *CUTIE.*
DON'T BE AFRAID, LITTLE YETI-SPAGHETTI. HERE YOU GO.
YOU'RE GIVING *BEER* TO A *CHILD?*
SAYS THE KIDNAPPER.
SUGAR RAE!
WHERE'S YOUR HASHTAG BADGE?

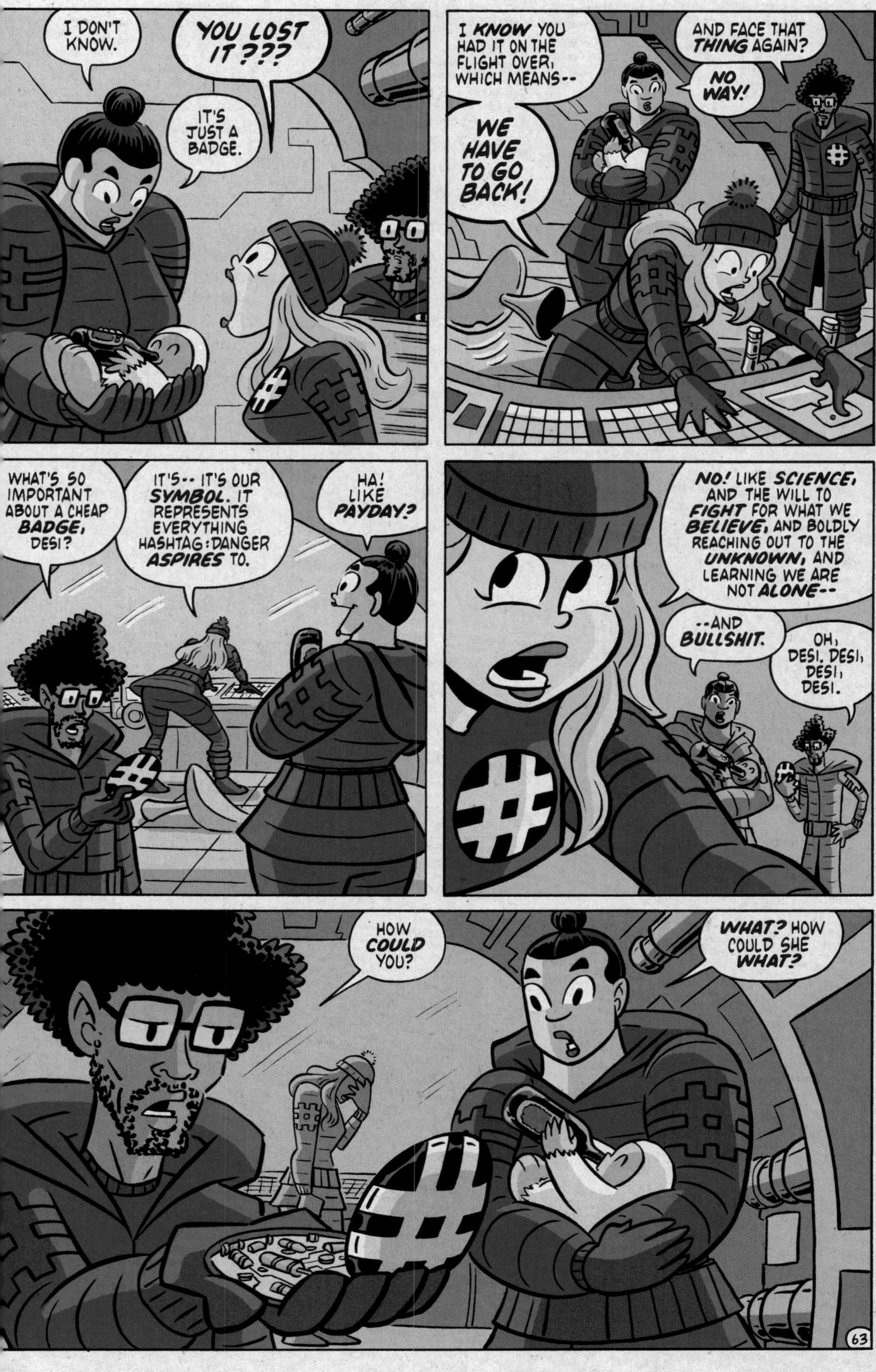

I DON'T KNOW.
YOU LOST IT???
IT'S JUST A BADGE.
I KNOW YOU HAD IT ON THE FLIGHT OVER, WHICH MEANS--
WE HAVE TO GO BACK!
AND FACE THAT THING AGAIN?
NO WAY!
WHAT'S SO IMPORTANT ABOUT A CHEAP BADGE, DESI?
IT'S-- IT'S OUR SYMBOL. IT REPRESENTS EVERYTHING HASHTAG:DANGER ASPIRES TO.
HA! LIKE PAYDAY?
NO! LIKE SCIENCE, AND THE WILL TO FIGHT FOR WHAT WE BELIEVE, AND BOLDLY REACHING OUT TO THE UNKNOWN, AND LEARNING WE ARE NOT ALONE--
--AND BULLSHIT.
OH, DESI. DESI, DESI, DESI.
HOW COULD YOU?
WHAT? HOW COULD SHE WHAT?

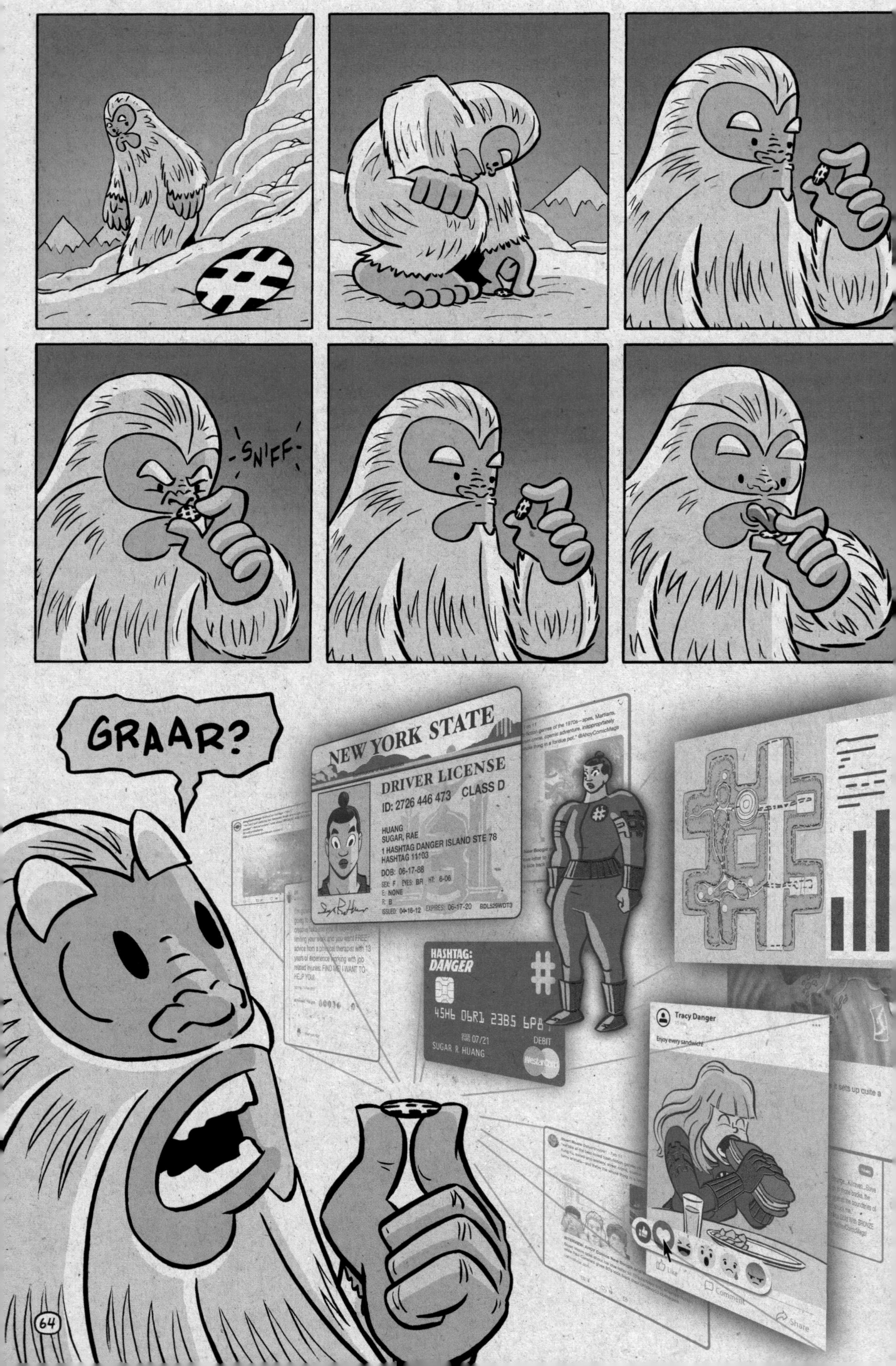
SNIFF
GRAAR?
NEW YORK STATE
DRIVER LICENSE
CLASS D
ID: 2726 446 473
HUANG
SUGAR, RAE
1 HASHTAG DANGER ISLAND STE 78
HASHTAG 11103
DOB: 06-17-88
HASHTAG: DANGER
07/21
DEBIT
SUGAR R. HUANG
Tracy Danger
Enjoy every sandwich!
Like
Comment
Share

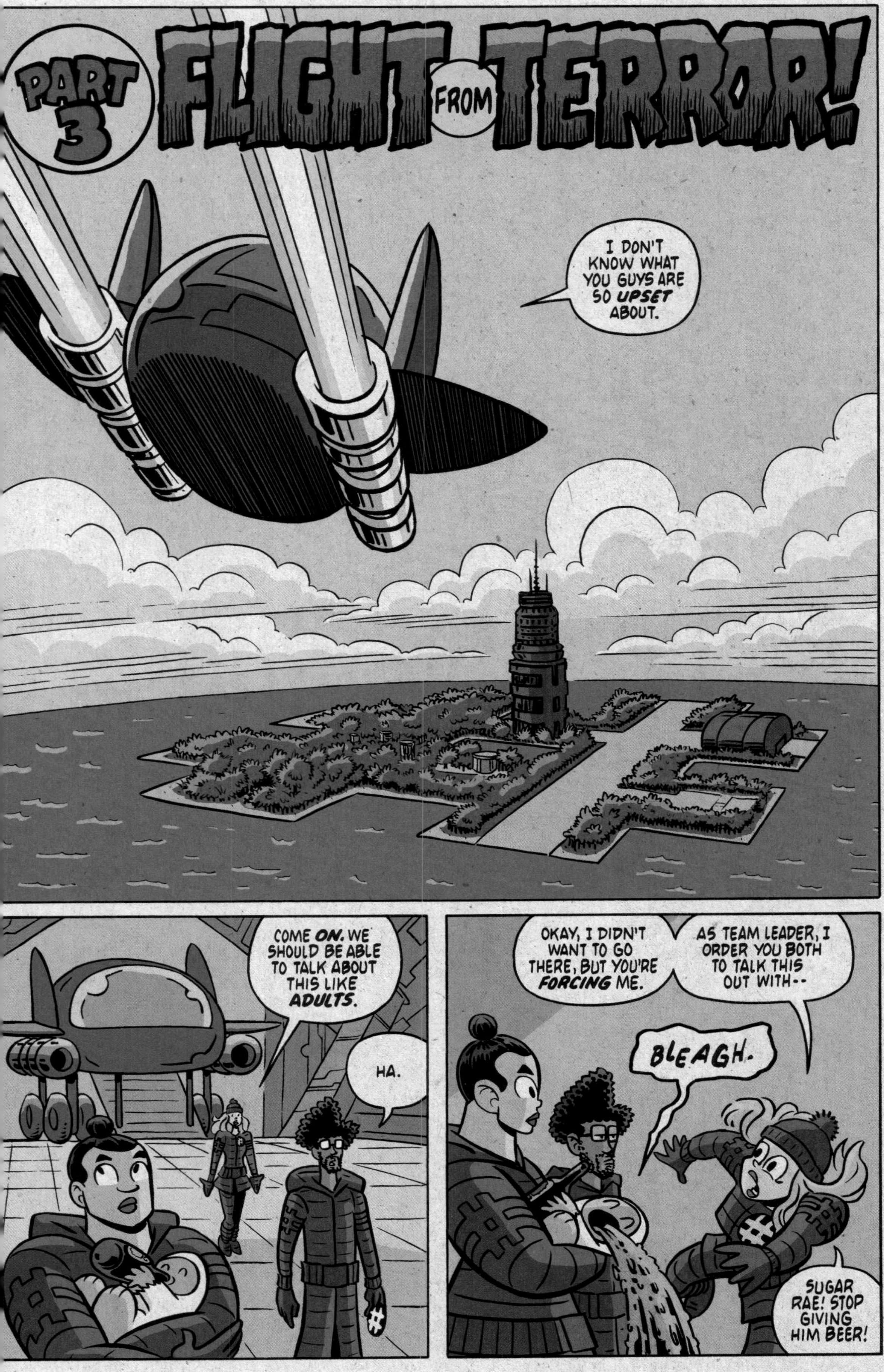
PART 3
FLIGHT FROM TERROR!
I DON'T KNOW WHAT YOU GUYS ARE SO UPSET ABOUT.
COME ON. WE SHOULD BE ABLE TO TALK ABOUT THIS LIKE ADULTS.
HA.
OKAY, I DIDN'T WANT TO GO THERE, BUT YOU'RE FORCING ME.
AS TEAM LEADER, I ORDER YOU BOTH TO TALK THIS OUT WITH--
BLEAGH.
SUGAR RAE! STOP GIVING HIM BEER!

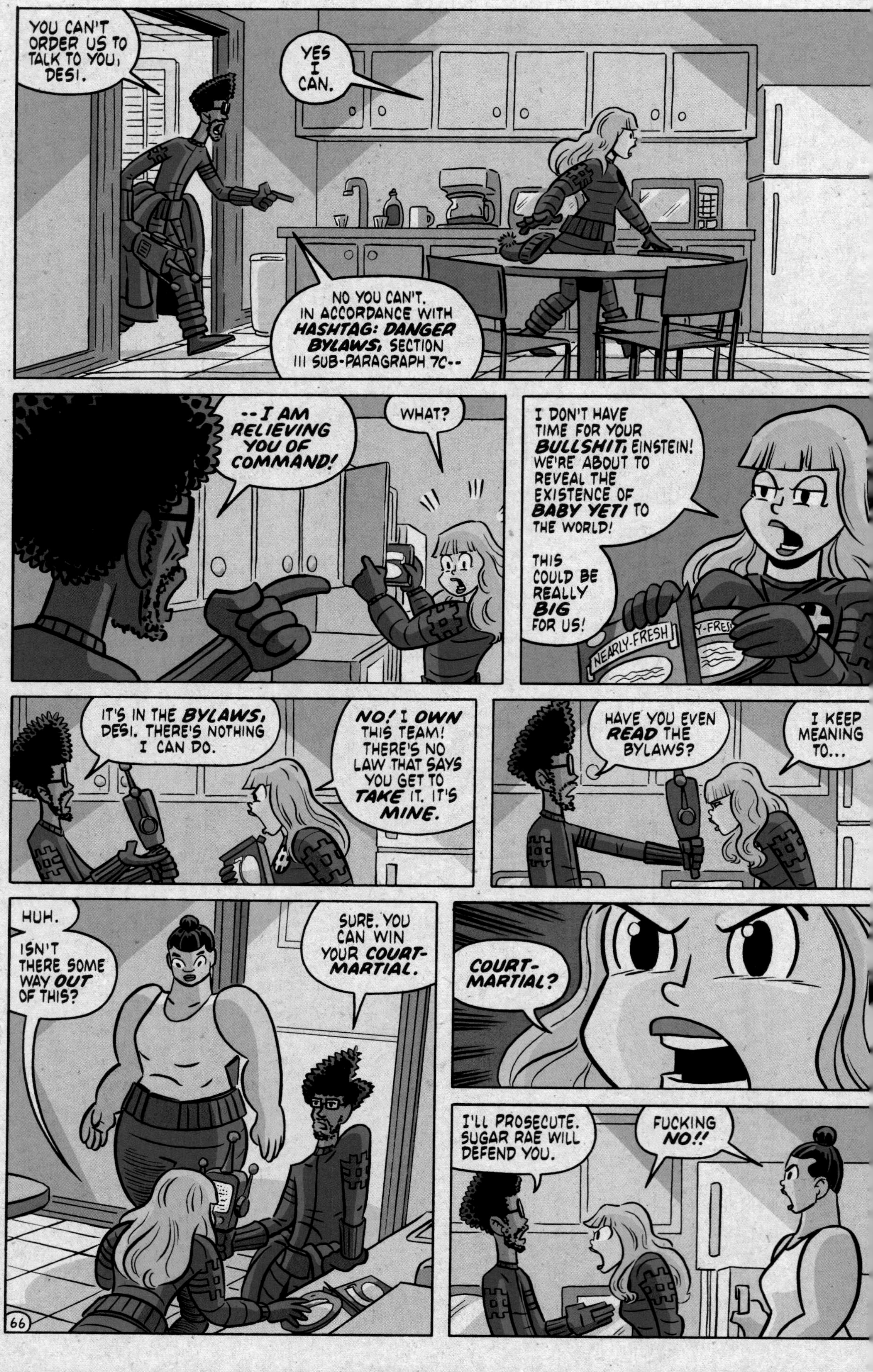
YOU CAN'T ORDER US TO TALK TO YOU, DESI.
YES I CAN.
NO YOU CAN'T. IN ACCORDANCE WITH HASHTAG: DANGER BYLAWS, SECTION III SUB-PARAGRAPH 7C--
--I AM RELIEVING YOU OF COMMAND!
WHAT?
I DON'T HAVE TIME FOR YOUR BULLSHIT, EINSTEIN! WE'RE ABOUT TO REVEAL THE EXISTENCE OF BABY YETI TO THE WORLD!
THIS COULD BE REALLY BIG FOR US!
NEARLY-FRESH
IT'S IN THE BYLAWS, DESI. THERE'S NOTHING I CAN DO.
NO! I OWN THIS TEAM! THERE'S NO LAW THAT SAYS YOU GET TO TAKE IT. IT'S MINE.
HAVE YOU EVEN READ THE BYLAWS?
I KEEP MEANING TO...
HUH.
ISN'T THERE SOME WAY OUT OF THIS?
SURE. YOU CAN WIN YOUR COURT-MARTIAL.
COURT-MARTIAL?
I'LL PROSECUTE. SUGAR RAE WILL DEFEND YOU.
FUCKING NO!!

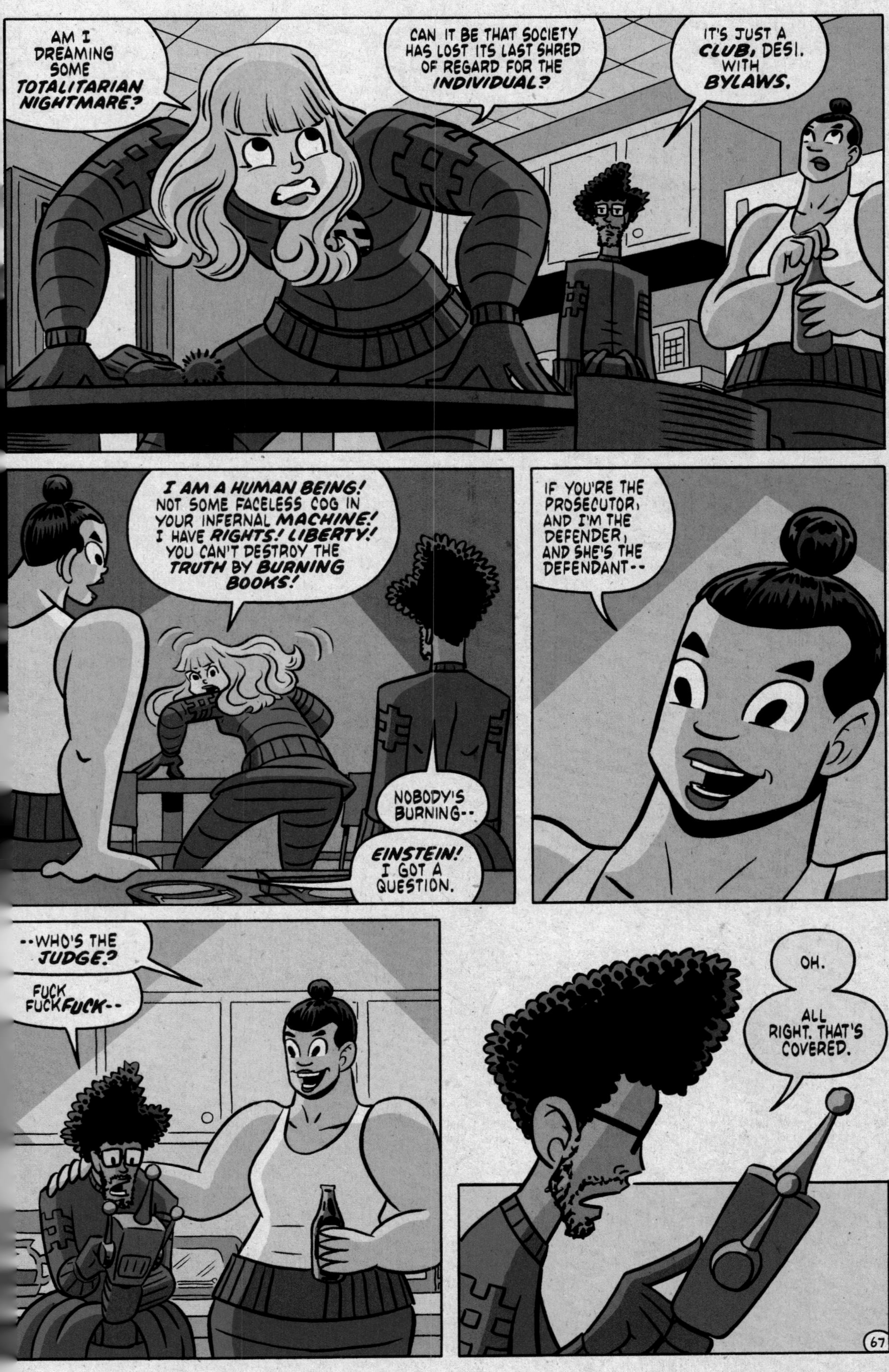
AM I DREAMING SOME TOTALITARIAN NIGHTMARE?
CAN IT BE THAT SOCIETY HAS LOST ITS LAST SHRED OF REGARD FOR THE INDIVIDUAL?
IT'S JUST A CLUB, DESI. WITH BYLAWS.
I AM A HUMAN BEING! NOT SOME FACELESS COG IN YOUR INFERNAL MACHINE! I HAVE RIGHTS! LIBERTY! YOU CAN'T DESTROY THE TRUTH BY BURNING BOOKS!
NOBODY'S BURNING--
EINSTEIN! I GOT A QUESTION.
IF YOU'RE THE PROSECUTOR, AND I'M THE DEFENDER, AND SHE'S THE DEFENDANT--
--WHO'S THE JUDGE?
FUCK FUCKFUCK--
OH.
ALL RIGHT. THAT'S COVERED.

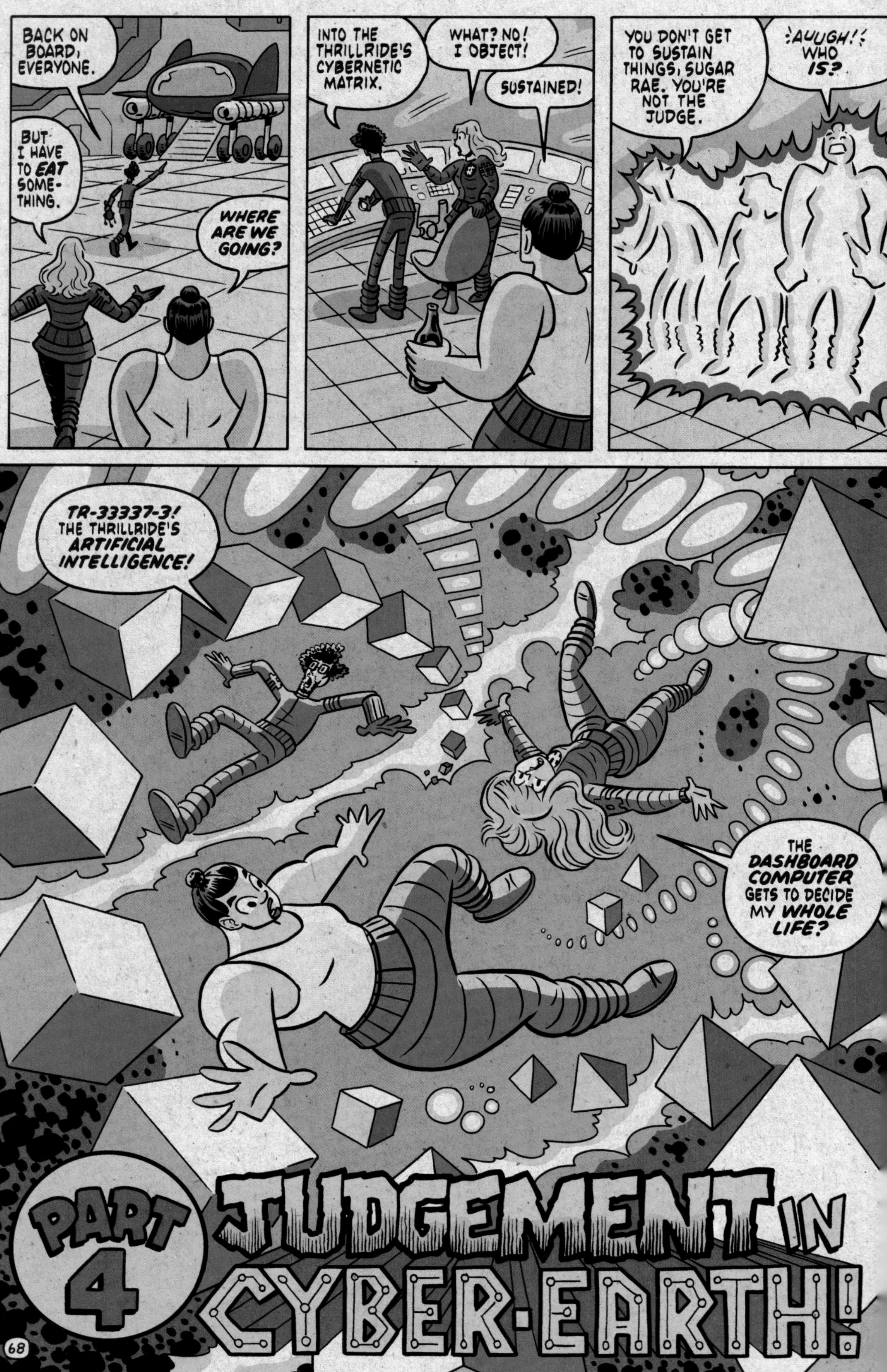
BACK ON BOARD, EVERYONE.
BUT I HAVE TO EAT SOMETHING.
WHERE ARE WE GOING?
INTO THE THRILLRIDE'S CYBERNETIC MATRIX.
WHAT? NO! I OBJECT!
SUSTAINED!
YOU DON'T GET TO SUSTAIN THINGS, SUGAR RAE. YOU'RE NOT THE JUDGE.
AUUGH! WHO IS?
TR-33337-3! THE THRILLRIDE'S ARTIFICIAL INTELLIGENCE!
THE DASHBOARD COMPUTER GETS TO DECIDE MY WHOLE LIFE?
PART 4
JUDGEMENT IN CYBER-EARTH!

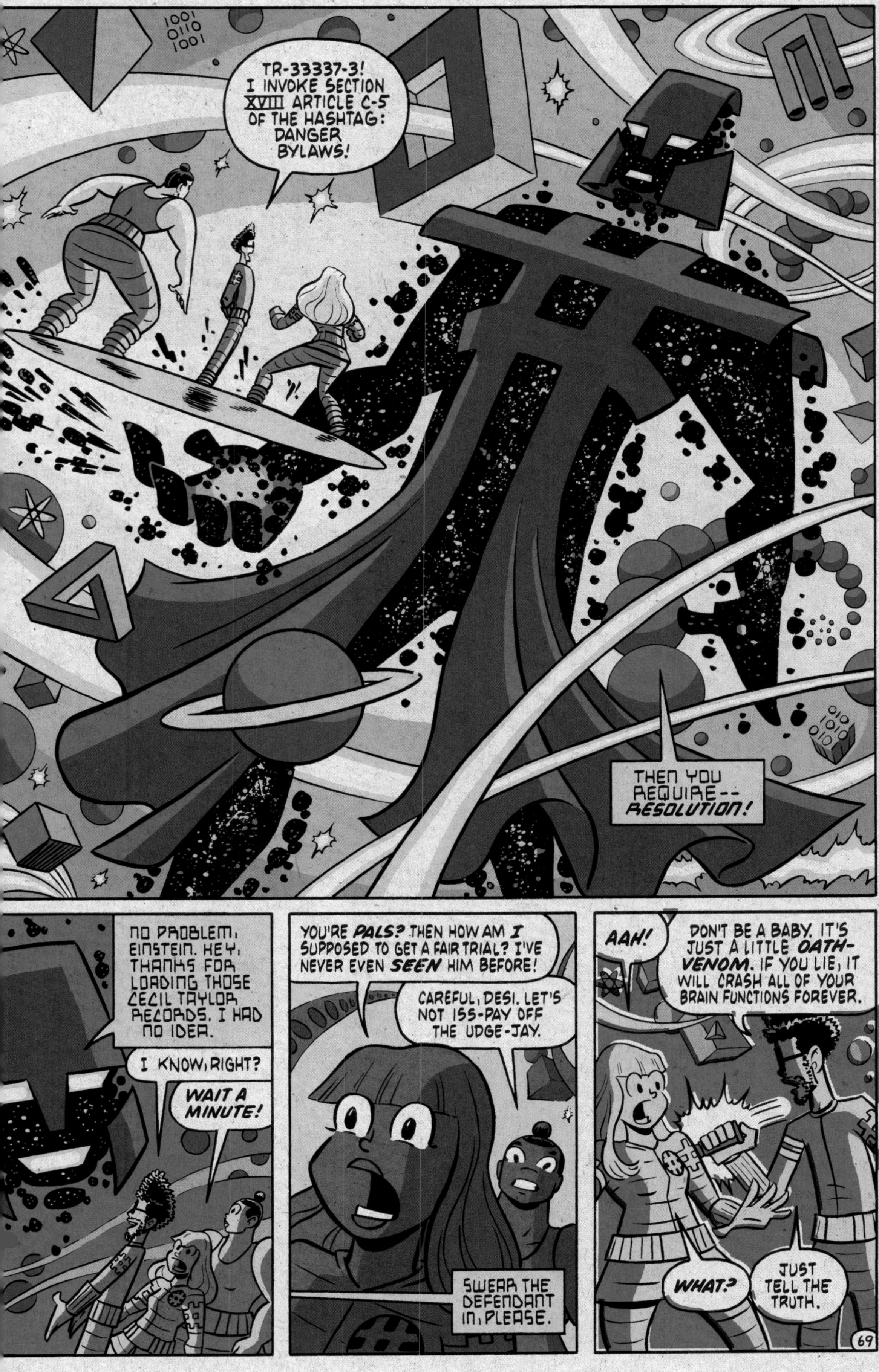

TR-33337-3! I INVOKE SECTION XVIII ARTICLE C-5 OF THE HASHTAG: DANGER BYLAWS!
THEN YOU REQUIRE-- RESOLUTION!
NO PROBLEM, EINSTEIN. HEY, THANKS FOR LOADING THOSE CECIL TAYLOR RECORDS. I HAD NO IDEA.
I KNOW, RIGHT?
WAIT A MINUTE!
YOU'RE PALS? THEN HOW AM I SUPPOSED TO GET A FAIR TRIAL? I'VE NEVER EVEN SEEN HIM BEFORE!
CAREFUL, DESI. LET'S NOT ISS-PAY OFF THE UDGE-JAY.
SWEAR THE DEFENDANT IN, PLEASE.
AAH!
DON'T BE A BABY. IT'S JUST A LITTLE OATH-VENOM. IF YOU LIE, IT WILL CRASH ALL OF YOUR BRAIN FUNCTIONS FOREVER.
WHAT?
JUST TELL THE TRUTH.

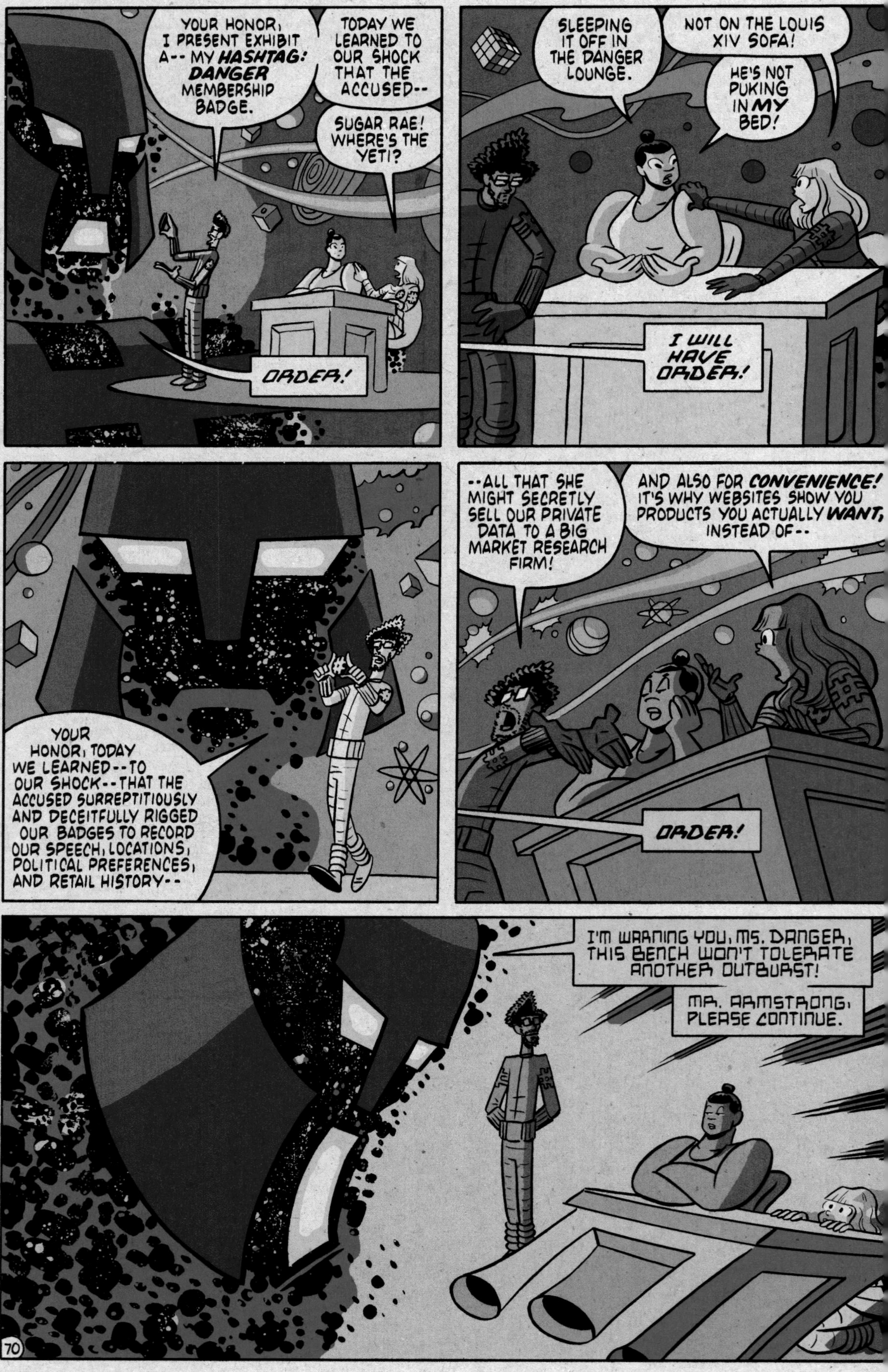
YOUR HONOR, I PRESENT EXHIBIT A-- MY HASHTAG: DANGER MEMBERSHIP BADGE.
TODAY WE LEARNED TO OUR SHOCK THAT THE ACCUSED--
SUGAR RAE! WHERE'S THE YETI?
ORDER!
SLEEPING IT OFF IN THE DANGER LOUNGE.
NOT ON THE LOUIS XIV SOFA!
HE'S NOT PUKING IN MY BED!
I WILL HAVE ORDER!
YOUR HONOR, TODAY WE LEARNED--TO OUR SHOCK--THAT THE ACCUSED SURREPTITIOUSLY AND DECEITFULLY RIGGED OUR BADGES TO RECORD OUR SPEECH, LOCATIONS, POLITICAL PREFERENCES, AND RETAIL HISTORY--
--ALL THAT SHE MIGHT SECRETLY SELL OUR PRIVATE DATA TO A BIG MARKET RESEARCH FIRM!
AND ALSO FOR CONVENIENCE! IT'S WHY WEBSITES SHOW YOU PRODUCTS YOU ACTUALLY WANT, INSTEAD OF--
ORDER!
I'M WARNING YOU, MS. DANGER, THIS BENCH WON'T TOLERATE ANOTHER OUTBURST!
MR. ARMSTRONG, PLEASE CONTINUE.

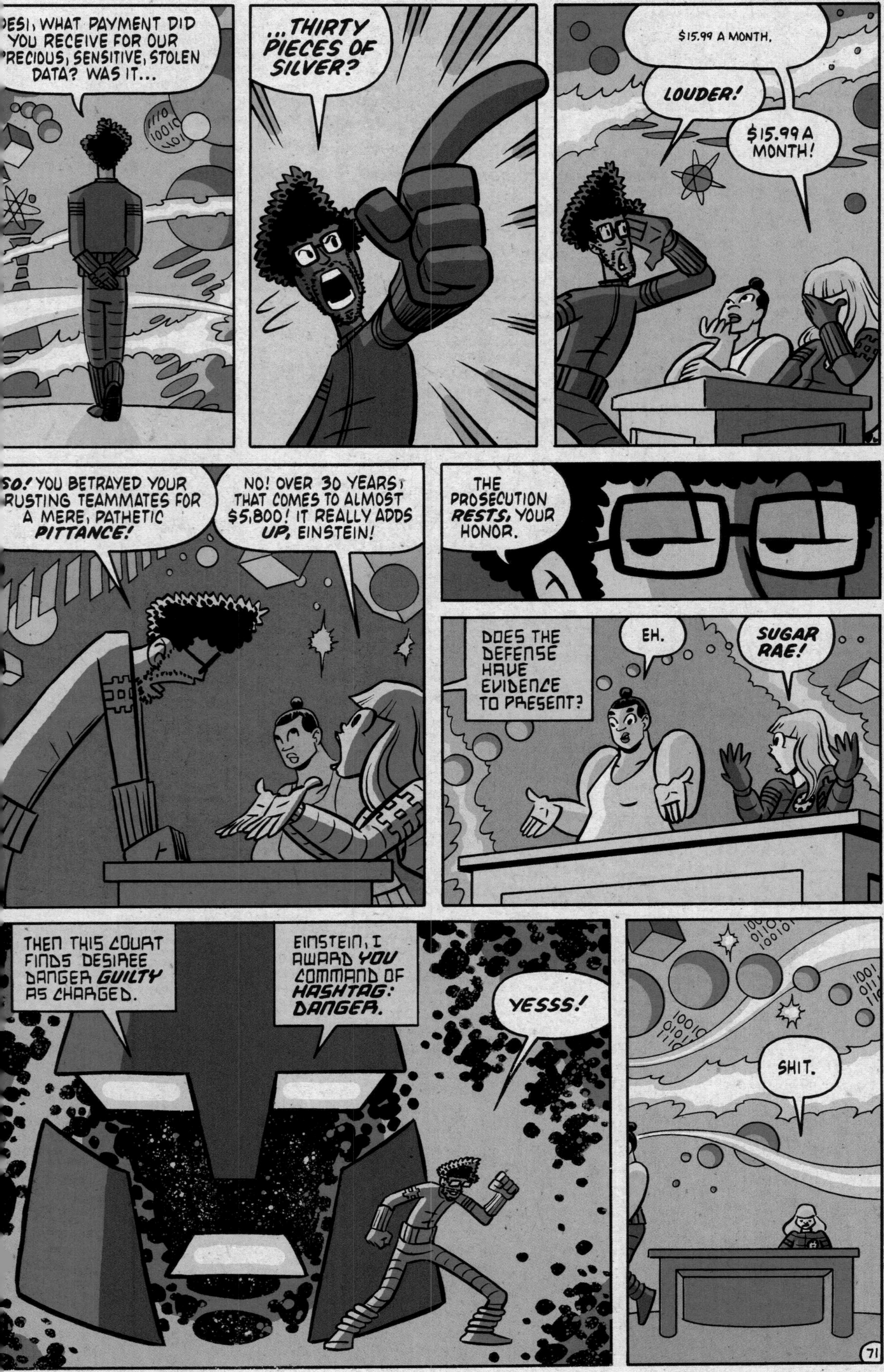

DESI, WHAT PAYMENT DID YOU RECEIVE FOR OUR PRECIOUS, SENSITIVE, STOLEN DATA? WAS IT...
...THIRTY PIECES OF SILVER?
$15.99 A MONTH.
LOUDER!
$15.99 A MONTH!
SO! YOU BETRAYED YOUR TRUSTING TEAMMATES FOR A MERE, PATHETIC PITTANCE!
NO! OVER 30 YEARS, THAT COMES TO ALMOST $5,800! IT REALLY ADDS UP, EINSTEIN!
THE PROSECUTION RESTS, YOUR HONOR.
DOES THE DEFENSE HAVE EVIDENCE TO PRESENT?
EH.
SUGAR RAE!
THEN THIS COURT FINDS DESIREE DANGER GUILTY AS CHARGED.
EINSTEIN, I AWARD YOU COMMAND OF HASHTAG: DANGER.
YESSS!
SHIT.

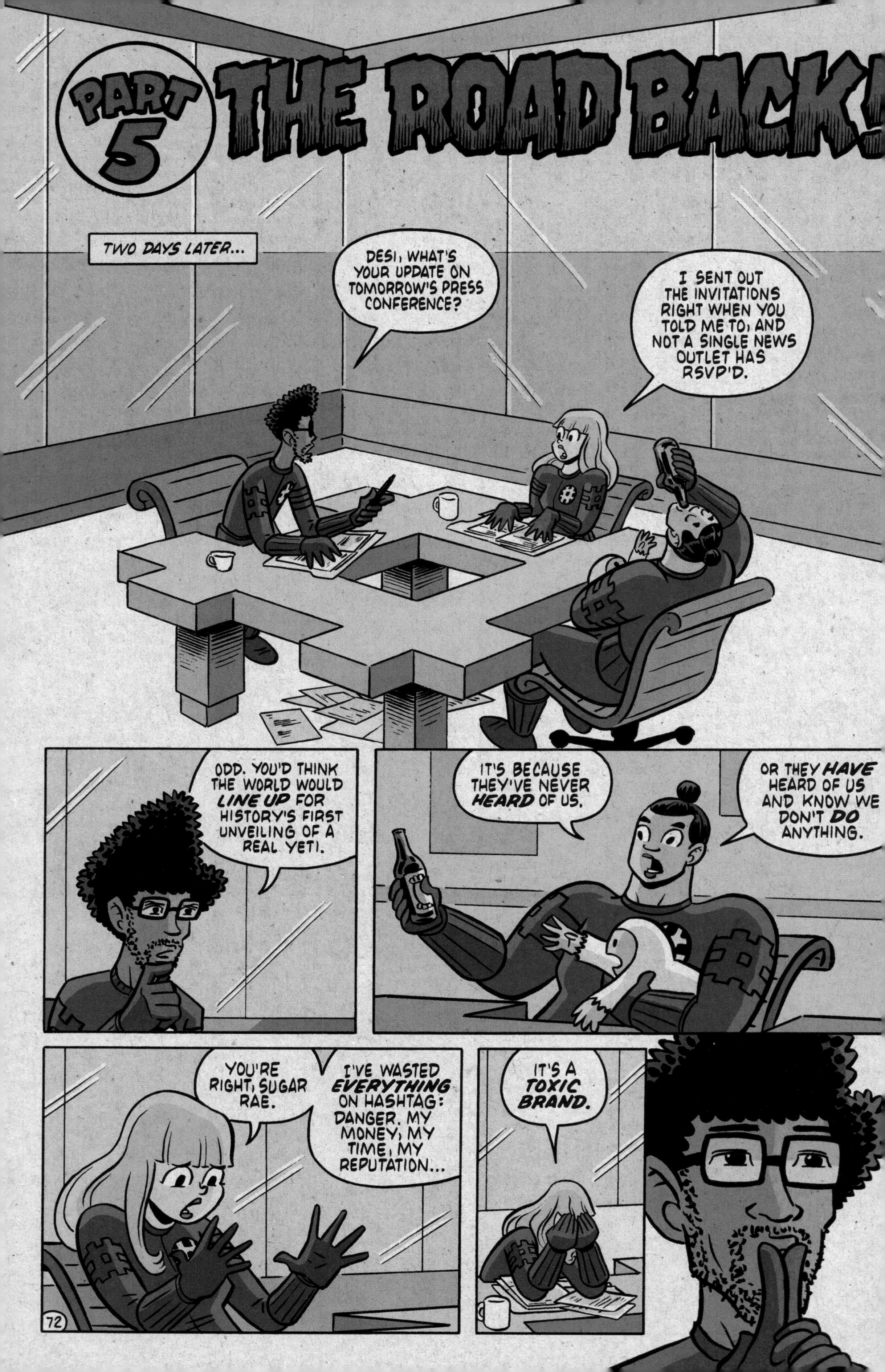

PART 5
THE ROAD BACK!
TWO DAYS LATER...
DESI, WHAT'S YOUR UPDATE ON TOMORROW'S PRESS CONFERENCE?
I SENT OUT THE INVITATIONS RIGHT WHEN YOU TOLD ME TO, AND NOT A SINGLE NEWS OUTLET HAS RSVP'D.
ODD. YOU'D THINK THE WORLD WOULD LINE UP FOR HISTORY'S FIRST UNVEILING OF A REAL YETI.
IT'S BECAUSE THEY'VE NEVER HEARD OF US.
OR THEY HAVE HEARD OF US AND KNOW WE DON'T DO ANYTHING.
YOU'RE RIGHT, SUGAR RAE.
I'VE WASTED EVERYTHING ON HASHTAG: DANGER. MY MONEY, MY TIME, MY REPUTATION...
IT'S A TOXIC BRAND.

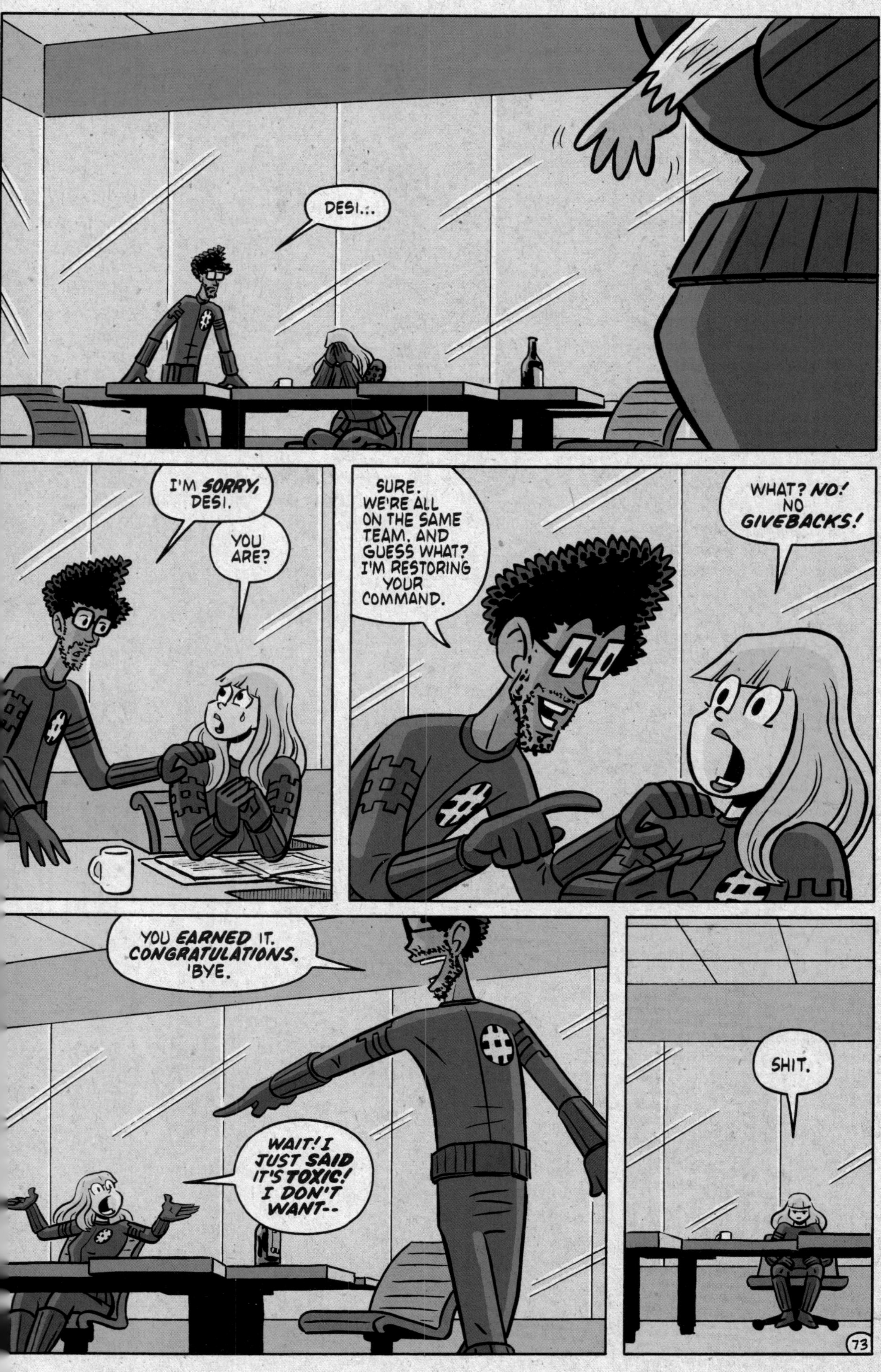
DESI...
I'M SORRY, DESI.
YOU ARE?
SURE. WE'RE ALL ON THE SAME TEAM. AND GUESS WHAT? I'M RESTORING YOUR COMMAND.
WHAT? NO! NO GIVEBACKS!
YOU EARNED IT. CONGRATULATIONS. 'BYE.
WAIT! I JUST SAID IT'S TOXIC! I DON'T WANT--
SHIT.

EPILOGUE

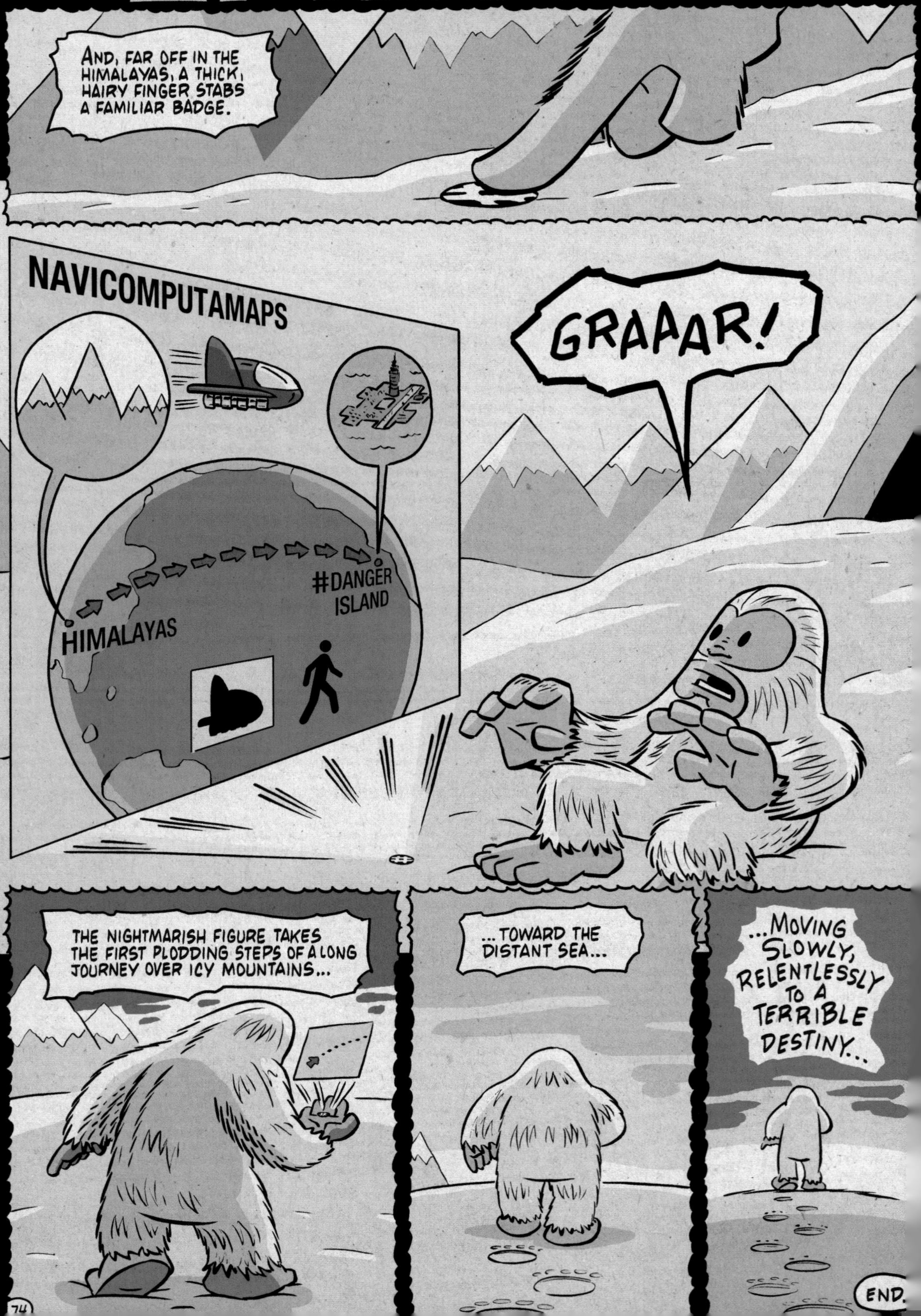

AND, FAR OFF IN THE HIMALAYAS, A THICK, HAIRY FINGER STABS A FAMILIAR BADGE.
NAVICOMPUTAMAPS
HIMALAYAS
#DANGER ISLAND
GRAAAR!
THE NIGHTMARISH FIGURE TAKES THE FIRST PLODDING STEPS OF A LONG JOURNEY OVER ICY MOUNTAINS...
...TOWARD THE DISTANT SEA...
...MOVING SLOWLY, RELENTLESSLY TO A TERRIBLE DESTINY...
END.

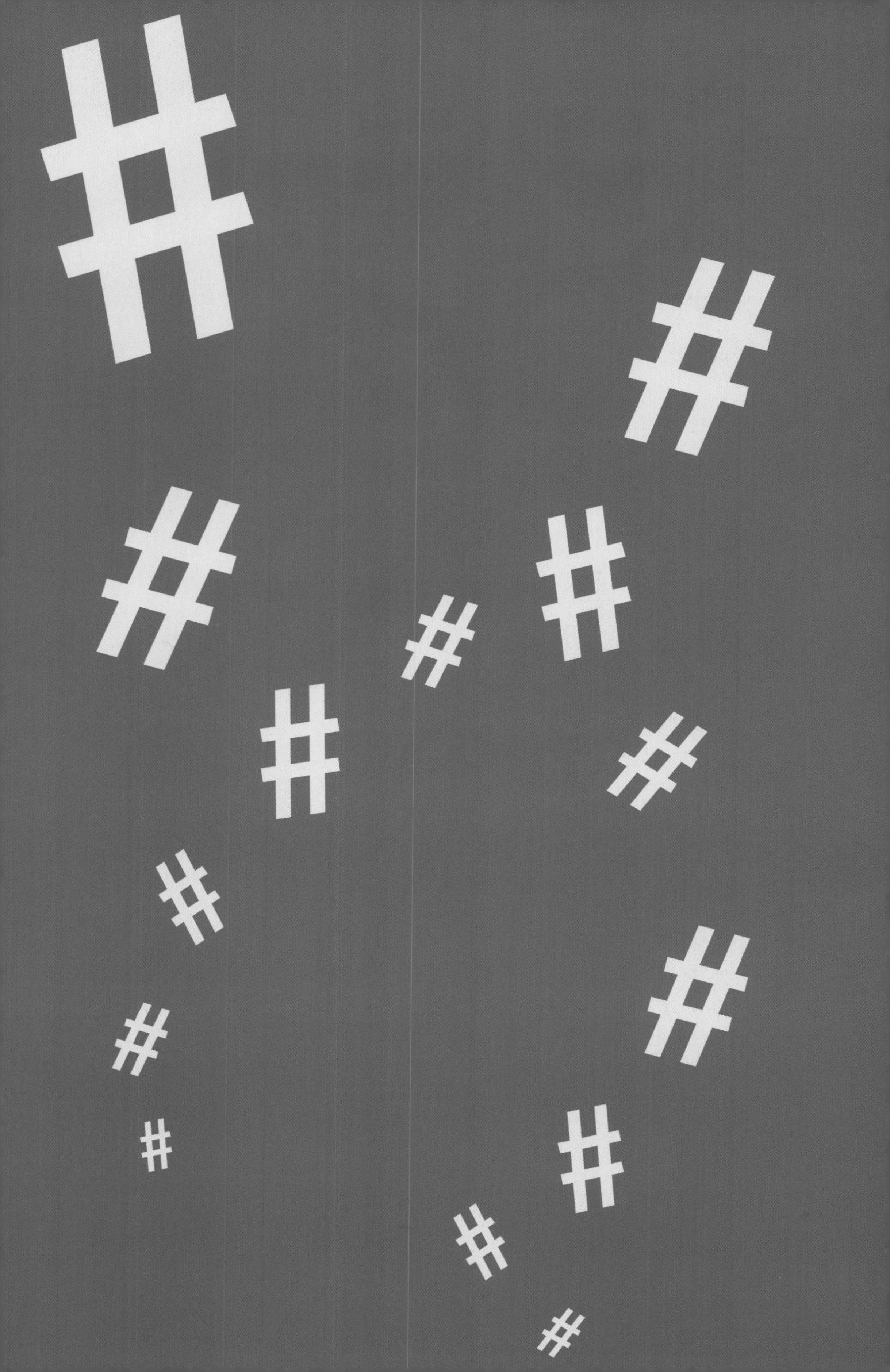

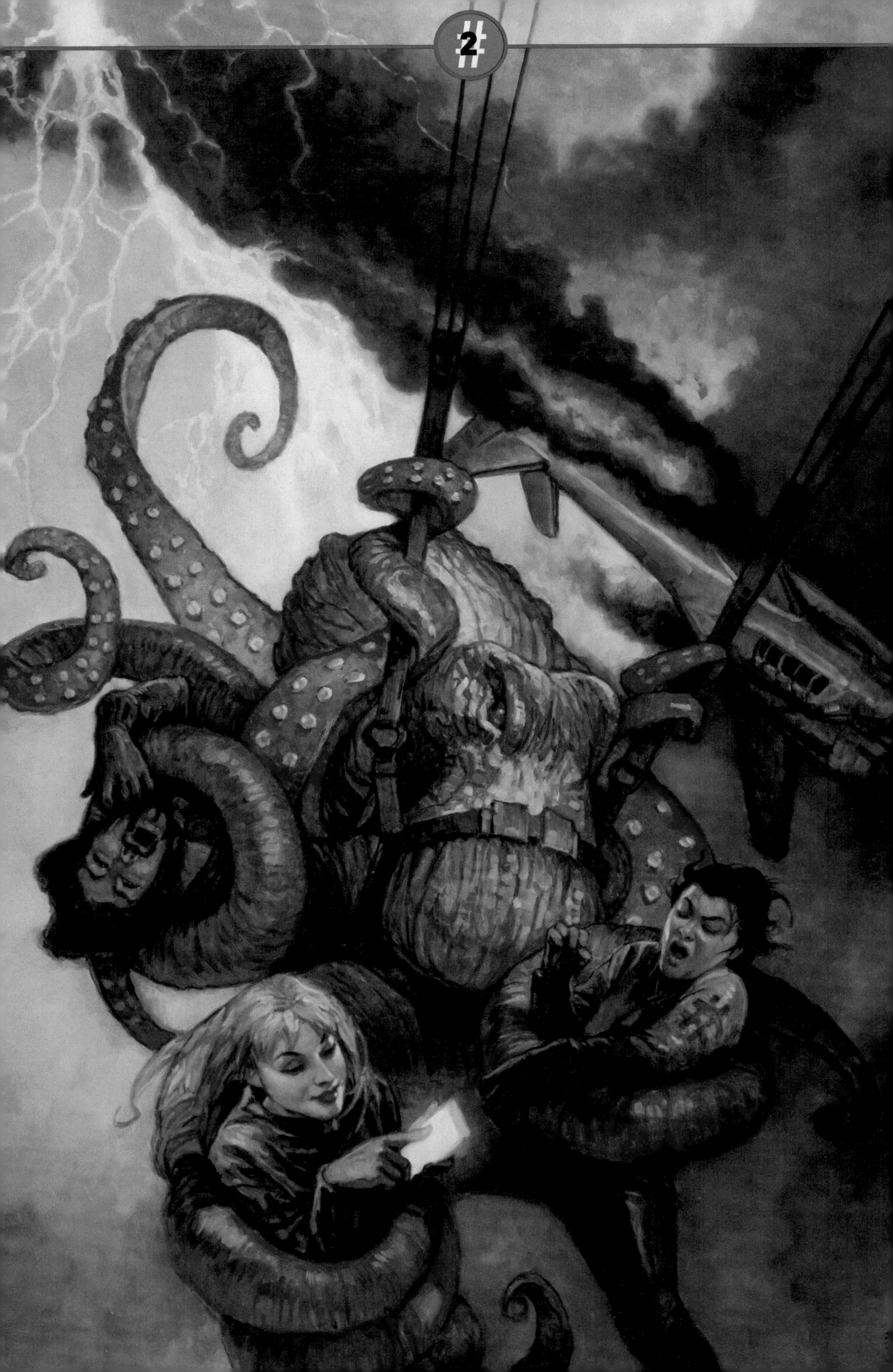

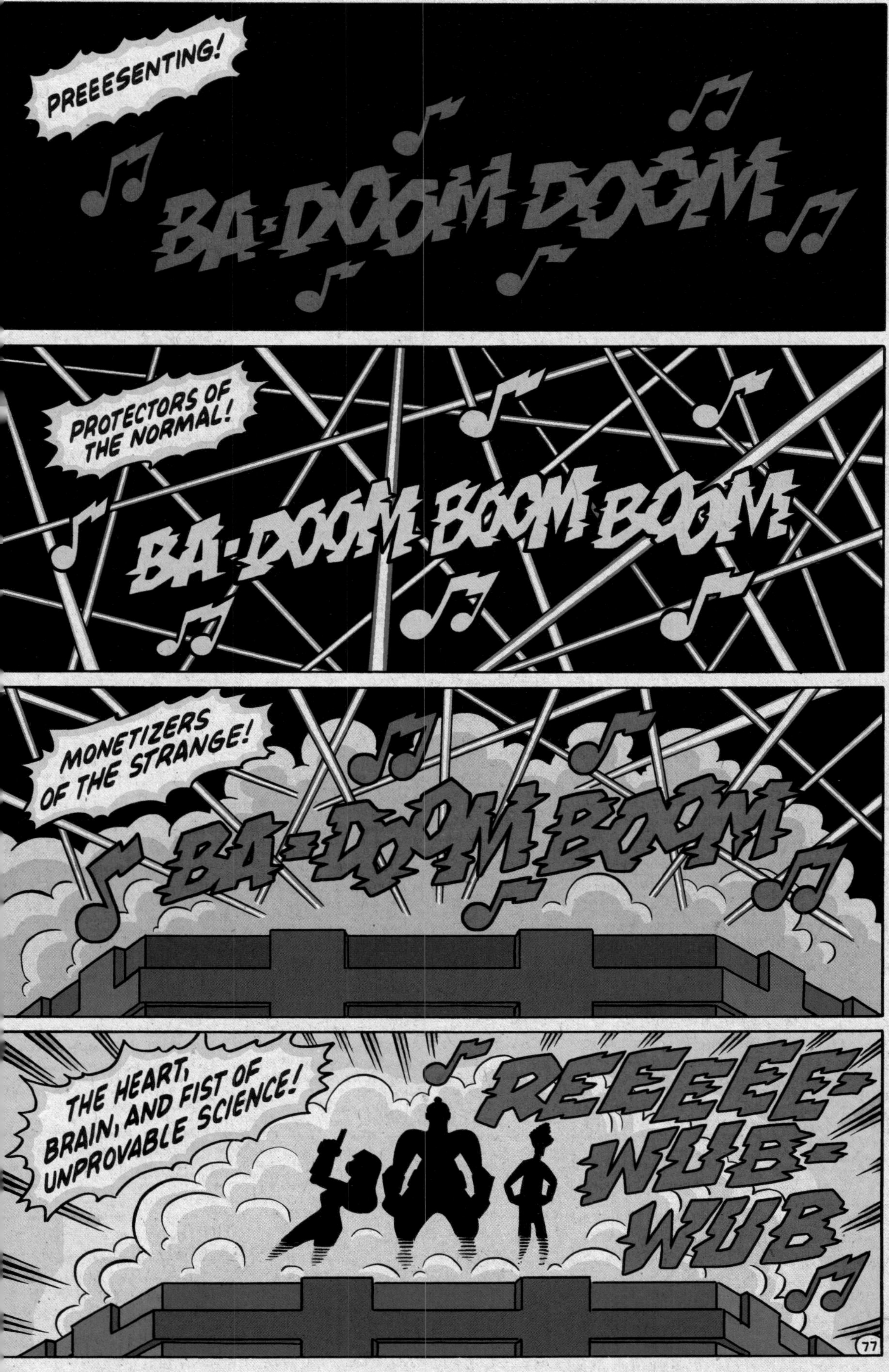
PREEESENTING!
BA-DOOM DOOM
PROTECTORS OF THE NORMAL!
BA-DOOM BOOM BOOM
MONETIZERS OF THE STRANGE!
BA-DOOM BOOM
THE HEART, BRAIN, AND FIST OF UNPROVABLE SCIENCE!
REEEEE-WUB-WUB

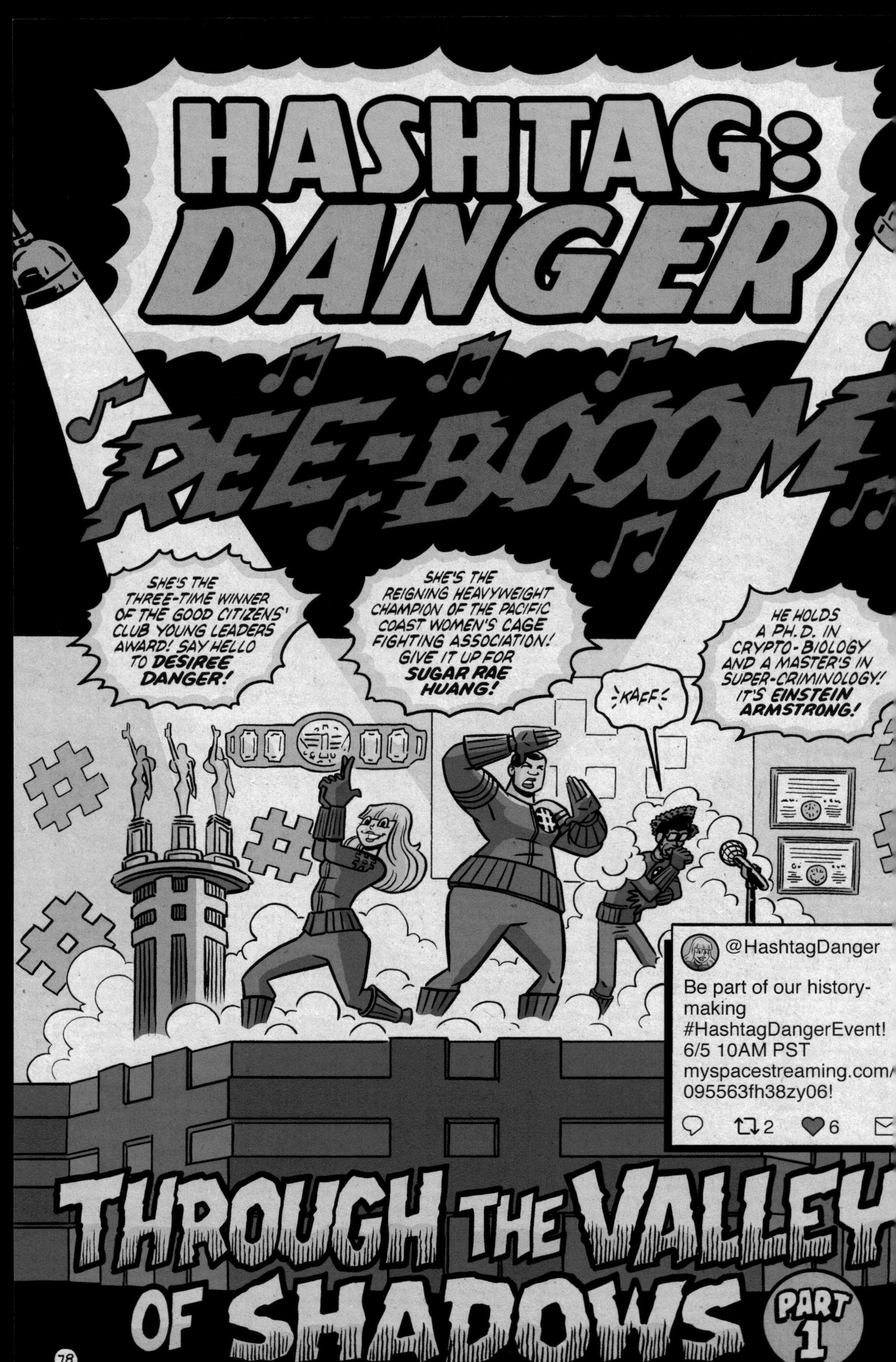
HASHTAG: DANGER
REE-BOOOM
SHE'S THE THREE-TIME WINNER OF THE GOOD CITIZENS' CLUB YOUNG LEADERS AWARD! SAY HELLO TO DESIREE DANGER!
SHE'S THE REIGNING HEAVYWEIGHT CHAMPION OF THE PACIFIC COAST WOMEN'S CAGE FIGHTING ASSOCIATION! GIVE IT UP FOR SUGAR RAE HUANG!
KAFF
HE HOLDS A PH.D. IN CRYPTO-BIOLOGY AND A MASTER'S IN SUPER-CRIMINOLOGY! IT'S EINSTEIN ARMSTRONG!
@HashtagDanger
Be part of our history-making #HashtagDangerEvent! 6/5 10AM PST myspacestreaming.com/095563fh38zy06!
2
6
THROUGH THE VALLEY OF SHADOWS
PART 1

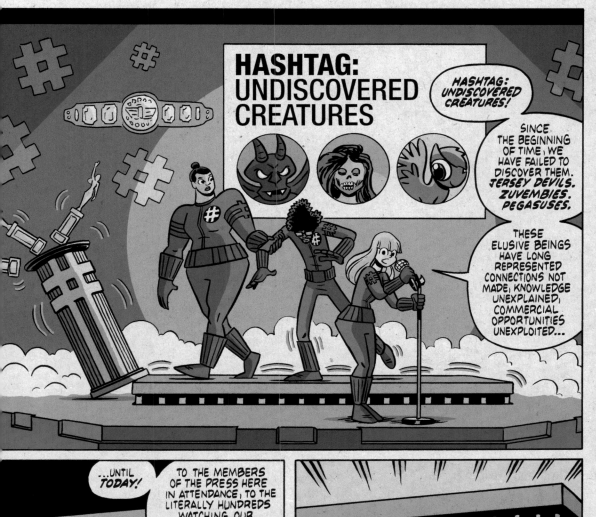

HASHTAG: UNDISCOVERED CREATURES

HASHTAG: UNDISCOVERED CREATURES!

SINCE THE BEGINNING OF TIME, WE HAVE FAILED TO DISCOVER THEM. *JERSEY DEVILS. ZUVEMBIES. PEGASUSES.*

THESE ELUSIVE BEINGS HAVE LONG REPRESENTED CONNECTIONS NOT MADE, KNOWLEDGE UNEXPLAINED, COMMERCIAL OPPORTUNITIES UNEXPLOITED...

...UNTIL *TODAY!*

TO THE MEMBERS OF THE PRESS HERE IN ATTENDANCE, TO THE LITERALLY HUNDREDS WATCHING OUR LIVESTREAM, *HASHTAG: DANGER* IS PROUD TO GIVE YOU...

HASHTAG: UNTIL TODAY!

...*YETI!*

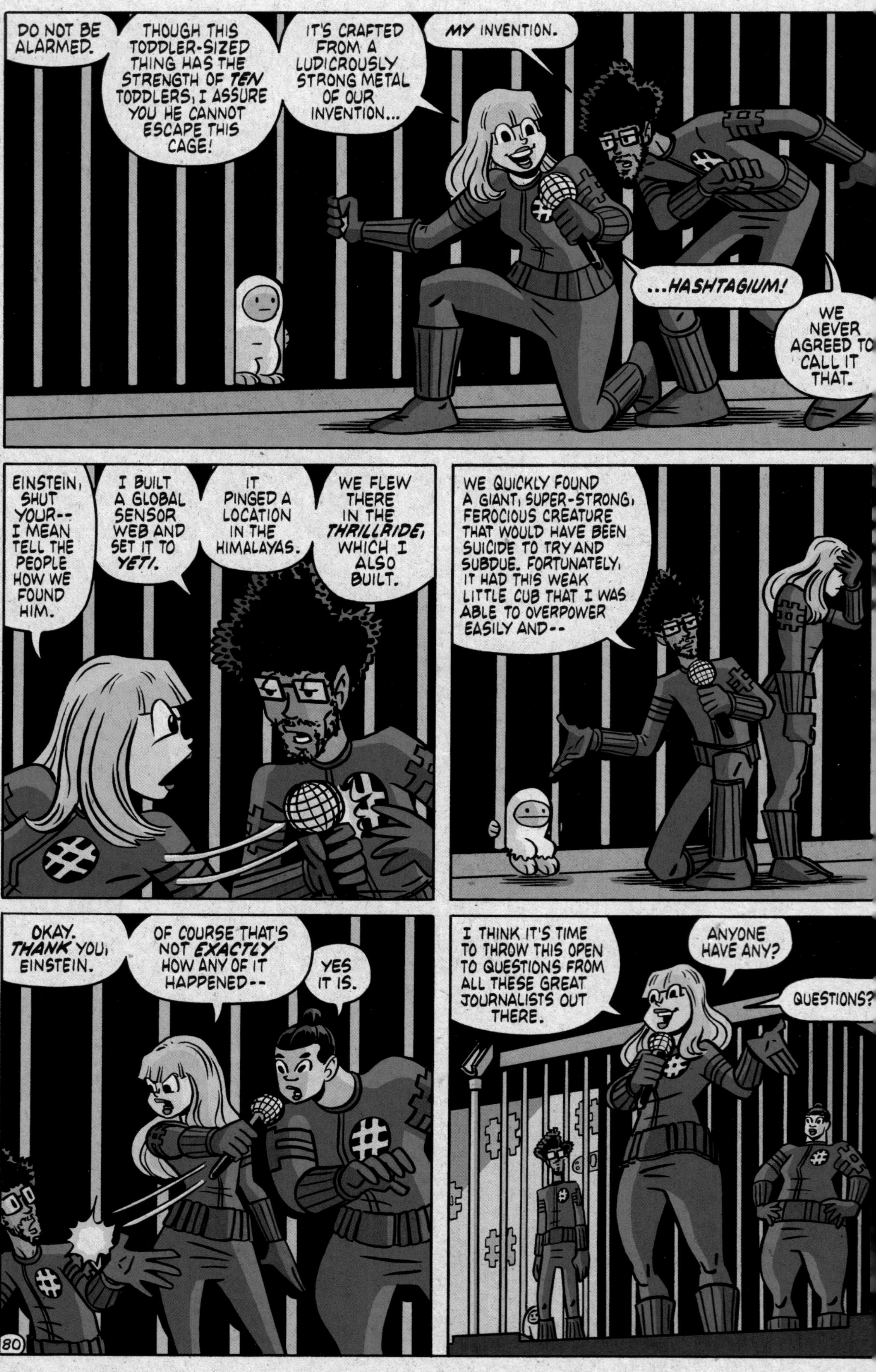

DO NOT BE ALARMED.
THOUGH THIS TODDLER-SIZED THING HAS THE STRENGTH OF *TEN* TODDLERS, I ASSURE YOU HE CANNOT ESCAPE THIS CAGE!
IT'S CRAFTED FROM A LUDICROUSLY STRONG METAL OF OUR INVENTION...
MY INVENTION.
...*HASHTAGIUM!*
WE NEVER AGREED TO CALL IT THAT.
EINSTEIN, SHUT YOUR-- I MEAN TELL THE PEOPLE HOW WE FOUND HIM.
I BUILT A GLOBAL SENSOR WEB AND SET IT TO *YETI*.
IT PINGED A LOCATION IN THE HIMALAYAS.
WE FLEW THERE IN THE *THRILLRIDE*, WHICH I ALSO BUILT.
WE QUICKLY FOUND A GIANT, SUPER-STRONG, FEROCIOUS CREATURE THAT WOULD HAVE BEEN SUICIDE TO TRY AND SUBDUE. FORTUNATELY, IT HAD THIS WEAK LITTLE CUB THAT I WAS ABLE TO OVERPOWER EASILY AND--
OKAY. *THANK* YOU, EINSTEIN.
OF COURSE THAT'S NOT *EXACTLY* HOW ANY OF IT HAPPENED--
YES IT IS.
I THINK IT'S TIME TO THROW THIS OPEN TO QUESTIONS FROM ALL THESE GREAT JOURNALISTS OUT THERE.
ANYONE HAVE ANY?
QUESTIONS?

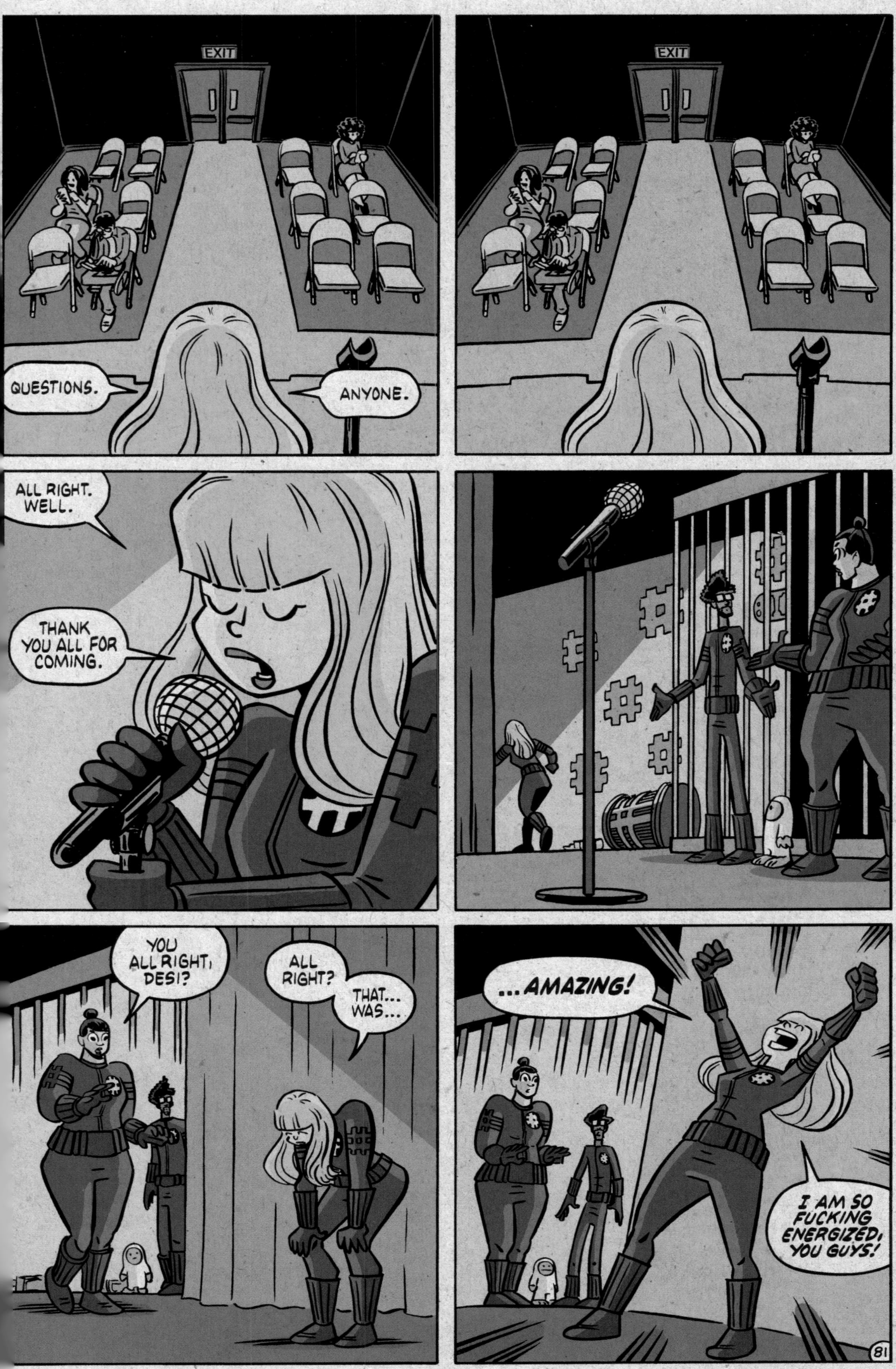
EXIT
QUESTIONS.
ANYONE.
EXIT
ALL RIGHT. WELL.
THANK YOU ALL FOR COMING.
YOU ALL RIGHT, DESI?
ALL RIGHT?
THAT... WAS...
...AMAZING!
I AM SO FUCKING ENERGIZED, YOU GUYS!

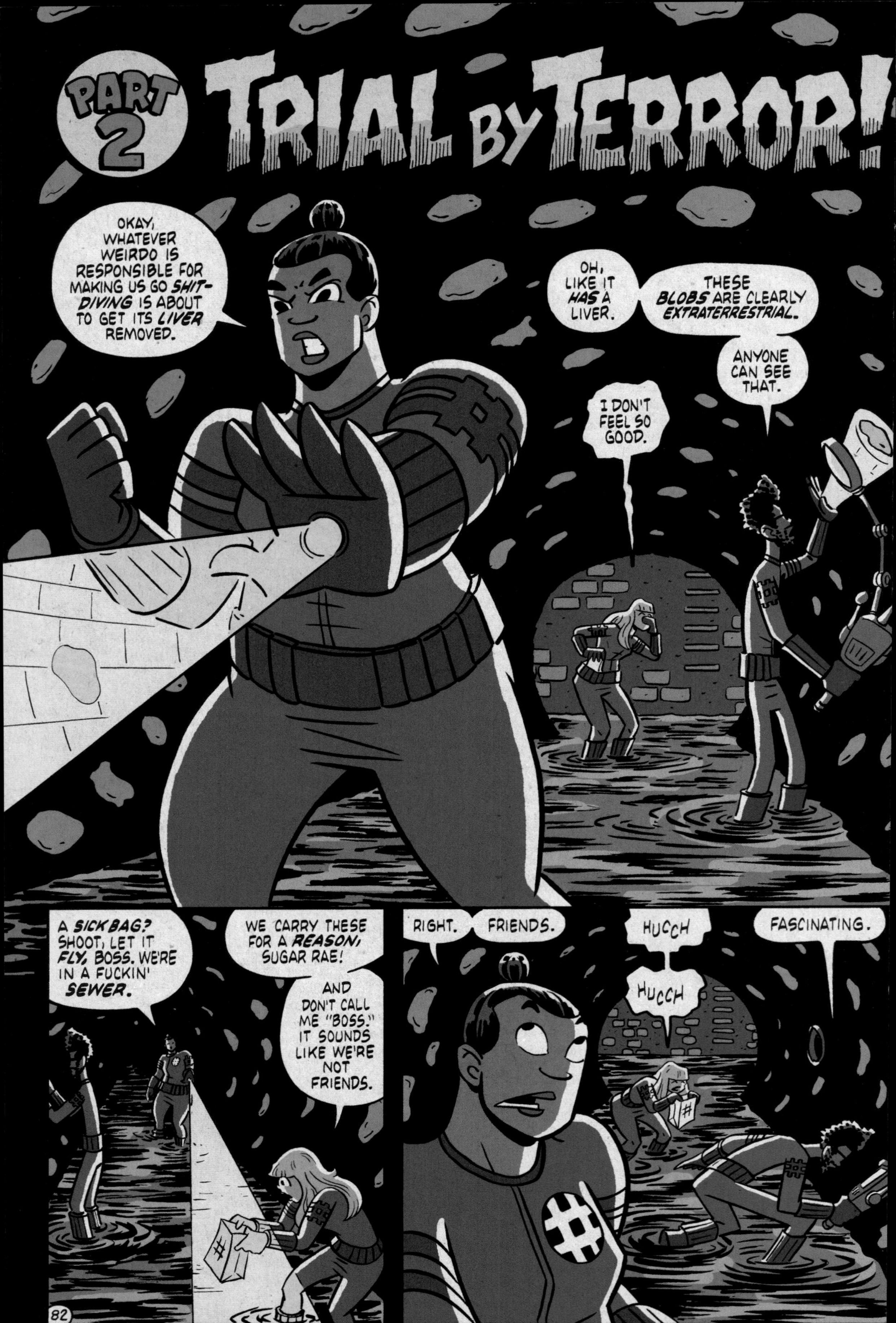
PART 2
TRIAL BY TERROR!
OKAY, WHATEVER WEIRDO IS RESPONSIBLE FOR MAKING US GO SHIT-DIVING IS ABOUT TO GET ITS LIVER REMOVED.
OH, LIKE IT HAS A LIVER.
THESE BLOBS ARE CLEARLY EXTRATERRESTRIAL.
ANYONE CAN SEE THAT.
I DON'T FEEL SO GOOD.
A SICK BAG? SHOOT, LET IT FLY, BOSS. WE'RE IN A FUCKIN' SEWER.
WE CARRY THESE FOR A REASON, SUGAR RAE!
AND DON'T CALL ME "BOSS." IT SOUNDS LIKE WE'RE NOT FRIENDS.
RIGHT.
FRIENDS.
HUCCH
HUCCH
FASCINATING.

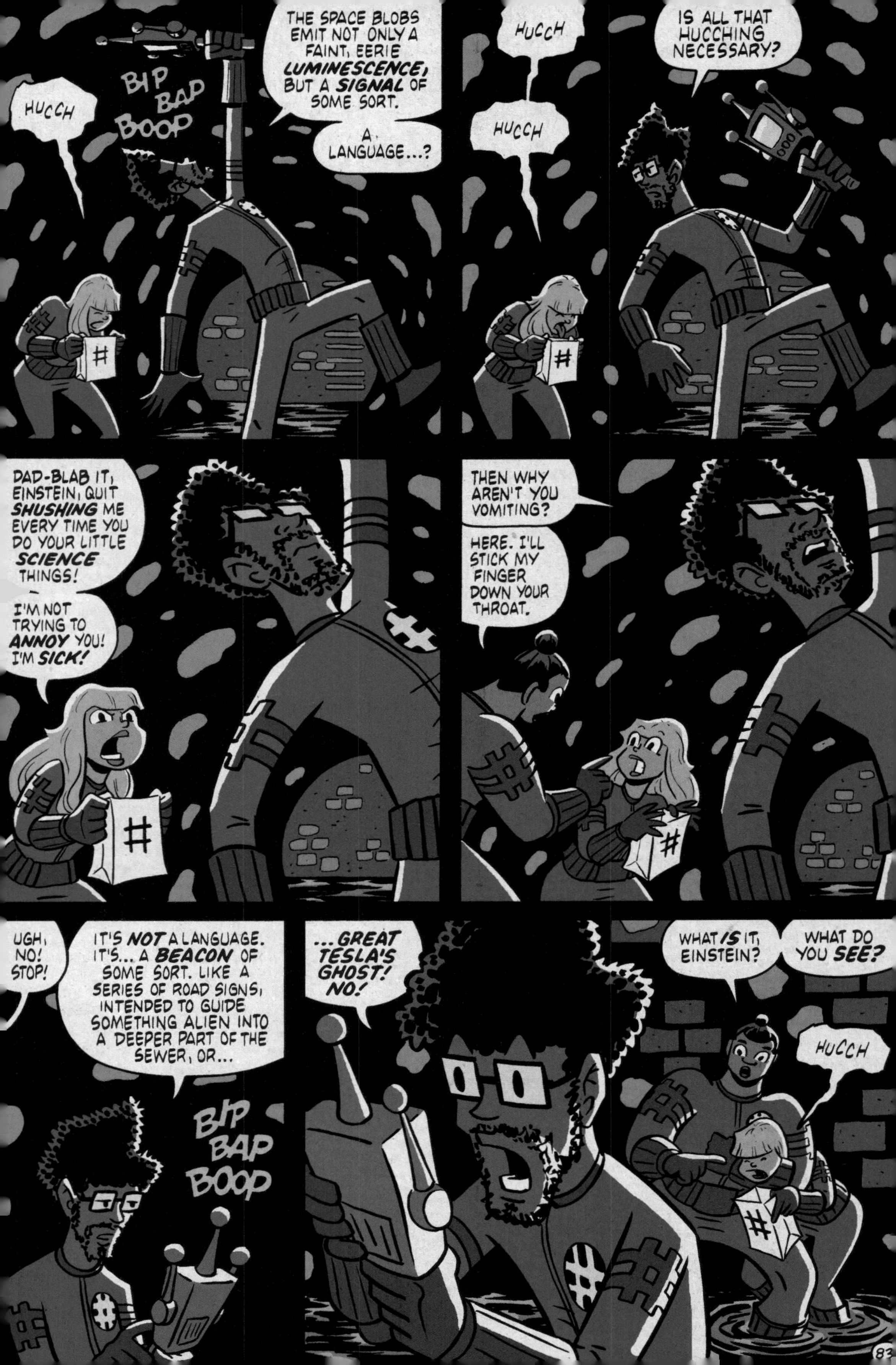
HUCCH
BIP BAP BOOP
THE SPACE BLOBS EMIT NOT ONLY A FAINT, EERIE LUMINESCENCE, BUT A SIGNAL OF SOME SORT.
A. LANGUAGE...?
HUCCH
HUCCH
IS ALL THAT HUCCHING NECESSARY?
DAD-BLAB IT, EINSTEIN, QUIT SHUSHING ME EVERY TIME YOU DO YOUR LITTLE SCIENCE THINGS!
I'M NOT TRYING TO ANNOY YOU! I'M SICK!
THEN WHY AREN'T YOU VOMITING?
HERE. I'LL STICK MY FINGER DOWN YOUR THROAT.
UGH, NO! STOP!
IT'S NOT A LANGUAGE. IT'S... A BEACON OF SOME SORT. LIKE A SERIES OF ROAD SIGNS, INTENDED TO GUIDE SOMETHING ALIEN INTO A DEEPER PART OF THE SEWER, OR...
BIP BAP BOOP
...GREAT TESLA'S GHOST! NO!
WHAT IS IT, EINSTEIN?
WHAT DO YOU SEE?
HUCCH

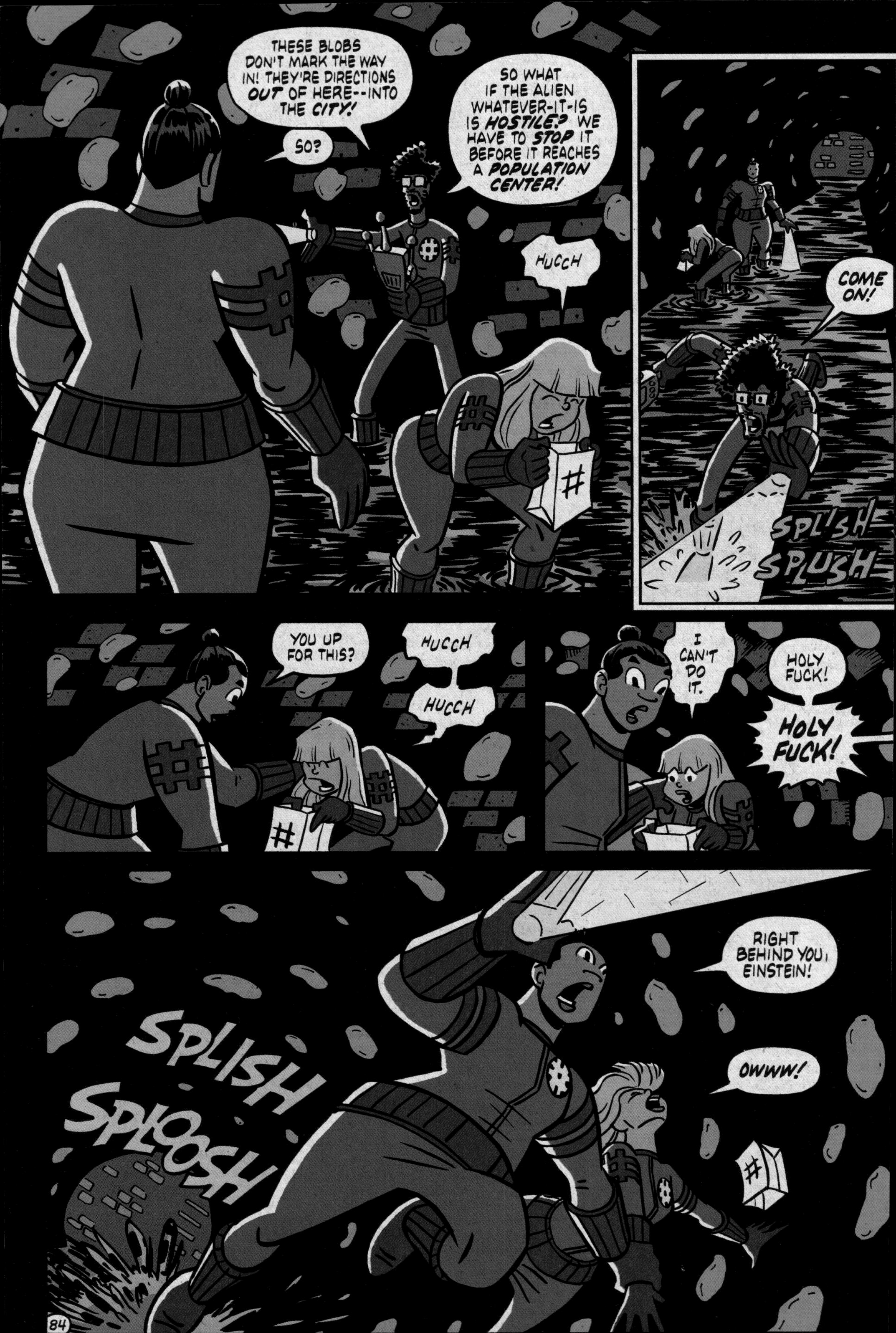
THESE BLOBS DON'T MARK THE WAY IN! THEY'RE DIRECTIONS OUT OF HERE--INTO THE CITY!
SO?
SO WHAT IF THE ALIEN WHATEVER-IT-IS IS HOSTILE? WE HAVE TO STOP IT BEFORE IT REACHES A POPULATION CENTER!
HUCCH
COME ON!
SPLUSH SPLUSH
YOU UP FOR THIS?
HUCCH
HUCCH
I CAN'T DO IT.
HOLY FUCK!
HOLY FUCK!
RIGHT BEHIND YOU, EINSTEIN!
OWWW!
SPLISH SPLOOSH

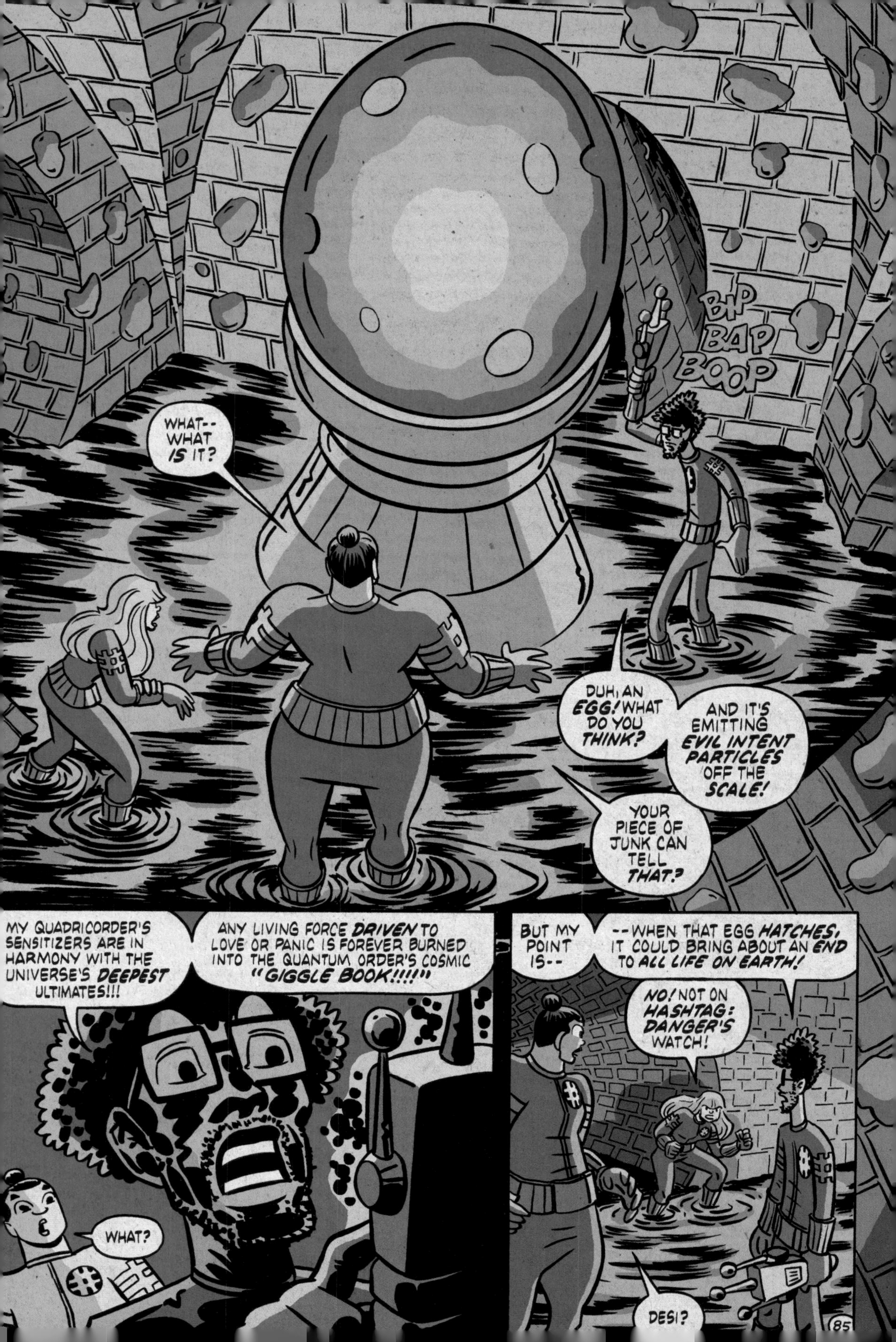
BIP BAP BOOP
WHAT-- WHAT *IS* IT?
DUH, AN *EGG!* WHAT DO YOU *THINK?*
AND IT'S EMITTING *EVIL INTENT PARTICLES* OFF THE *SCALE!*
YOUR PIECE OF JUNK CAN TELL *THAT?*
MY QUADRICORDER'S SENSITIZERS ARE IN HARMONY WITH THE UNIVERSE'S *DEEPEST* ULTIMATES!!!
ANY LIVING FORCE *DRIVEN* TO LOVE OR PANIC IS FOREVER BURNED INTO THE QUANTUM ORDER'S COSMIC *"GIGGLE BOOK!!!!"*
WHAT?
BUT MY POINT IS--
--WHEN THAT EGG *HATCHES*, IT COULD BRING ABOUT AN *END* TO *ALL LIFE ON EARTH!*
NO! NOT ON *HASHTAG: DANGER'S* WATCH!
DESI?

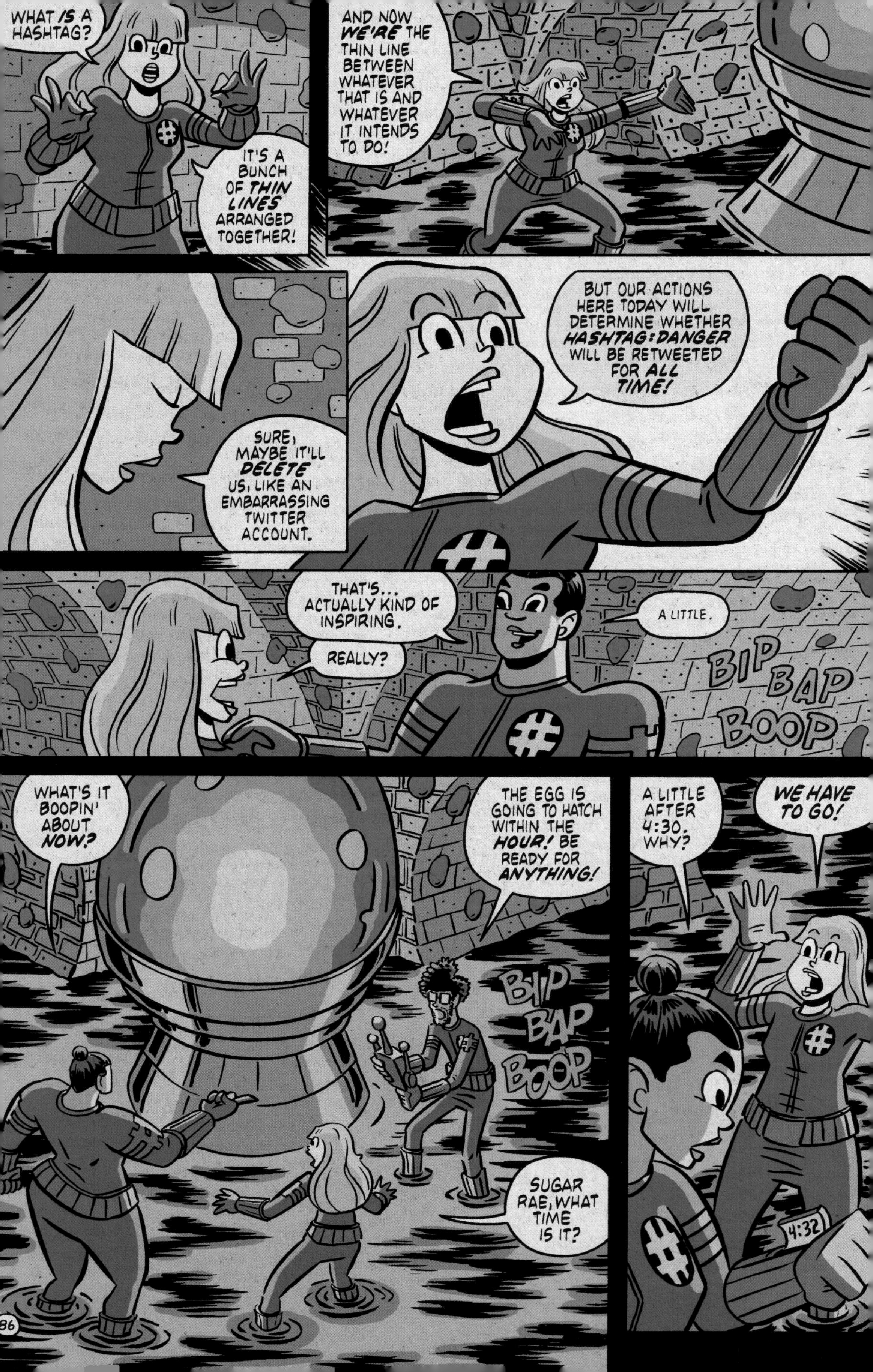
WHAT IS A HASHTAG?
IT'S A BUNCH OF THIN LINES ARRANGED TOGETHER!
AND NOW WE'RE THE THIN LINE BETWEEN WHATEVER THAT IS AND WHATEVER IT INTENDS TO DO!
SURE, MAYBE IT'LL DELETE US, LIKE AN EMBARRASSING TWITTER ACCOUNT.
BUT OUR ACTIONS HERE TODAY WILL DETERMINE WHETHER HASHTAG:DANGER WILL BE RETWEETED FOR ALL TIME!
THAT'S... ACTUALLY KIND OF INSPIRING.
REALLY?
A LITTLE.
BIP BAP BOOP
WHAT'S IT BOOPIN' ABOUT NOW?
THE EGG IS GOING TO HATCH WITHIN THE HOUR! BE READY FOR ANYTHING!
BIP BAP BOOP
SUGAR RAE, WHAT TIME IS IT?
A LITTLE AFTER 4:30. WHY?
4:32
WE HAVE TO GO!

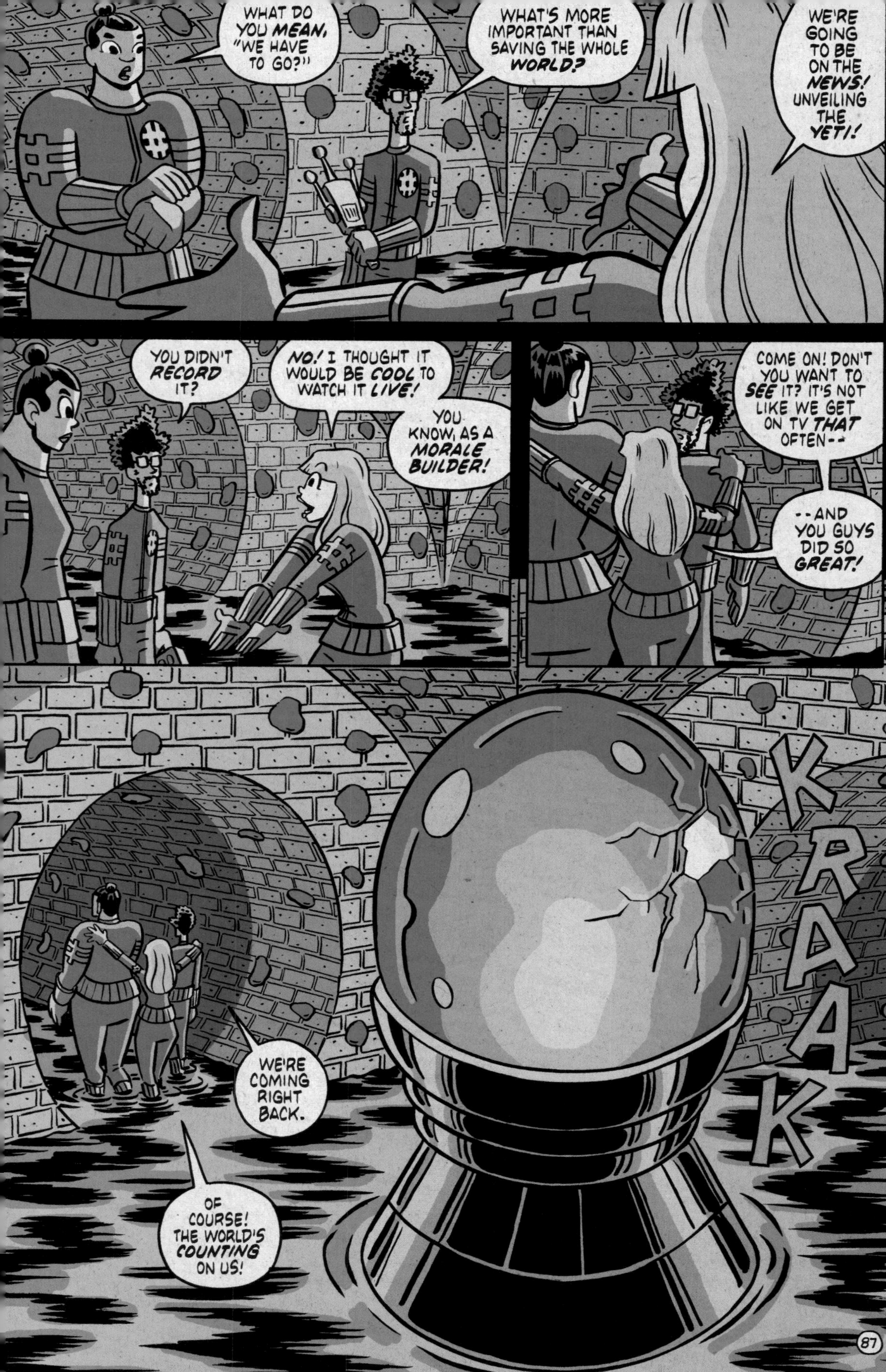
WHAT DO YOU MEAN, "WE HAVE TO GO?"
WHAT'S MORE IMPORTANT THAN SAVING THE WHOLE WORLD?
WE'RE GOING TO BE ON THE NEWS! UNVEILING THE YETI!
YOU DIDN'T RECORD IT?
NO! I THOUGHT IT WOULD BE COOL TO WATCH IT LIVE!
YOU KNOW, AS A MORALE BUILDER!
COME ON! DON'T YOU WANT TO SEE IT? IT'S NOT LIKE WE GET ON TV THAT OFTEN--
--AND YOU GUYS DID SO GREAT!
KRAAK
WE'RE COMING RIGHT BACK.
OF COURSE! THE WORLD'S COUNTING ON US!

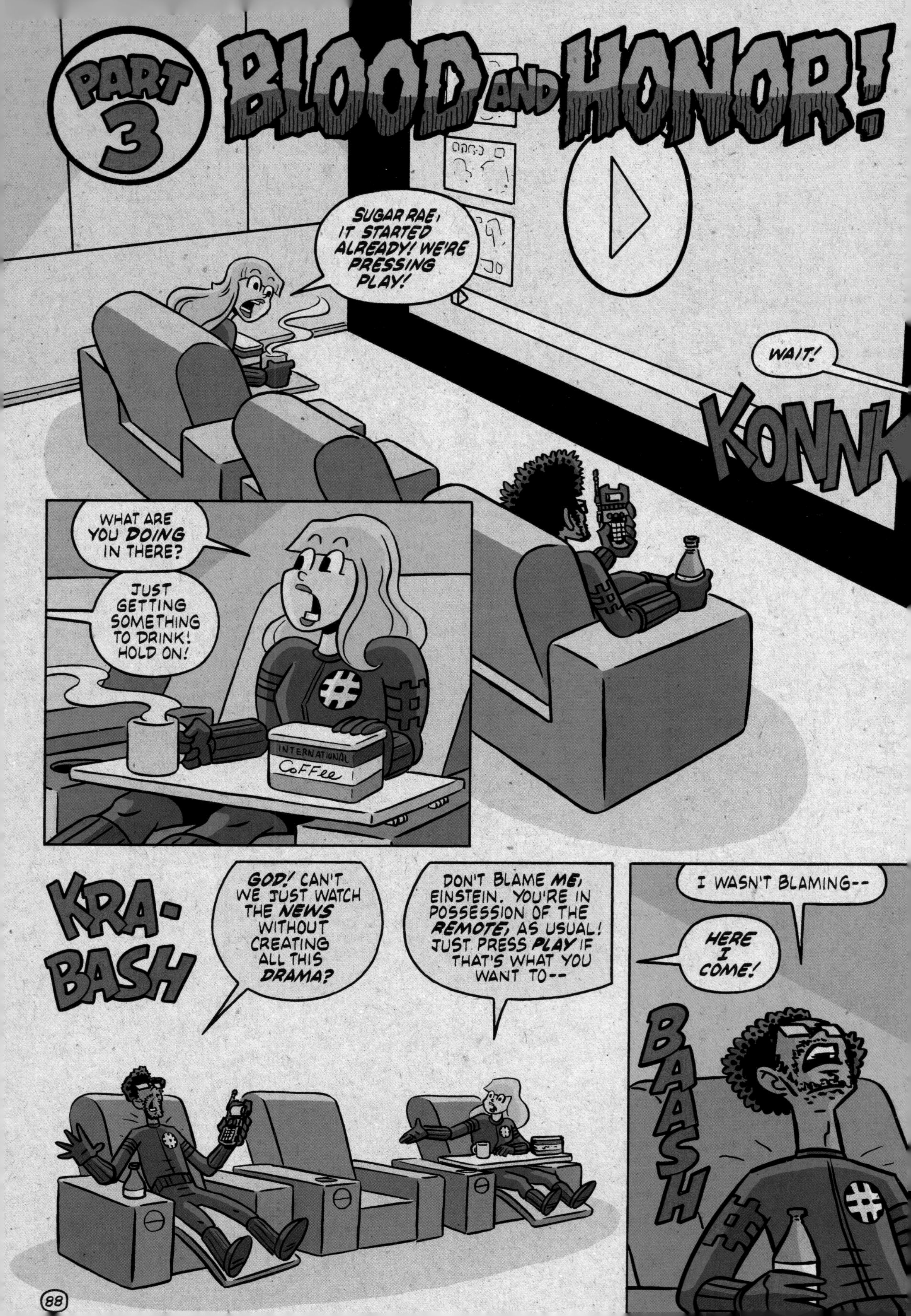
PART 3
BLOOD AND HONOR!
SUGAR RAE, IT STARTED ALREADY! WE'RE PRESSING PLAY!
WAIT!
KONNK
WHAT ARE YOU DOING IN THERE?
JUST GETTING SOMETHING TO DRINK! HOLD ON!
INTERNATIONAL
CoFFee
KRA-BASH
GOD! CAN'T WE JUST WATCH THE NEWS WITHOUT CREATING ALL THIS DRAMA?
DON'T BLAME ME, EINSTEIN. YOU'RE IN POSSESSION OF THE REMOTE, AS USUAL! JUST PRESS PLAY IF THAT'S WHAT YOU WANT TO--
I WASN'T BLAMING--
HERE I COME!
BAASH

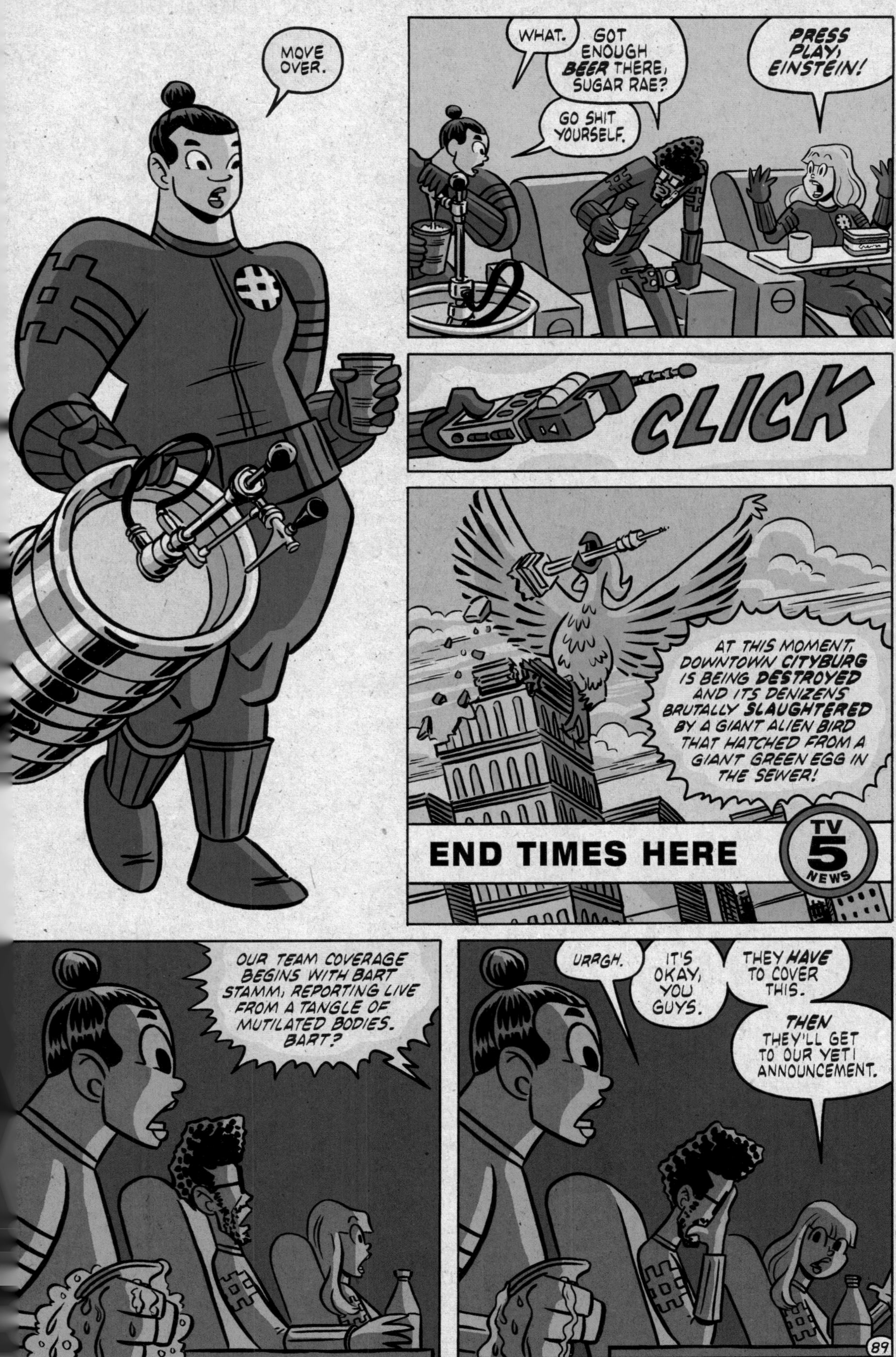
MOVE OVER.
WHAT.
GOT ENOUGH BEER THERE, SUGAR RAE?
GO SHIT YOURSELF.
PRESS PLAY, EINSTEIN!
CLICK
AT THIS MOMENT, DOWNTOWN CITYBURG IS BEING DESTROYED AND ITS DENIZENS BRUTALLY SLAUGHTERED BY A GIANT ALIEN BIRD THAT HATCHED FROM A GIANT GREEN EGG IN THE SEWER!
END TIMES HERE
TV 5 NEWS
OUR TEAM COVERAGE BEGINS WITH BART STAMM, REPORTING LIVE FROM A TANGLE OF MUTILATED BODIES. BART?
URRGH.
IT'S OKAY, YOU GUYS.
THEY HAVE TO COVER THIS.
THEN THEY'LL GET TO OUR YETI ANNOUNCEMENT.

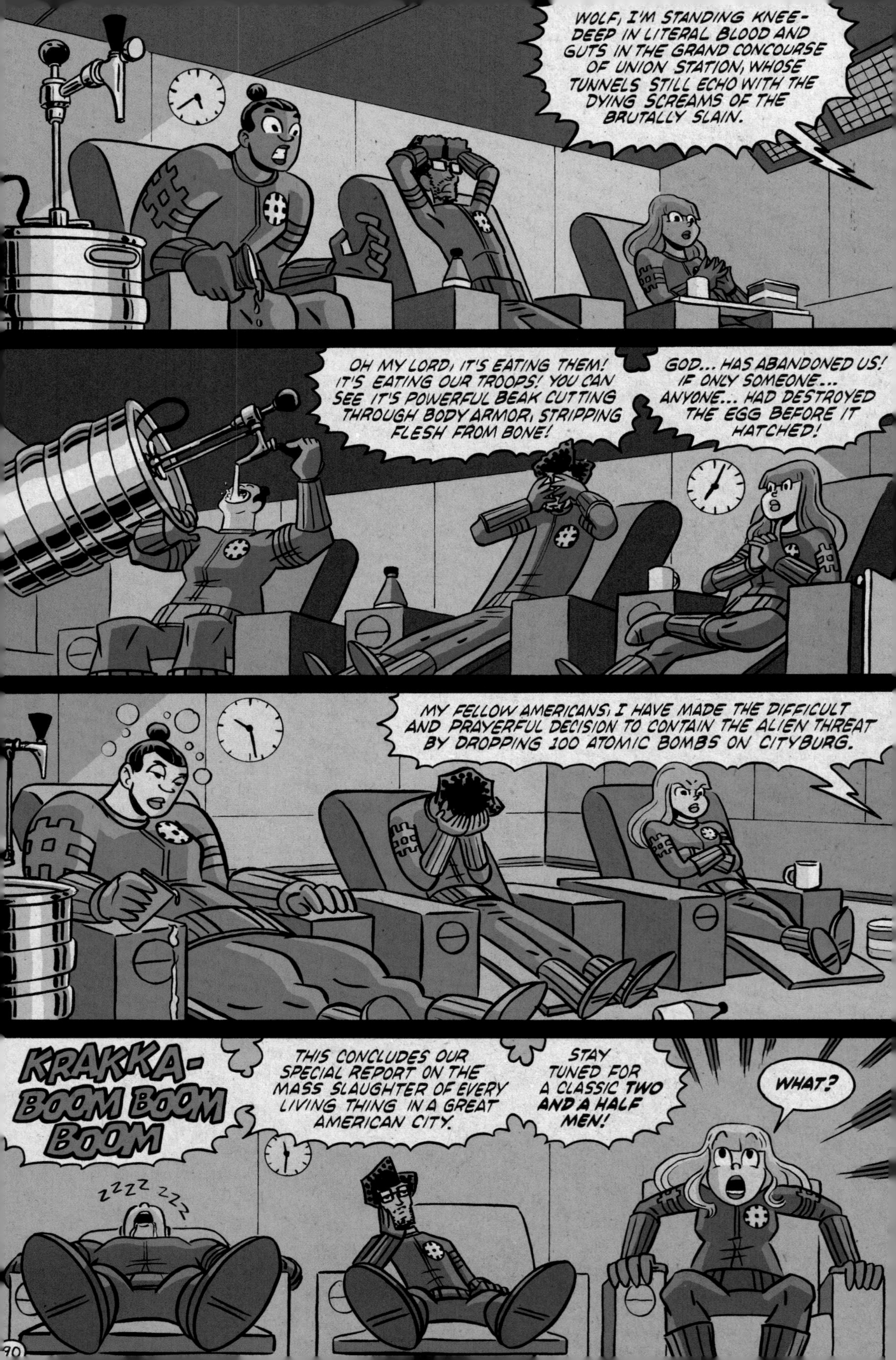
WOLF, I'M STANDING KNEE-DEEP IN LITERAL BLOOD AND GUTS IN THE GRAND CONCOURSE OF UNION STATION, WHOSE TUNNELS STILL ECHO WITH THE DYING SCREAMS OF THE BRUTALLY SLAIN.
OH MY LORD, IT'S EATING THEM! IT'S EATING OUR TROOPS! YOU CAN SEE IT'S POWERFUL BEAK CUTTING THROUGH BODY ARMOR, STRIPPING FLESH FROM BONE!
GOD... HAS ABANDONED US! IF ONLY SOMEONE... ANYONE... HAD DESTROYED THE EGG BEFORE IT HATCHED!
MY FELLOW AMERICANS, I HAVE MADE THE DIFFICULT AND PRAYERFUL DECISION TO CONTAIN THE ALIEN THREAT BY DROPPING 100 ATOMIC BOMBS ON CITYBURG.
KRAKKA-BOOM BOOM BOOM
THIS CONCLUDES OUR SPECIAL REPORT ON THE MASS SLAUGHTER OF EVERY LIVING THING IN A GREAT AMERICAN CITY.
STAY TUNED FOR A CLASSIC **TWO AND A HALF MEN!**
WHAT?
ZZZZ ZZZ

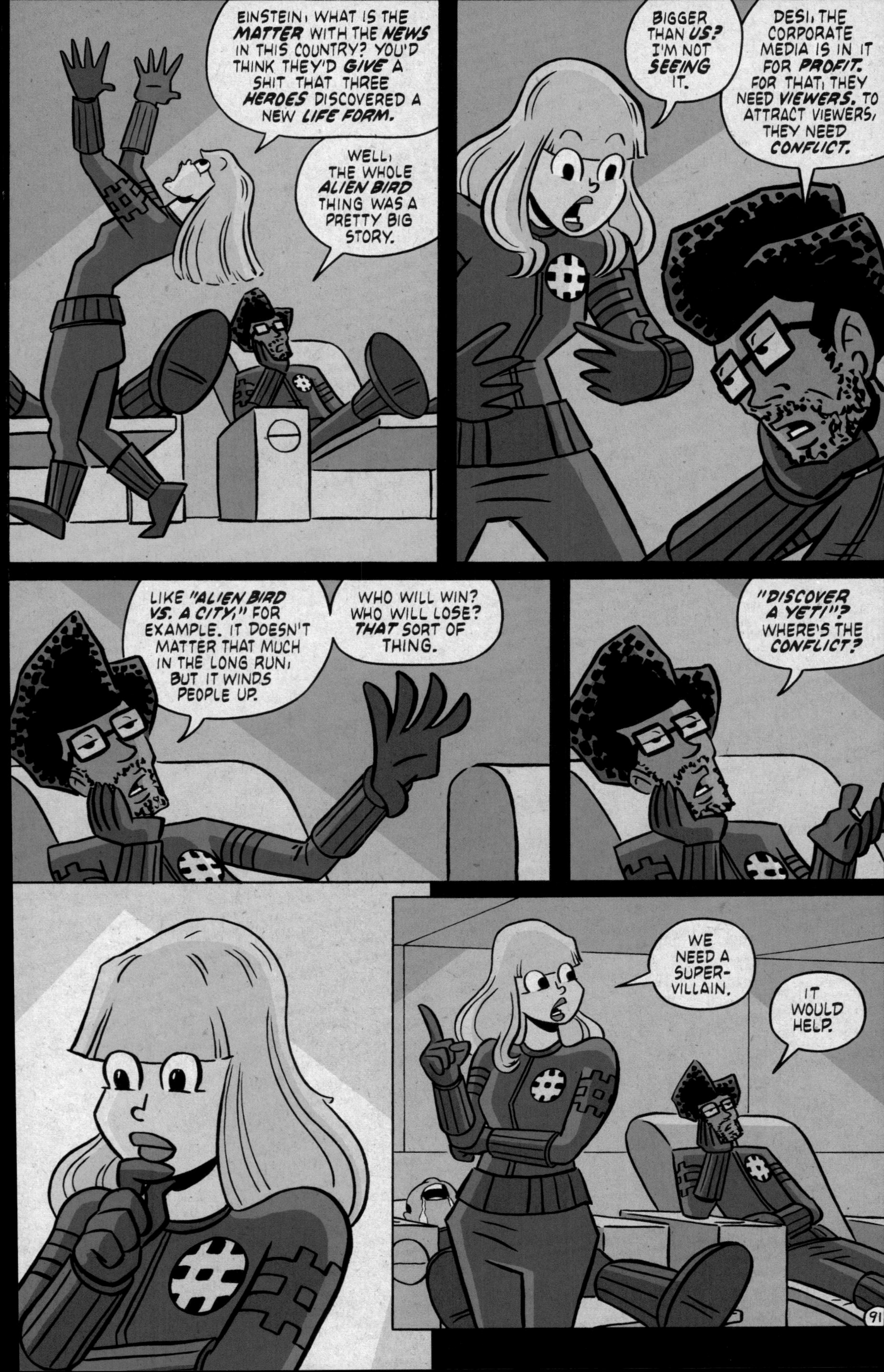
EINSTEIN, WHAT IS THE MATTER WITH THE NEWS IN THIS COUNTRY? YOU'D THINK THEY'D GIVE A SHIT THAT THREE HEROES DISCOVERED A NEW LIFE FORM.
WELL, THE WHOLE ALIEN BIRD THING WAS A PRETTY BIG STORY.
BIGGER THAN US? I'M NOT SEEING IT.
DESI, THE CORPORATE MEDIA IS IN IT FOR PROFIT. FOR THAT, THEY NEED VIEWERS. TO ATTRACT VIEWERS, THEY NEED CONFLICT.
LIKE "ALIEN BIRD VS. A CITY," FOR EXAMPLE. IT DOESN'T MATTER THAT MUCH IN THE LONG RUN, BUT IT WINDS PEOPLE UP.
WHO WILL WIN? WHO WILL LOSE? THAT SORT OF THING.
"DISCOVER A YETI"? WHERE'S THE CONFLICT?
WE NEED A SUPER-VILLAIN.
IT WOULD HELP.
91

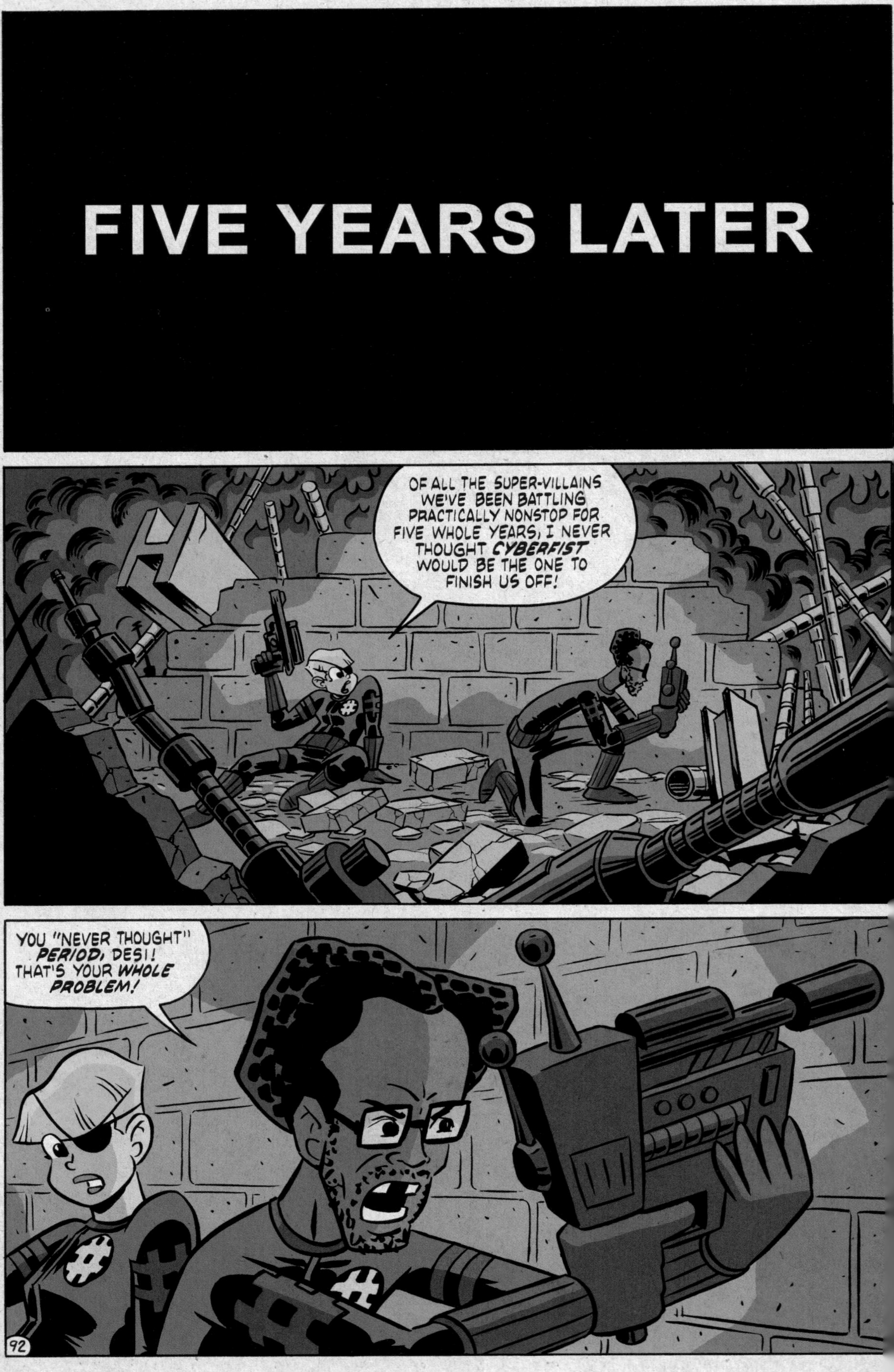
FIVE YEARS LATER
OF ALL THE SUPER-VILLAINS WE'VE BEEN BATTLING PRACTICALLY NONSTOP FOR FIVE WHOLE YEARS, I NEVER THOUGHT CYBERFIST WOULD BE THE ONE TO FINISH US OFF!
YOU "NEVER THOUGHT" PERIOD, DESI! THAT'S YOUR WHOLE PROBLEM!
92

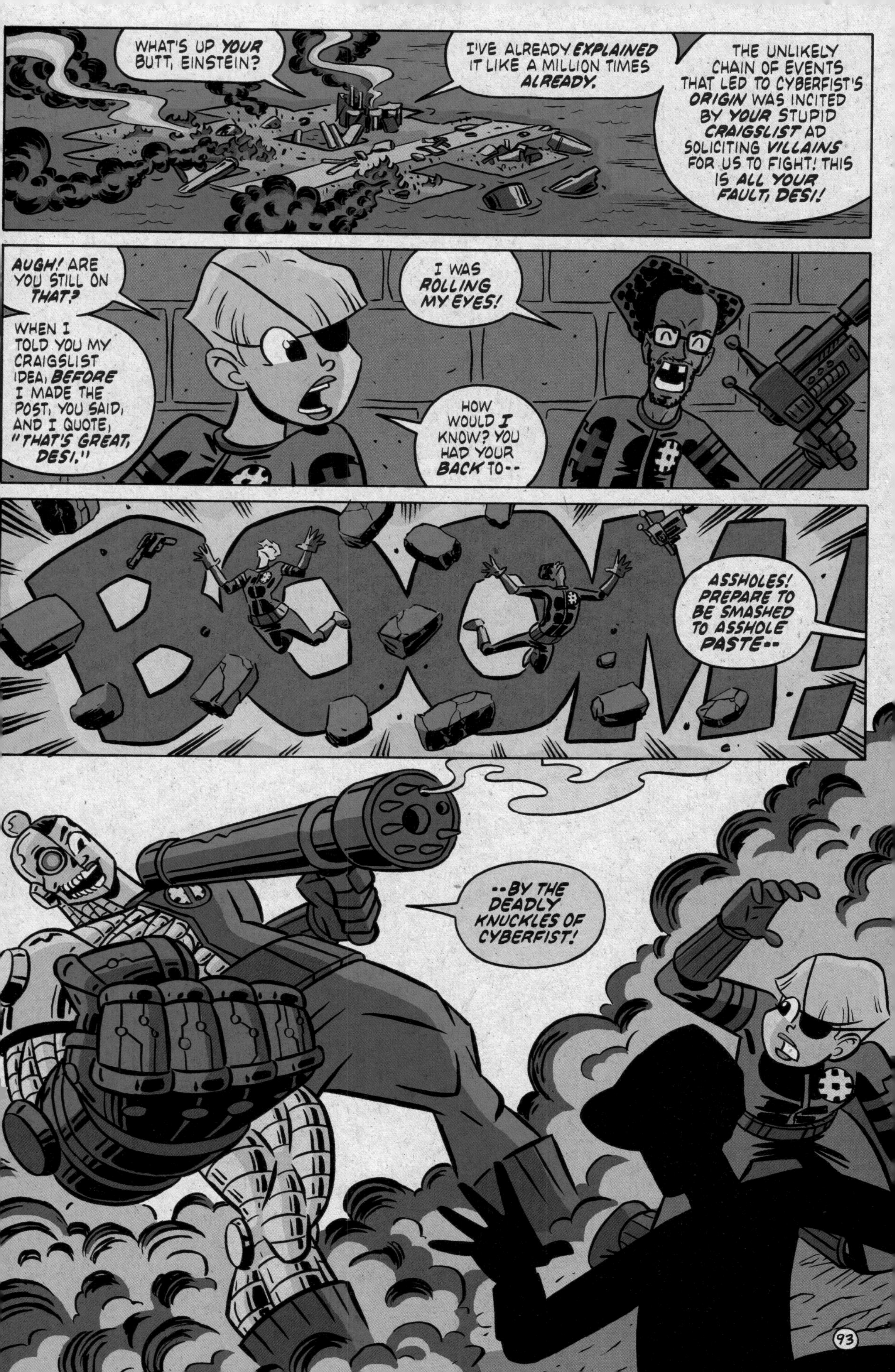
WHAT'S UP YOUR BUTT, EINSTEIN?
I'VE ALREADY EXPLAINED IT LIKE A MILLION TIMES ALREADY.
THE UNLIKELY CHAIN OF EVENTS THAT LED TO CYBERFIST'S ORIGIN WAS INCITED BY YOUR STUPID CRAIGSLIST AD SOLICITING VILLAINS FOR US TO FIGHT! THIS IS ALL YOUR FAULT, DESI!
AUGH! ARE YOU STILL ON THAT?
WHEN I TOLD YOU MY CRAIGSLIST IDEA, BEFORE I MADE THE POST, YOU SAID, AND I QUOTE, "THAT'S GREAT, DESI."
I WAS ROLLING MY EYES!
HOW WOULD I KNOW? YOU HAD YOUR BACK TO--
BOOM!
ASSHOLES! PREPARE TO BE SMASHED TO ASSHOLE PASTE--
--BY THE DEADLY KNUCKLES OF CYBERFIST!

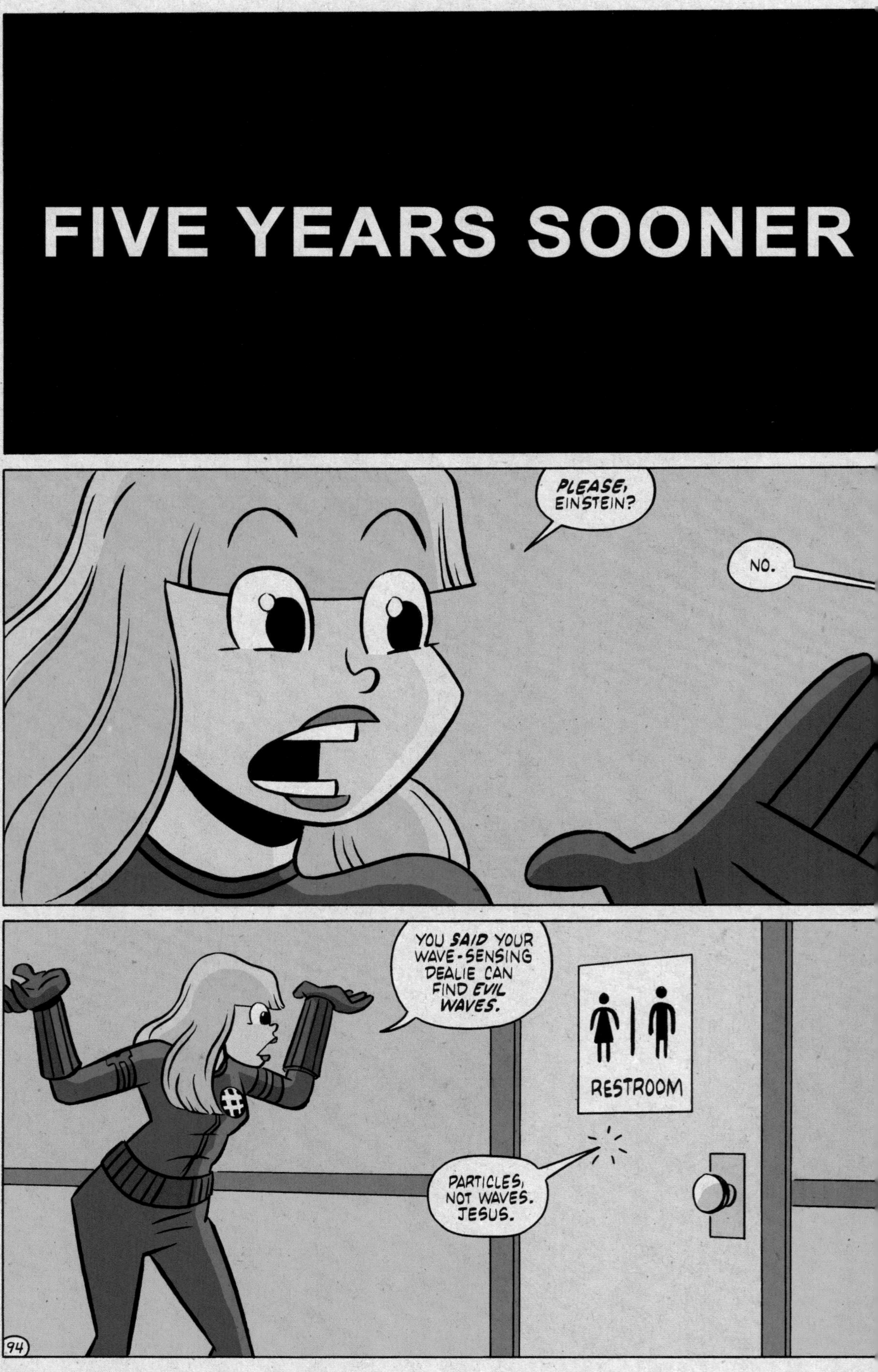
FIVE YEARS SOONER
PLEASE, EINSTEIN?
NO.
YOU SAID YOUR WAVE-SENSING DEALIE CAN FIND EVIL WAVES.
RESTROOM
PARTICLES, NOT WAVES. JESUS.

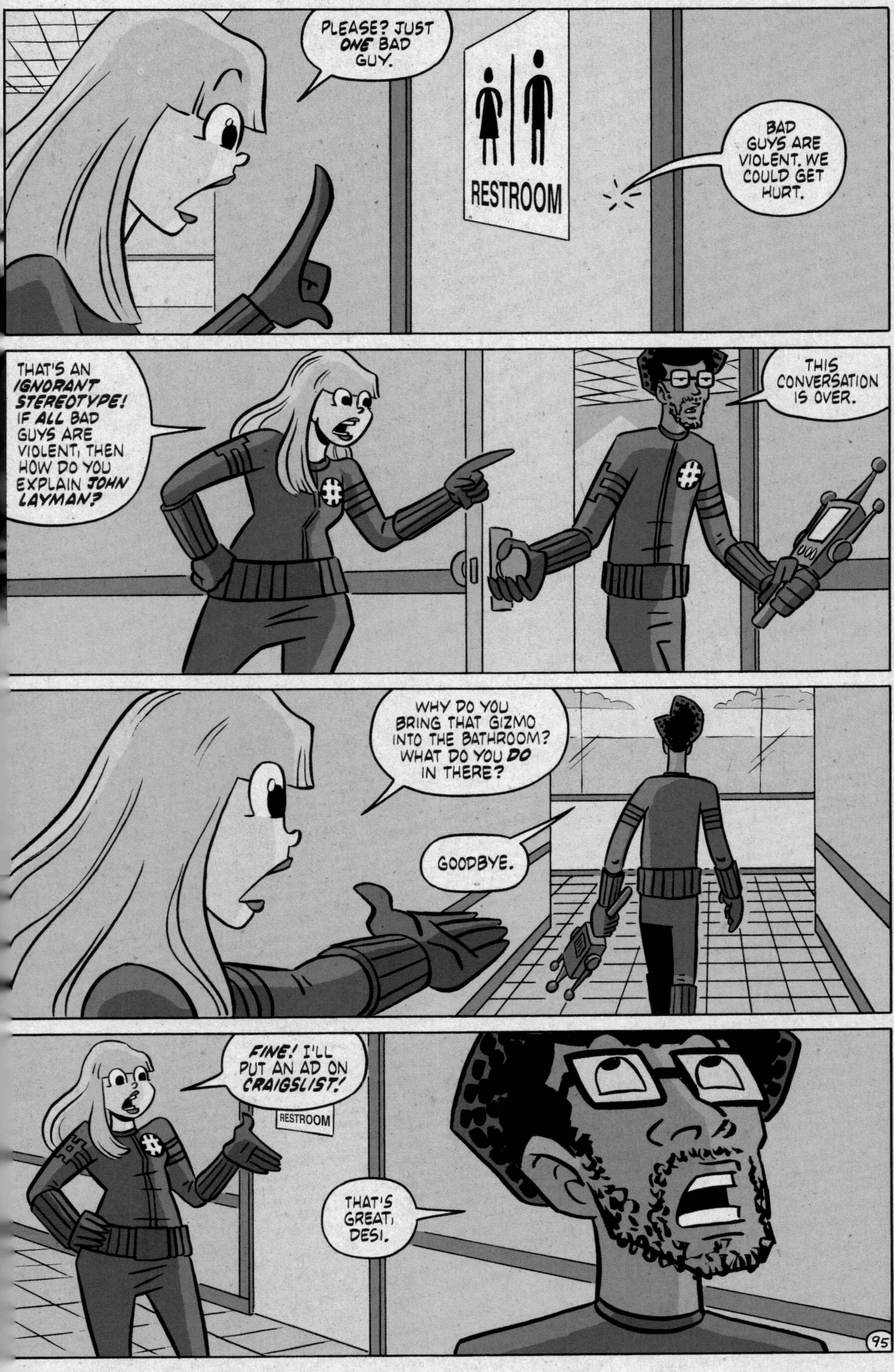
PLEASE? JUST ONE BAD GUY.
RESTROOM
BAD GUYS ARE VIOLENT. WE COULD GET HURT.
THAT'S AN IGNORANT STEREOTYPE! IF ALL BAD GUYS ARE VIOLENT, THEN HOW DO YOU EXPLAIN JOHN LAYMAN?
THIS CONVERSATION IS OVER.
WHY DO YOU BRING THAT GIZMO INTO THE BATHROOM? WHAT DO YOU DO IN THERE?
GOODBYE.
FINE! I'LL PUT AN AD ON CRAIGSLIST!
RESTROOM
THAT'S GREAT, DESI.

EPILOGUE

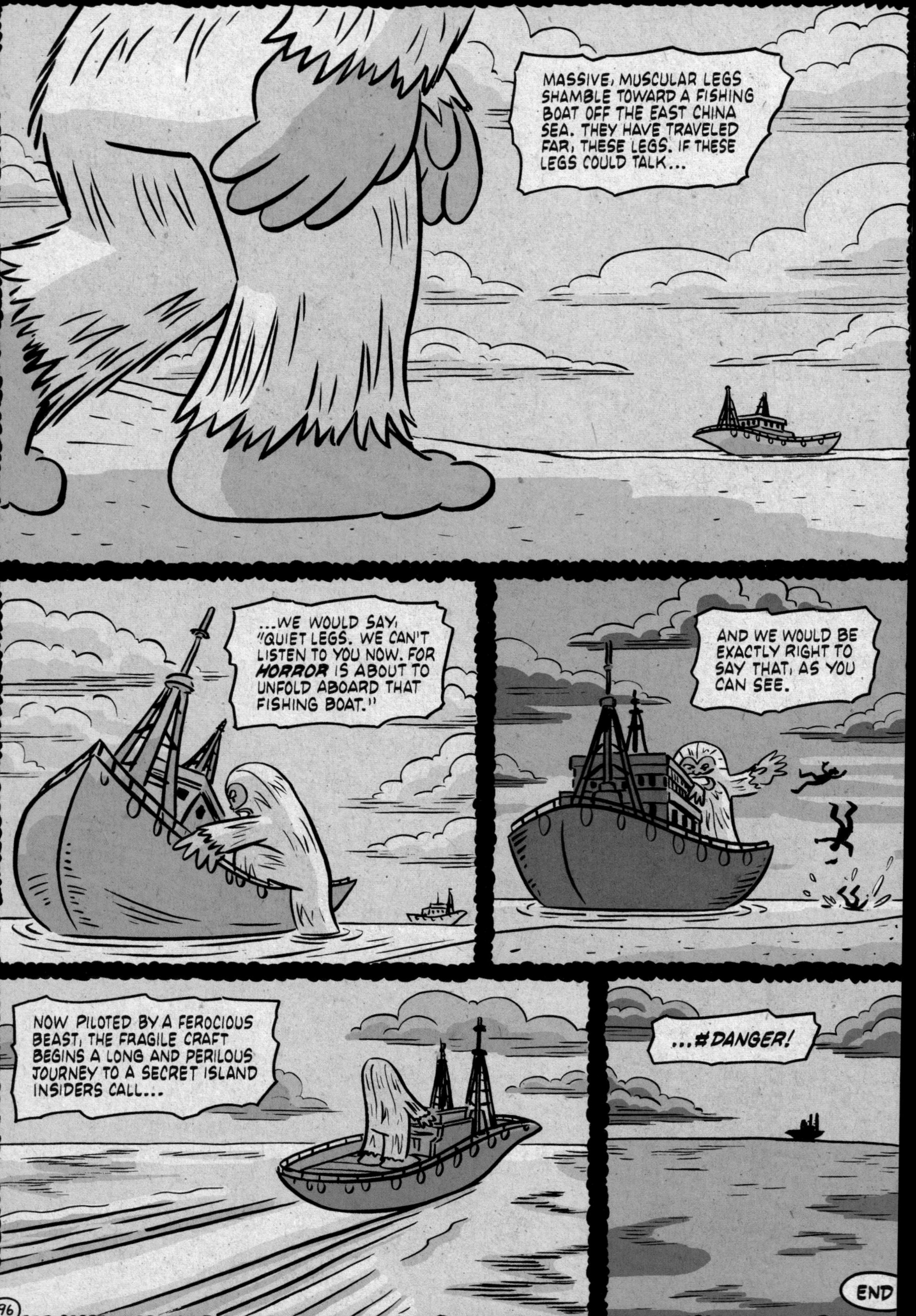
MASSIVE, MUSCULAR LEGS SHAMBLE TOWARD A FISHING BOAT OFF THE EAST CHINA SEA. THEY HAVE TRAVELED FAR, THESE LEGS. IF THESE LEGS COULD TALK...
...WE WOULD SAY, "QUIET LEGS. WE CAN'T LISTEN TO YOU NOW. FOR HORROR IS ABOUT TO UNFOLD ABOARD THAT FISHING BOAT."
AND WE WOULD BE EXACTLY RIGHT TO SAY THAT, AS YOU CAN SEE.
NOW PILOTED BY A FEROCIOUS BEAST, THE FRAGILE CRAFT BEGINS A LONG AND PERILOUS JOURNEY TO A SECRET ISLAND INSIDERS CALL...
...#DANGER!
END

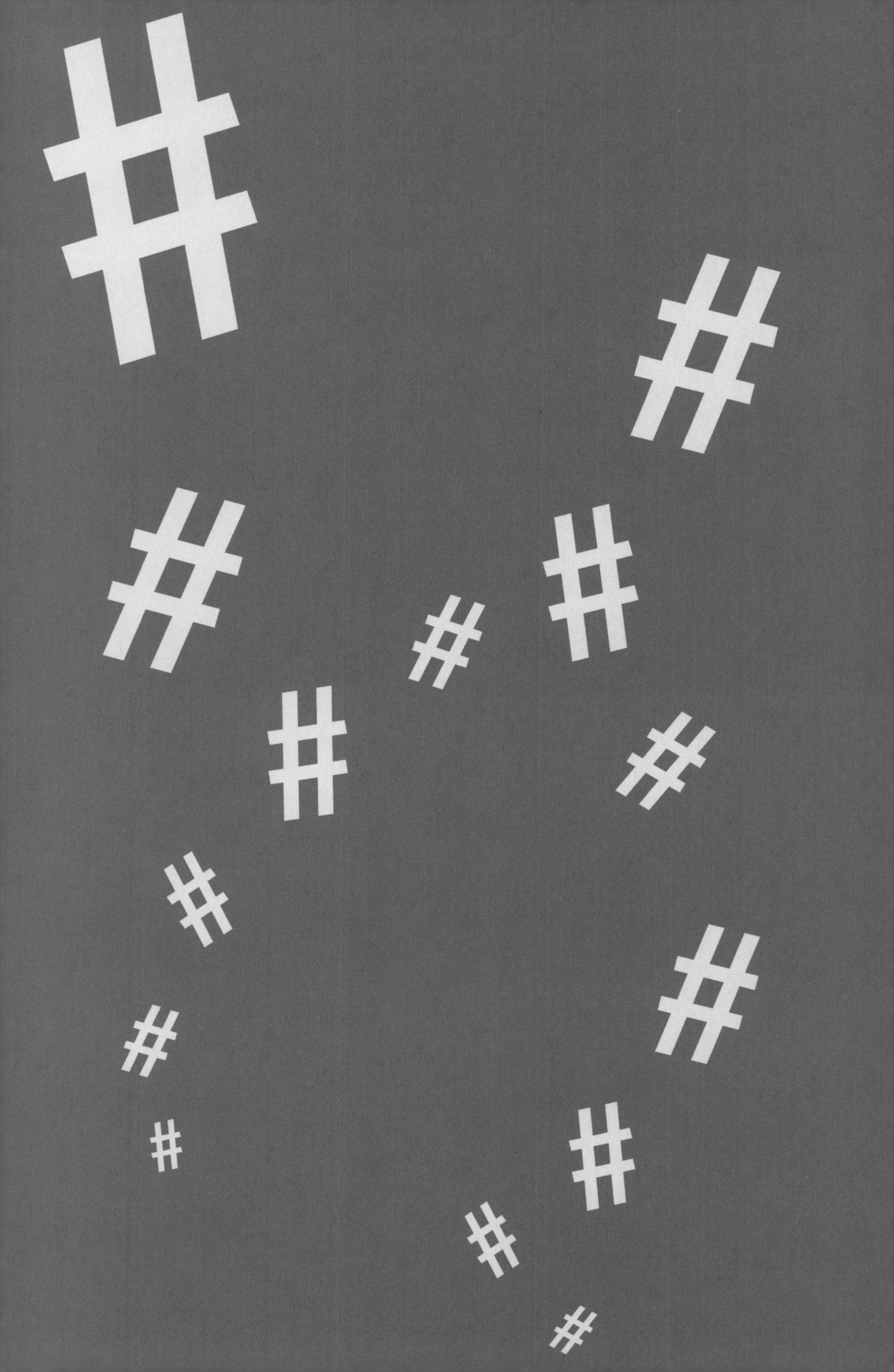

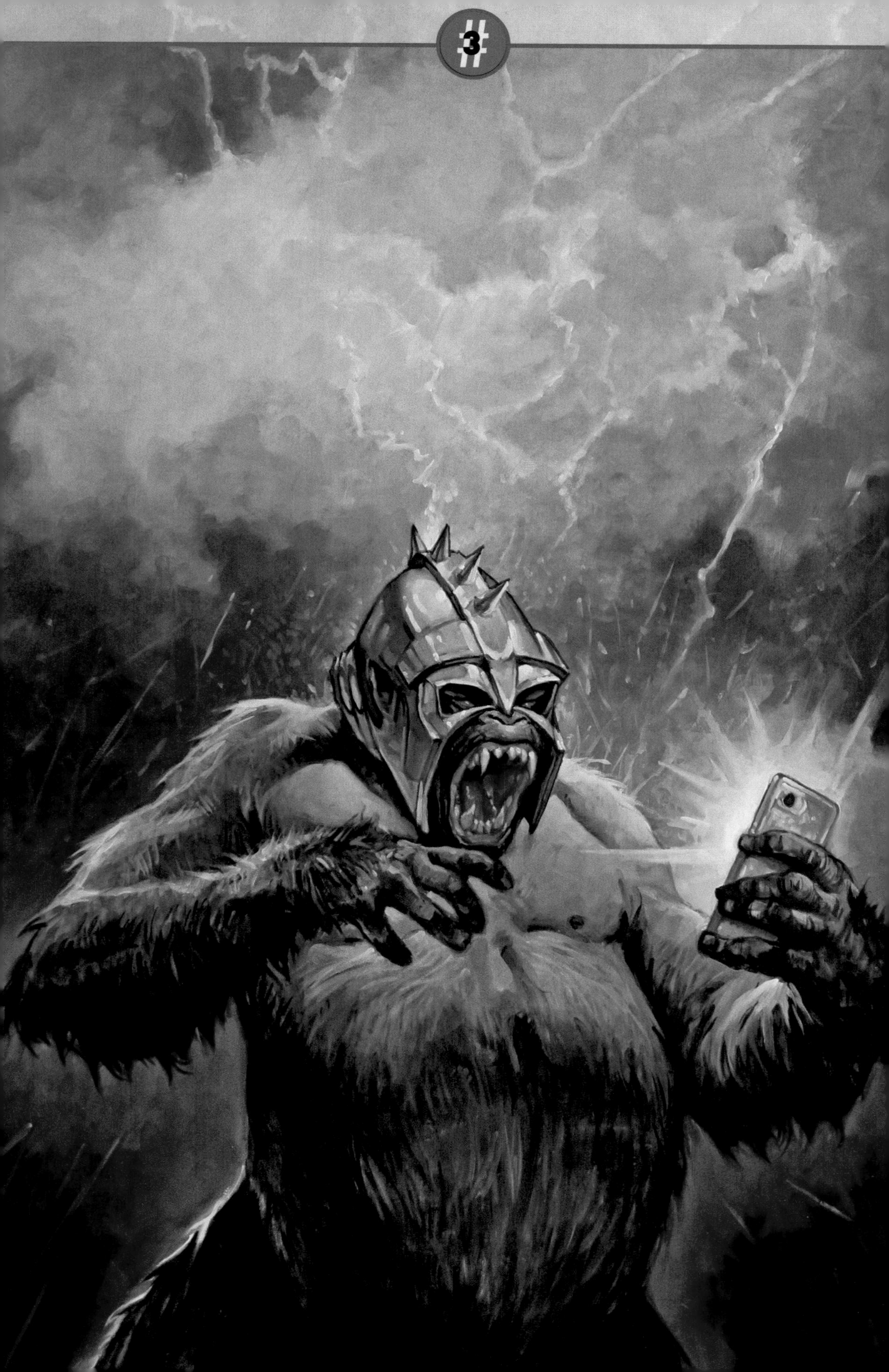
#3

EINSTEIN ARMSTRONG
PH.D. CRYPTO-BIOLOGY
MS SUPER-CRIMINOLOGY

SUGAR RAE HUANG
REIGNING HEAVYWEIGHT CHAMPION:
PACIFIC COAST WOMEN'S CAGE FIGHTING ASSN.

DESIREE DANGER
THREE-TIME WINNER : GOOD CITIZENS'
CLUB YOUNG LEADER AWARD

TOGETHER THEY ANSWER THE DESPERATE CRY...

HASHTAG: DANGER

MISSION 000011:

THE APE IN THE IRON MASK!

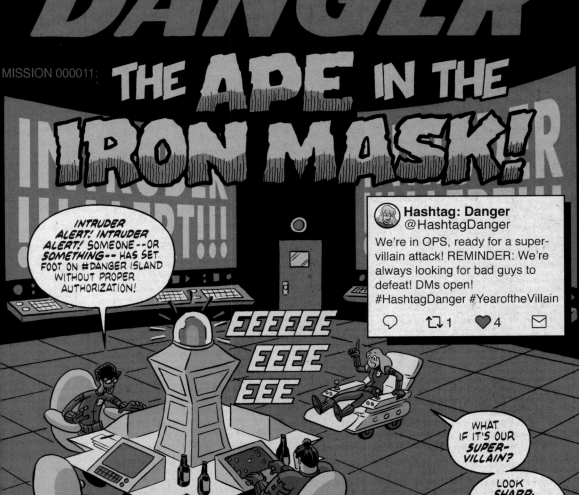

INTRUDER ALERT! INTRUDER ALERT! SOMEONE--OR SOMETHING-- HAS SET FOOT ON #DANGER ISLAND WITHOUT PROPER AUTHORIZATION!

Hashtag: Danger
@HashtagDanger

We're in OPS, ready for a super-villain attack! REMINDER: We're always looking for bad guys to defeat! DMs open!
#HashtagDanger #YearoftheVillain

💬   ⟲ 1   ♥ 4   ✉

EEEEEE EEEE EEE

WHAT IF IT'S OUR SUPER-VILLAIN?

LOOK SHARP, EVERYBODY! THIS COULD GET US ON THE NEWS!

99

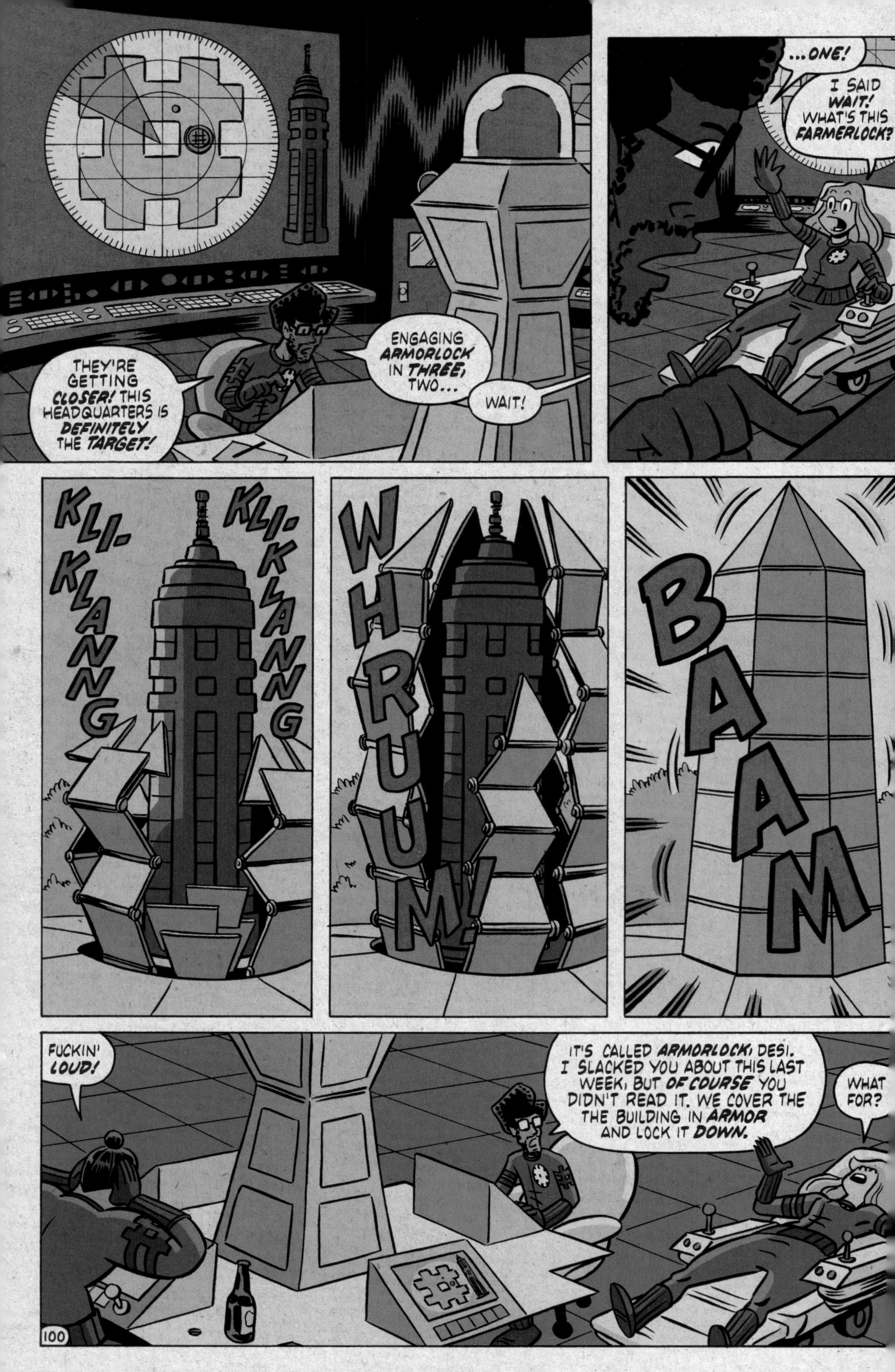
THEY'RE GETTING CLOSER! THIS HEADQUARTERS IS DEFINITELY THE TARGET!
ENGAGING ARMORLOCK IN THREE, TWO...
WAIT!
...ONE!
I SAID WAIT! WHAT'S THIS FARMERLOCK?
KLI-KLANNG
KLI-KLANNG
WHRRUUM!
BAAM
FUCKIN' LOUD!
IT'S CALLED ARMORLOCK, DESI. I SLACKED YOU ABOUT THIS LAST WEEK, BUT OF COURSE YOU DIDN'T READ IT. WE COVER THE THE BUILDING IN ARMOR AND LOCK IT DOWN.
WHAT FOR?

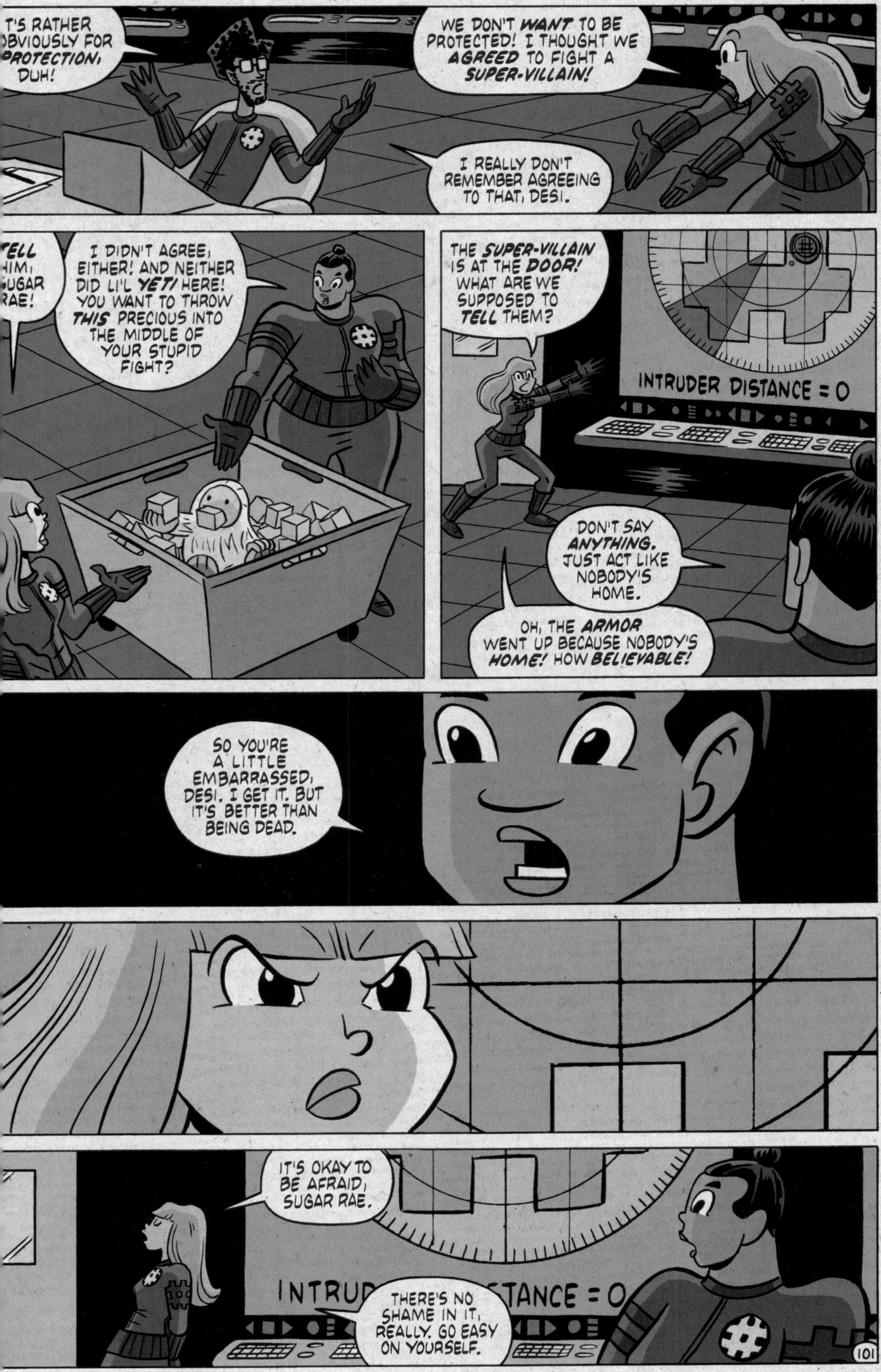
T'S RATHER OBVIOUSLY FOR PROTECTION, DUH!
WE DON'T WANT TO BE PROTECTED! I THOUGHT WE AGREED TO FIGHT A SUPER-VILLAIN!
I REALLY DON'T REMEMBER AGREEING TO THAT, DESI.
TELL HIM, SUGAR RAE!
I DIDN'T AGREE, EITHER! AND NEITHER DID LI'L YETI HERE! YOU WANT TO THROW THIS PRECIOUS INTO THE MIDDLE OF YOUR STUPID FIGHT?
THE SUPER-VILLAIN IS AT THE DOOR! WHAT ARE WE SUPPOSED TO TELL THEM?
INTRUDER DISTANCE = 0
DON'T SAY ANYTHING. JUST ACT LIKE NOBODY'S HOME.
OH, THE ARMOR WENT UP BECAUSE NOBODY'S HOME! HOW BELIEVABLE!
SO YOU'RE A LITTLE EMBARRASSED, DESI. I GET IT. BUT IT'S BETTER THAN BEING DEAD.
IT'S OKAY TO BE AFRAID, SUGAR RAE.
INTRUD STANCE = 0
THERE'S NO SHAME IN IT, REALLY. GO EASY ON YOURSELF.

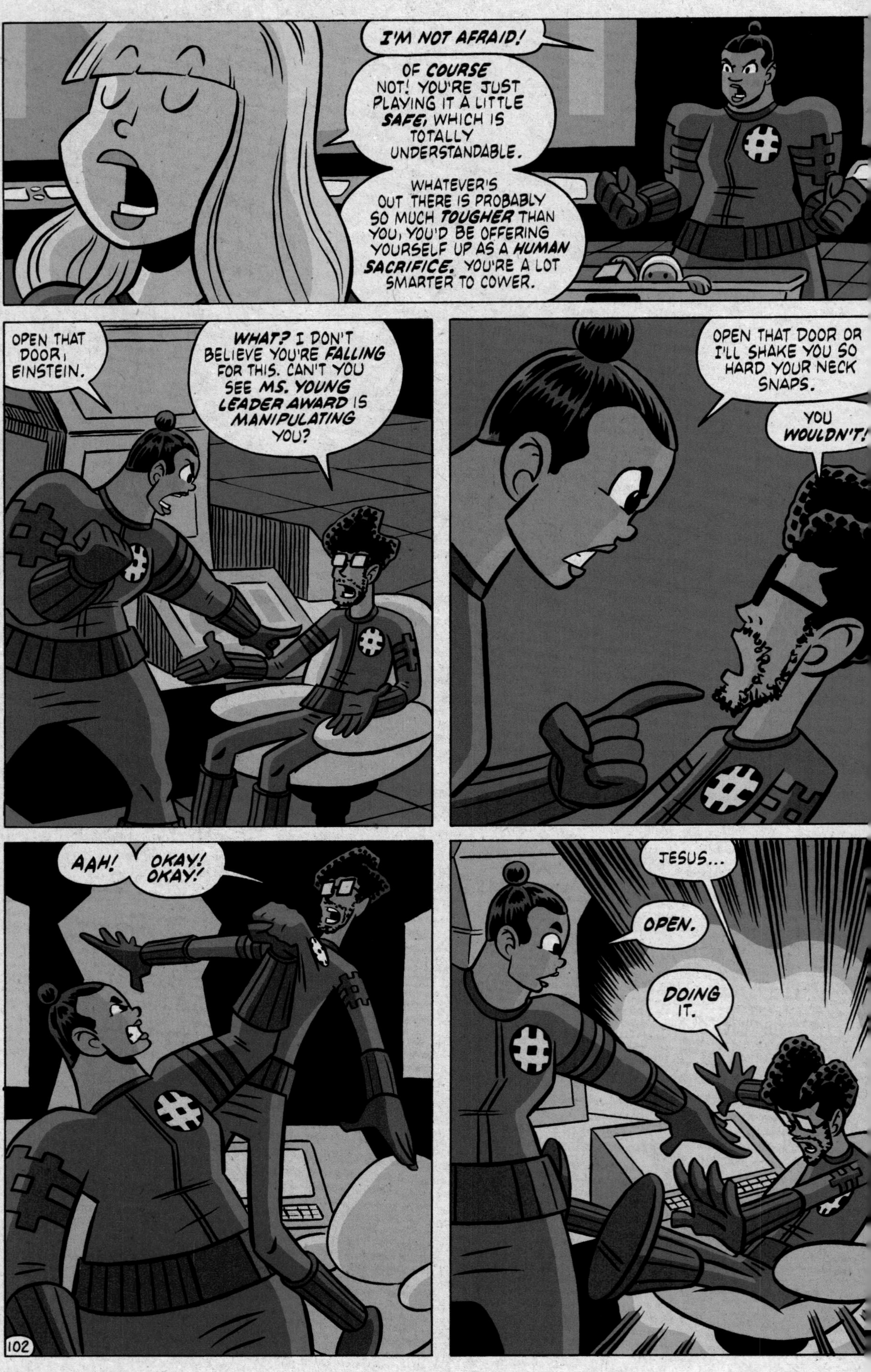
I'M NOT AFRAID!
OF COURSE NOT! YOU'RE JUST PLAYING IT A LITTLE SAFE, WHICH IS TOTALLY UNDERSTANDABLE.
WHATEVER'S OUT THERE IS PROBABLY SO MUCH TOUGHER THAN YOU, YOU'D BE OFFERING YOURSELF UP AS A HUMAN SACRIFICE. YOU'RE A LOT SMARTER TO COWER.
OPEN THAT DOOR, EINSTEIN.
WHAT? I DON'T BELIEVE YOU'RE FALLING FOR THIS. CAN'T YOU SEE MS. YOUNG LEADER AWARD IS MANIPULATING YOU?
OPEN THAT DOOR OR I'LL SHAKE YOU SO HARD YOUR NECK SNAPS.
YOU WOULDN'T!
AAH!
OKAY! OKAY!
JESUS...
OPEN.
DOING IT.

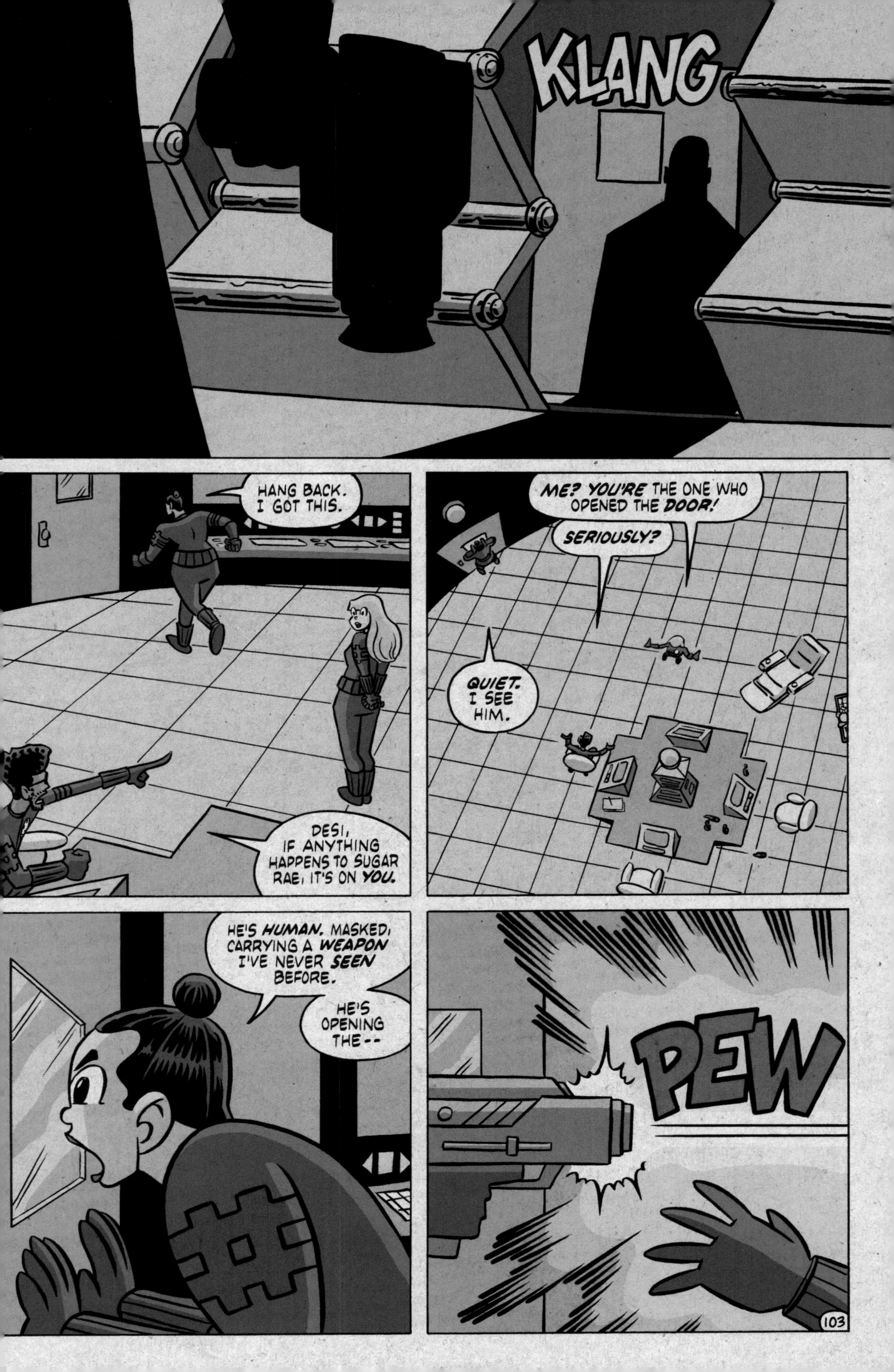
KLANG
HANG BACK. I GOT THIS.
DESI, IF ANYTHING HAPPENS TO SUGAR RAE, IT'S ON YOU.
ME? YOU'RE THE ONE WHO OPENED THE DOOR!
SERIOUSLY?
QUIET. I SEE HIM.
HE'S HUMAN. MASKED, CARRYING A WEAPON I'VE NEVER SEEN BEFORE.
HE'S OPENING THE--
PEW

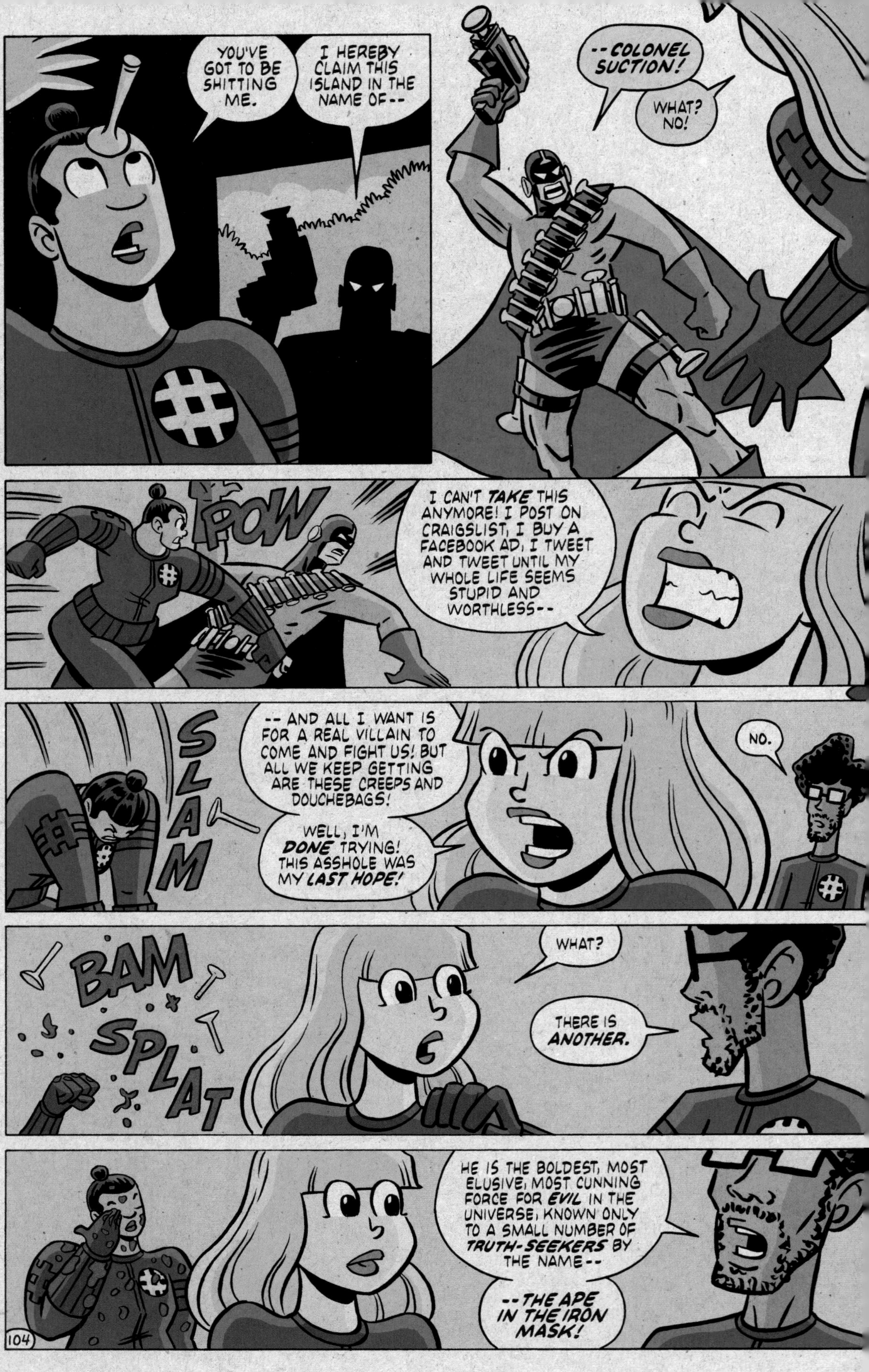
YOU'VE GOT TO BE SHITTING ME.
I HEREBY CLAIM THIS ISLAND IN THE NAME OF--
--COLONEL SUCTION!
WHAT? NO!
POW
I CAN'T TAKE THIS ANYMORE! I POST ON CRAIGSLIST, I BUY A FACEBOOK AD, I TWEET AND TWEET UNTIL MY WHOLE LIFE SEEMS STUPID AND WORTHLESS--
SLAM
--AND ALL I WANT IS FOR A REAL VILLAIN TO COME AND FIGHT US! BUT ALL WE KEEP GETTING ARE THESE CREEPS AND DOUCHEBAGS!
WELL, I'M DONE TRYING! THIS ASSHOLE WAS MY LAST HOPE!
NO.
BAM
SPLAT
WHAT?
THERE IS ANOTHER.
HE IS THE BOLDEST, MOST ELUSIVE, MOST CUNNING FORCE FOR EVIL IN THE UNIVERSE, KNOWN ONLY TO A SMALL NUMBER OF TRUTH-SEEKERS BY THE NAME--
--THE APE IN THE IRON MASK!

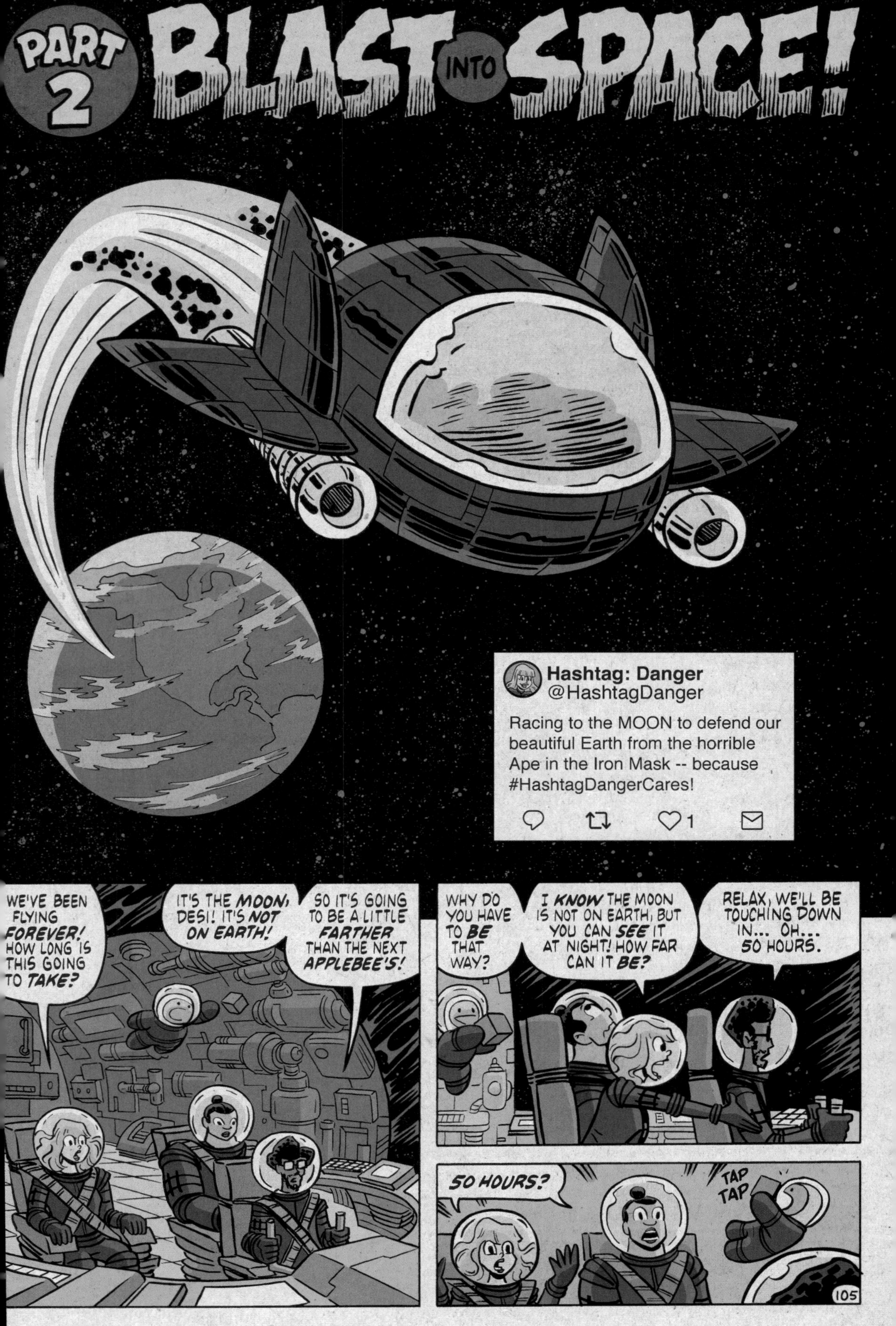
PART 2 BLAST INTO SPACE!
Hashtag: Danger
@HashtagDanger
Racing to the MOON to defend our beautiful Earth from the horrible Ape in the Iron Mask -- because #HashtagDangerCares!
1
WE'VE BEEN FLYING FOREVER! HOW LONG IS THIS GOING TO TAKE?
IT'S THE MOON, DESI! IT'S NOT ON EARTH!
SO IT'S GOING TO BE A LITTLE FARTHER THAN THE NEXT APPLEBEE'S!
WHY DO YOU HAVE TO BE THAT WAY?
I KNOW THE MOON IS NOT ON EARTH, BUT YOU CAN SEE IT AT NIGHT! HOW FAR CAN IT BE?
RELAX, WE'LL BE TOUCHING DOWN IN... OH... 50 HOURS.
50 HOURS?
TAP TAP

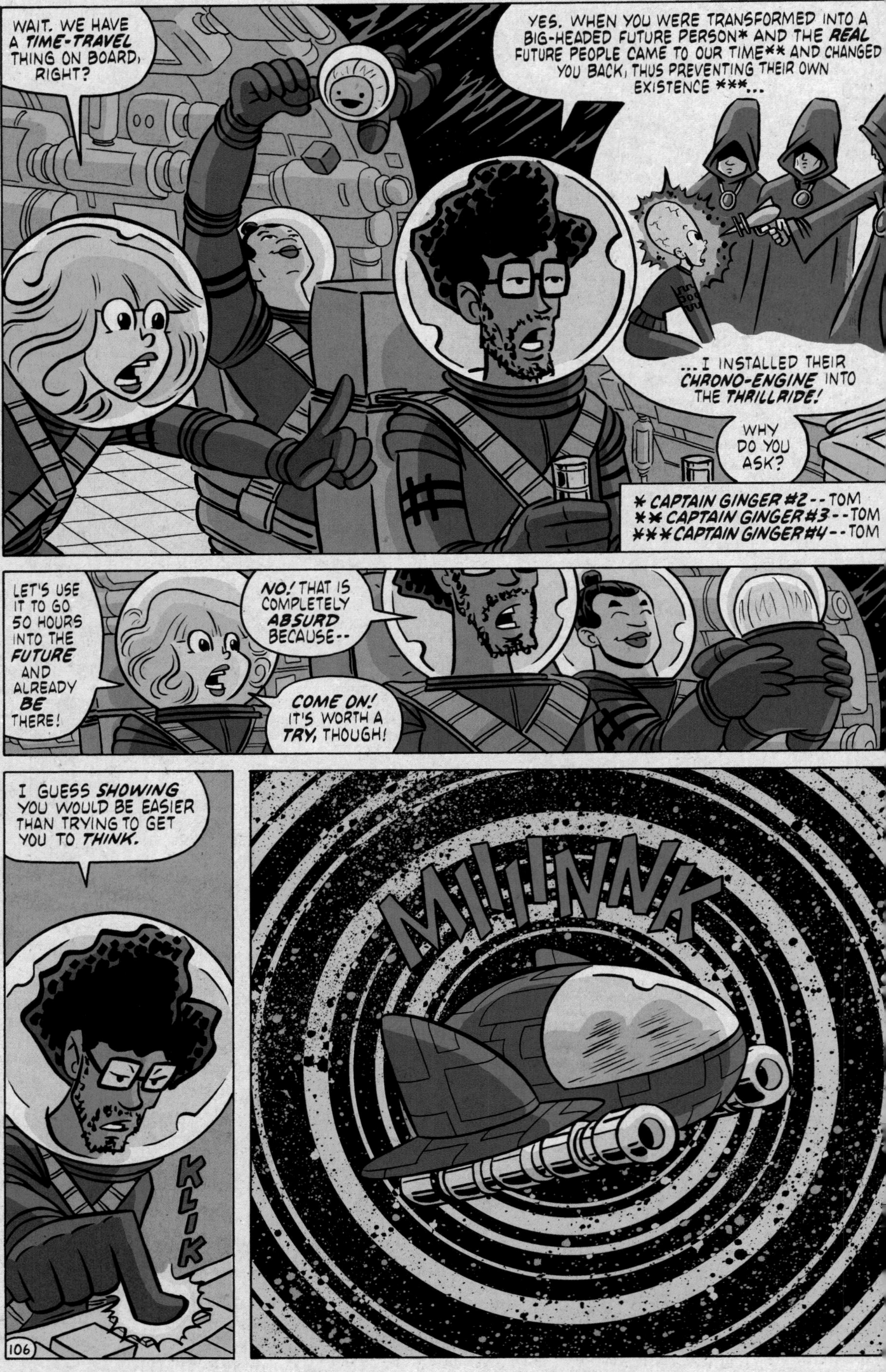

WAIT. WE HAVE A TIME-TRAVEL THING ON BOARD, RIGHT?
YES. WHEN YOU WERE TRANSFORMED INTO A BIG-HEADED FUTURE PERSON* AND THE REAL FUTURE PEOPLE CAME TO OUR TIME** AND CHANGED YOU BACK, THUS PREVENTING THEIR OWN EXISTENCE ***...
...I INSTALLED THEIR CHRONO-ENGINE INTO THE THRILLRIDE!
WHY DO YOU ASK?
* CAPTAIN GINGER #2 -- TOM
** CAPTAIN GINGER #3 -- TOM
*** CAPTAIN GINGER #4 -- TOM
LET'S USE IT TO GO 50 HOURS INTO THE FUTURE AND ALREADY BE THERE!
NO! THAT IS COMPLETELY ABSURD BECAUSE--
COME ON! IT'S WORTH A TRY, THOUGH!
I GUESS SHOWING YOU WOULD BE EASIER THAN TRYING TO GET YOU TO THINK.
KLIK
MIIIINNK

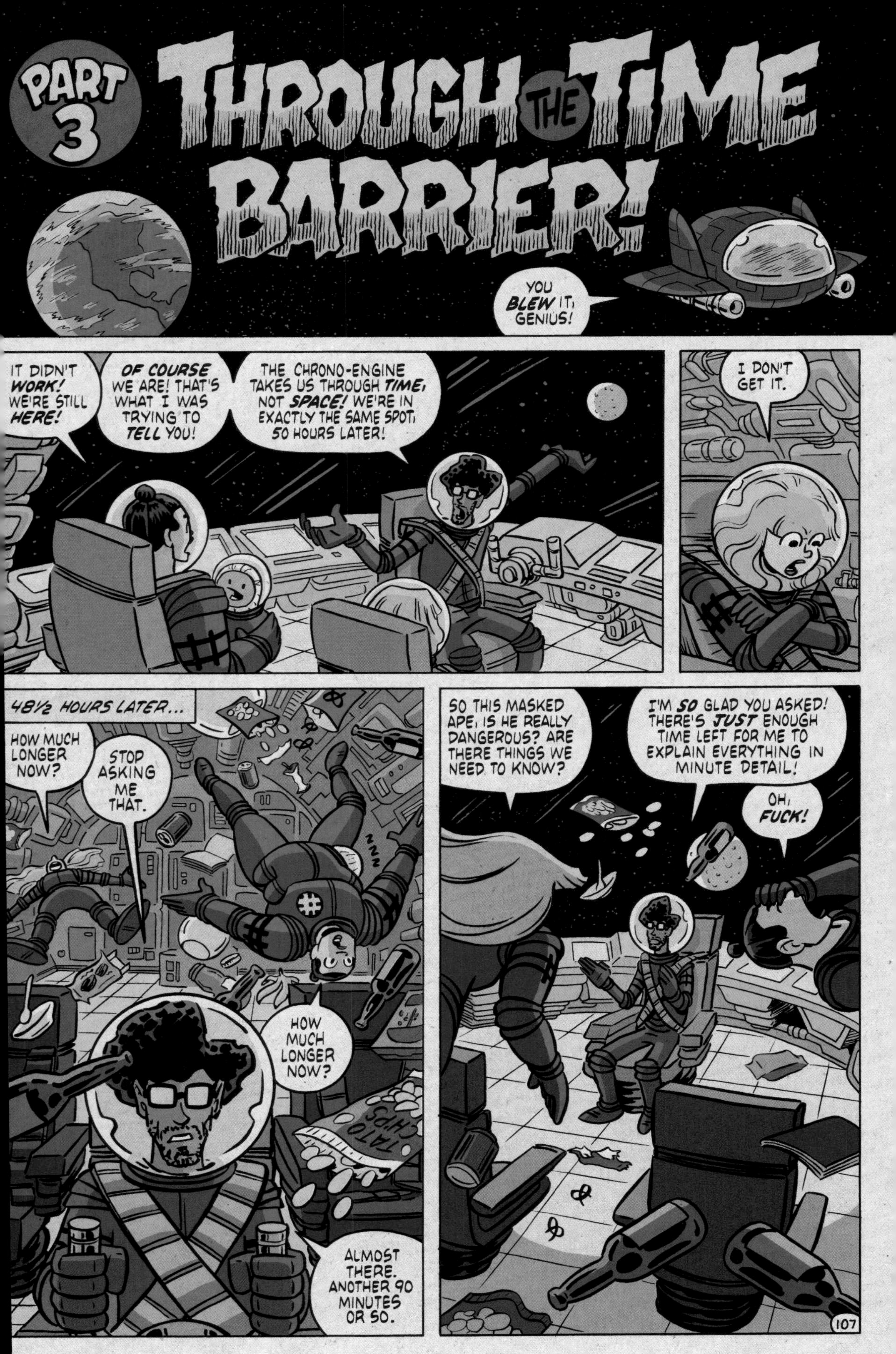
PART 3
THROUGH THE TIME BARRIER!
YOU BLEW IT, GENIUS!
IT DIDN'T WORK! WE'RE STILL HERE!
OF COURSE WE ARE! THAT'S WHAT I WAS TRYING TO TELL YOU!
THE CHRONO-ENGINE TAKES US THROUGH TIME, NOT SPACE! WE'RE IN EXACTLY THE SAME SPOT, 50 HOURS LATER!
I DON'T GET IT.
48½ HOURS LATER...
HOW MUCH LONGER NOW?
STOP ASKING ME THAT.
HOW MUCH LONGER NOW?
ALMOST THERE. ANOTHER 90 MINUTES OR SO.
SO THIS MASKED APE, IS HE REALLY DANGEROUS? ARE THERE THINGS WE NEED TO KNOW?
I'M SO GLAD YOU ASKED! THERE'S JUST ENOUGH TIME LEFT FOR ME TO EXPLAIN EVERYTHING IN MINUTE DETAIL!
OH, FUCK!

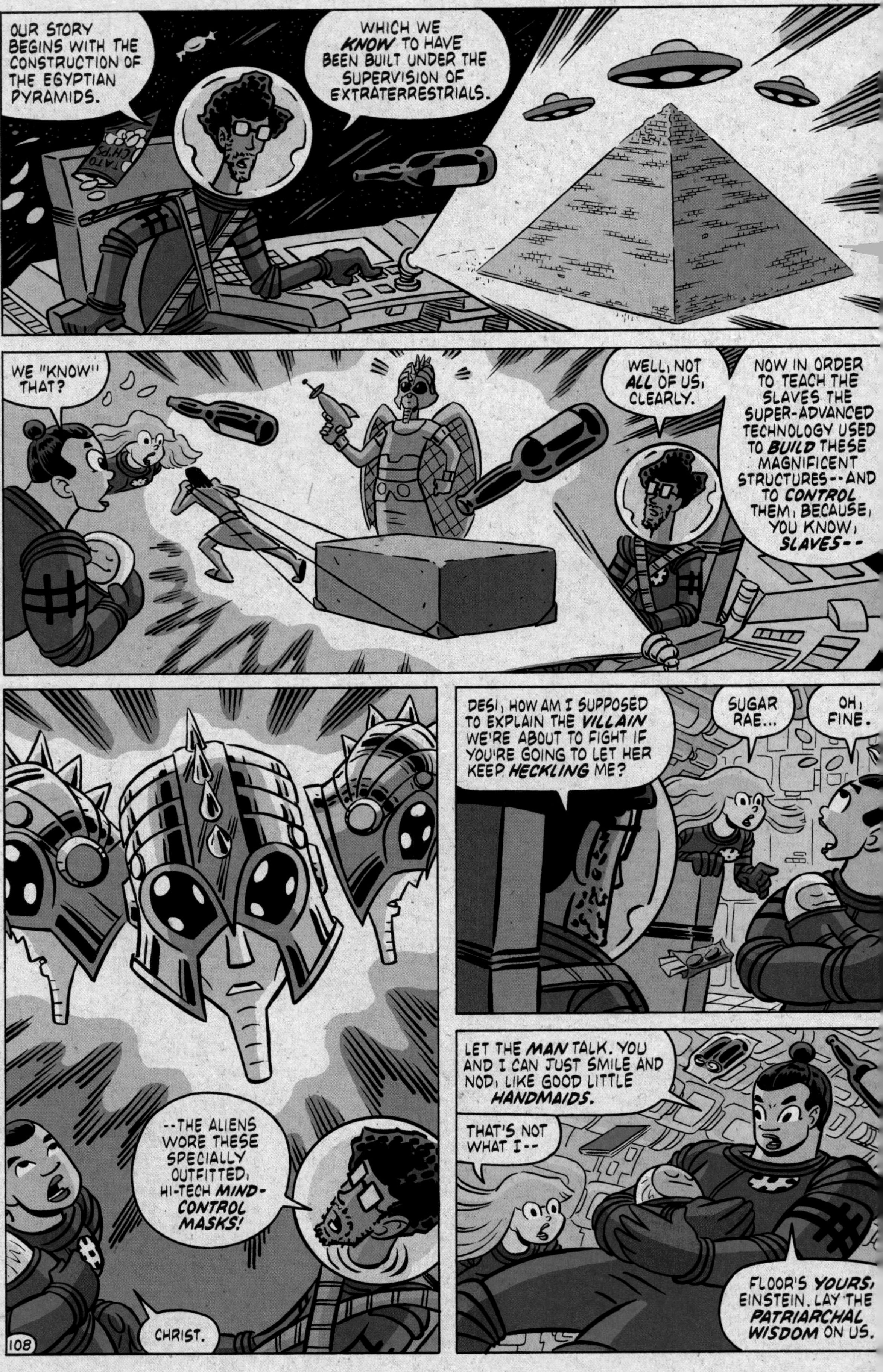

OUR STORY BEGINS WITH THE CONSTRUCTION OF THE EGYPTIAN PYRAMIDS.
WHICH WE KNOW TO HAVE BEEN BUILT UNDER THE SUPERVISION OF EXTRATERRESTRIALS.
WE "KNOW" THAT?
WELL, NOT ALL OF US, CLEARLY.
NOW IN ORDER TO TEACH THE SLAVES THE SUPER-ADVANCED TECHNOLOGY USED TO BUILD THESE MAGNIFICENT STRUCTURES--AND TO CONTROL THEM, BECAUSE, YOU KNOW, SLAVES--
--THE ALIENS WORE THESE SPECIALLY OUTFITTED, HI-TECH MIND-CONTROL MASKS!
CHRIST.
DESI, HOW AM I SUPPOSED TO EXPLAIN THE VILLAIN WE'RE ABOUT TO FIGHT IF YOU'RE GOING TO LET HER KEEP HECKLING ME?
SUGAR RAE...
OH, FINE.
LET THE MAN TALK. YOU AND I CAN JUST SMILE AND NOD, LIKE GOOD LITTLE HANDMAIDS.
THAT'S NOT WHAT I--
FLOOR'S YOURS, EINSTEIN. LAY THE PATRIARCHAL WISDOM ON US.

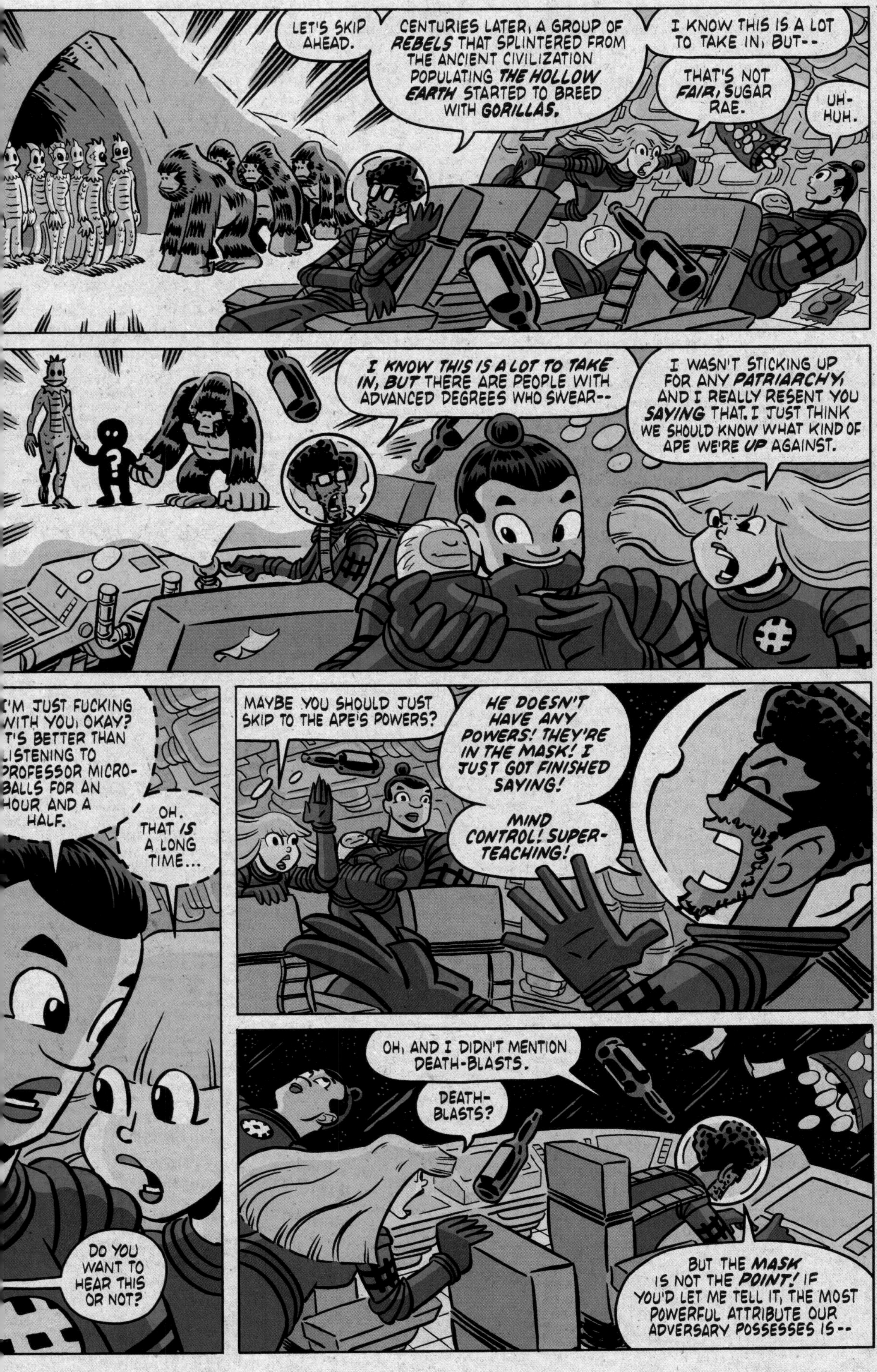
LET'S SKIP AHEAD.
CENTURIES LATER, A GROUP OF REBELS THAT SPLINTERED FROM THE ANCIENT CIVILIZATION POPULATING THE HOLLOW EARTH STARTED TO BREED WITH GORILLAS.
I KNOW THIS IS A LOT TO TAKE IN, BUT--
THAT'S NOT FAIR, SUGAR RAE.
UH-HUH.
I KNOW THIS IS A LOT TO TAKE IN, BUT THERE ARE PEOPLE WITH ADVANCED DEGREES WHO SWEAR--
I WASN'T STICKING UP FOR ANY PATRIARCHY, AND I REALLY RESENT YOU SAYING THAT. I JUST THINK WE SHOULD KNOW WHAT KIND OF APE WE'RE UP AGAINST.
?
I'M JUST FUCKING WITH YOU, OKAY? IT'S BETTER THAN LISTENING TO PROFESSOR MICRO-BALLS FOR AN HOUR AND A HALF.
OH. THAT IS A LONG TIME...
DO YOU WANT TO HEAR THIS OR NOT?
MAYBE YOU SHOULD JUST SKIP TO THE APE'S POWERS?
HE DOESN'T HAVE ANY POWERS! THEY'RE IN THE MASK! I JUST GOT FINISHED SAYING!
MIND CONTROL! SUPER-TEACHING!
OH, AND I DIDN'T MENTION DEATH-BLASTS.
DEATH-BLASTS?
BUT THE MASK IS NOT THE POINT! IF YOU'D LET ME TELL IT, THE MOST POWERFUL ATTRIBUTE OUR ADVERSARY POSSESSES IS--

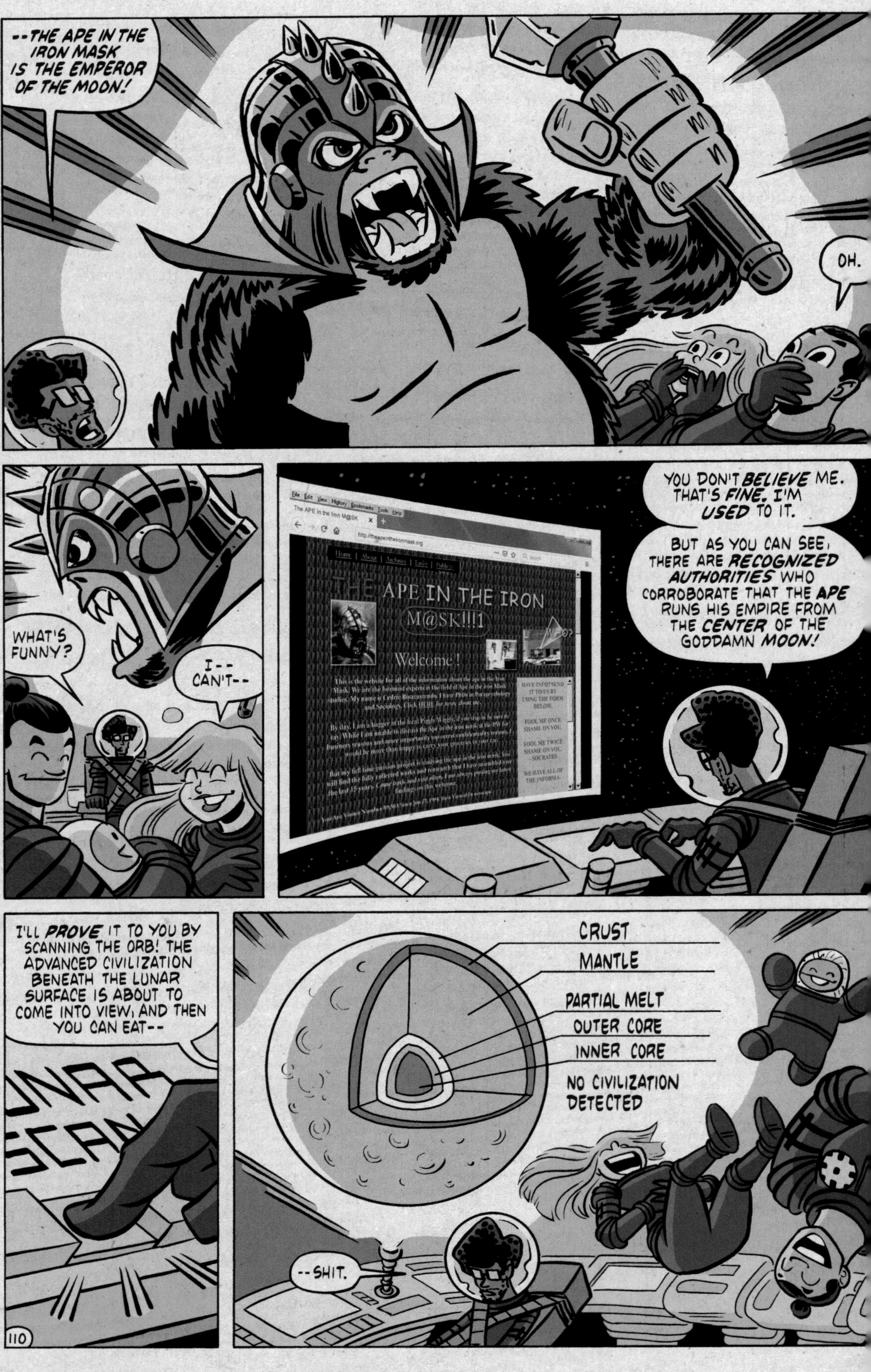
--THE APE IN THE IRON MASK IS THE EMPEROR OF THE MOON!
OH.
WHAT'S FUNNY?
I-- CAN'T--
File Edit View History Bookmarks Tools Help
The APE In the Iron M@SK
http://theapeintheironmask.org
Home | About | Archives | Links | Publica...
THE APE IN THE IRON M@SK!!!1
WHO?
Welcome !
This is the website for all of the information about the ape in the Iron Mask. We are the foremost experts in the field of Ape in the iron Mask studies. My name is Cedric Boszcaxcendo. I have PhDs in Parapsychology and Sociology. Click HERE for more about me.
By day, I am a bagger at the local Piggly Wiggly, if you stop in be sure to say. While I am unable to discuss the Ape in the iron mask at the PW for business reasons and more importantly top-secret confidentiality reasons, I would be more than happy to carry your groceries to your car.
But my full time passion project is studying the ape in the iron mask. You will find the fully collected works and research that I have assembled over the last 15 years. Come back and visit often. I am always posting my latest findings on this webzone.
HAVE INFO? SEND IT TO US BY USING THE FORM BELOW.
FOOL ME ONCE SHAME ON YOU. FOOL ME TWICE SHAME ON YOU. - SOCRATES
WE HAVE ALL OF THE INFORMA-
YOU DON'T BELIEVE ME. THAT'S FINE. I'M USED TO IT.
BUT AS YOU CAN SEE, THERE ARE RECOGNIZED AUTHORITIES WHO CORROBORATE THAT THE APE RUNS HIS EMPIRE FROM THE CENTER OF THE GODDAMN MOON!
I'LL PROVE IT TO YOU BY SCANNING THE ORB! THE ADVANCED CIVILIZATION BENEATH THE LUNAR SURFACE IS ABOUT TO COME INTO VIEW, AND THEN YOU CAN EAT--
UNAR SCAN
CRUST
MANTLE
PARTIAL MELT
OUTER CORE
INNER CORE
NO CIVILIZATION DETECTED
--SHIT.

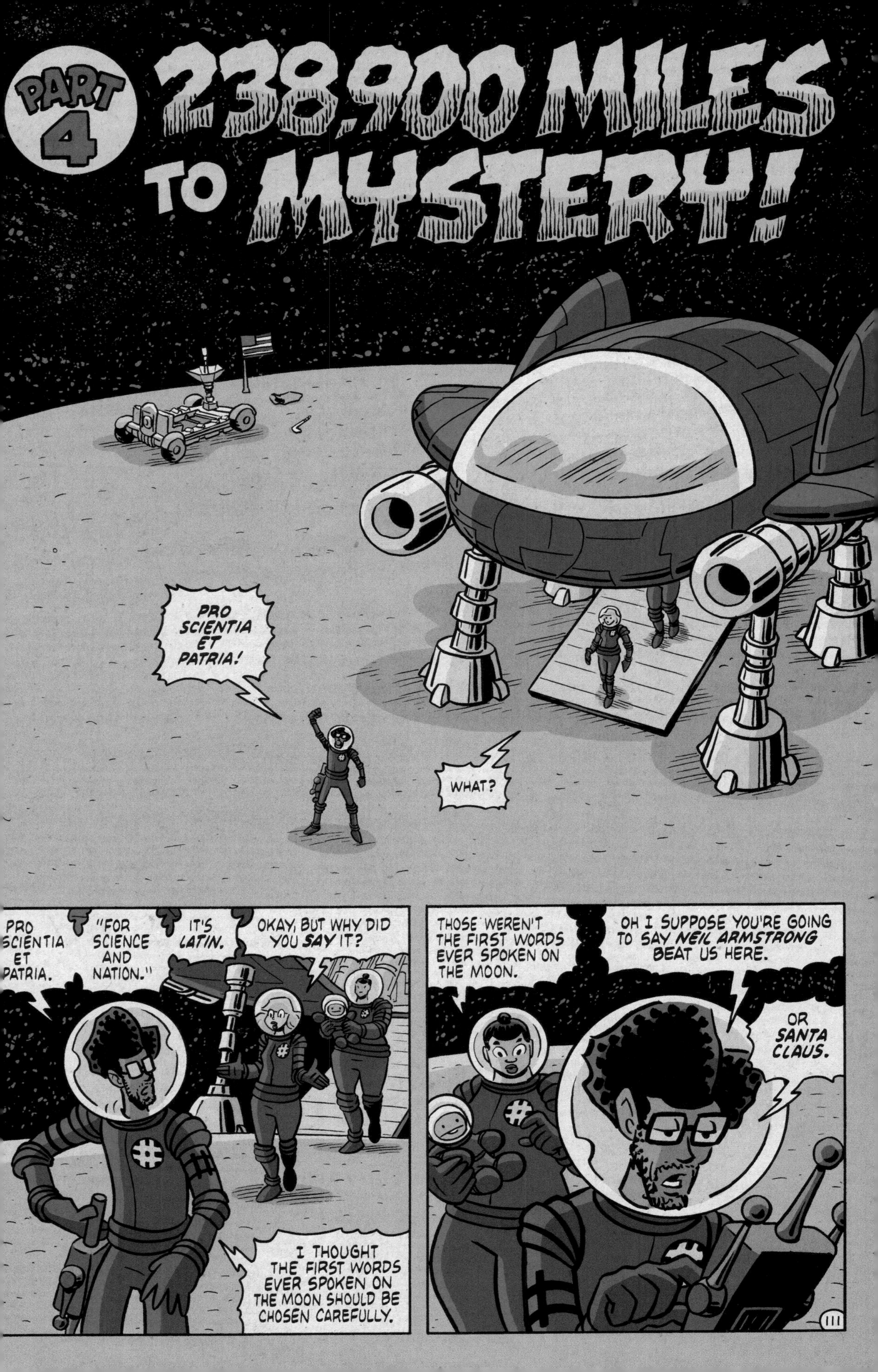
PART 4
238,900 MILES TO MYSTERY!
PRO SCIENTIA ET PATRIA!
WHAT?
PRO SCIENTIA ET PATRIA.
"FOR SCIENCE AND NATION."
IT'S LATIN.
OKAY, BUT WHY DID YOU SAY IT?
I THOUGHT THE FIRST WORDS EVER SPOKEN ON THE MOON SHOULD BE CHOSEN CAREFULLY.
THOSE WEREN'T THE FIRST WORDS EVER SPOKEN ON THE MOON.
OH I SUPPOSE YOU'RE GOING TO SAY NEIL ARMSTRONG BEAT US HERE.
OR SANTA CLAUS.

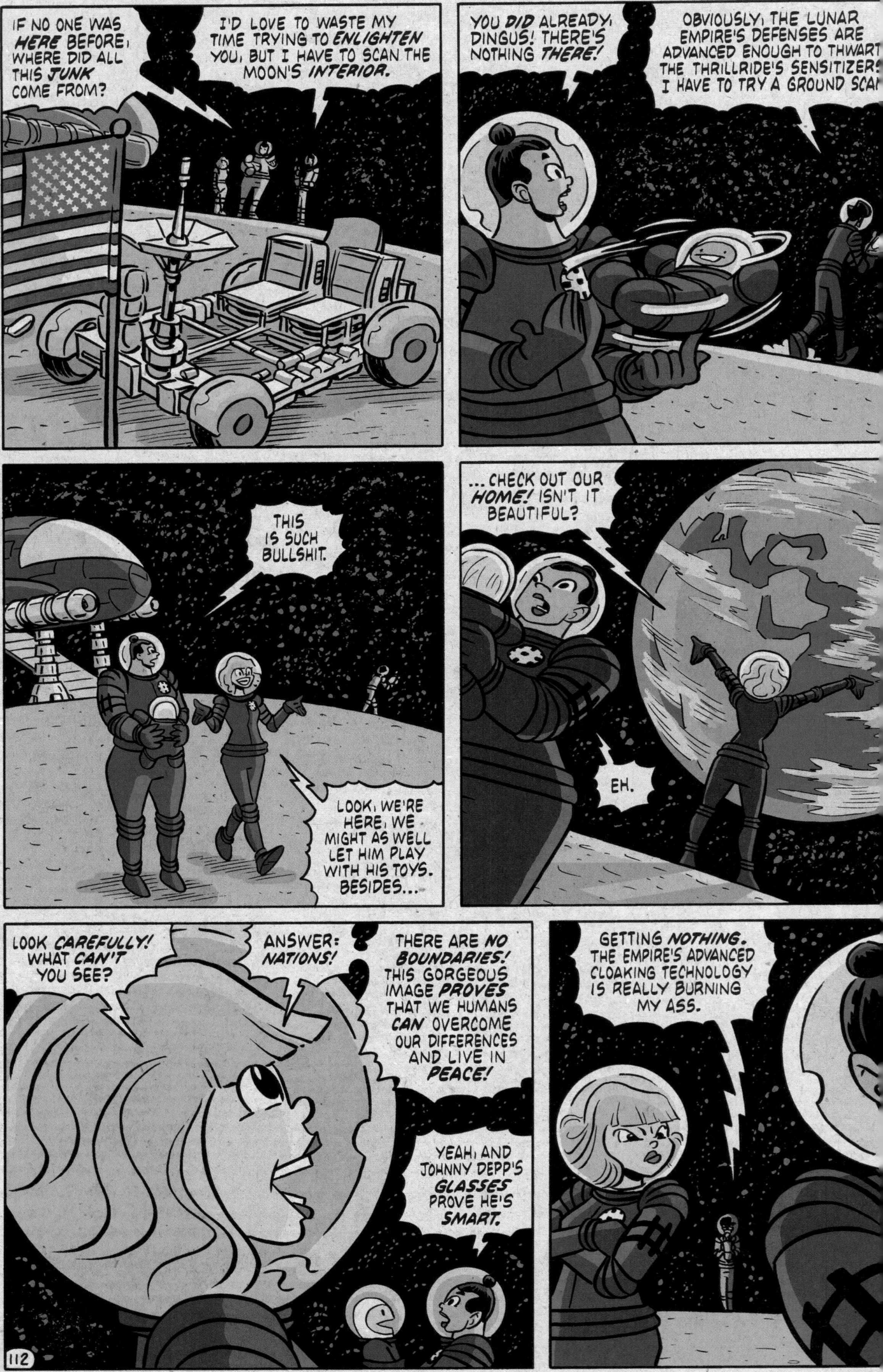
IF NO ONE WAS HERE BEFORE, WHERE DID ALL THIS JUNK COME FROM?
I'D LOVE TO WASTE MY TIME TRYING TO ENLIGHTEN YOU, BUT I HAVE TO SCAN THE MOON'S INTERIOR.
YOU DID ALREADY, DINGUS! THERE'S NOTHING THERE!
OBVIOUSLY, THE LUNAR EMPIRE'S DEFENSES ARE ADVANCED ENOUGH TO THWART THE THRILLRIDE'S SENSITIZERS I HAVE TO TRY A GROUND SCA
THIS IS SUCH BULLSHIT.
LOOK, WE'RE HERE, WE MIGHT AS WELL LET HIM PLAY WITH HIS TOYS. BESIDES...
...CHECK OUT OUR HOME! ISN'T IT BEAUTIFUL?
EH.
LOOK CAREFULLY! WHAT CAN'T YOU SEE?
ANSWER: NATIONS!
THERE ARE NO BOUNDARIES! THIS GORGEOUS IMAGE PROVES THAT WE HUMANS CAN OVERCOME OUR DIFFERENCES AND LIVE IN PEACE!
YEAH, AND JOHNNY DEPP'S GLASSES PROVE HE'S SMART.
GETTING NOTHING. THE EMPIRE'S ADVANCED CLOAKING TECHNOLOGY IS REALLY BURNING MY ASS.

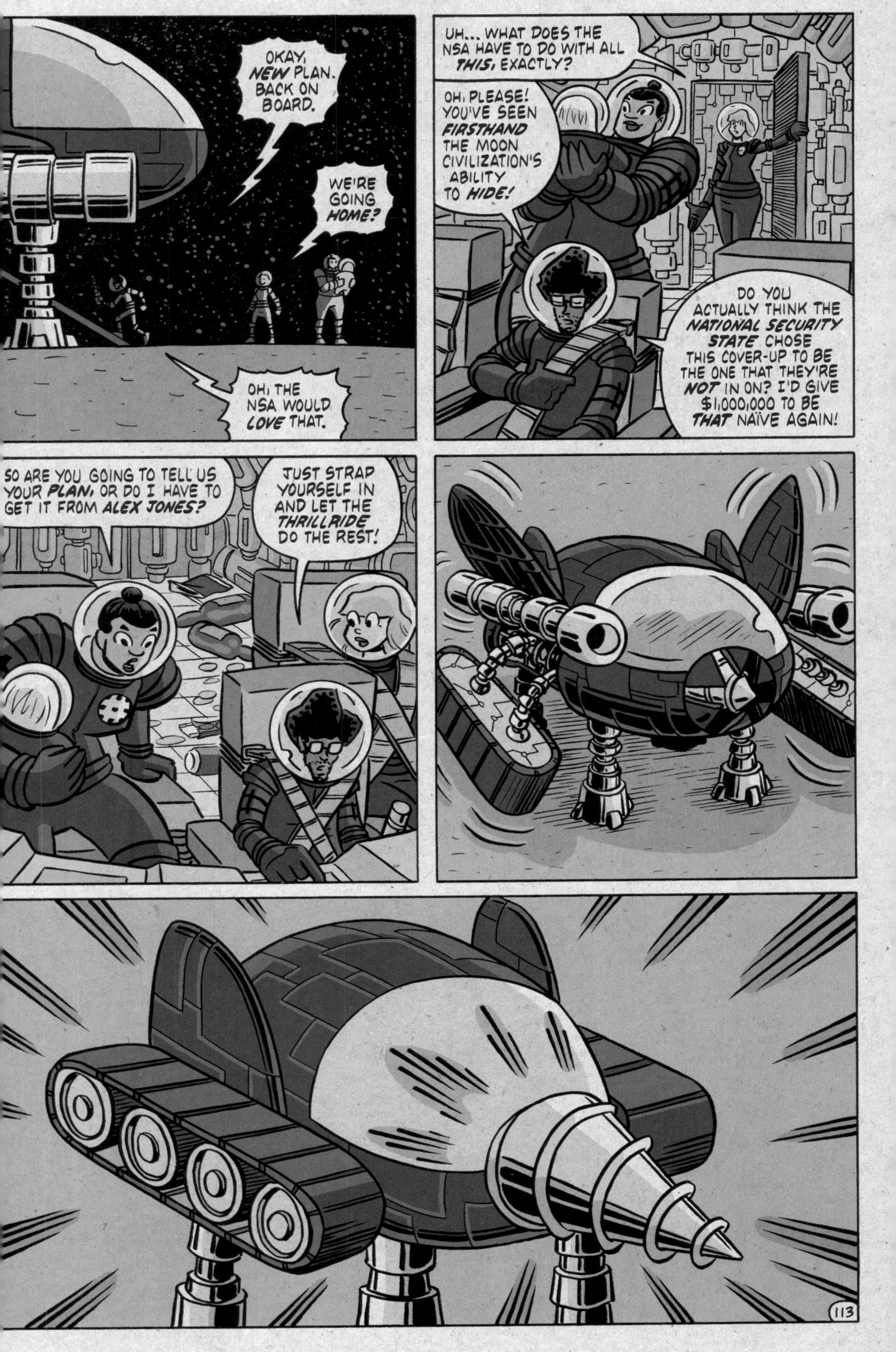
OKAY, NEW PLAN. BACK ON BOARD.
WE'RE GOING HOME?
OH, THE NSA WOULD LOVE THAT.
UH... WHAT DOES THE NSA HAVE TO DO WITH ALL THIS, EXACTLY?
OH, PLEASE! YOU'VE SEEN FIRSTHAND THE MOON CIVILIZATION'S ABILITY TO HIDE!
DO YOU ACTUALLY THINK THE NATIONAL SECURITY STATE CHOSE THIS COVER-UP TO BE THE ONE THAT THEY'RE NOT IN ON? I'D GIVE $1,000,000 TO BE THAT NAÏVE AGAIN!
SO ARE YOU GOING TO TELL US YOUR PLAN, OR DO I HAVE TO GET IT FROM ALEX JONES?
JUST STRAP YOURSELF IN AND LET THE THRILLRIDE DO THE REST!
113

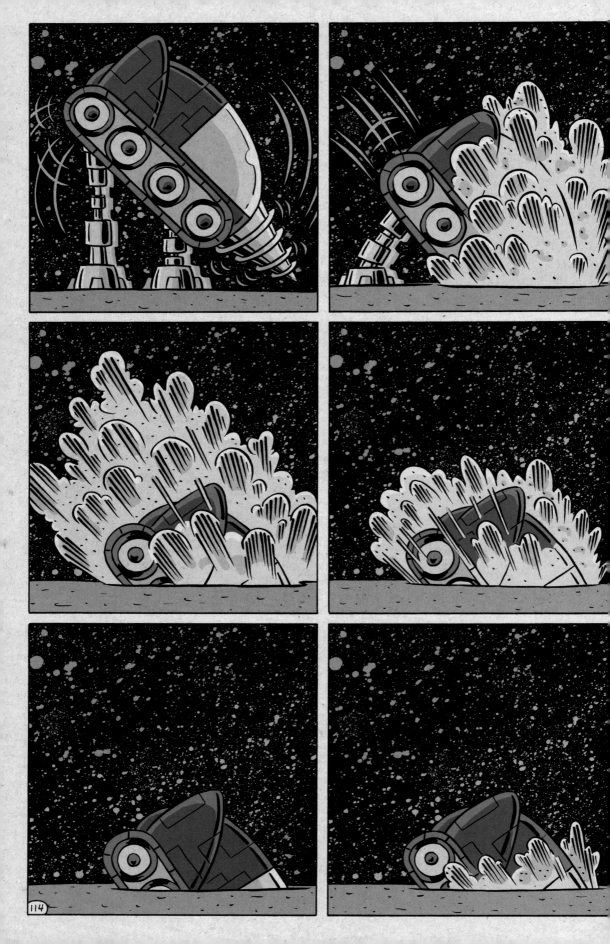

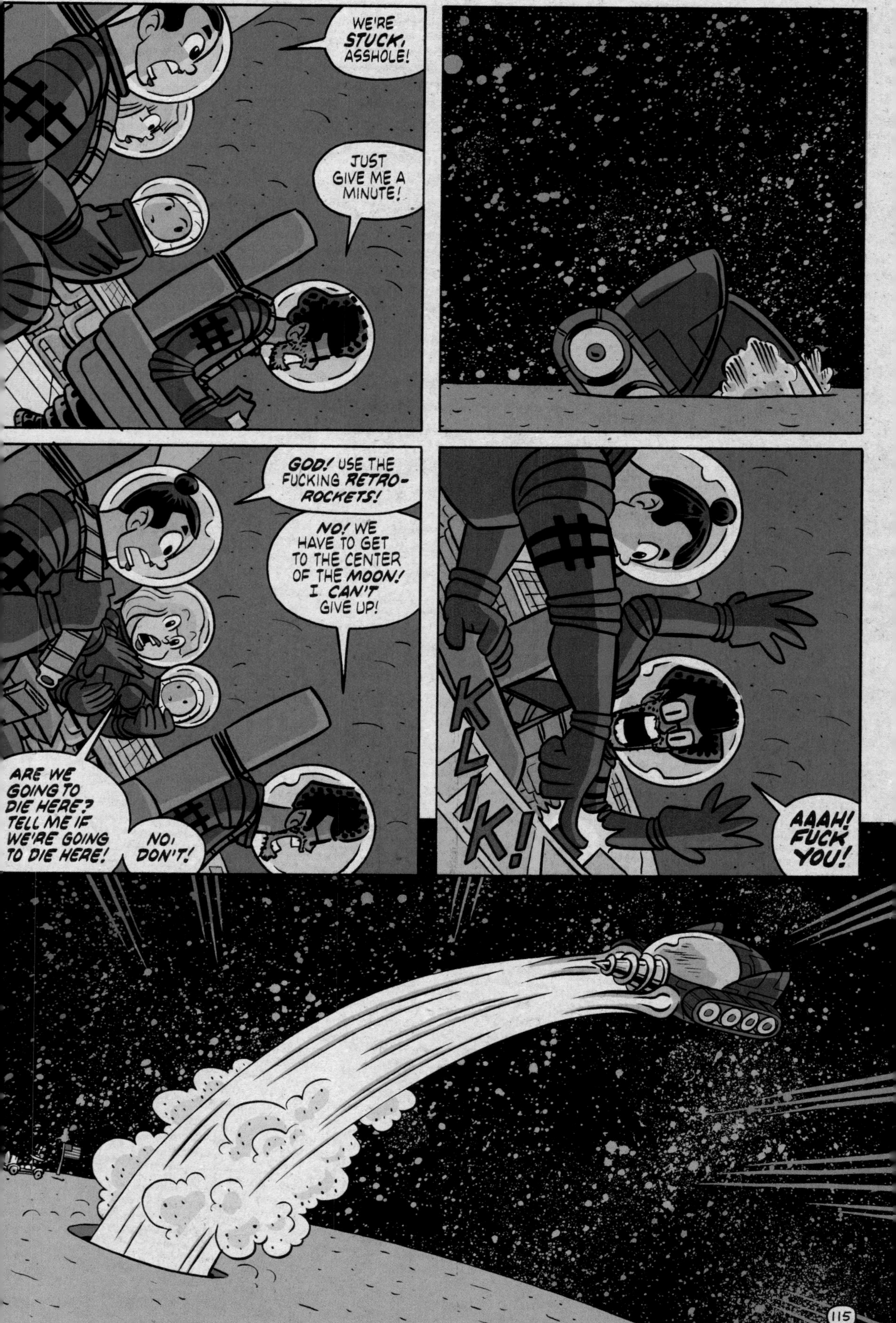
WE'RE STUCK, ASSHOLE!
JUST GIVE ME A MINUTE!
GOD! USE THE FUCKING RETRO-ROCKETS!
NO! WE HAVE TO GET TO THE CENTER OF THE MOON! I CAN'T GIVE UP!
ARE WE GOING TO DIE HERE? TELL ME IF WE'RE GOING TO DIE HERE!
NO, DON'T!
KLIK!
AAAH! FUCK YOU!

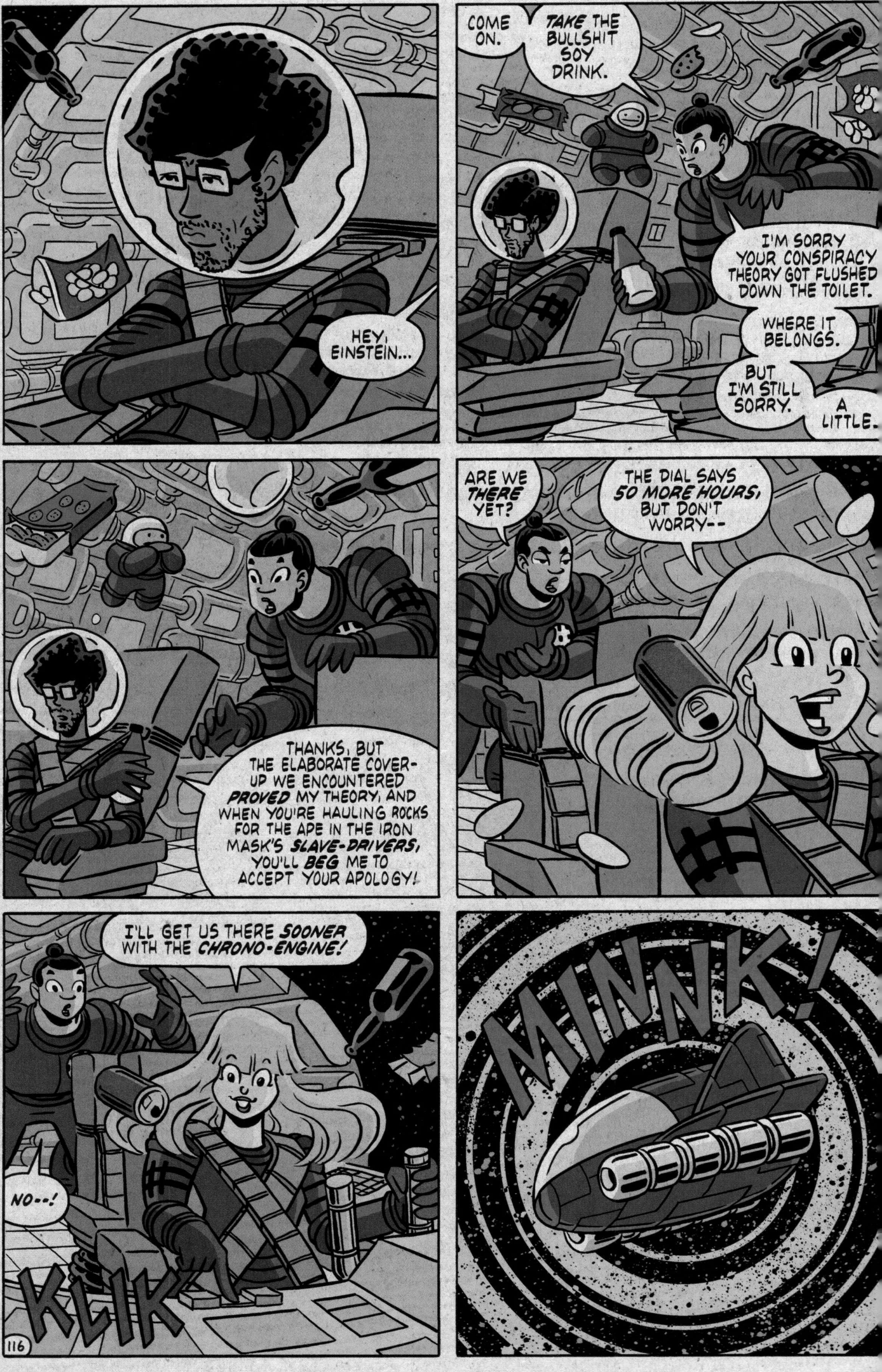
HEY, EINSTEIN...
COME ON.
TAKE THE BULLSHIT SOY DRINK.
I'M SORRY YOUR CONSPIRACY THEORY GOT FLUSHED DOWN THE TOILET.
WHERE IT BELONGS.
BUT I'M STILL SORRY.
A LITTLE.
THANKS, BUT THE ELABORATE COVER-UP WE ENCOUNTERED PROVED MY THEORY, AND WHEN YOU'RE HAULING ROCKS FOR THE APE IN THE IRON MASK'S SLAVE-DRIVERS, YOU'LL BEG ME TO ACCEPT YOUR APOLOGY!
ARE WE THERE YET?
THE DIAL SAYS 50 MORE HOURS, BUT DON'T WORRY--
I'LL GET US THERE SOONER WITH THE CHRONO-ENGINE!
NO--!
KLIK
MINNK!

EPILOGUE

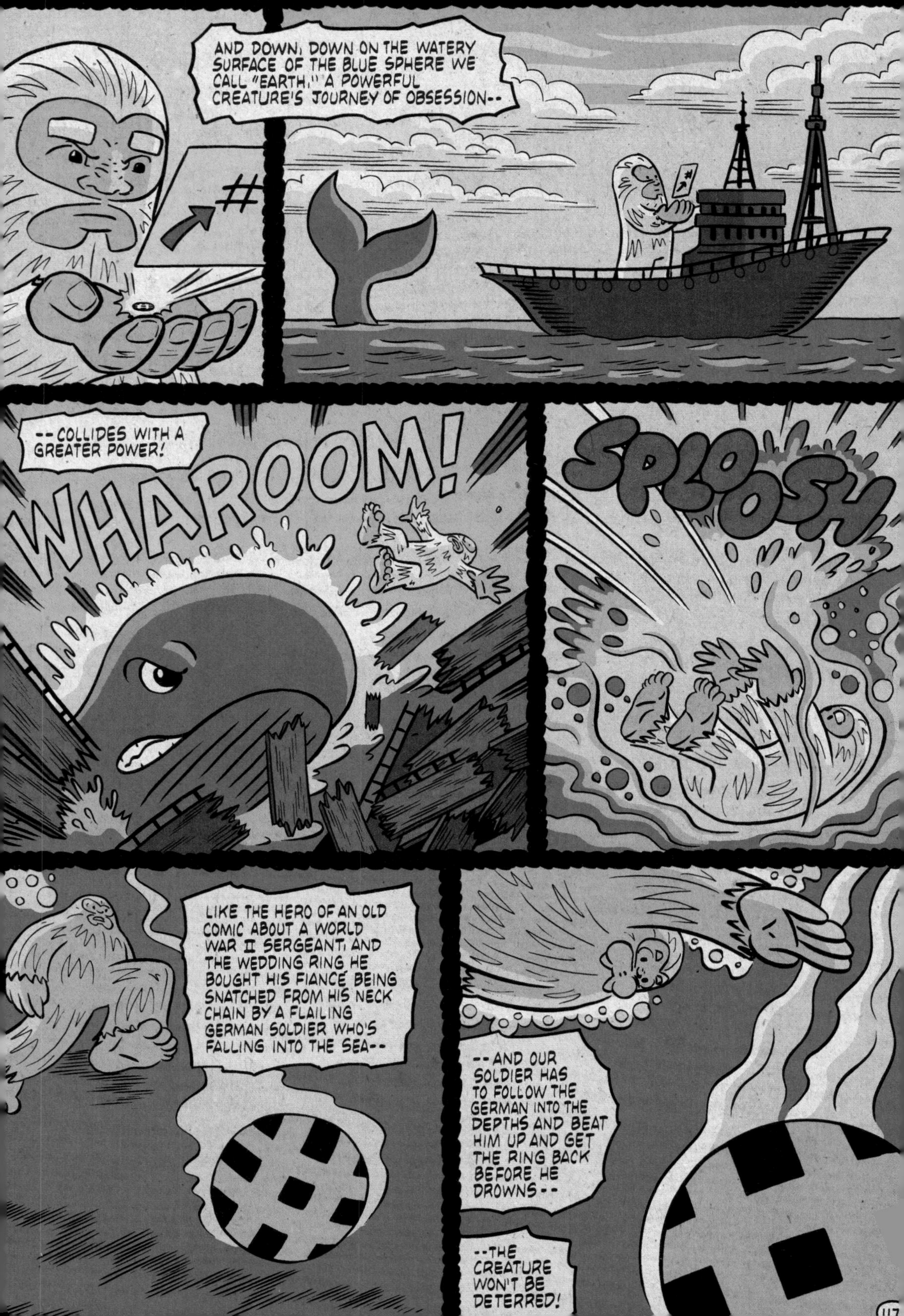

AND DOWN, DOWN ON THE WATERY SURFACE OF THE BLUE SPHERE WE CALL "EARTH," A POWERFUL CREATURE'S JOURNEY OF OBSESSION--
--COLLIDES WITH A GREATER POWER!
WHAROOM!
SPLOOSH
LIKE THE HERO OF AN OLD COMIC ABOUT A WORLD WAR II SERGEANT, AND THE WEDDING RING HE BOUGHT HIS FIANCÉ BEING SNATCHED FROM HIS NECK CHAIN BY A FLAILING GERMAN SOLDIER WHO'S FALLING INTO THE SEA--
--AND OUR SOLDIER HAS TO FOLLOW THE GERMAN INTO THE DEPTHS AND BEAT HIM UP AND GET THE RING BACK BEFORE HE DROWNS--
--THE CREATURE WON'T BE DETERRED!

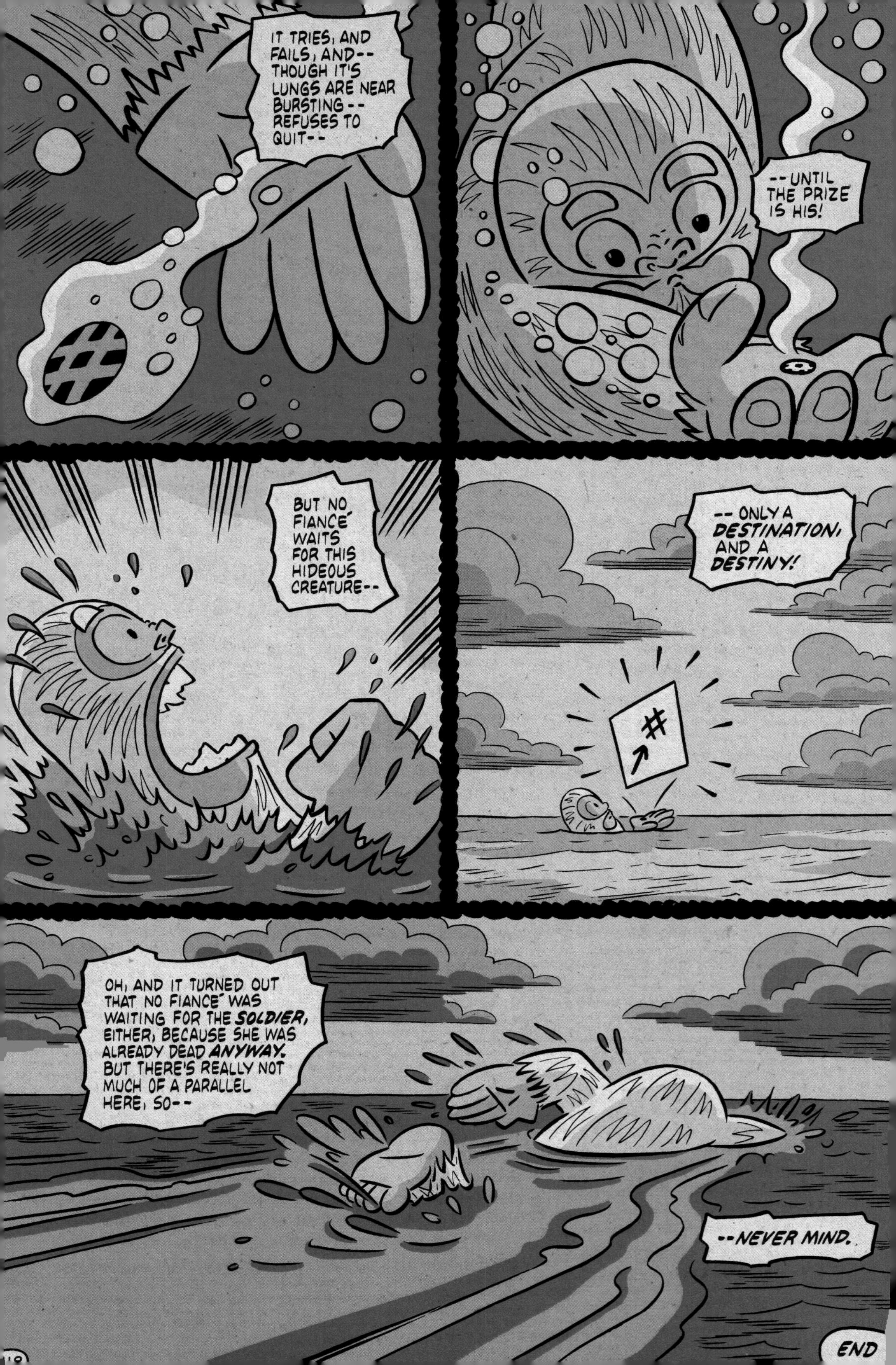
IT TRIES, AND FAILS, AND-- THOUGH IT'S LUNGS ARE NEAR BURSTING-- REFUSES TO QUIT--
--UNTIL THE PRIZE IS HIS!
BUT NO FIANCÉ WAITS FOR THIS HIDEOUS CREATURE--
-- ONLY A DESTINATION, AND A DESTINY!
OH, AND IT TURNED OUT THAT NO FIANCÉ WAS WAITING FOR THE SOLDIER, EITHER, BECAUSE SHE WAS ALREADY DEAD ANYWAY. BUT THERE'S REALLY NOT MUCH OF A PARALLEL HERE, SO--
--NEVER MIND.
END

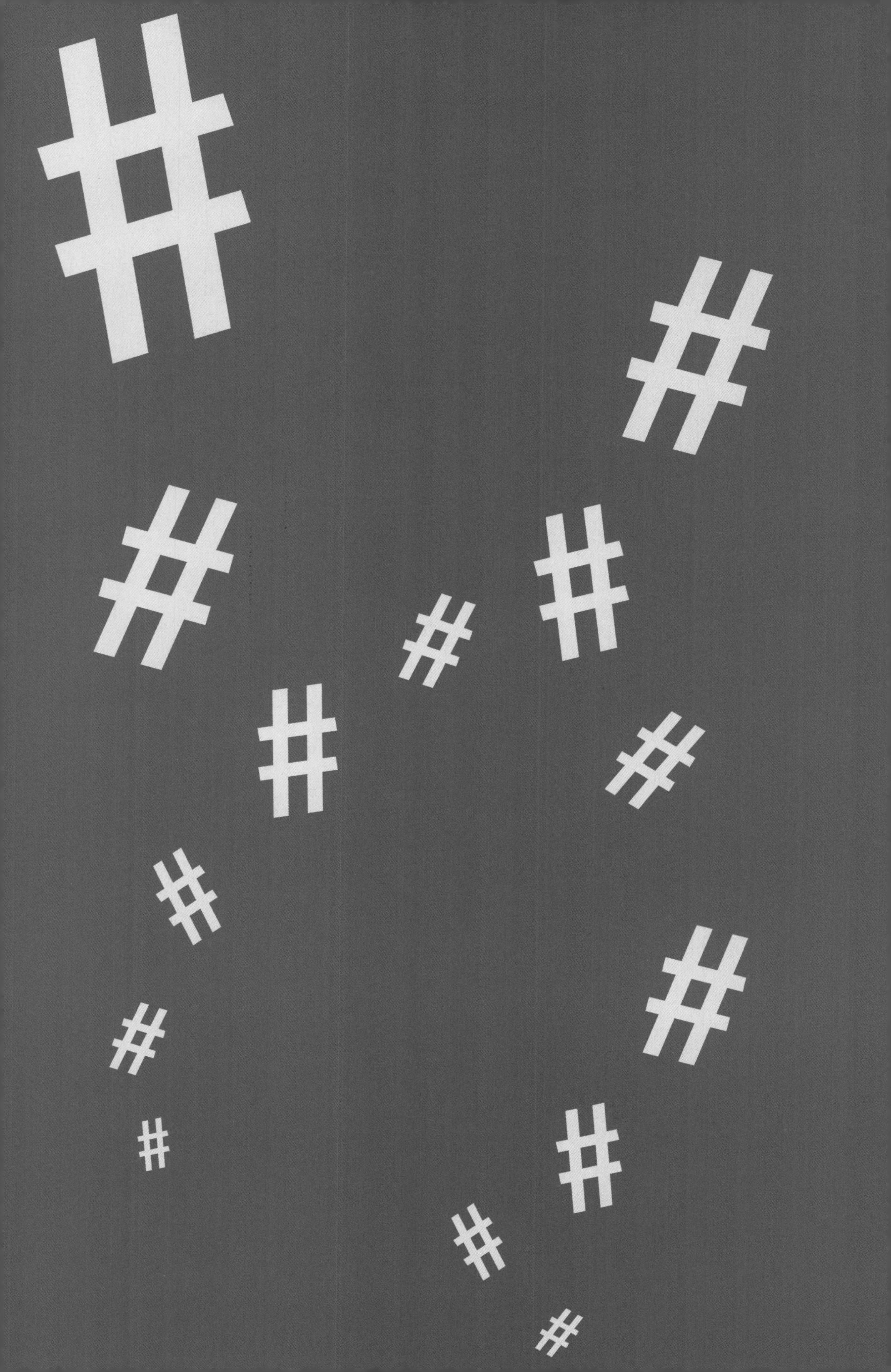

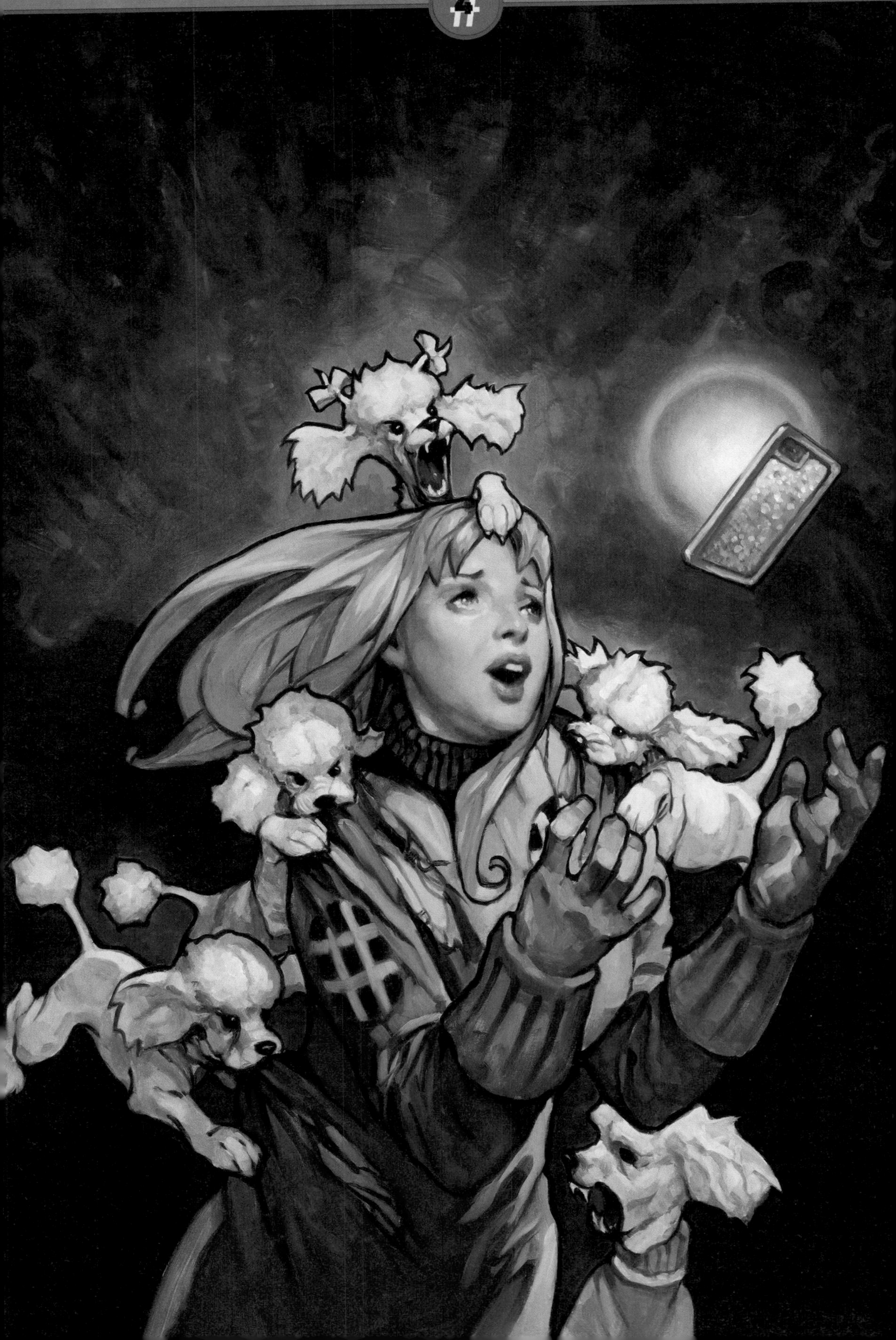

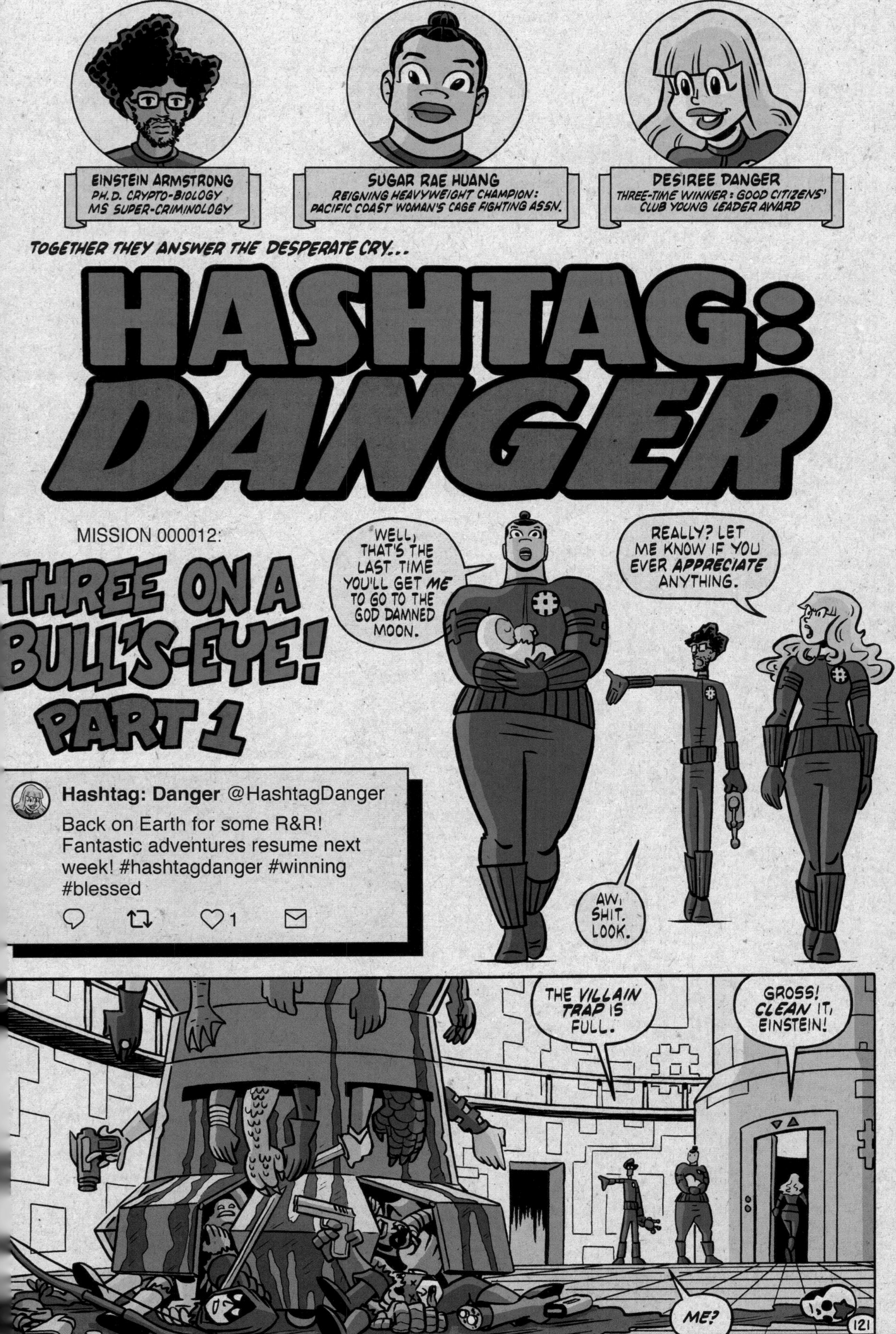
EINSTEIN ARMSTRONG
PH.D. CRYPTO-BIOLOGY
MS SUPER-CRIMINOLOGY
SUGAR RAE HUANG
REIGNING HEAVYWEIGHT CHAMPION:
PACIFIC COAST WOMAN'S CAGE FIGHTING ASSN.
DESIREE DANGER
THREE-TIME WINNER: GOOD CITIZENS' CLUB YOUNG LEADER AWARD
TOGETHER THEY ANSWER THE DESPERATE CRY...
HASHTAG: DANGER
MISSION 000012:
THREE ON A BULL'S-EYE! PART 1
WELL, THAT'S THE LAST TIME YOU'LL GET ME TO GO TO THE GOD DAMNED MOON.
REALLY? LET ME KNOW IF YOU EVER APPRECIATE ANYTHING.
Hashtag: Danger @HashtagDanger
Back on Earth for some R&R! Fantastic adventures resume next week! #hashtagdanger #winning #blessed
1
AW, SHIT. LOOK.
THE VILLAIN TRAP IS FULL.
GROSS! CLEAN IT, EINSTEIN!
ME?

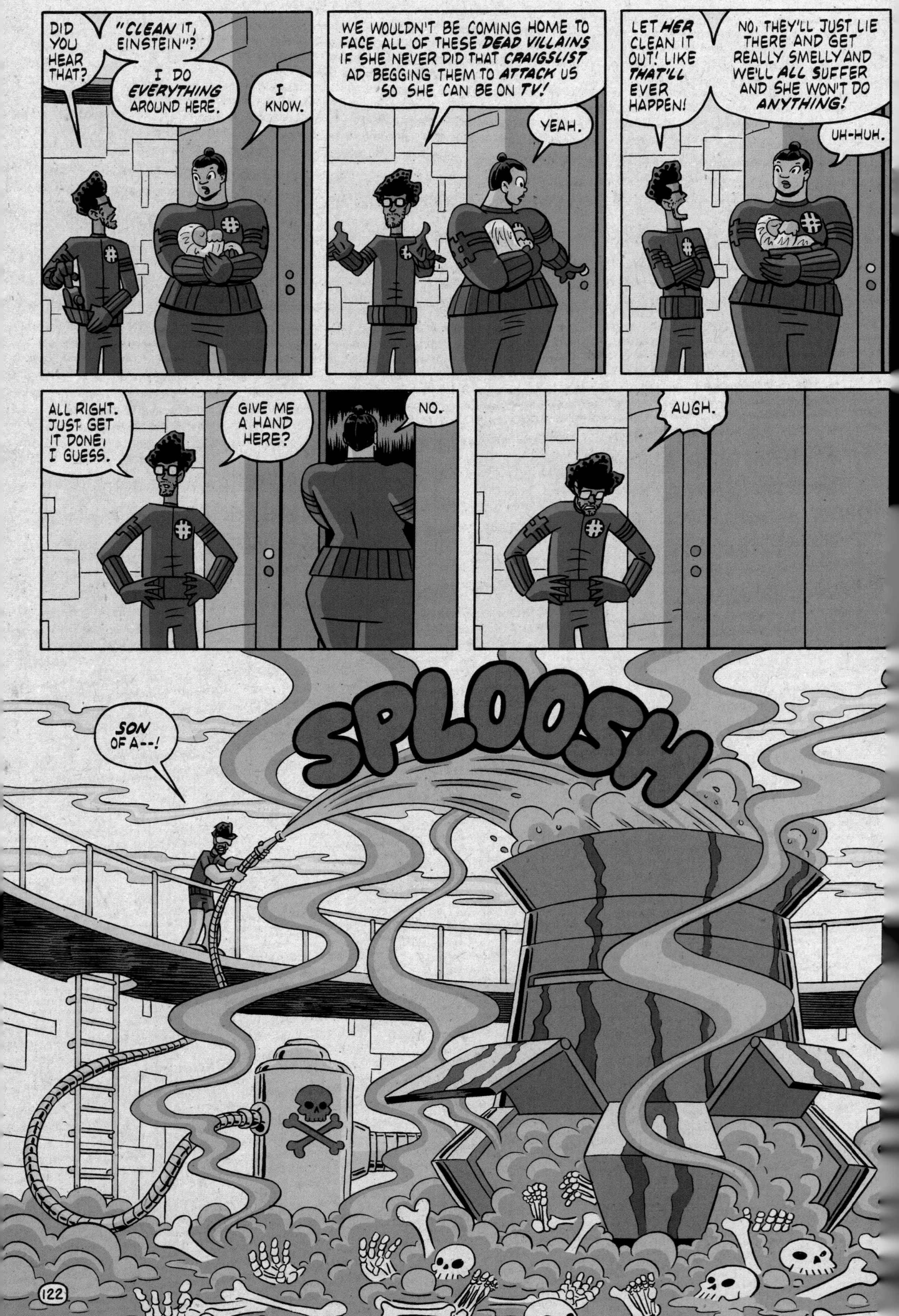
DID YOU HEAR THAT?
"CLEAN IT, EINSTEIN"?
I DO EVERYTHING AROUND HERE.
I KNOW.
WE WOULDN'T BE COMING HOME TO FACE ALL OF THESE DEAD VILLAINS IF SHE NEVER DID THAT CRAIGSLIST AD BEGGING THEM TO ATTACK US SO SHE CAN BE ON TV!
YEAH.
LET HER CLEAN IT OUT! LIKE THAT'LL EVER HAPPEN!
NO, THEY'LL JUST LIE THERE AND GET REALLY SMELLY AND WE'LL ALL SUFFER AND SHE WON'T DO ANYTHING!
UH-HUH.
ALL RIGHT. JUST GET IT DONE, I GUESS.
GIVE ME A HAND HERE?
NO.
AUGH.
SPLOOSH
SON OF A--!

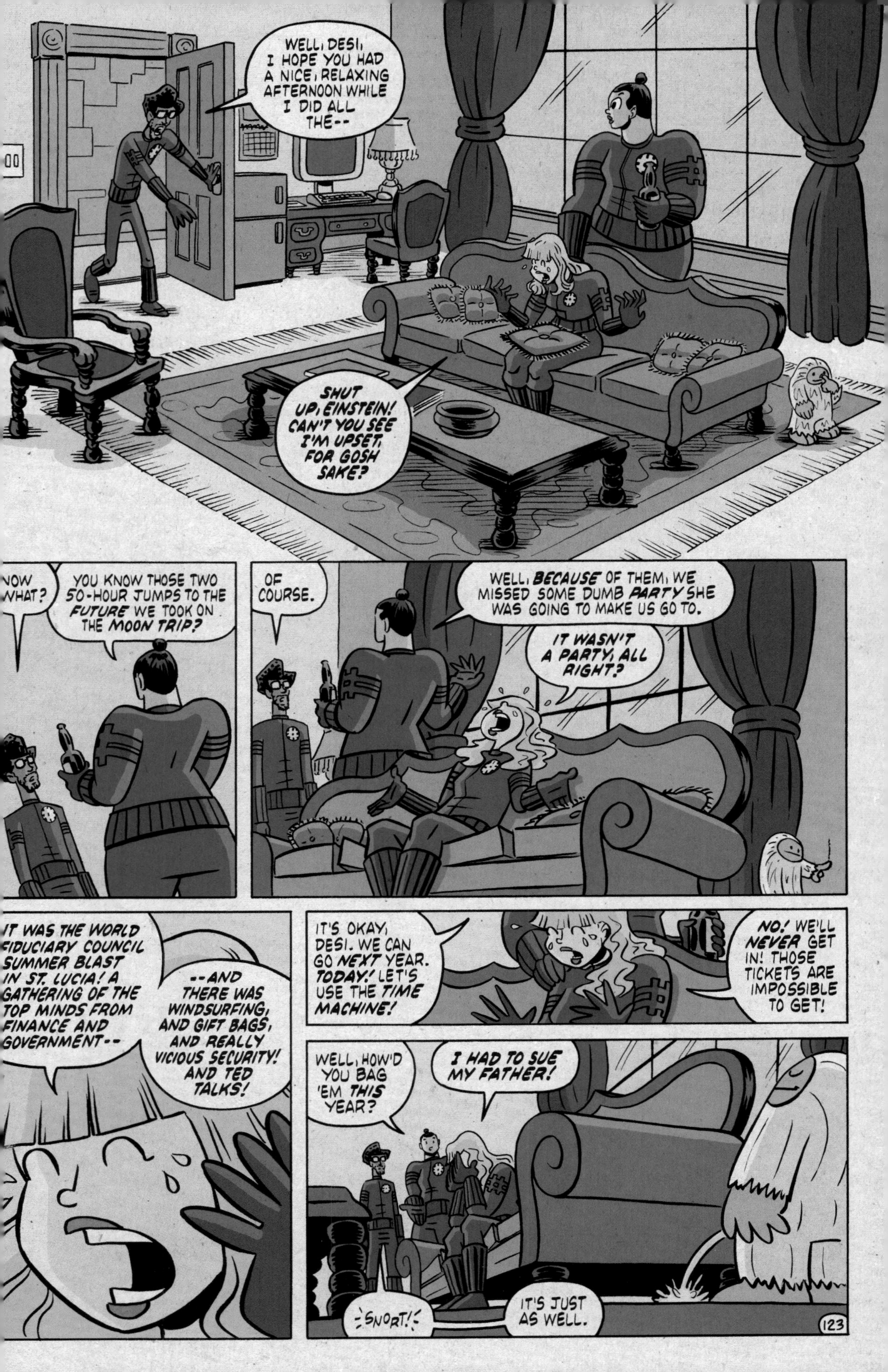
WELL, DESI, I HOPE YOU HAD A NICE, RELAXING AFTERNOON WHILE I DID ALL THE--
SHUT UP, EINSTEIN! CAN'T YOU SEE I'M UPSET, FOR GOSH SAKE?
NOW WHAT?
YOU KNOW THOSE TWO 50-HOUR JUMPS TO THE FUTURE WE TOOK ON THE MOON TRIP?
OF COURSE.
WELL, BECAUSE OF THEM, WE MISSED SOME DUMB PARTY SHE WAS GOING TO MAKE US GO TO.
IT WASN'T A PARTY, ALL RIGHT?
IT WAS THE WORLD FIDUCIARY COUNCIL SUMMER BLAST IN ST. LUCIA! A GATHERING OF THE TOP MINDS FROM FINANCE AND GOVERNMENT--
--AND THERE WAS WINDSURFING, AND GIFT BAGS, AND REALLY VICIOUS SECURITY! AND TED TALKS!
IT'S OKAY, DESI. WE CAN GO NEXT YEAR. TODAY! LET'S USE THE TIME MACHINE!
NO! WE'LL NEVER GET IN! THOSE TICKETS ARE IMPOSSIBLE TO GET!
WELL, HOW'D YOU BAG 'EM THIS YEAR?
I HAD TO SUE MY FATHER!
SNORT!
IT'S JUST AS WELL.

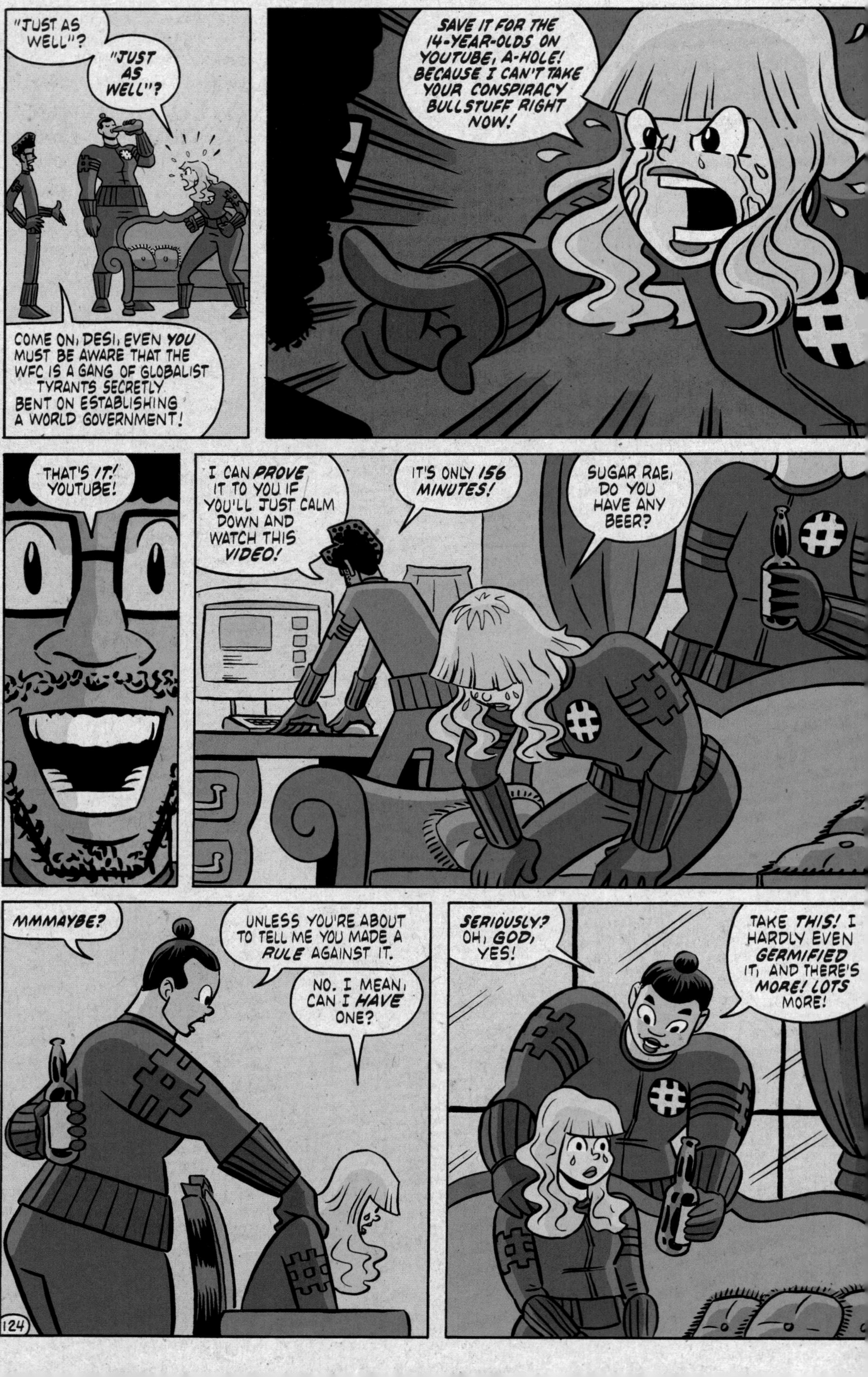
"JUST AS WELL"?
"JUST AS WELL"?
COME ON, DESI, EVEN YOU MUST BE AWARE THAT THE WFC IS A GANG OF GLOBALIST TYRANTS SECRETLY BENT ON ESTABLISHING A WORLD GOVERNMENT!
SAVE IT FOR THE 14-YEAR-OLDS ON YOUTUBE, A-HOLE! BECAUSE I CAN'T TAKE YOUR CONSPIRACY BULLSTUFF RIGHT NOW!
THAT'S IT! YOUTUBE!
I CAN PROVE IT TO YOU IF YOU'LL JUST CALM DOWN AND WATCH THIS VIDEO!
IT'S ONLY 156 MINUTES!
SUGAR RAE, DO YOU HAVE ANY BEER?
MMMAYBE?
UNLESS YOU'RE ABOUT TO TELL ME YOU MADE A RULE AGAINST IT.
NO. I MEAN, CAN I HAVE ONE?
SERIOUSLY? OH, GOD, YES!
TAKE THIS! I HARDLY EVEN GERMIFIED IT, AND THERE'S MORE! LOTS MORE!

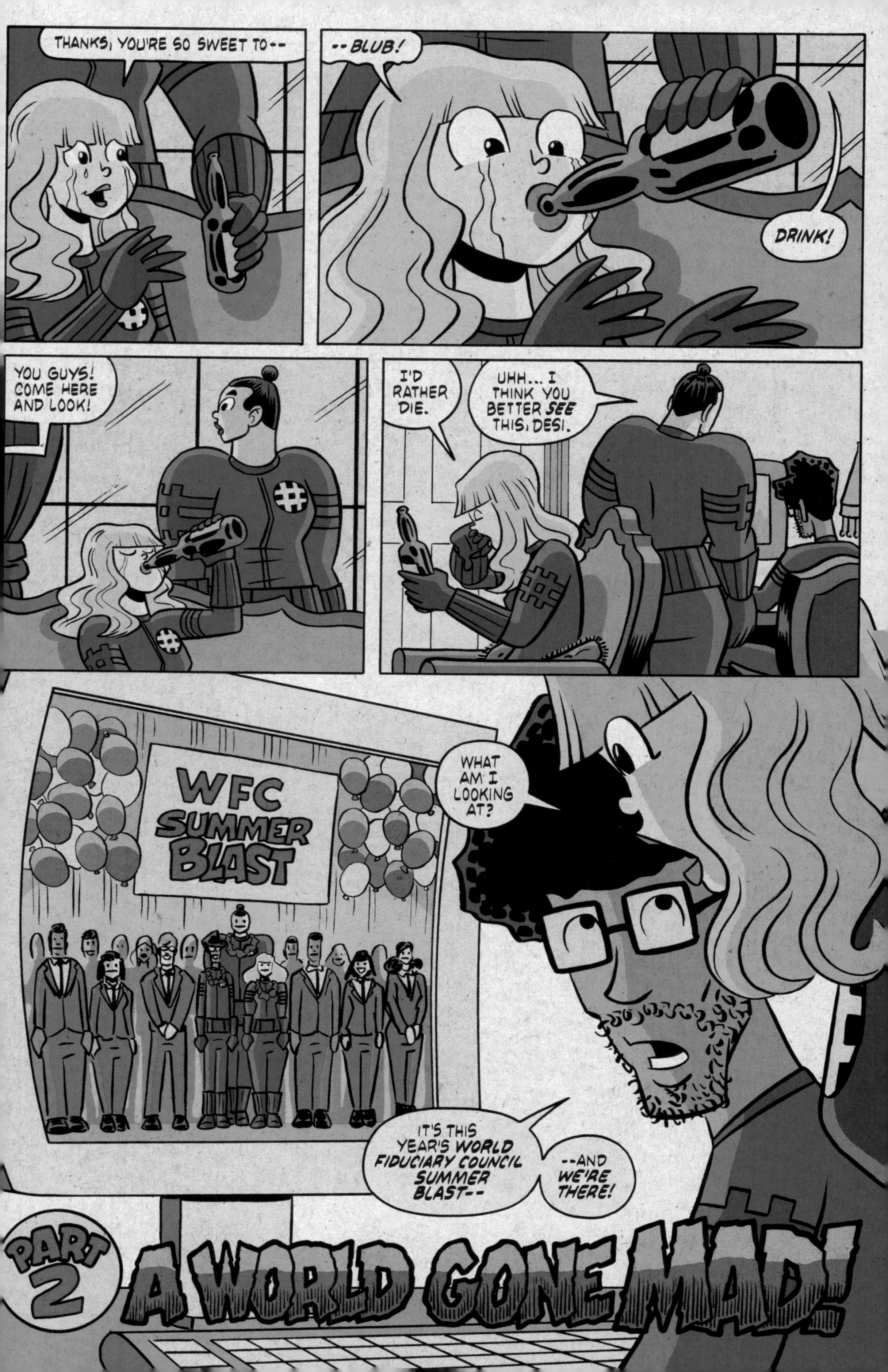
THANKS, YOU'RE SO SWEET TO--
--BLUB!
DRINK!
YOU GUYS! COME HERE AND LOOK!
I'D RATHER DIE.
UHH... I THINK YOU BETTER SEE THIS, DESI.
WFC SUMMER BLAST
WHAT AM I LOOKING AT?
IT'S THIS YEAR'S WORLD FIDUCIARY COUNCIL SUMMER BLAST--
--AND WE'RE THERE!
PART 2
A WORLD GONE MAD!

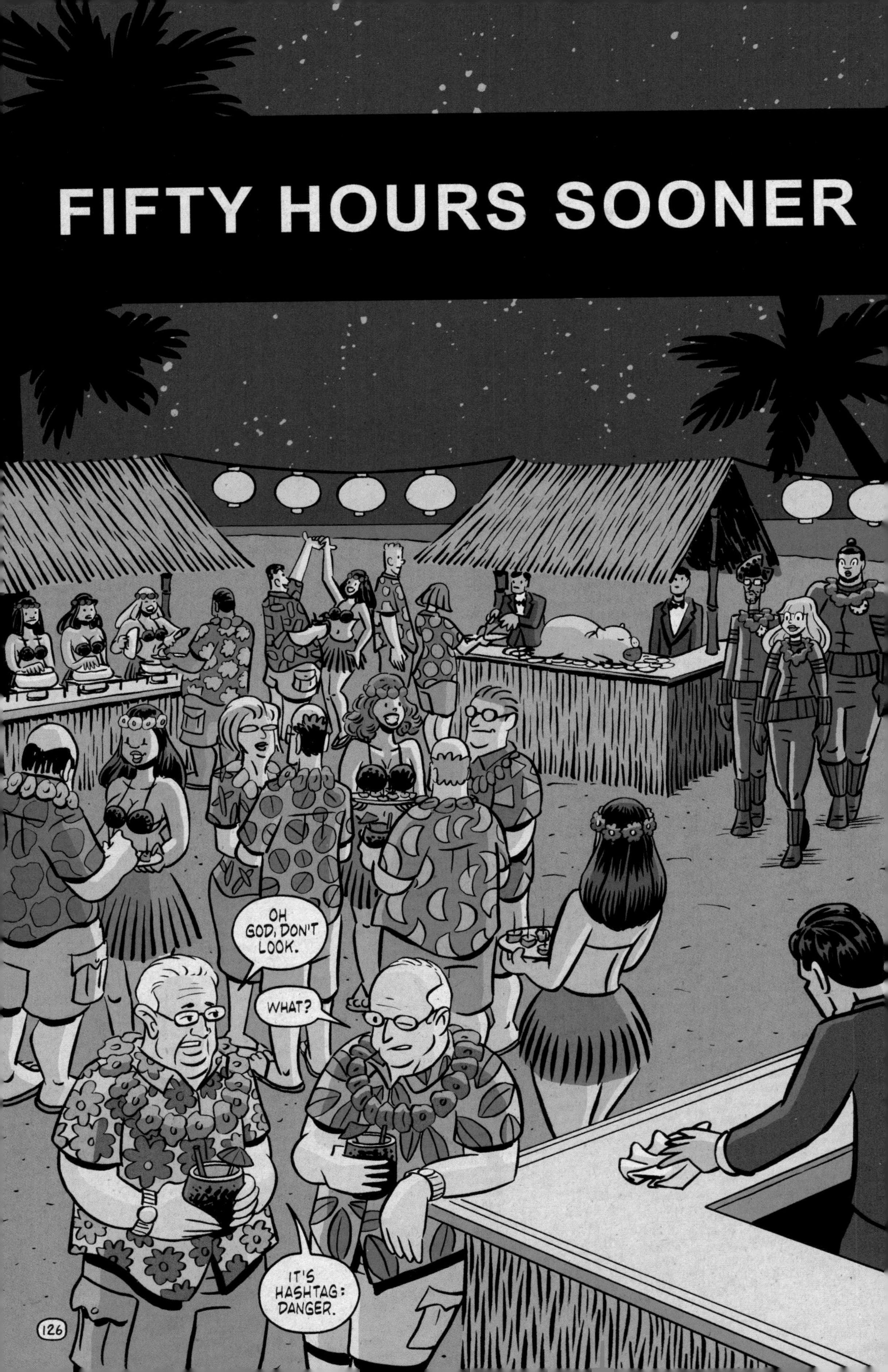
FIFTY HOURS SOONER
OH GOD, DON'T LOOK.
WHAT?
IT'S HASHTAG: DANGER.

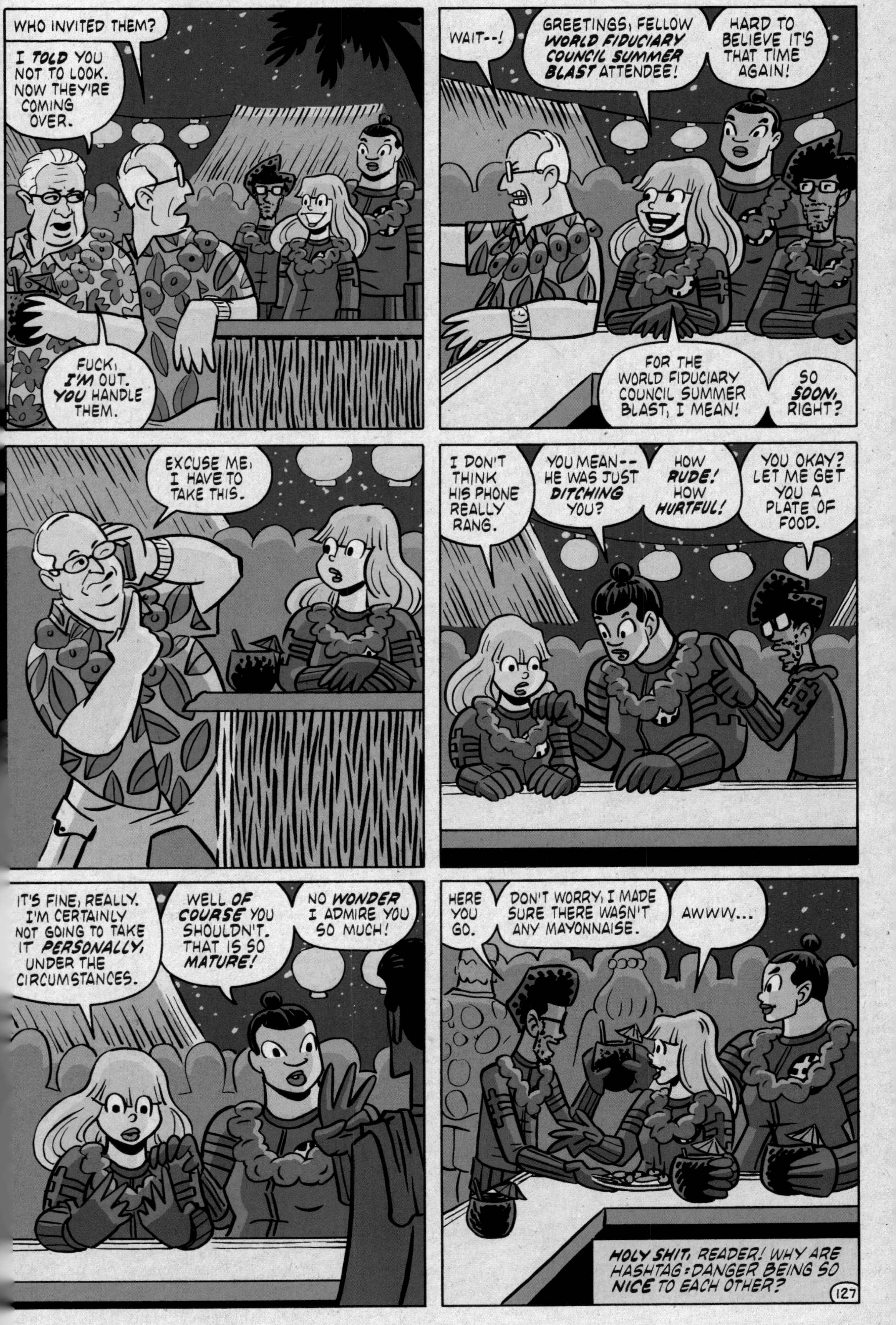
WHO INVITED THEM?
I TOLD YOU NOT TO LOOK. NOW THEY'RE COMING OVER.
FUCK, I'M OUT. YOU HANDLE THEM.
WAIT--!
GREETINGS, FELLOW WORLD FIDUCIARY COUNCIL SUMMER BLAST ATTENDEE!
HARD TO BELIEVE IT'S THAT TIME AGAIN!
FOR THE WORLD FIDUCIARY COUNCIL SUMMER BLAST, I MEAN!
SO SOON, RIGHT?
EXCUSE ME, I HAVE TO TAKE THIS.
I DON'T THINK HIS PHONE REALLY RANG.
YOU MEAN-- HE WAS JUST DITCHING YOU?
HOW RUDE! HOW HURTFUL!
YOU OKAY? LET ME GET YOU A PLATE OF FOOD.
IT'S FINE, REALLY. I'M CERTAINLY NOT GOING TO TAKE IT PERSONALLY, UNDER THE CIRCUMSTANCES.
WELL OF COURSE YOU SHOULDN'T. THAT IS SO MATURE!
NO WONDER I ADMIRE YOU SO MUCH!
HERE YOU GO.
DON'T WORRY, I MADE SURE THERE WASN'T ANY MAYONNAISE.
AWWW...
HOLY SHIT, READER! WHY ARE HASHTAG:DANGER BEING SO NICE TO EACH OTHER?
127

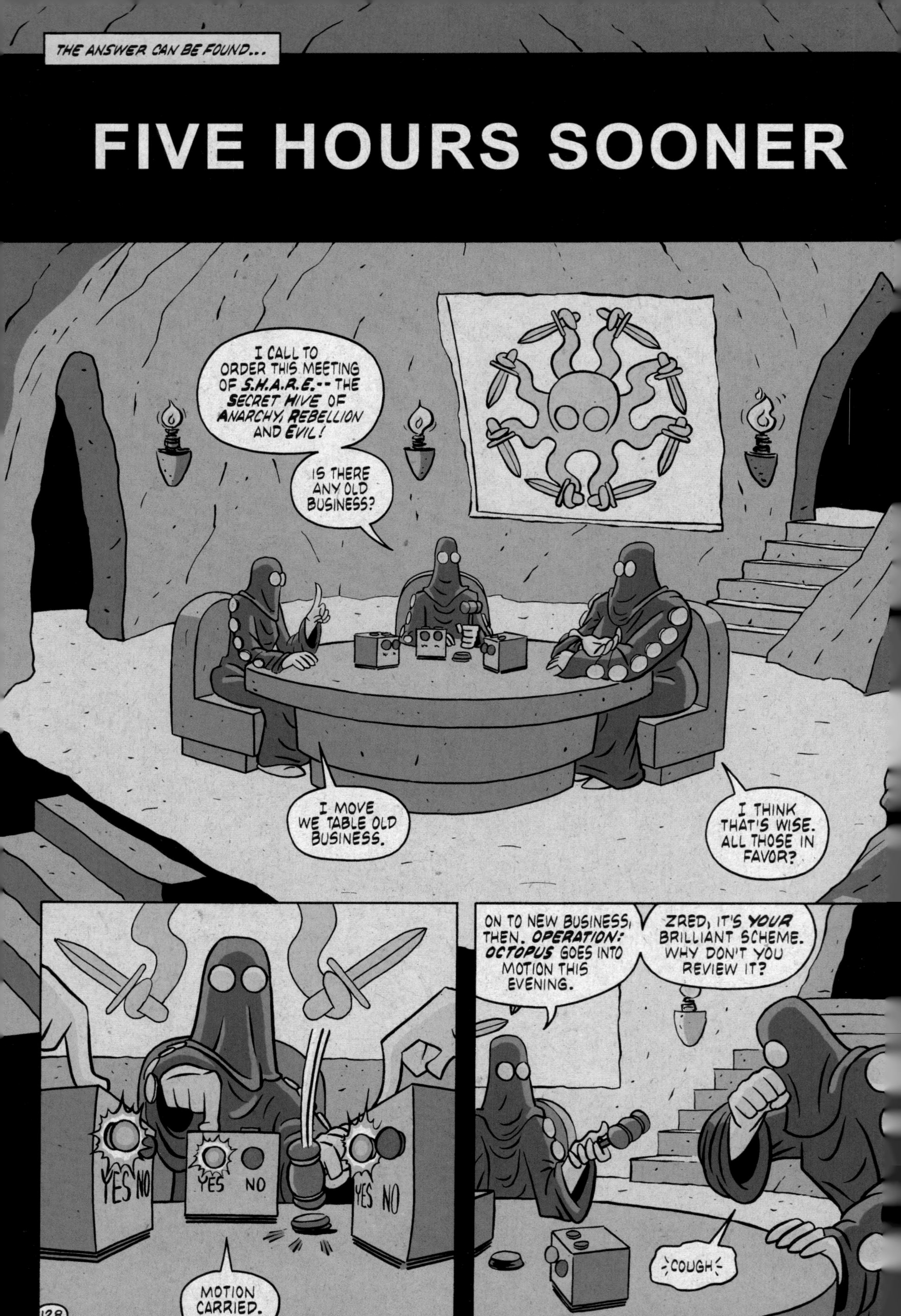
THE ANSWER CAN BE FOUND...
FIVE HOURS SOONER
I CALL TO ORDER THIS MEETING OF S.H.A.R.E.-- THE SECRET HIVE OF ANARCHY, REBELLION AND EVIL!
IS THERE ANY OLD BUSINESS?
I MOVE WE TABLE OLD BUSINESS.
I THINK THAT'S WISE. ALL THOSE IN FAVOR?
YES NO
YES NO
YES NO
MOTION CARRIED.
ON TO NEW BUSINESS, THEN. OPERATION: OCTOPUS GOES INTO MOTION THIS EVENING.
ZRED, IT'S YOUR BRILLIANT SCHEME. WHY DON'T YOU REVIEW IT?
COUGH

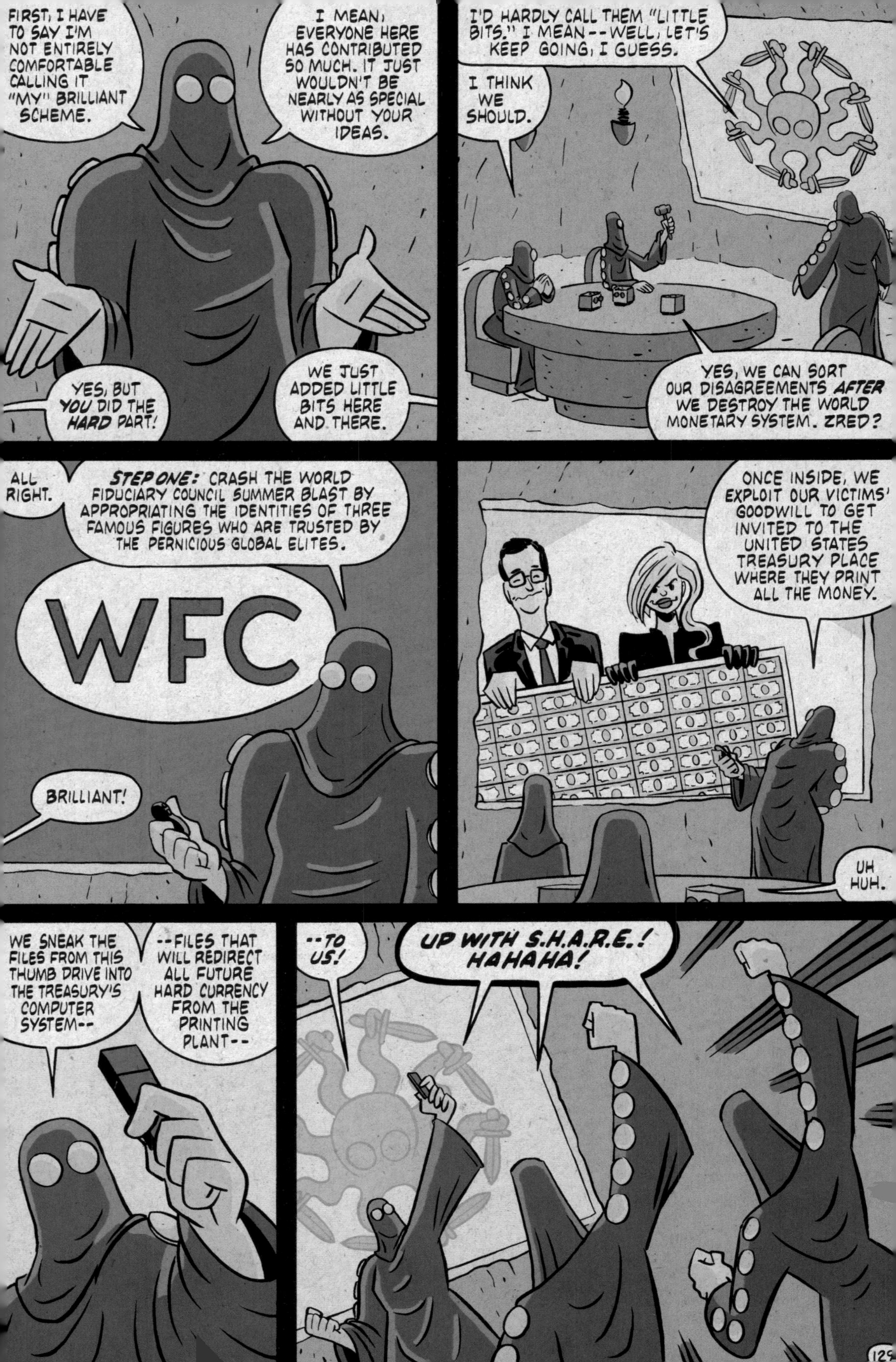
FIRST, I HAVE TO SAY I'M NOT ENTIRELY COMFORTABLE CALLING IT "MY" BRILLIANT SCHEME.
I MEAN, EVERYONE HERE HAS CONTRIBUTED SO MUCH. IT JUST WOULDN'T BE NEARLY AS SPECIAL WITHOUT YOUR IDEAS.
YES, BUT *YOU* DID THE *HARD* PART!
WE JUST ADDED LITTLE BITS HERE AND THERE.
I'D HARDLY CALL THEM "LITTLE BITS." I MEAN--WELL, LET'S KEEP GOING, I GUESS.
I THINK WE SHOULD.
YES, WE CAN SORT OUR DISAGREEMENTS *AFTER* WE DESTROY THE WORLD MONETARY SYSTEM. ZRED?
ALL RIGHT.
STEP ONE: CRASH THE WORLD FIDUCIARY COUNCIL SUMMER BLAST BY APPROPRIATING THE IDENTITIES OF THREE FAMOUS FIGURES WHO ARE TRUSTED BY THE PERNICIOUS GLOBAL ELITES.
WFC
BRILLIANT!
ONCE INSIDE, WE EXPLOIT OUR VICTIMS' GOODWILL TO GET INVITED TO THE UNITED STATES TREASURY PLACE WHERE THEY PRINT ALL THE MONEY.
UH HUH.
WE SNEAK THE FILES FROM THIS THUMB DRIVE INTO THE TREASURY'S COMPUTER SYSTEM--
--FILES THAT WILL REDIRECT ALL FUTURE HARD CURRENCY FROM THE PRINTING PLANT--
--TO US!
UP WITH S.H.A.R.E.! HAHAHA!

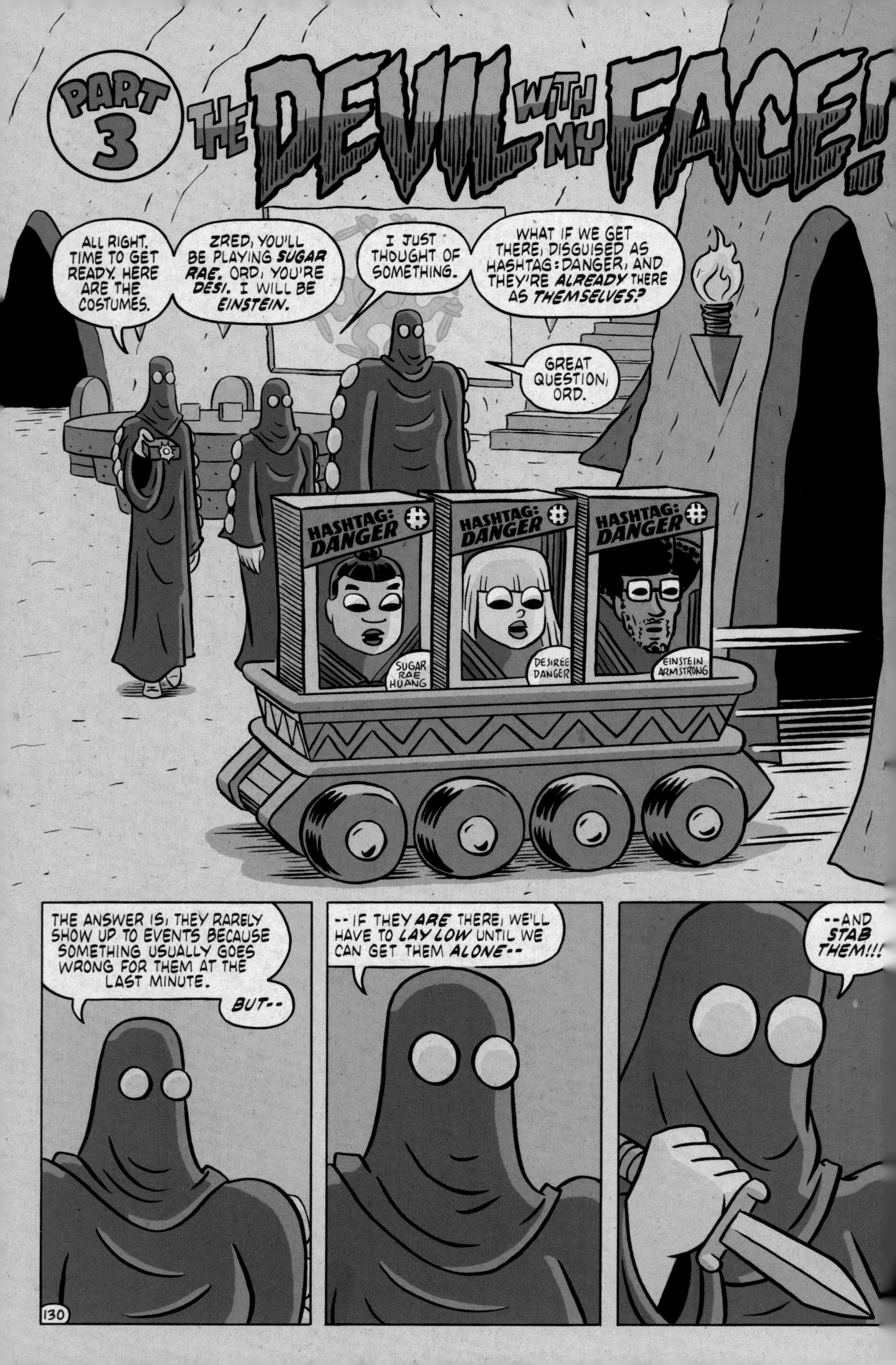
PART 3
THE DEVIL WITH MY FACE!
ALL RIGHT. TIME TO GET READY. HERE ARE THE COSTUMES.
ZRED, YOU'LL BE PLAYING SUGAR RAE. ORD, YOU'RE DESI. I WILL BE EINSTEIN.
I JUST THOUGHT OF SOMETHING.
WHAT IF WE GET THERE, DISGUISED AS HASHTAG:DANGER, AND THEY'RE ALREADY THERE AS THEMSELVES?
GREAT QUESTION, ORD.
HASHTAG: DANGER
SUGAR RAE HUANG
HASHTAG: DANGER
DESIREE DANGER
HASHTAG: DANGER
EINSTEIN ARMSTRONG
THE ANSWER IS, THEY RARELY SHOW UP TO EVENTS BECAUSE SOMETHING USUALLY GOES WRONG FOR THEM AT THE LAST MINUTE.
BUT--
--IF THEY ARE THERE, WE'LL HAVE TO LAY LOW UNTIL WE CAN GET THEM ALONE--
--AND STAB THEM!!!

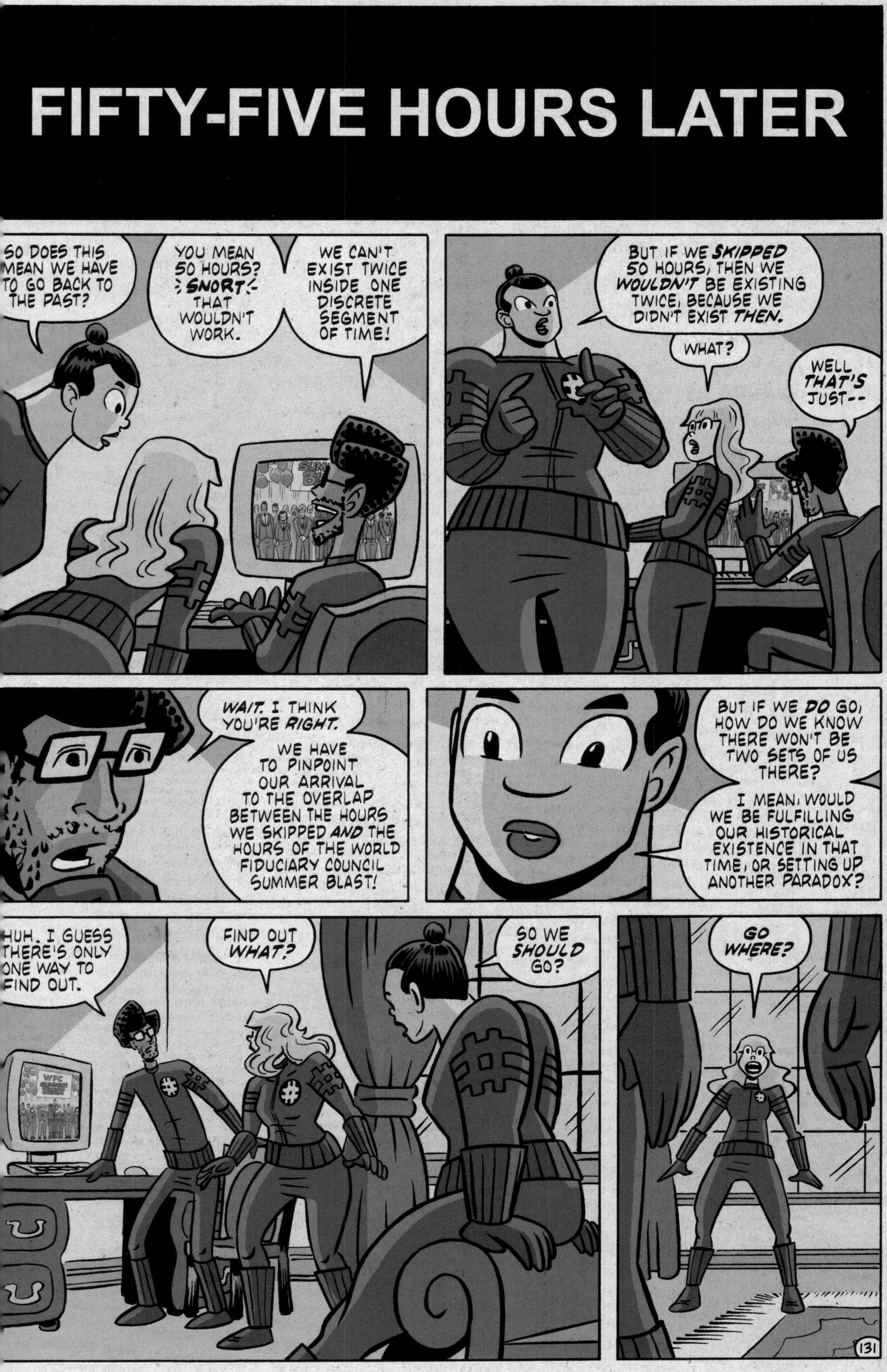
FIFTY-FIVE HOURS LATER
SO DOES THIS MEAN WE HAVE TO GO BACK TO THE PAST?
YOU MEAN 50 HOURS? *SNORT* THAT WOULDN'T WORK.
WE CAN'T EXIST TWICE INSIDE ONE DISCRETE SEGMENT OF TIME!
BUT IF WE SKIPPED 50 HOURS, THEN WE WOULDN'T BE EXISTING TWICE, BECAUSE WE DIDN'T EXIST THEN.
WHAT?
WELL THAT'S JUST--
WAIT. I THINK YOU'RE RIGHT.
WE HAVE TO PINPOINT OUR ARRIVAL TO THE OVERLAP BETWEEN THE HOURS WE SKIPPED AND THE HOURS OF THE WORLD FIDUCIARY COUNCIL SUMMER BLAST!
BUT IF WE DO GO, HOW DO WE KNOW THERE WON'T BE TWO SETS OF US THERE?
I MEAN, WOULD WE BE FULFILLING OUR HISTORICAL EXISTENCE IN THAT TIME, OR SETTING UP ANOTHER PARADOX?
HUH. I GUESS THERE'S ONLY ONE WAY TO FIND OUT.
FIND OUT WHAT?
SO WE SHOULD GO?
GO WHERE?

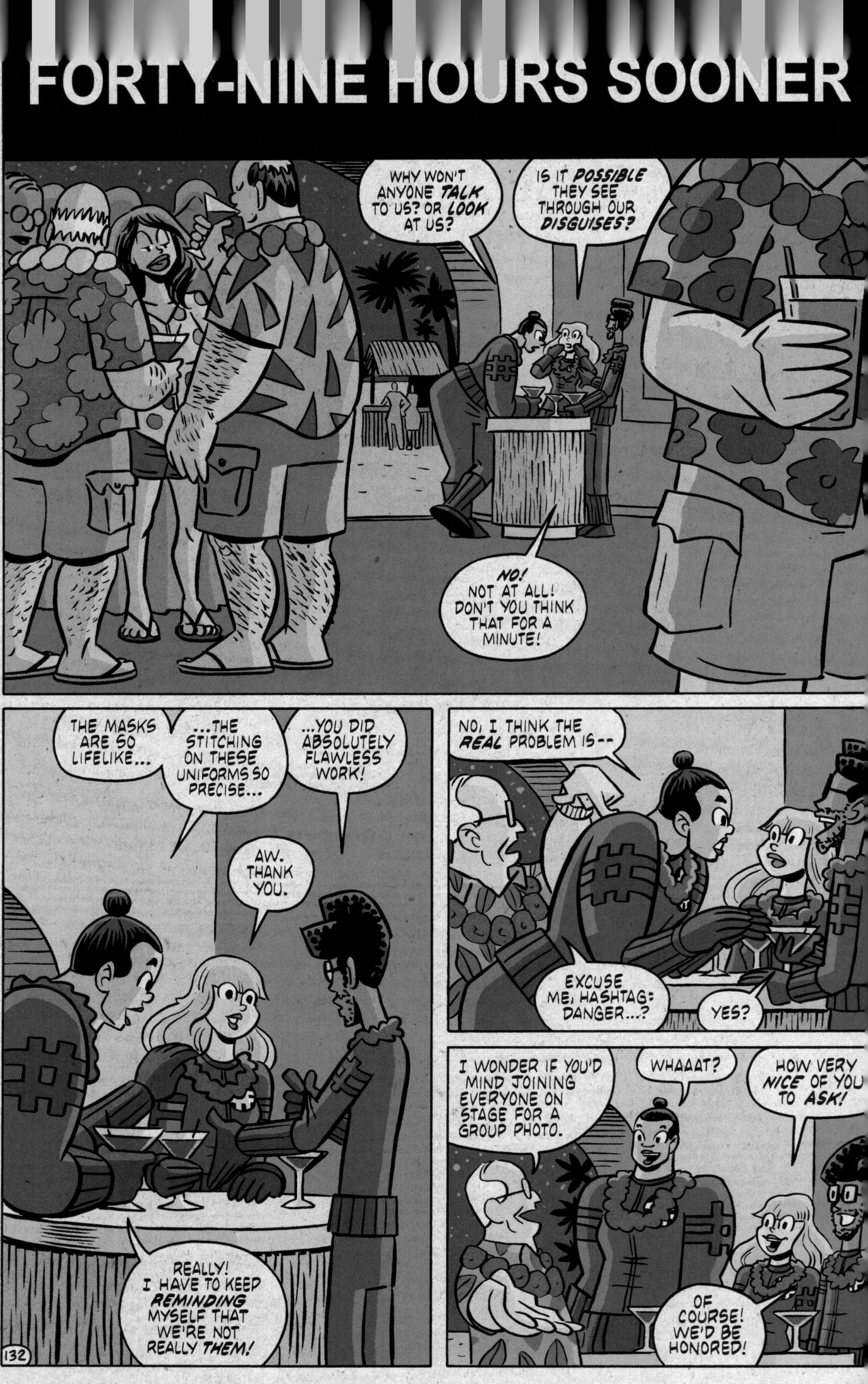
FORTY-NINE HOURS SOONER
WHY WON'T ANYONE TALK TO US? OR LOOK AT US?
IS IT POSSIBLE THEY SEE THROUGH OUR DISGUISES?
NO! NOT AT ALL! DON'T YOU THINK THAT FOR A MINUTE!
THE MASKS ARE SO LIFELIKE...
...THE STITCHING ON THESE UNIFORMS SO PRECISE...
...YOU DID ABSOLUTELY FLAWLESS WORK!
AW. THANK YOU.
REALLY! I HAVE TO KEEP REMINDING MYSELF THAT WE'RE NOT REALLY THEM!
NO, I THINK THE REAL PROBLEM IS--
EXCUSE ME, HASHTAG: DANGER...?
YES?
I WONDER IF YOU'D MIND JOINING EVERYONE ON STAGE FOR A GROUP PHOTO.
WHAAAT?
HOW VERY NICE OF YOU TO ASK!
OF COURSE! WE'D BE HONORED!

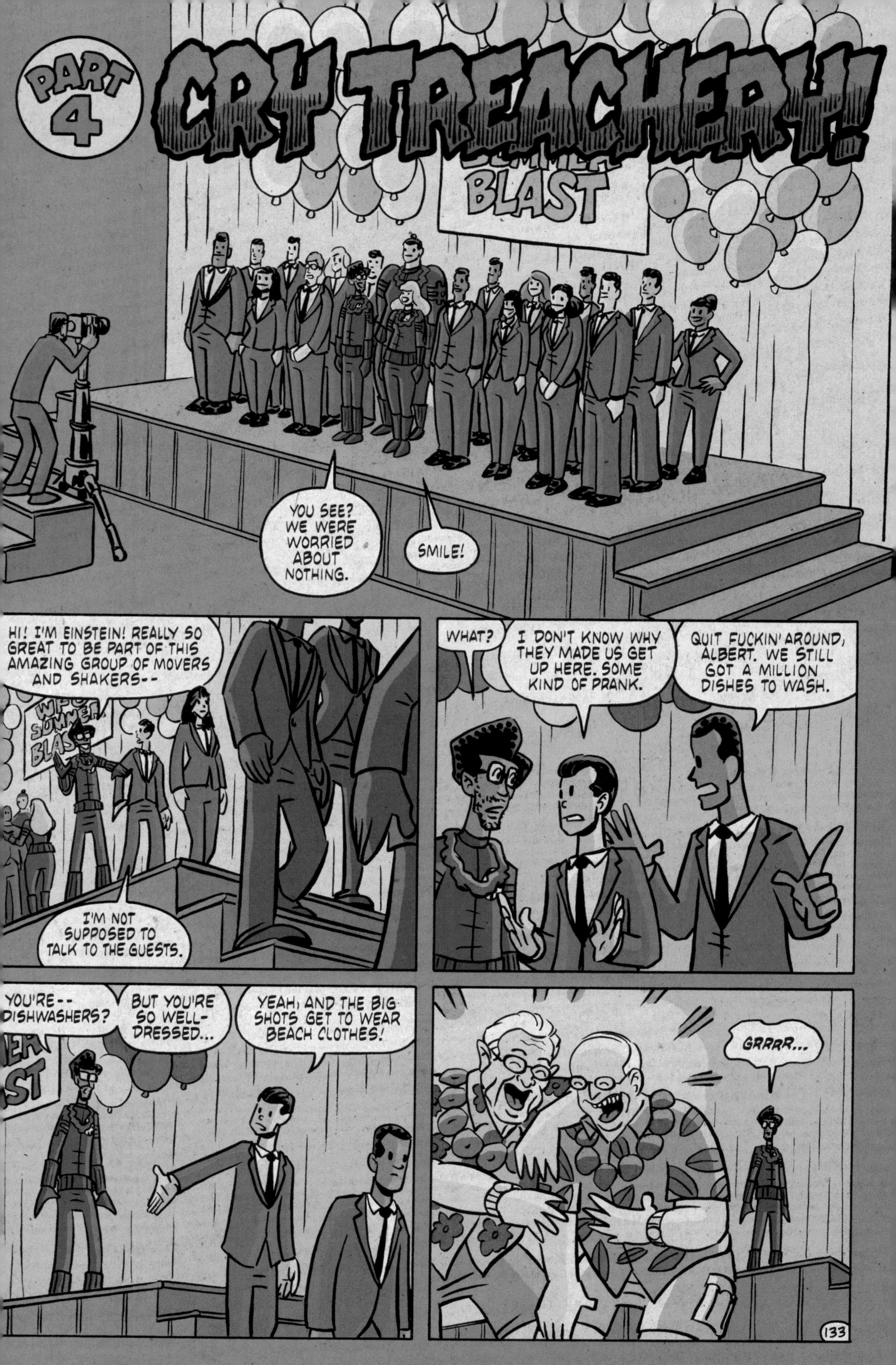
PART 4
CRY TREACHERY!
BLAST
YOU SEE? WE WERE WORRIED ABOUT NOTHING.
SMILE!
HI! I'M EINSTEIN! REALLY SO GREAT TO BE PART OF THIS AMAZING GROUP OF MOVERS AND SHAKERS--
I'M NOT SUPPOSED TO TALK TO THE GUESTS.
WHAT?
I DON'T KNOW WHY THEY MADE US GET UP HERE. SOME KIND OF PRANK.
QUIT FUCKIN' AROUND, ALBERT. WE STILL GOT A MILLION DISHES TO WASH.
YOU'RE-- DISHWASHERS?
BUT YOU'RE SO WELL-DRESSED...
YEAH, AND THE BIG SHOTS GET TO WEAR BEACH CLOTHES!
GRRRR...

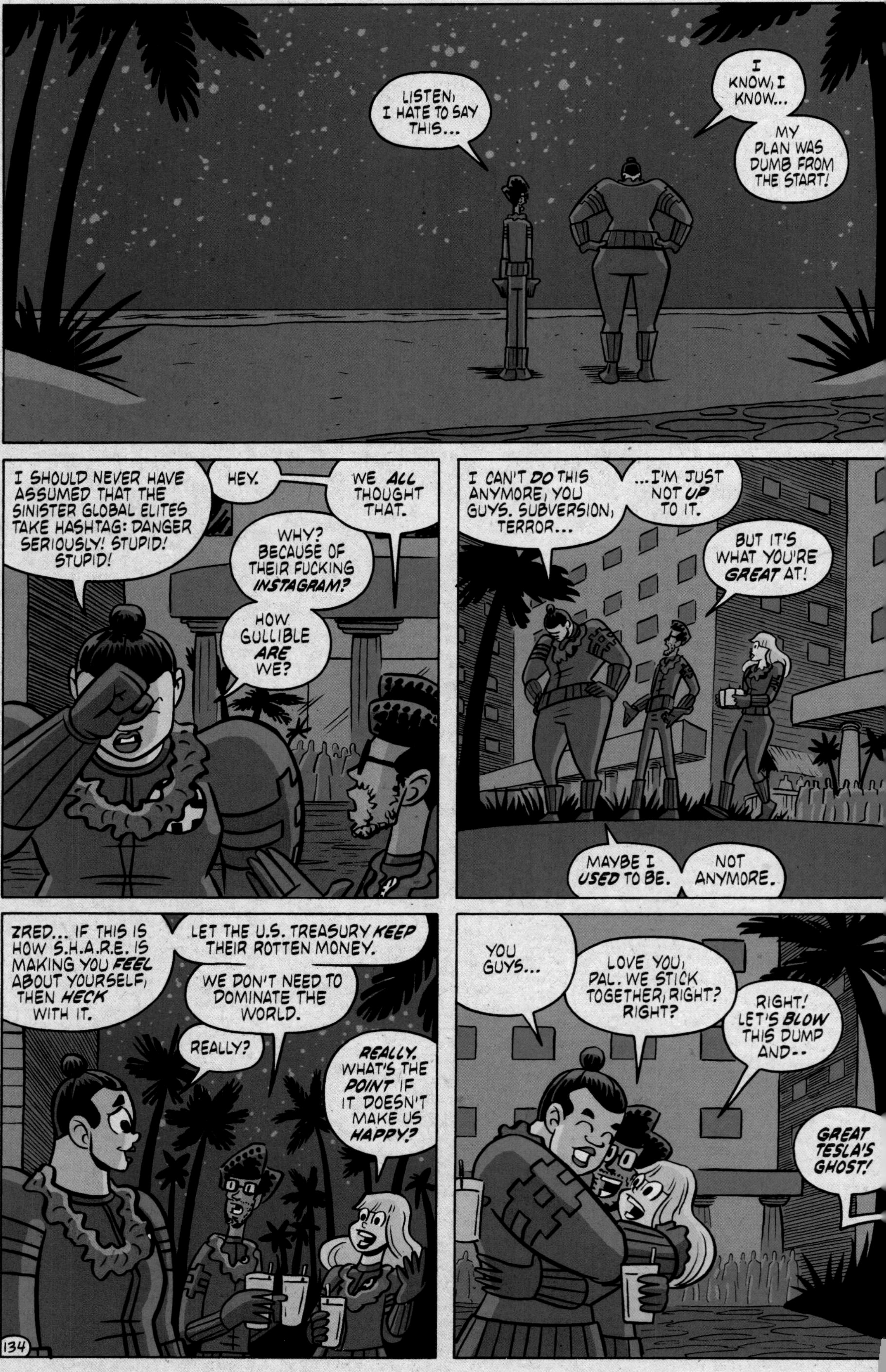
LISTEN, I HATE TO SAY THIS...
I KNOW, I KNOW...
MY PLAN WAS DUMB FROM THE START!
I SHOULD NEVER HAVE ASSUMED THAT THE SINISTER GLOBAL ELITES TAKE HASHTAG: DANGER SERIOUSLY! STUPID! STUPID!
HEY.
WE ALL THOUGHT THAT.
WHY? BECAUSE OF THEIR FUCKING INSTAGRAM?
HOW GULLIBLE ARE WE?
I CAN'T DO THIS ANYMORE, YOU GUYS. SUBVERSION, TERROR...
...I'M JUST NOT UP TO IT.
BUT IT'S WHAT YOU'RE GREAT AT!
MAYBE I USED TO BE.
NOT ANYMORE.
ZRED... IF THIS IS HOW S.H.A.R.E. IS MAKING YOU FEEL ABOUT YOURSELF, THEN HECK WITH IT.
LET THE U.S. TREASURY KEEP THEIR ROTTEN MONEY.
WE DON'T NEED TO DOMINATE THE WORLD.
REALLY?
REALLY. WHAT'S THE POINT IF IT DOESN'T MAKE US HAPPY?
YOU GUYS...
LOVE YOU, PAL. WE STICK TOGETHER, RIGHT? RIGHT?
RIGHT! LET'S BLOW THIS DUMP AND--
GREAT TESLA'S GHOST!

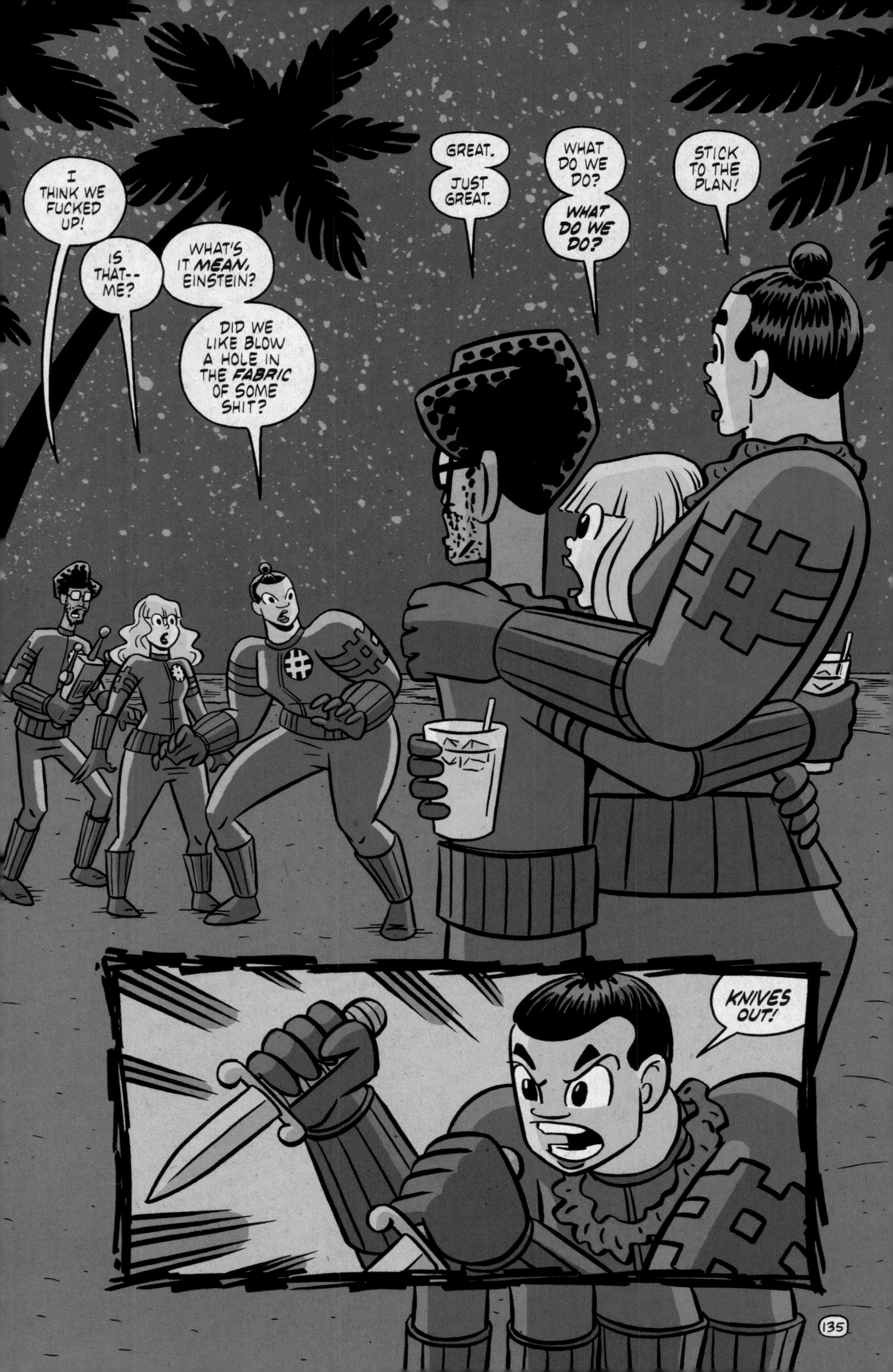
I THINK WE FUCKED UP!
IS THAT-- ME?
WHAT'S IT MEAN, EINSTEIN?
DID WE LIKE BLOW A HOLE IN THE FABRIC OF SOME SHIT?
GREAT.
JUST GREAT.
WHAT DO WE DO?
WHAT DO WE DO?
STICK TO THE PLAN!
KNIVES OUT!

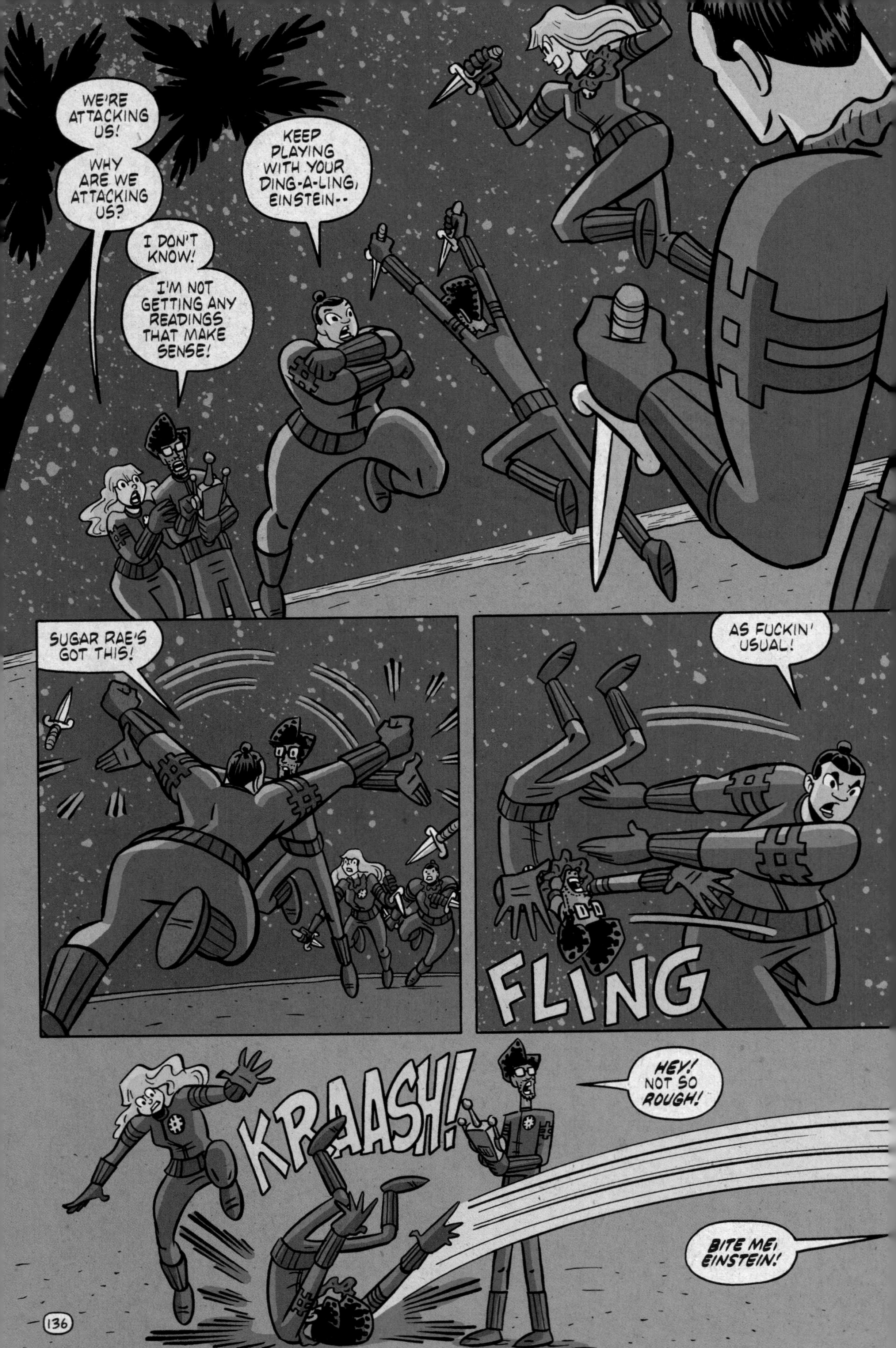
WE'RE ATTACKING US!
WHY ARE WE ATTACKING US?
I DON'T KNOW!
I'M NOT GETTING ANY READINGS THAT MAKE SENSE!
KEEP PLAYING WITH YOUR DING-A-LING, EINSTEIN--
SUGAR RAE'S GOT THIS!
AS FUCKIN' USUAL!
FLING
KRAASH!
HEY! NOT SO ROUGH!
BITE ME, EINSTEIN!

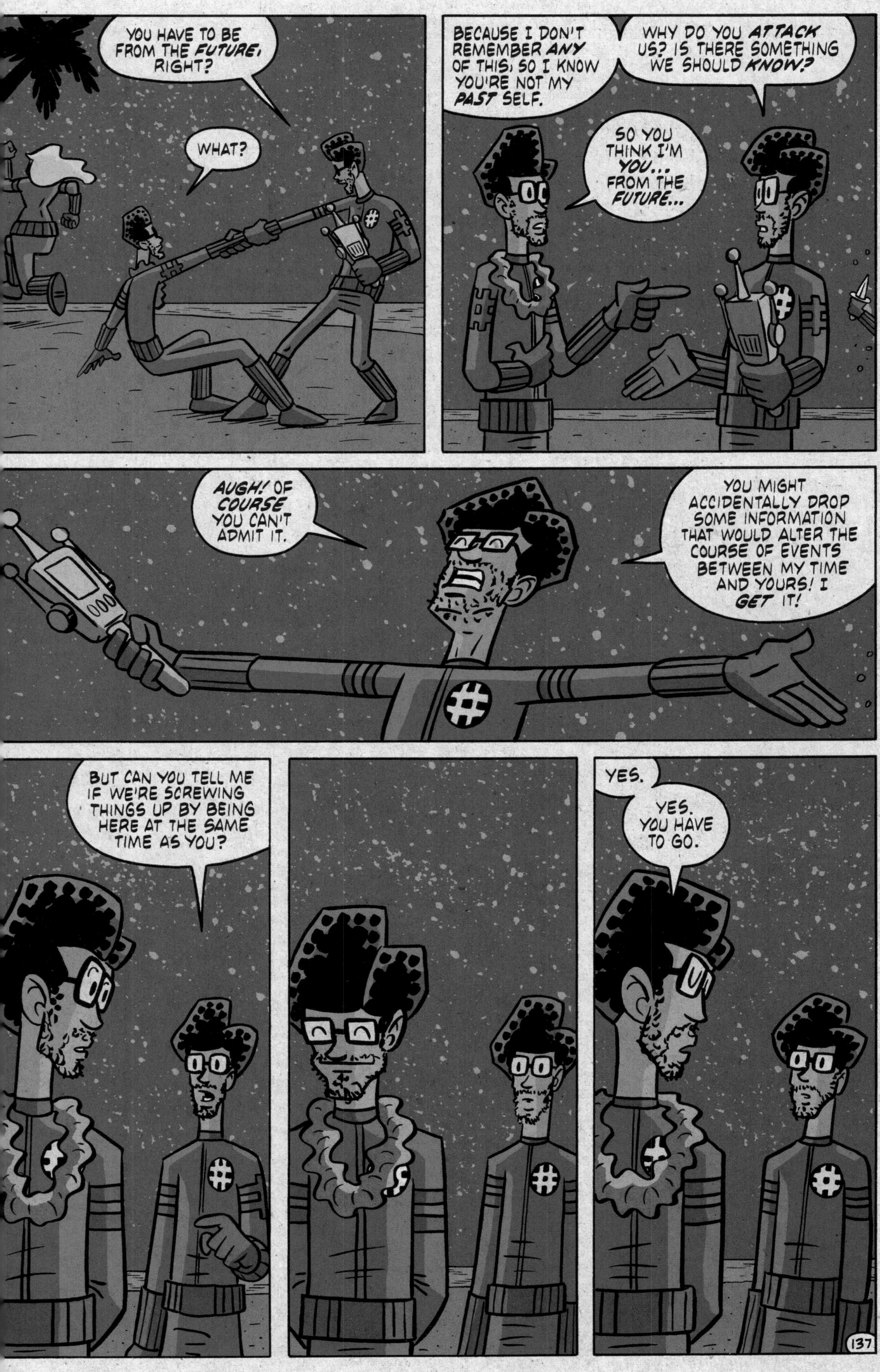
YOU HAVE TO BE FROM THE *FUTURE*, RIGHT?
WHAT?
BECAUSE I DON'T REMEMBER *ANY* OF THIS, SO I KNOW YOU'RE NOT MY *PAST* SELF.
WHY DO YOU *ATTACK* US? IS THERE SOMETHING WE SHOULD *KNOW?*
SO YOU THINK I'M *YOU*... FROM THE *FUTURE*...
AUGH! OF *COURSE* YOU CAN'T ADMIT IT.
YOU MIGHT ACCIDENTALLY DROP SOME INFORMATION THAT WOULD ALTER THE COURSE OF EVENTS BETWEEN MY TIME AND YOURS! I *GET* IT!
BUT CAN YOU TELL ME IF WE'RE SCREWING THINGS UP BY BEING HERE AT THE SAME TIME AS YOU?
YES.
YES. YOU HAVE TO GO.

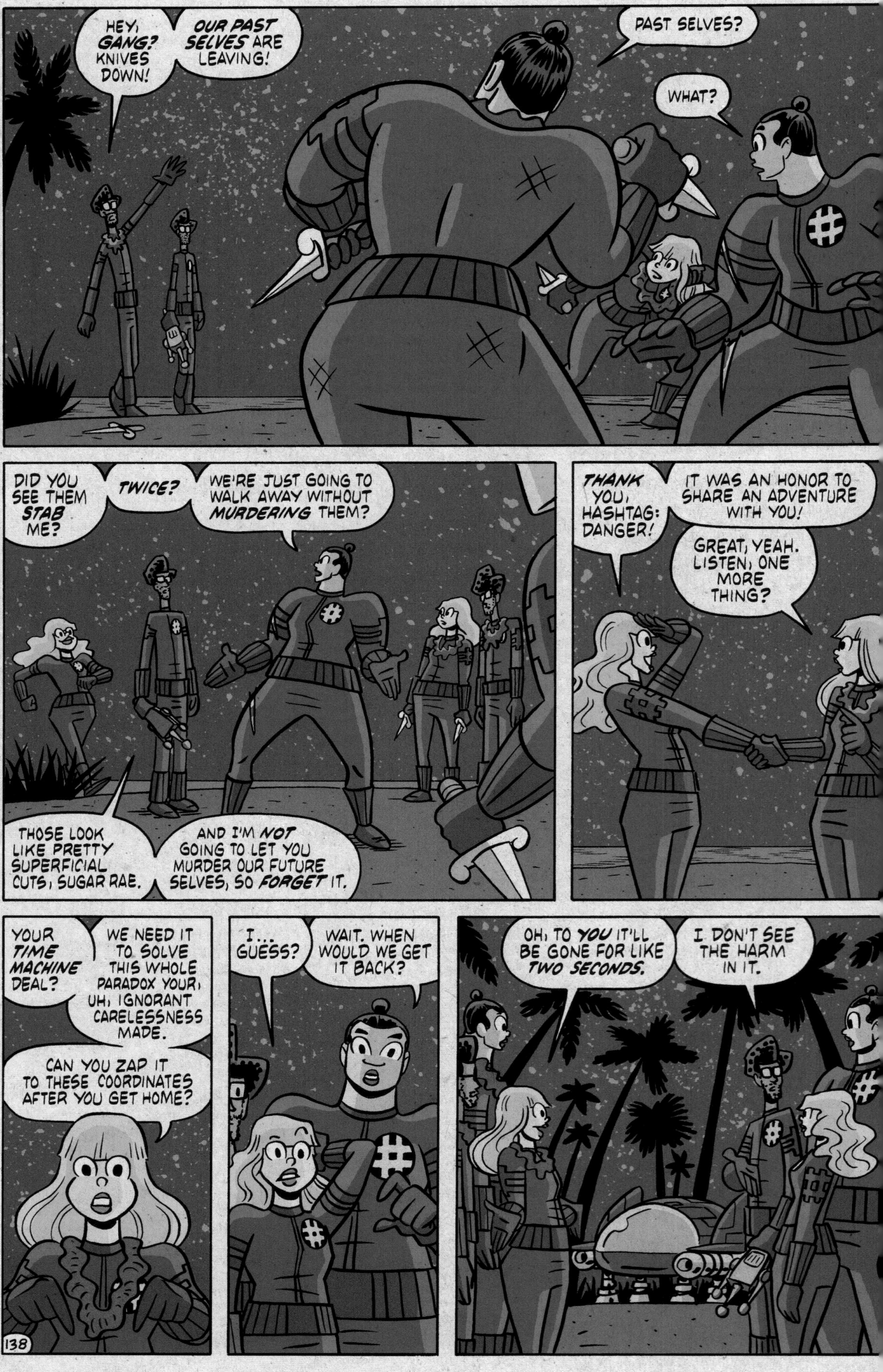

HEY, GANG? KNIVES DOWN!
OUR PAST SELVES ARE LEAVING!
PAST SELVES?
WHAT?
DID YOU SEE THEM STAB ME?
TWICE?
WE'RE JUST GOING TO WALK AWAY WITHOUT MURDERING THEM?
THOSE LOOK LIKE PRETTY SUPERFICIAL CUTS, SUGAR RAE.
AND I'M NOT GOING TO LET YOU MURDER OUR FUTURE SELVES, SO FORGET IT.
THANK YOU, HASHTAG: DANGER!
IT WAS AN HONOR TO SHARE AN ADVENTURE WITH YOU!
GREAT, YEAH. LISTEN, ONE MORE THING?
YOUR TIME MACHINE DEAL?
WE NEED IT TO SOLVE THIS WHOLE PARADOX YOUR, UH, IGNORANT CARELESSNESS MADE.
CAN YOU ZAP IT TO THESE COORDINATES AFTER YOU GET HOME?
I... GUESS?
WAIT. WHEN WOULD WE GET IT BACK?
OH, TO YOU IT'LL BE GONE FOR LIKE TWO SECONDS.
I DON'T SEE THE HARM IN IT.

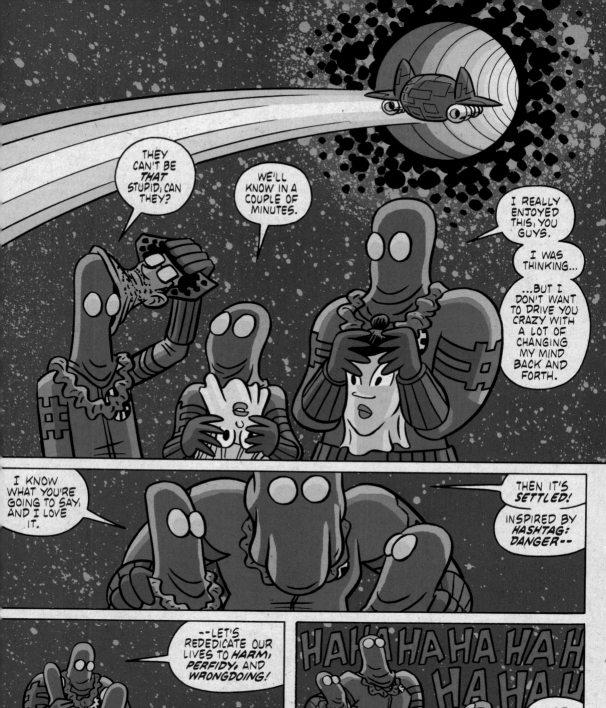

THEY CAN'T BE *THAT* STUPID, CAN THEY?

WE'LL KNOW IN A COUPLE OF MINUTES.

I REALLY ENJOYED THIS, YOU GUYS.

I WAS THINKING...

...BUT I DON'T WANT TO DRIVE YOU CRAZY WITH A LOT OF CHANGING MY MIND BACK AND FORTH.

I KNOW WHAT YOU'RE GOING TO SAY, AND I LOVE IT.

THEN IT'S *SETTLED!*

INSPIRED BY *HASHTAG: DANGER--*

--LET'S REDEDICATE OUR LIVES TO *HARM, PERFIDY,* AND *WRONGDOING!*

MINK

HA HA HA HA HA HA HA U

MORE LIKE HASHTAG: *DIPSHIT,* RIGHT?

139

EPILOGUE

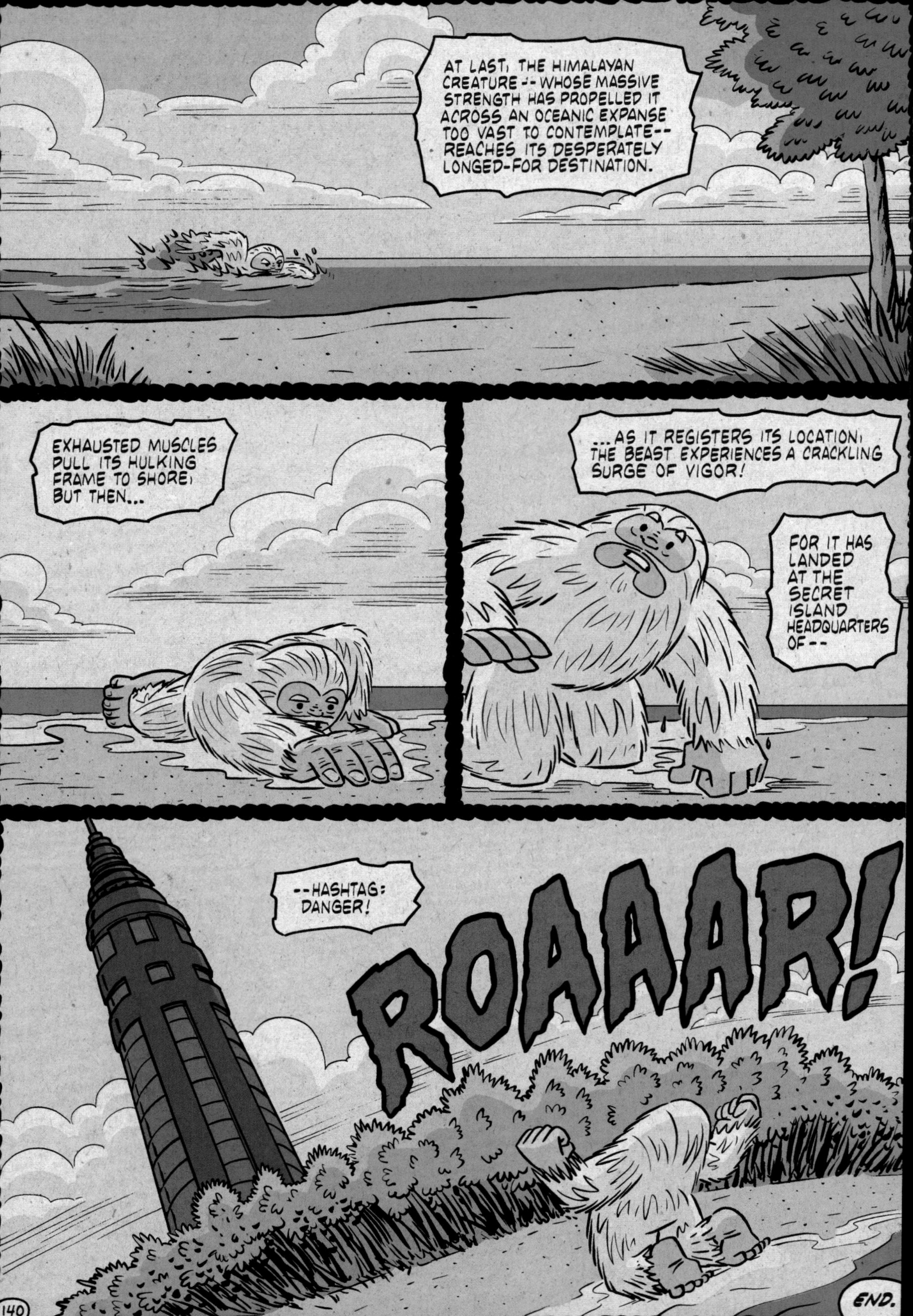
AT LAST, THE HIMALAYAN CREATURE -- WHOSE MASSIVE STRENGTH HAS PROPELLED IT ACROSS AN OCEANIC EXPANSE TOO VAST TO CONTEMPLATE -- REACHES ITS DESPERATELY LONGED-FOR DESTINATION.
EXHAUSTED MUSCLES PULL ITS HULKING FRAME TO SHORE, BUT THEN...
...AS IT REGISTERS ITS LOCATION, THE BEAST EXPERIENCES A CRACKLING SURGE OF VIGOR!
FOR IT HAS LANDED AT THE SECRET ISLAND HEADQUARTERS OF --
--HASHTAG: DANGER!
ROAAAR!
END.

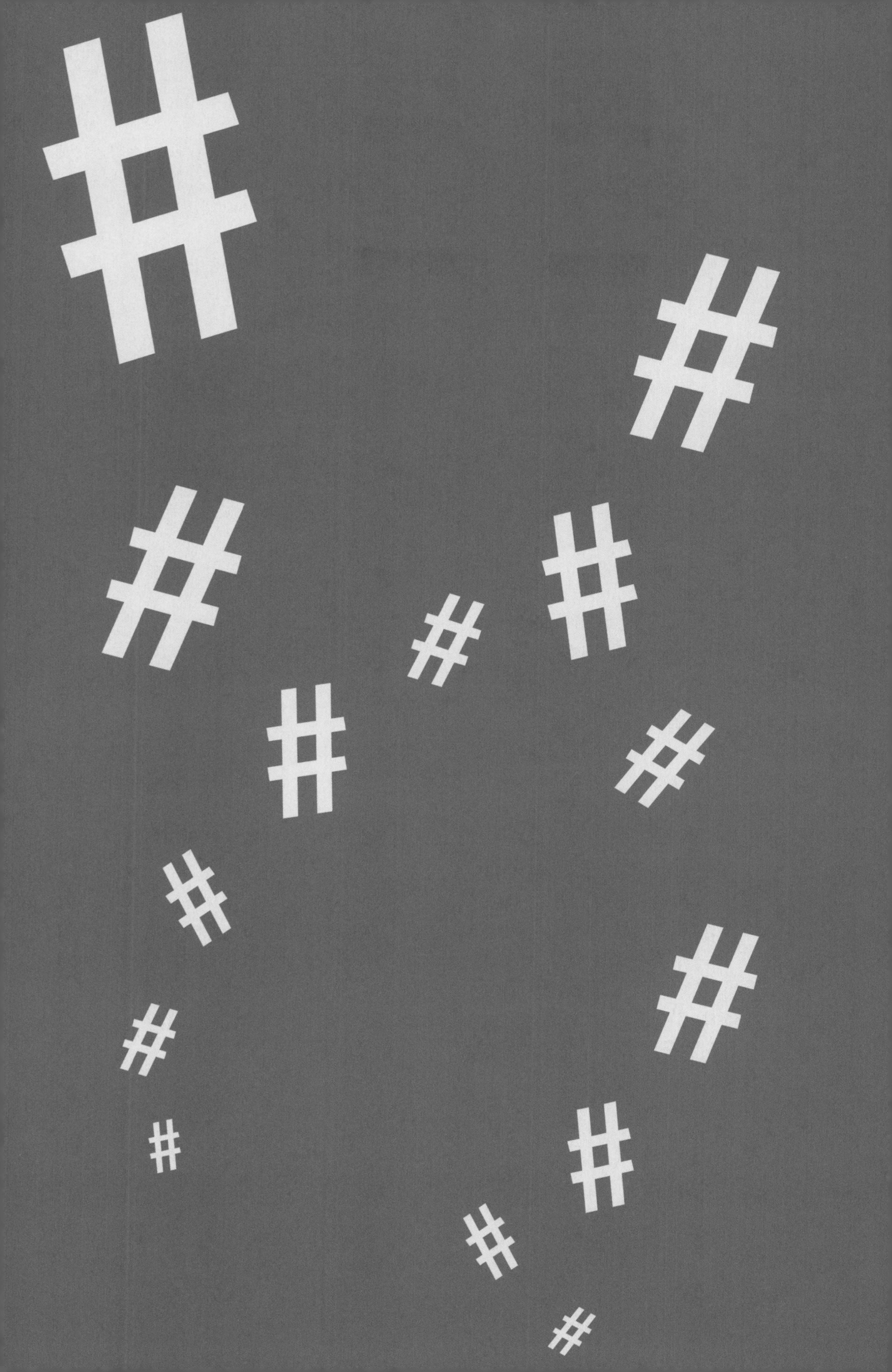

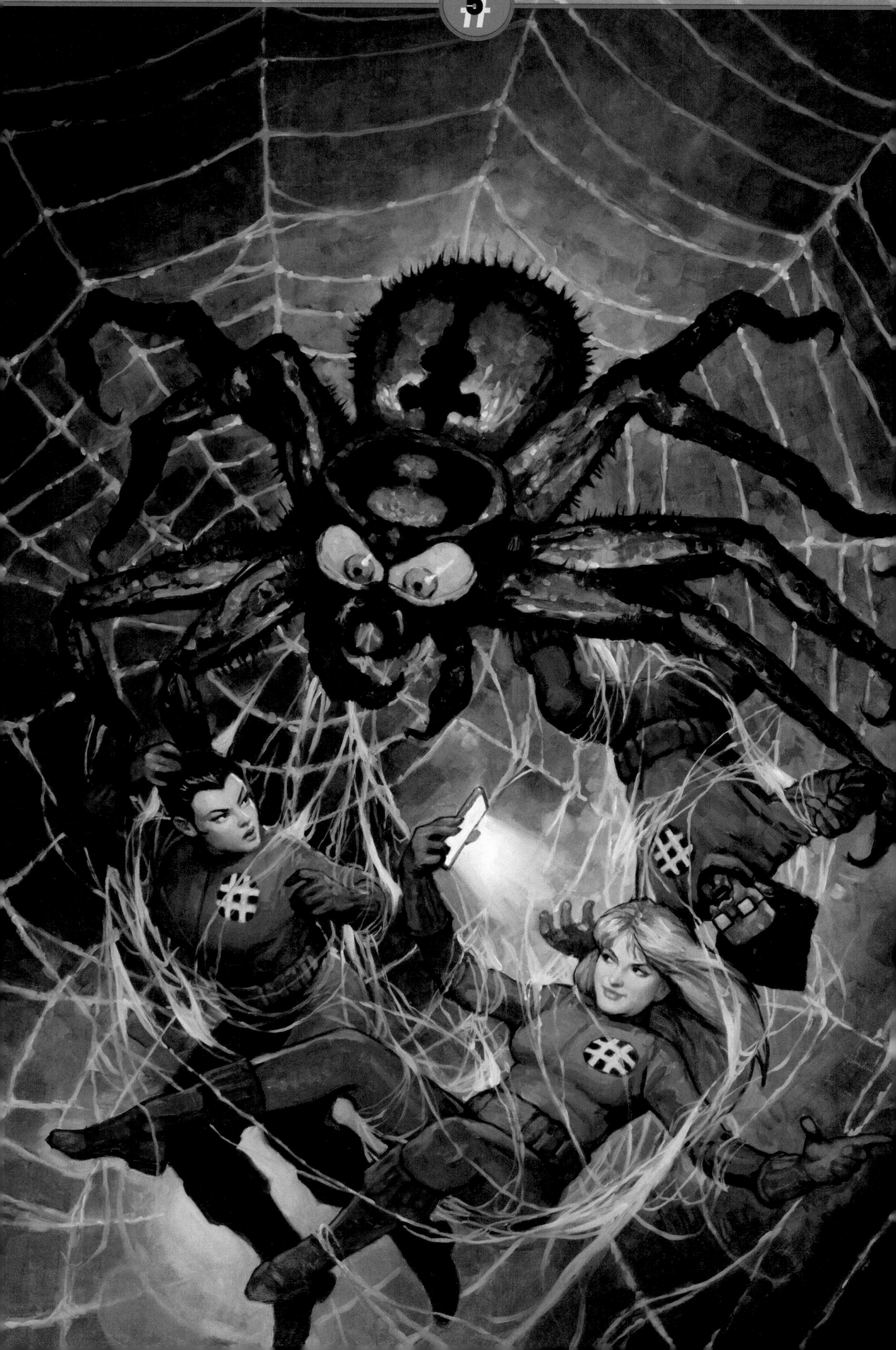

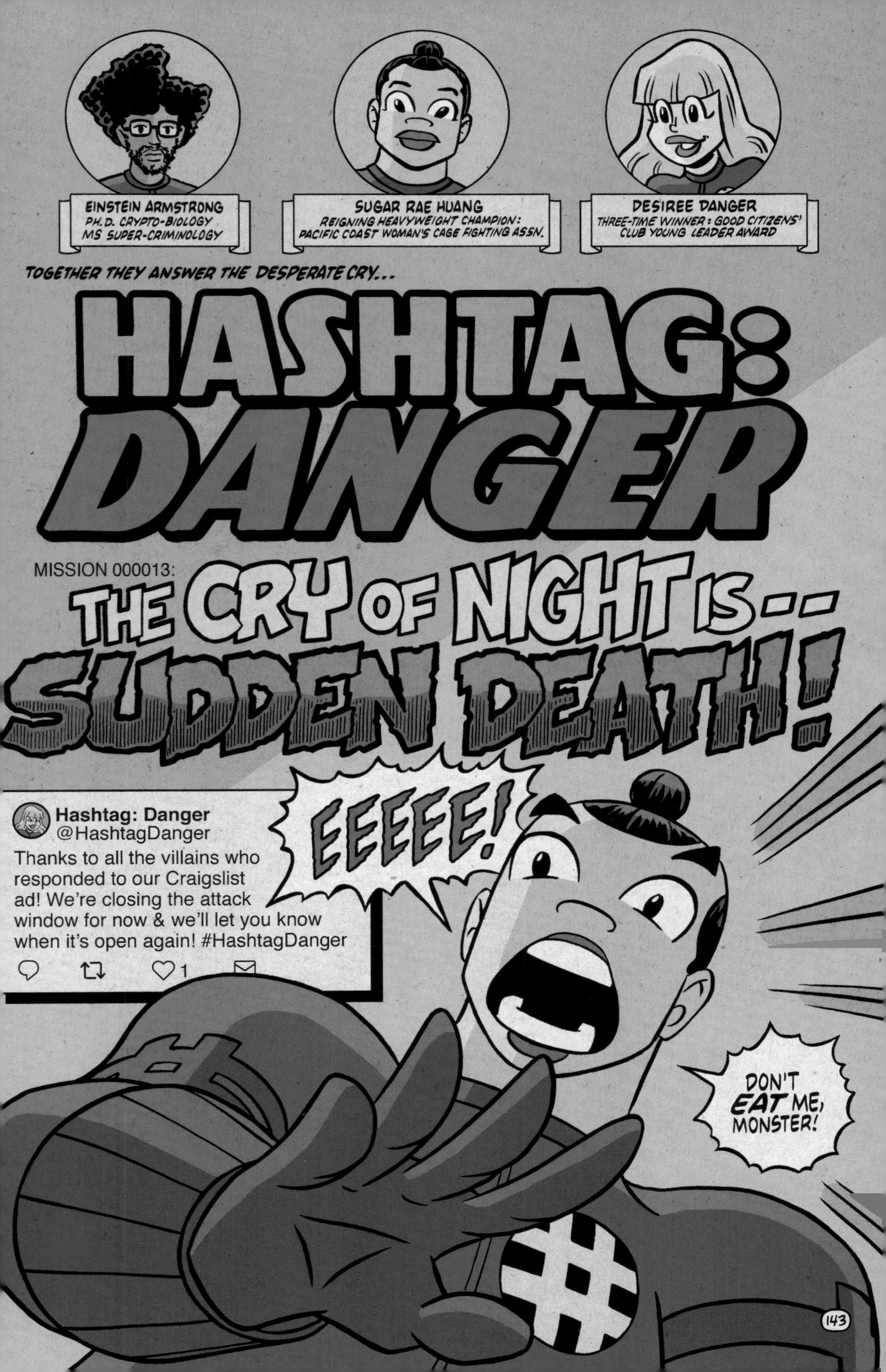

EINSTEIN ARMSTRONG
PH.D. CRYPTO-BIOLOGY
MS SUPER-CRIMINOLOGY
SUGAR RAE HUANG
REIGNING HEAVYWEIGHT CHAMPION:
PACIFIC COAST WOMAN'S CAGE FIGHTING ASSN.
DESIREE DANGER
THREE-TIME WINNER: GOOD CITIZENS' CLUB YOUNG LEADER AWARD
TOGETHER THEY ANSWER THE DESPERATE CRY...
HASHTAG: DANGER
MISSION 000013:
THE CRY OF NIGHT IS... SUDDEN DEATH!
Hashtag: Danger
@HashtagDanger
Thanks to all the villains who responded to our Craigslist ad! We're closing the attack window for now & we'll let you know when it's open again! #HashtagDanger
1
EEEEE!
DON'T EAT ME, MONSTER!

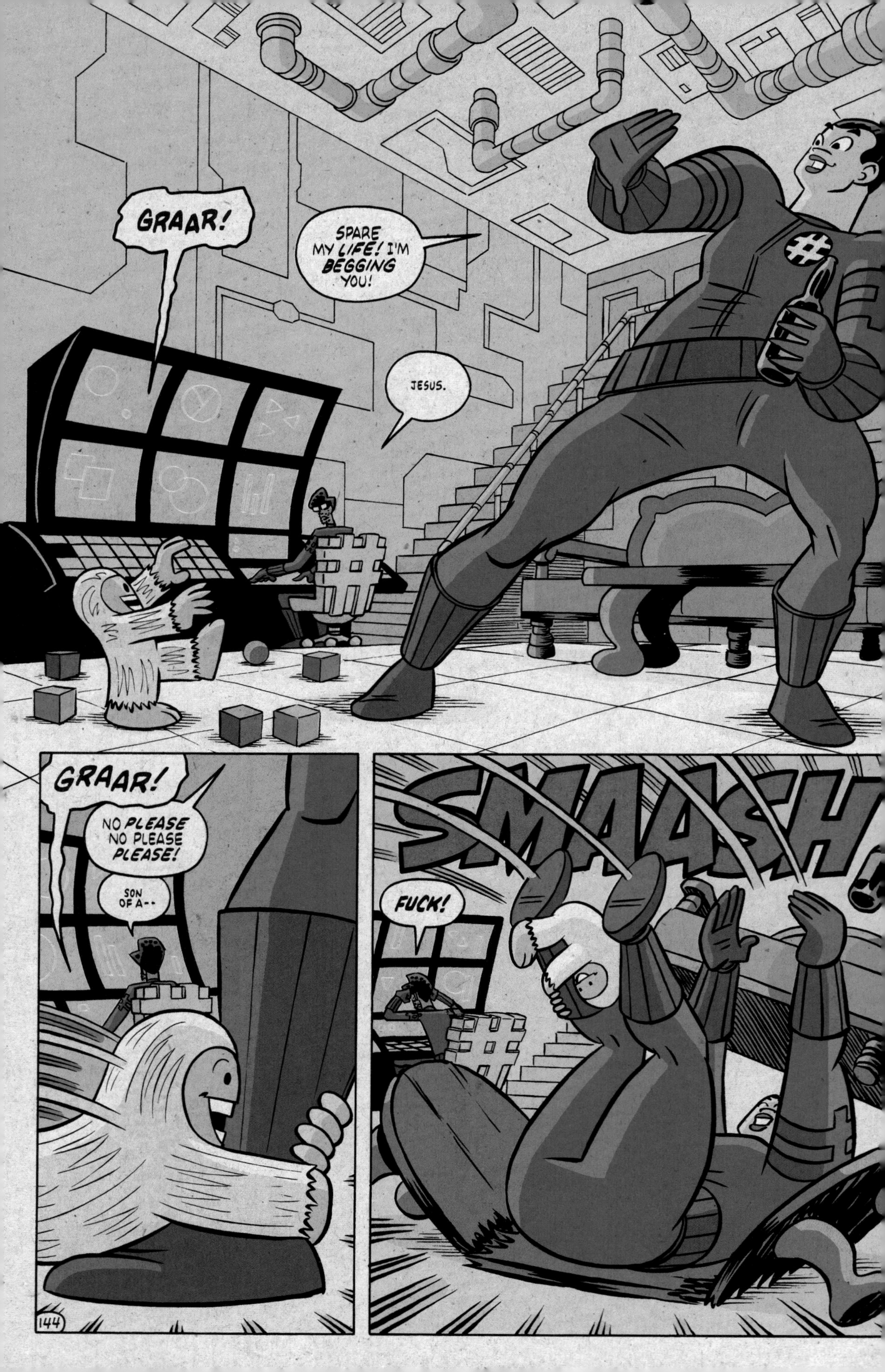
GRAAR!
SPARE MY LIFE! I'M BEGGING YOU!
JESUS.
GRAAR!
NO PLEASE NO PLEASE PLEASE!
SON OF A--
SMAASH
FUCK!

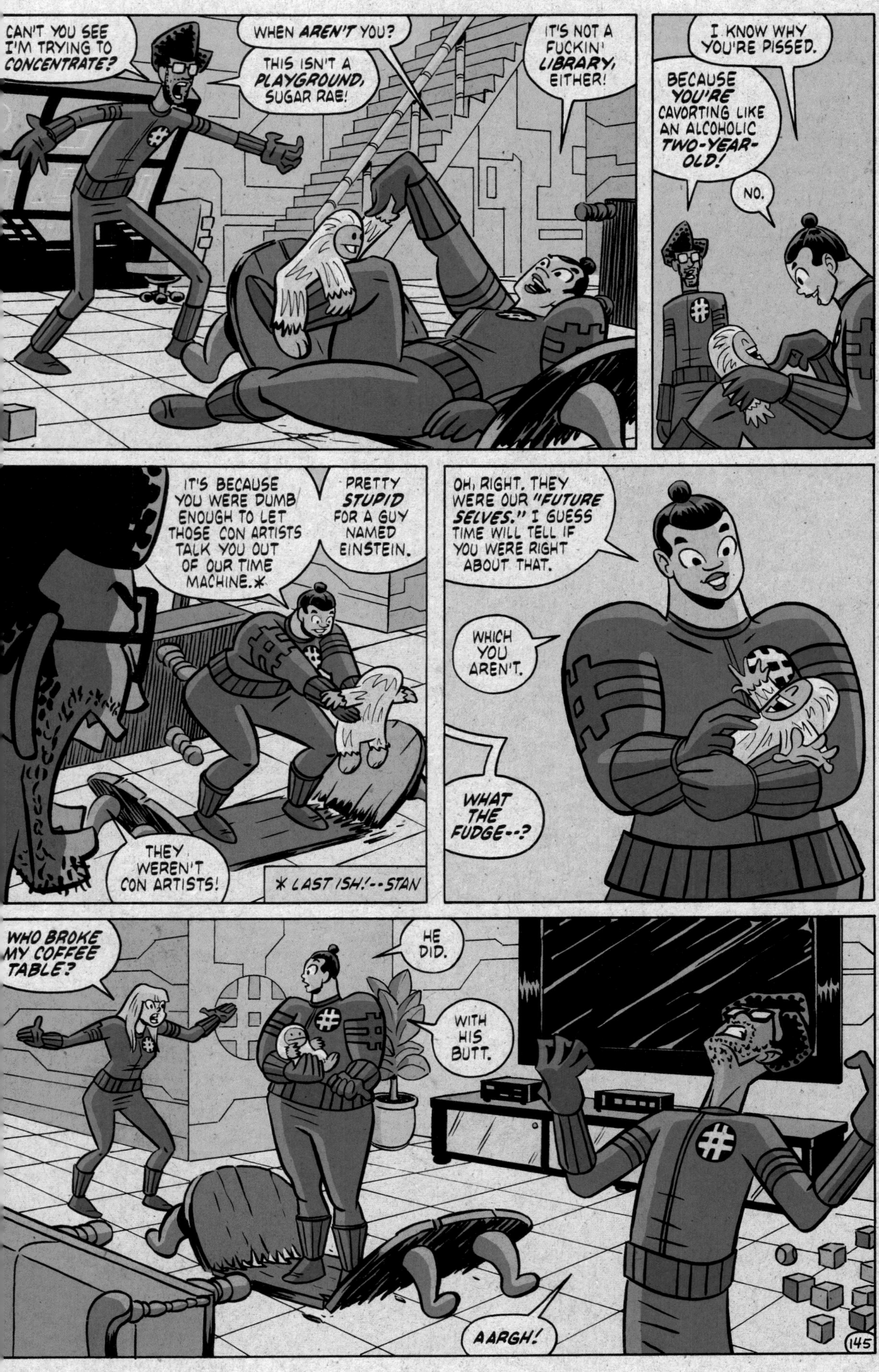
CAN'T YOU SEE I'M TRYING TO CONCENTRATE?
WHEN AREN'T YOU?
THIS ISN'T A PLAYGROUND, SUGAR RAE!
IT'S NOT A FUCKIN' LIBRARY, EITHER!
I KNOW WHY YOU'RE PISSED.
BECAUSE YOU'RE CAVORTING LIKE AN ALCOHOLIC TWO-YEAR-OLD!
NO.
IT'S BECAUSE YOU WERE DUMB ENOUGH TO LET THOSE CON ARTISTS TALK YOU OUT OF OUR TIME MACHINE.*
PRETTY STUPID FOR A GUY NAMED EINSTEIN.
THEY WEREN'T CON ARTISTS!
* LAST ISH!--STAN
OH, RIGHT. THEY WERE OUR "FUTURE SELVES." I GUESS TIME WILL TELL IF YOU WERE RIGHT ABOUT THAT.
WHICH YOU AREN'T.
WHAT THE FUDGE--?
WHO BROKE MY COFFEE TABLE?
HE DID.
WITH HIS BUTT.
AARGH!

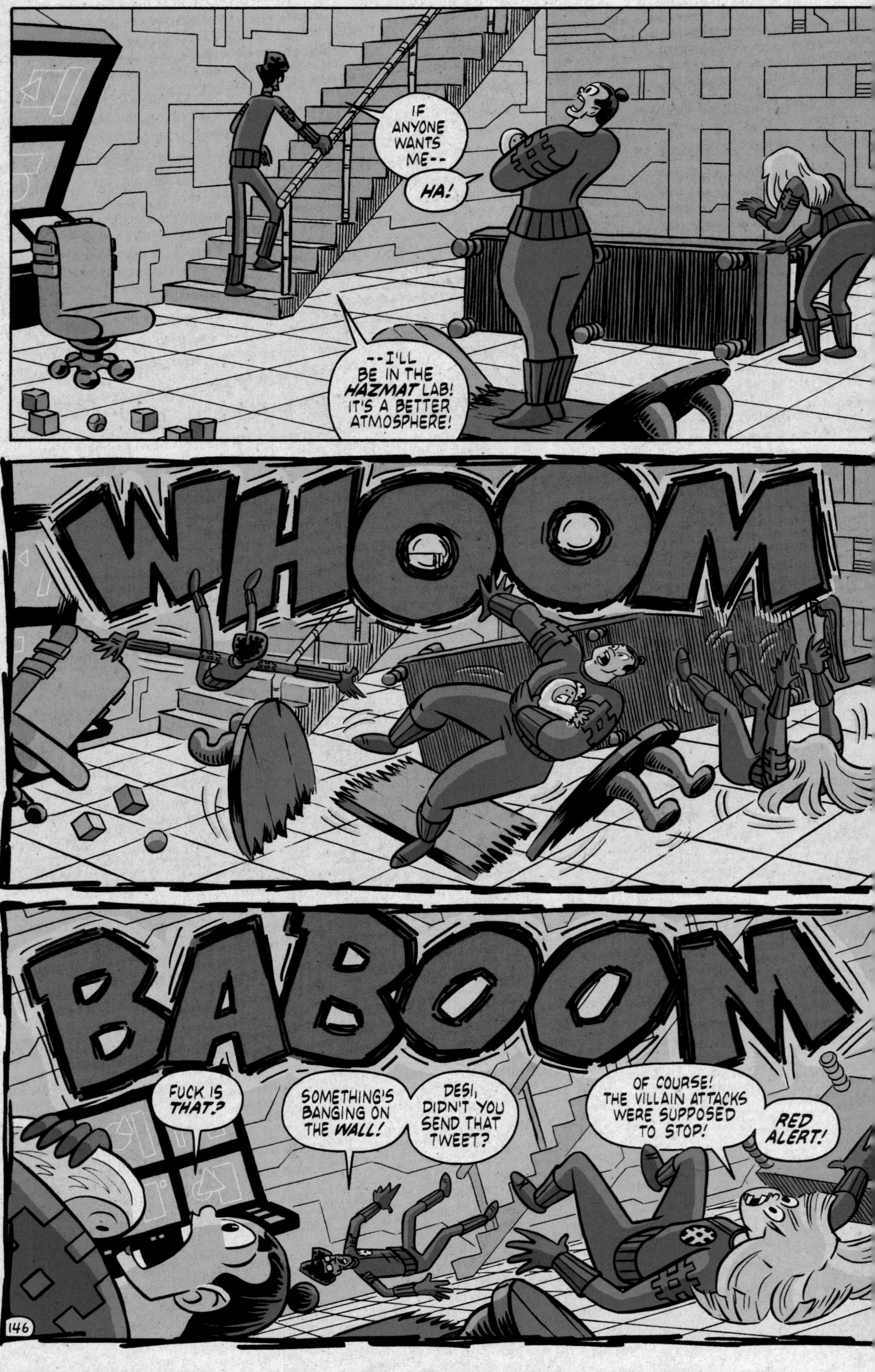
IF ANYONE WANTS ME--
HA!
--I'LL BE IN THE HAZMAT LAB! IT'S A BETTER ATMOSPHERE!
WHOOM
BABOOM
FUCK IS THAT?
SOMETHING'S BANGING ON THE WALL!
DESI, DIDN'T YOU SEND THAT TWEET?
OF COURSE! THE VILLAIN ATTACKS WERE SUPPOSED TO STOP!
RED ALERT!

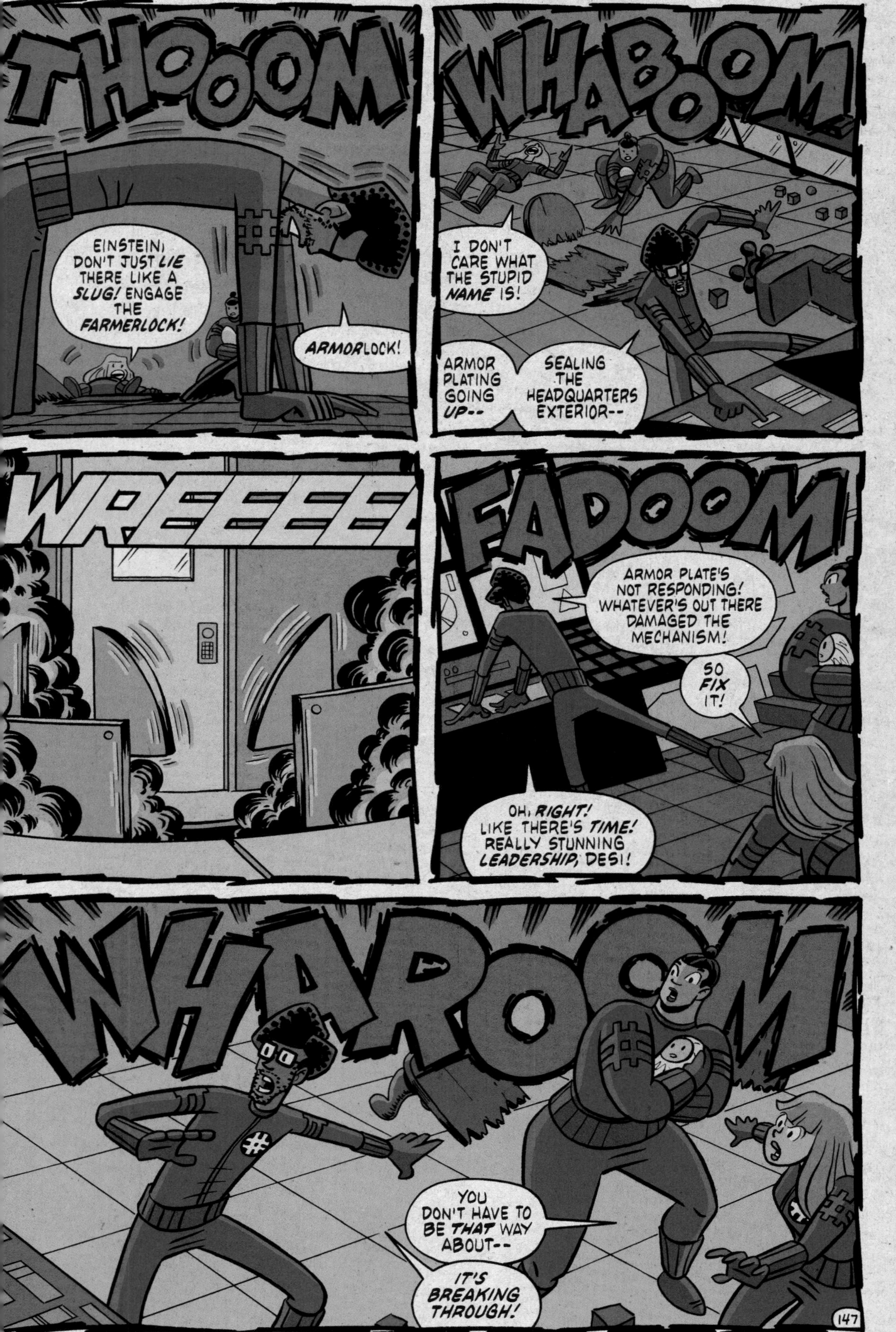
THOOOM
EINSTEIN, DON'T JUST LIE THERE LIKE A SLUG! ENGAGE THE FARMERLOCK!
ARMORLOCK!
WHABOOM
I DON'T CARE WHAT THE STUPID NAME IS!
ARMOR PLATING GOING UP--
SEALING THE HEADQUARTERS EXTERIOR--
WREEEEE
FADOOM
ARMOR PLATE'S NOT RESPONDING! WHATEVER'S OUT THERE DAMAGED THE MECHANISM!
SO FIX IT!
OH, RIGHT! LIKE THERE'S TIME! REALLY STUNNING LEADERSHIP, DESI!
WHAROOM
YOU DON'T HAVE TO BE THAT WAY ABOUT--
IT'S BREAKING THROUGH!

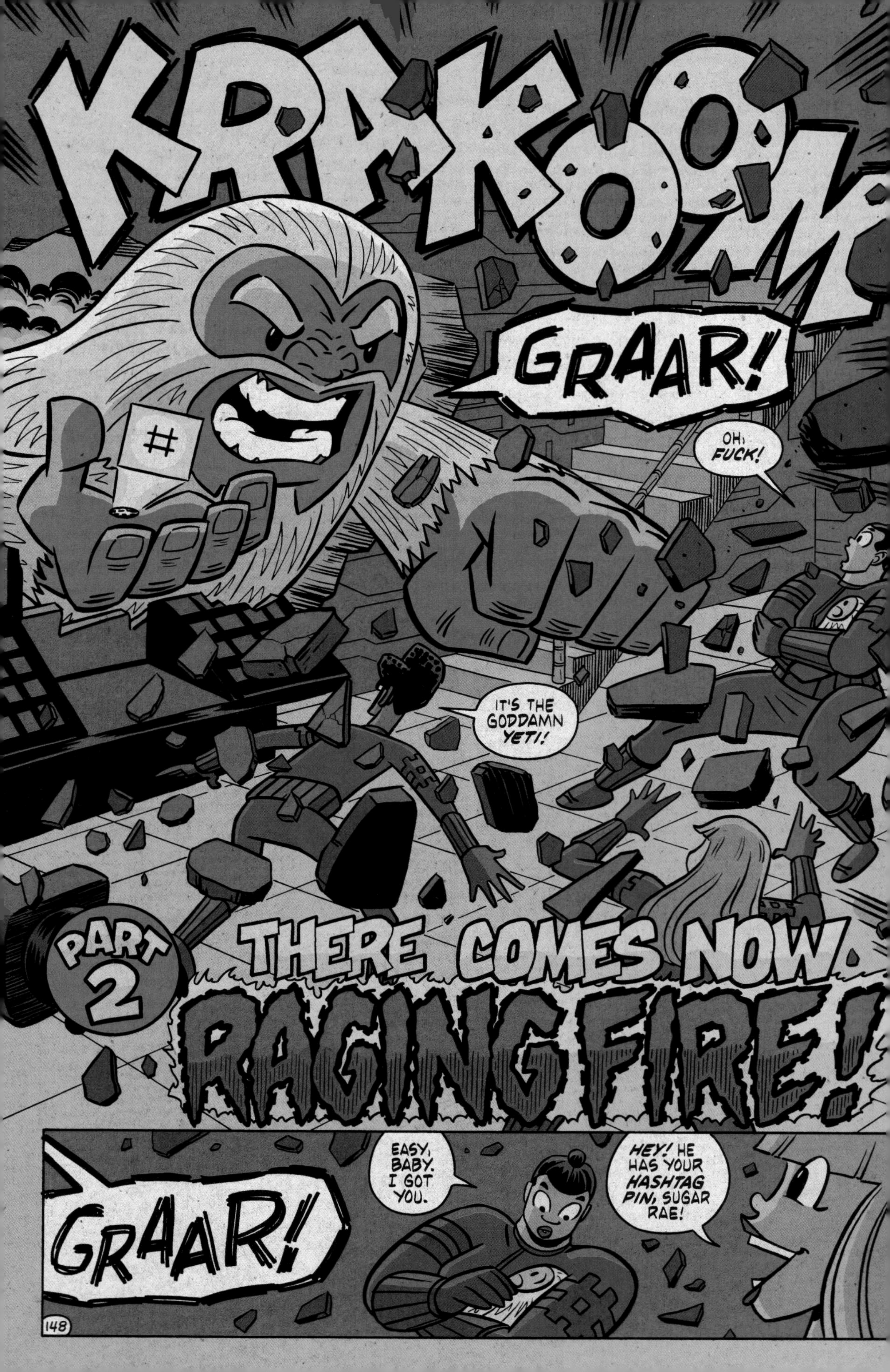
KRAKOOM
GRAAR!
OH, FUCK!
IT'S THE GODDAMN YETI!
PART 2 THERE COMES NOW RAGING FIRE!
GRAAR!
EASY, BABY. I GOT YOU.
HEY! HE HAS YOUR HASHTAG PIN, SUGAR RAE!

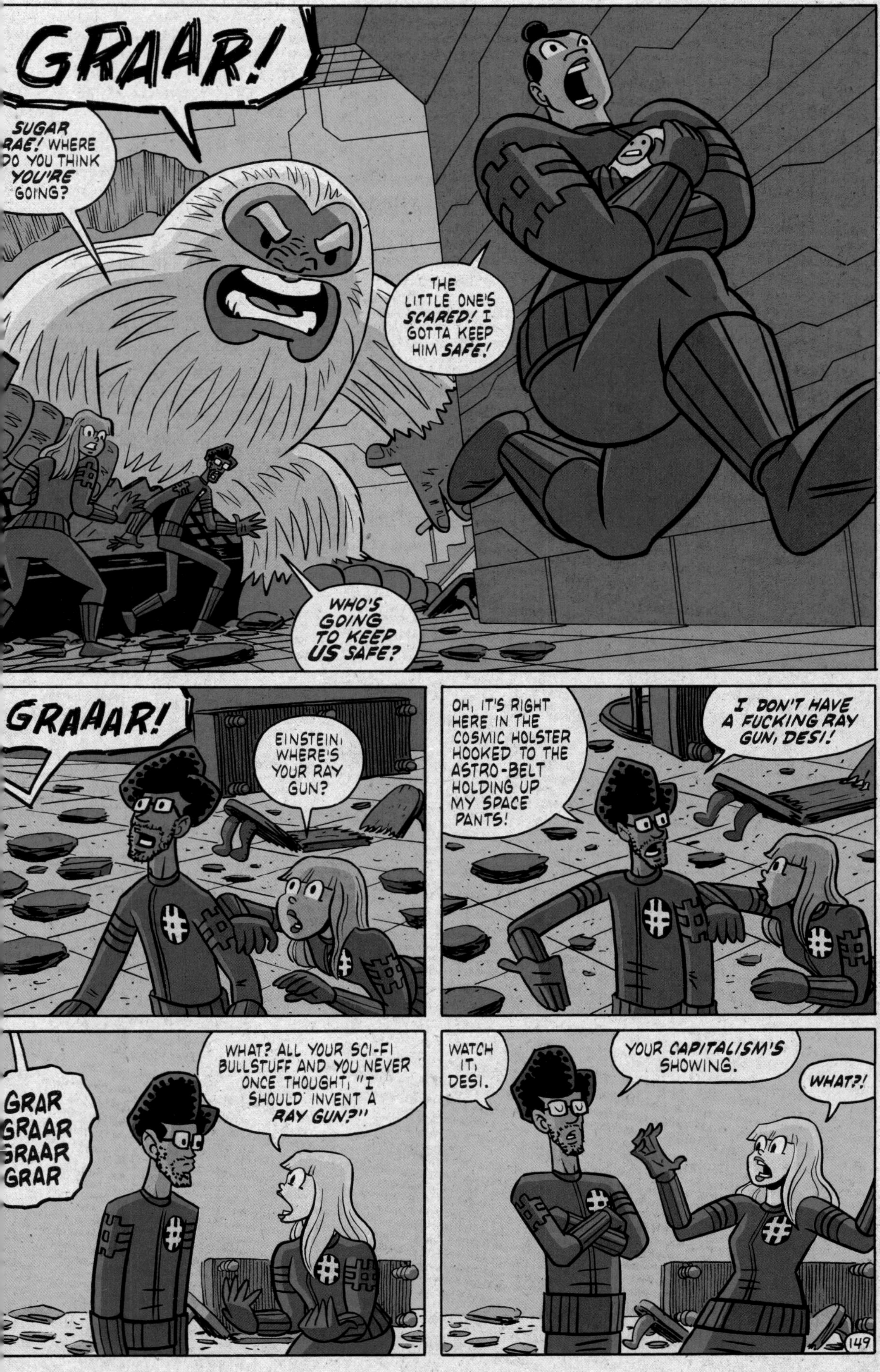
GRAAR!
SUGAR RAE! WHERE DO YOU THINK YOU'RE GOING?
THE LITTLE ONE'S SCARED! I GOTTA KEEP HIM SAFE!
WHO'S GOING TO KEEP US SAFE?
GRAAAR!
EINSTEIN, WHERE'S YOUR RAY GUN?
OH, IT'S RIGHT HERE IN THE COSMIC HOLSTER HOOKED TO THE ASTRO-BELT HOLDING UP MY SPACE PANTS!
I DON'T HAVE A FUCKING RAY GUN, DESI!
GRAR GRAAR GRAAR GRAR
WHAT? ALL YOUR SCI-FI BULLSTUFF AND YOU NEVER ONCE THOUGHT, "I SHOULD INVENT A RAY GUN?"
WATCH IT, DESI.
YOUR CAPITALISM'S SHOWING.
WHAT?!
149

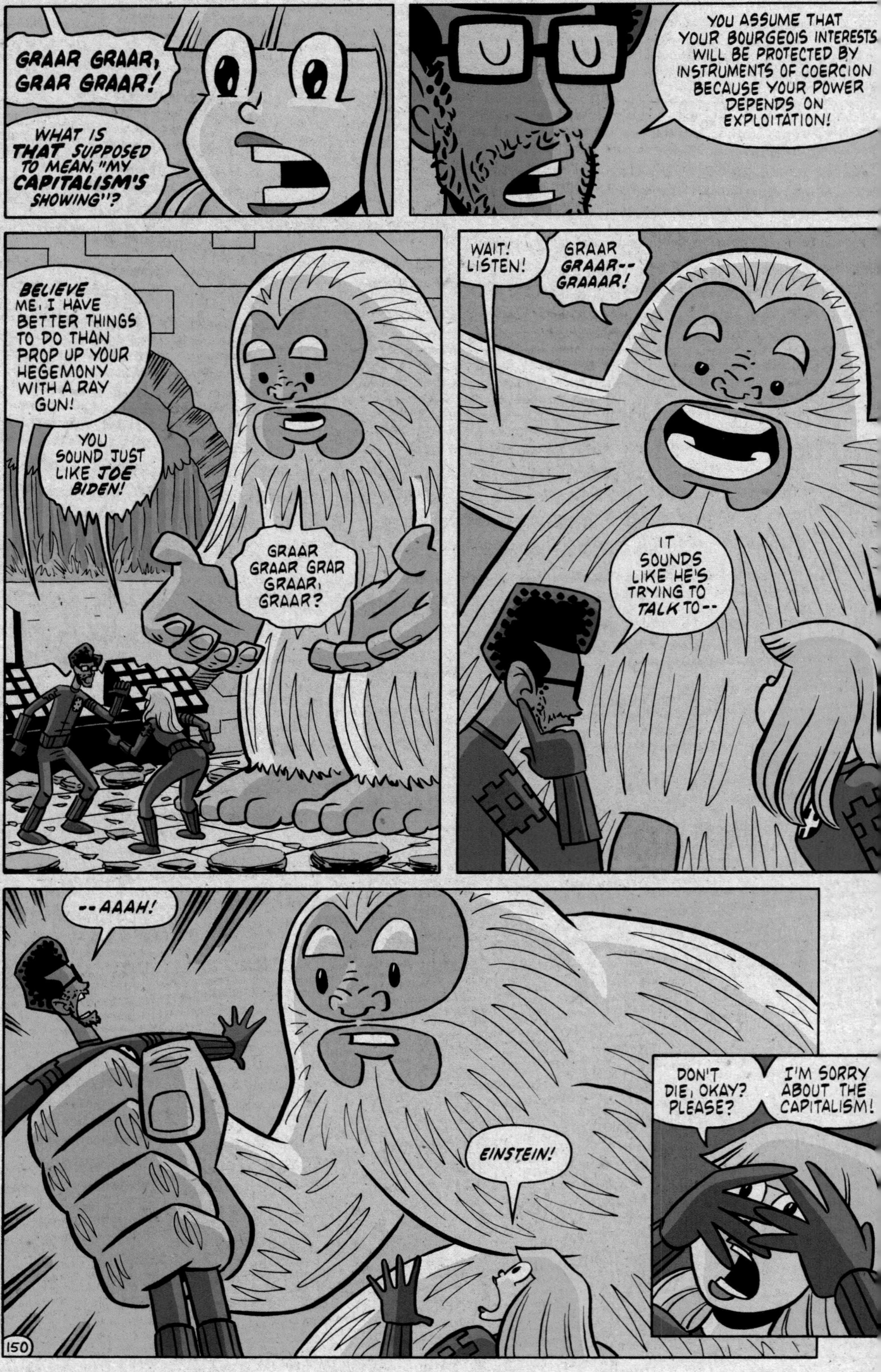
GRAAR GRAAR, GRAR GRAAR!
WHAT IS THAT SUPPOSED TO MEAN, "MY CAPITALISM'S SHOWING"?
YOU ASSUME THAT YOUR BOURGEOIS INTERESTS WILL BE PROTECTED BY INSTRUMENTS OF COERCION BECAUSE YOUR POWER DEPENDS ON EXPLOITATION!
BELIEVE ME, I HAVE BETTER THINGS TO DO THAN PROP UP YOUR HEGEMONY WITH A RAY GUN!
YOU SOUND JUST LIKE JOE BIDEN!
GRAAR GRAAR GRAR GRAAR, GRAAR?
WAIT! LISTEN!
GRAAR GRAAR-- GRAAAR!
IT SOUNDS LIKE HE'S TRYING TO TALK TO--
--AAAH!
EINSTEIN!
DON'T DIE, OKAY? PLEASE?
I'M SORRY ABOUT THE CAPITALISM!

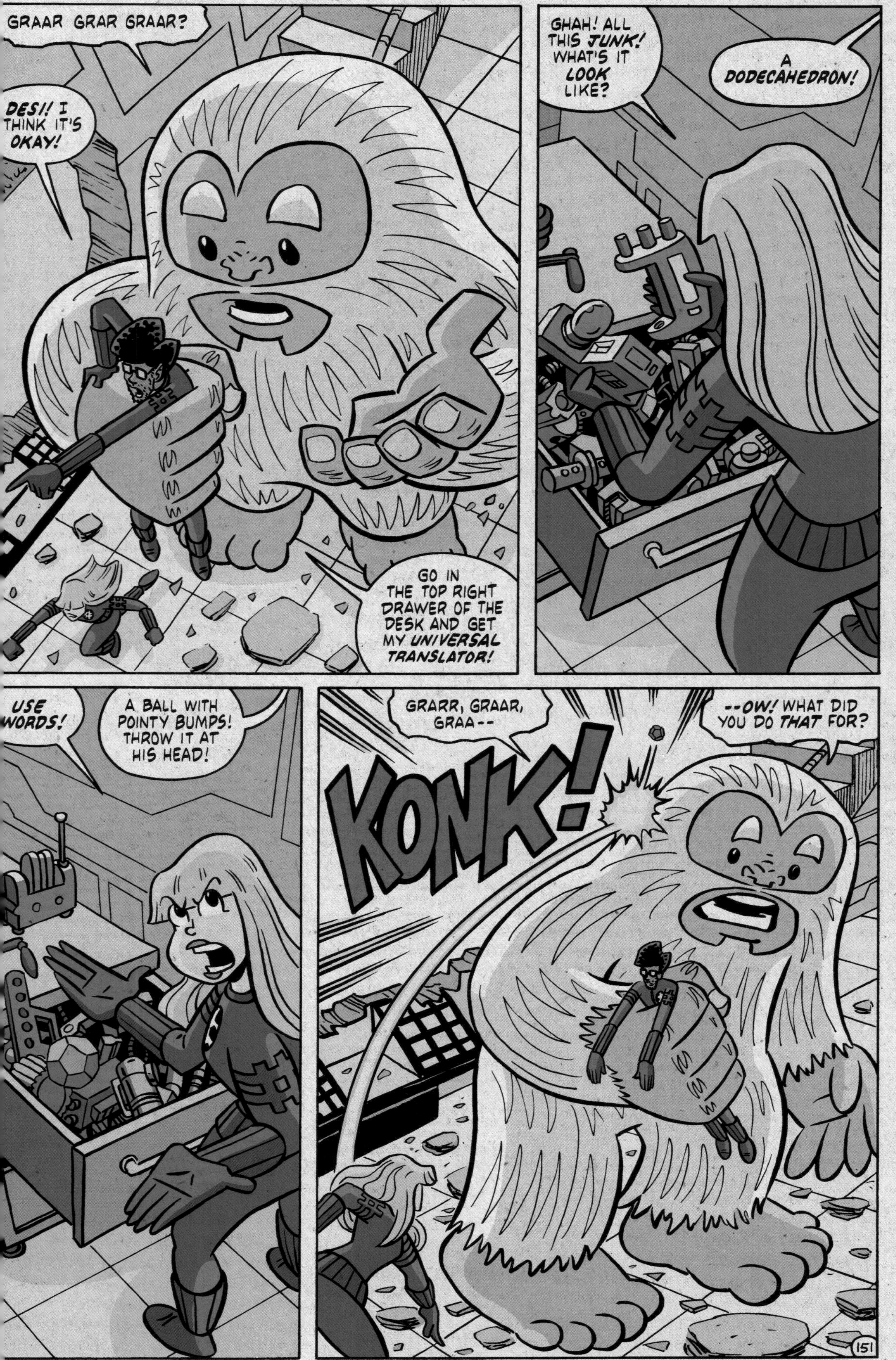
GRAAR GRAR GRAAR?
DES!! I THINK IT'S OKAY!
GO IN THE TOP RIGHT DRAWER OF THE DESK AND GET MY UNIVERSAL TRANSLATOR!
GHAH! ALL THIS JUNK! WHAT'S IT LOOK LIKE?
A DODECAHEDRON!
USE WORDS!
A BALL WITH POINTY BUMPS! THROW IT AT HIS HEAD!
GRARR, GRAAR, GRAA--
KONK!
--OW! WHAT DID YOU DO THAT FOR?

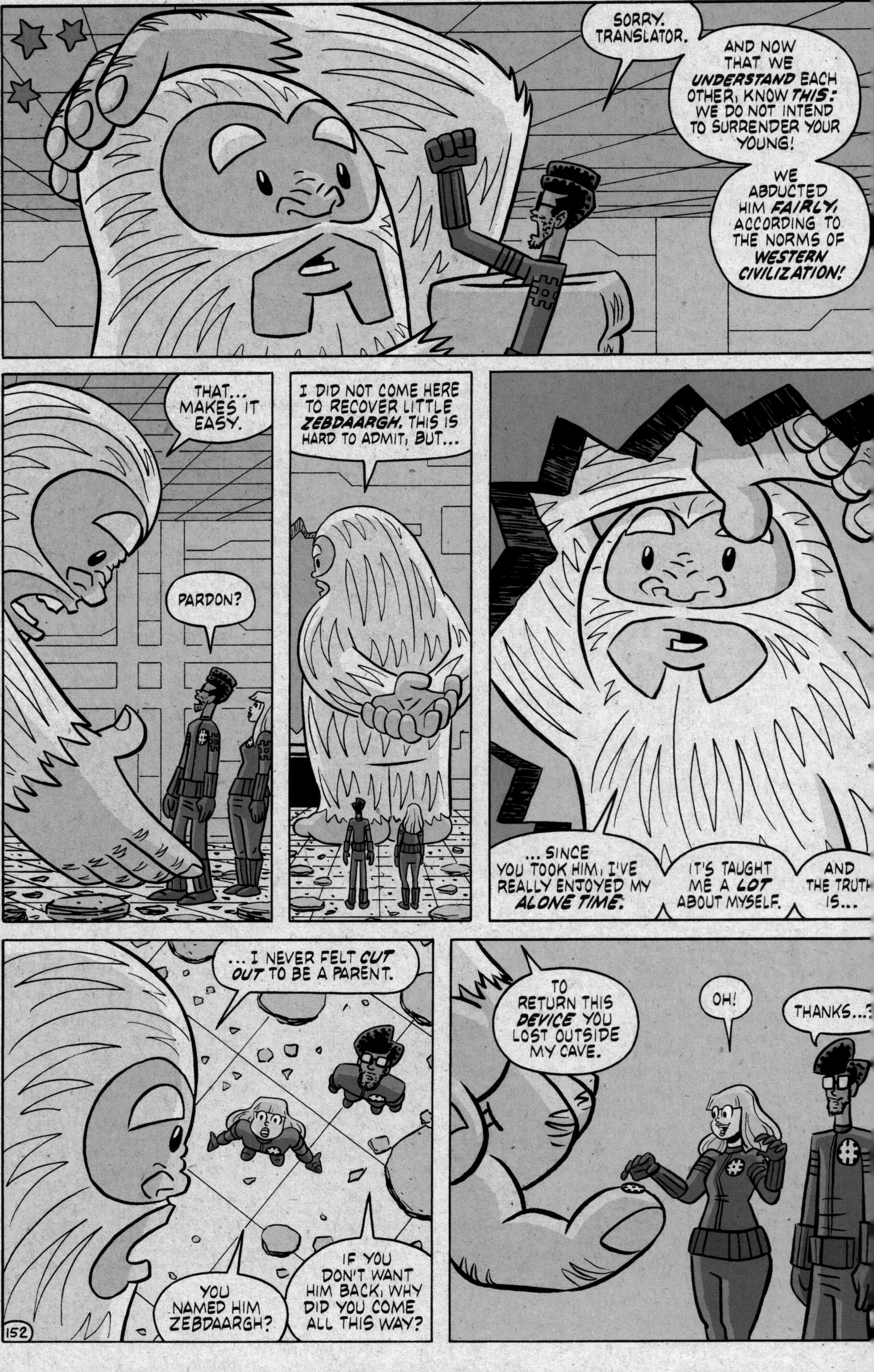
SORRY. TRANSLATOR.
AND NOW THAT WE UNDERSTAND EACH OTHER, KNOW THIS: WE DO NOT INTEND TO SURRENDER YOUR YOUNG!
WE ABDUCTED HIM FAIRLY, ACCORDING TO THE NORMS OF WESTERN CIVILIZATION!
THAT... MAKES IT EASY.
PARDON?
I DID NOT COME HERE TO RECOVER LITTLE ZEBDAARGH. THIS IS HARD TO ADMIT, BUT...
...SINCE YOU TOOK HIM, I'VE REALLY ENJOYED MY ALONE TIME.
IT'S TAUGHT ME A LOT ABOUT MYSELF.
AND THE TRUTH IS...
...I NEVER FELT CUT OUT TO BE A PARENT.
YOU NAMED HIM ZEBDAARGH?
IF YOU DON'T WANT HIM BACK, WHY DID YOU COME ALL THIS WAY?
TO RETURN THIS DEVICE YOU LOST OUTSIDE MY CAVE.
OH!
THANKS...?

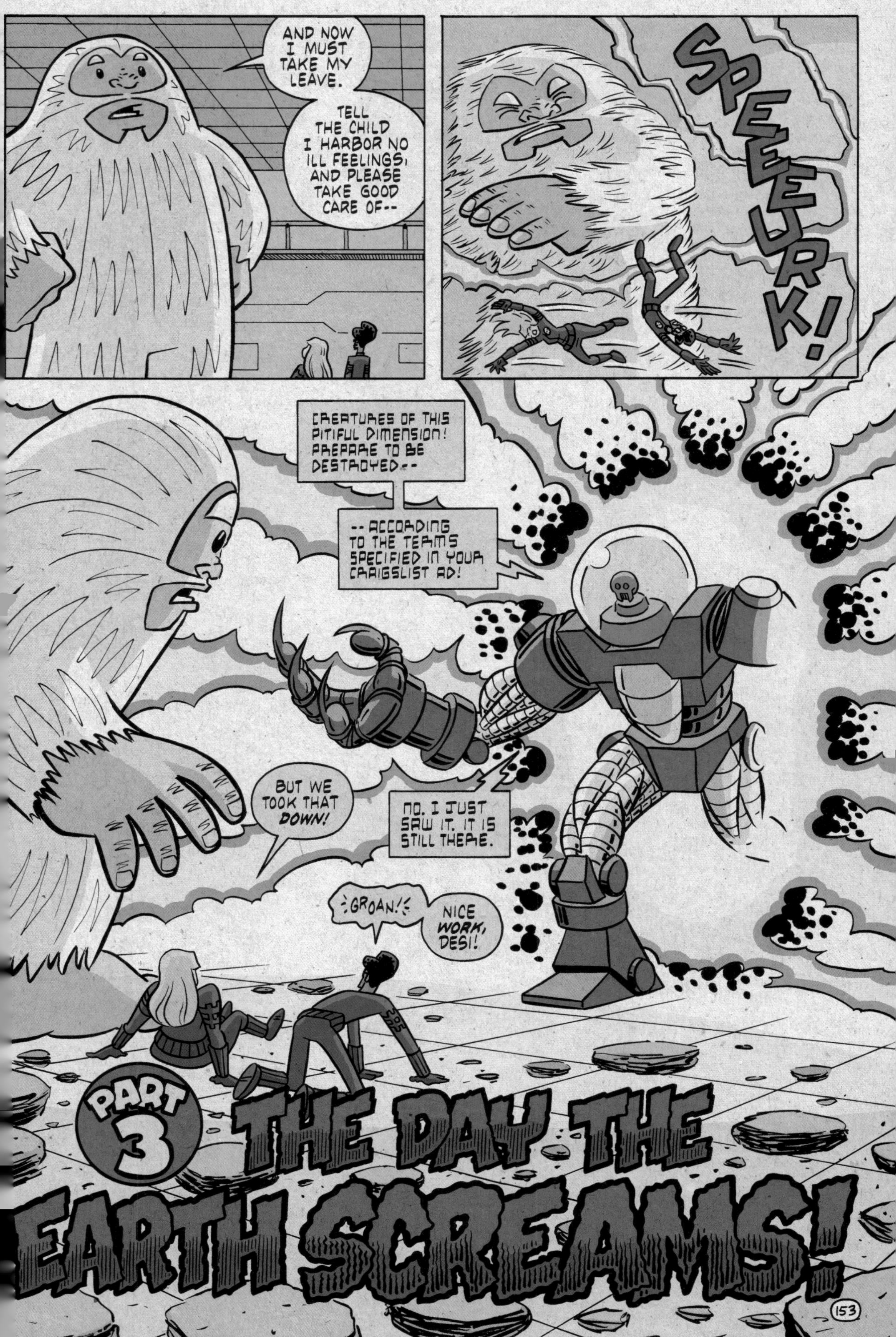
AND NOW I MUST TAKE MY LEAVE.
TELL THE CHILD I HARBOR NO ILL FEELINGS, AND PLEASE TAKE GOOD CARE OF--
SPEEEURK!
CREATURES OF THIS PITIFUL DIMENSION! PREPARE TO BE DESTROYED--
--ACCORDING TO THE TERMS SPECIFIED IN YOUR CRAIGSLIST AD!
BUT WE TOOK THAT DOWN!
NO. I JUST SAW IT. IT IS STILL THERE.
GROAN!
NICE WORK, DESI!
PART 3
THE DAY THE EARTH SCREAMS!

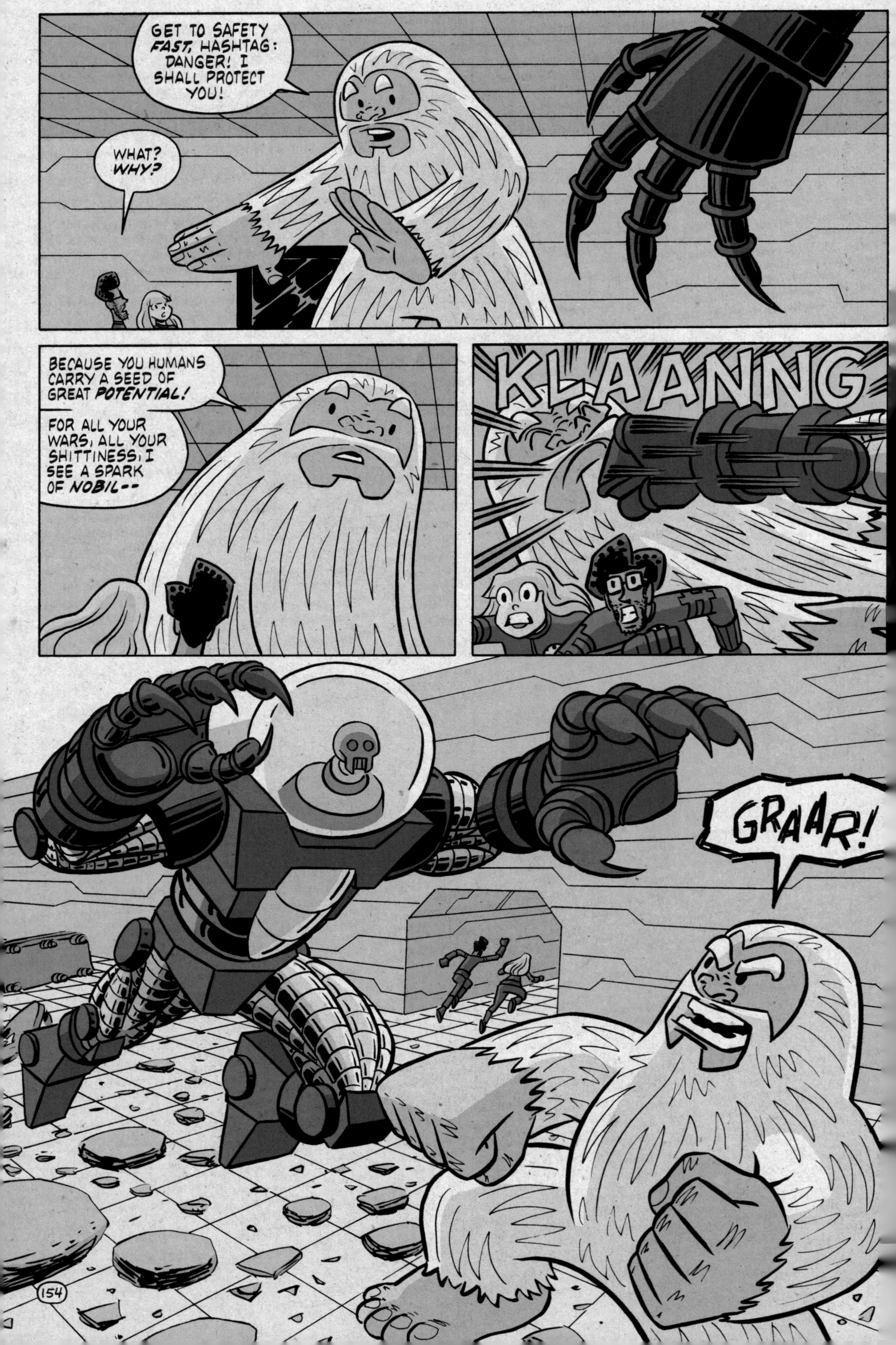
GET TO SAFETY FAST, HASHTAG: DANGER! I SHALL PROTECT YOU!
WHAT? WHY?
BECAUSE YOU HUMANS CARRY A SEED OF GREAT POTENTIAL!
FOR ALL YOUR WARS, ALL YOUR SHITTINESS, I SEE A SPARK OF NOBIL--
KLAANNG
GRAAR!

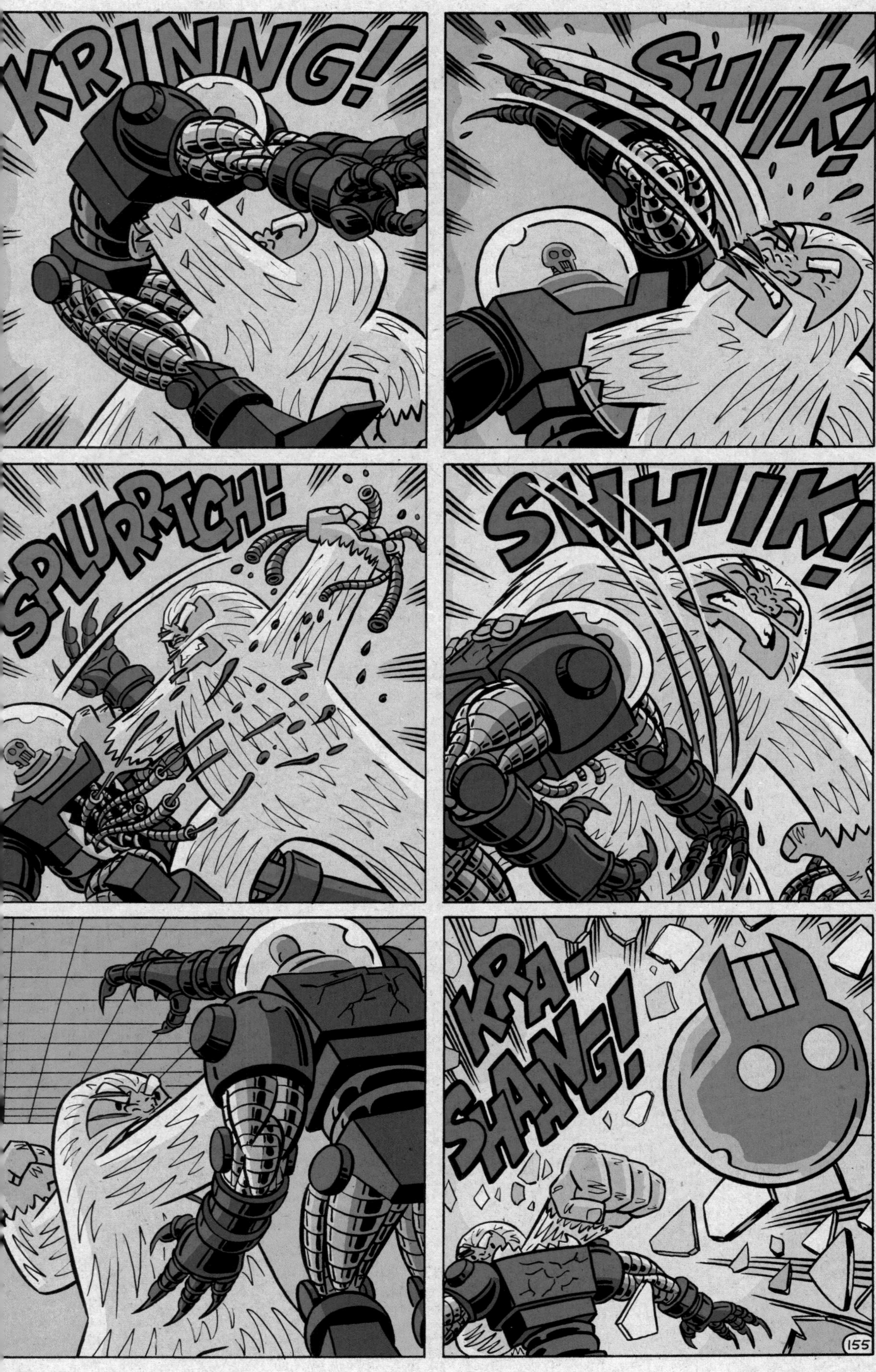
KRINNG!
SHIK!
SPLURRTCH!
SHHIIK!
KRA-SHANG!

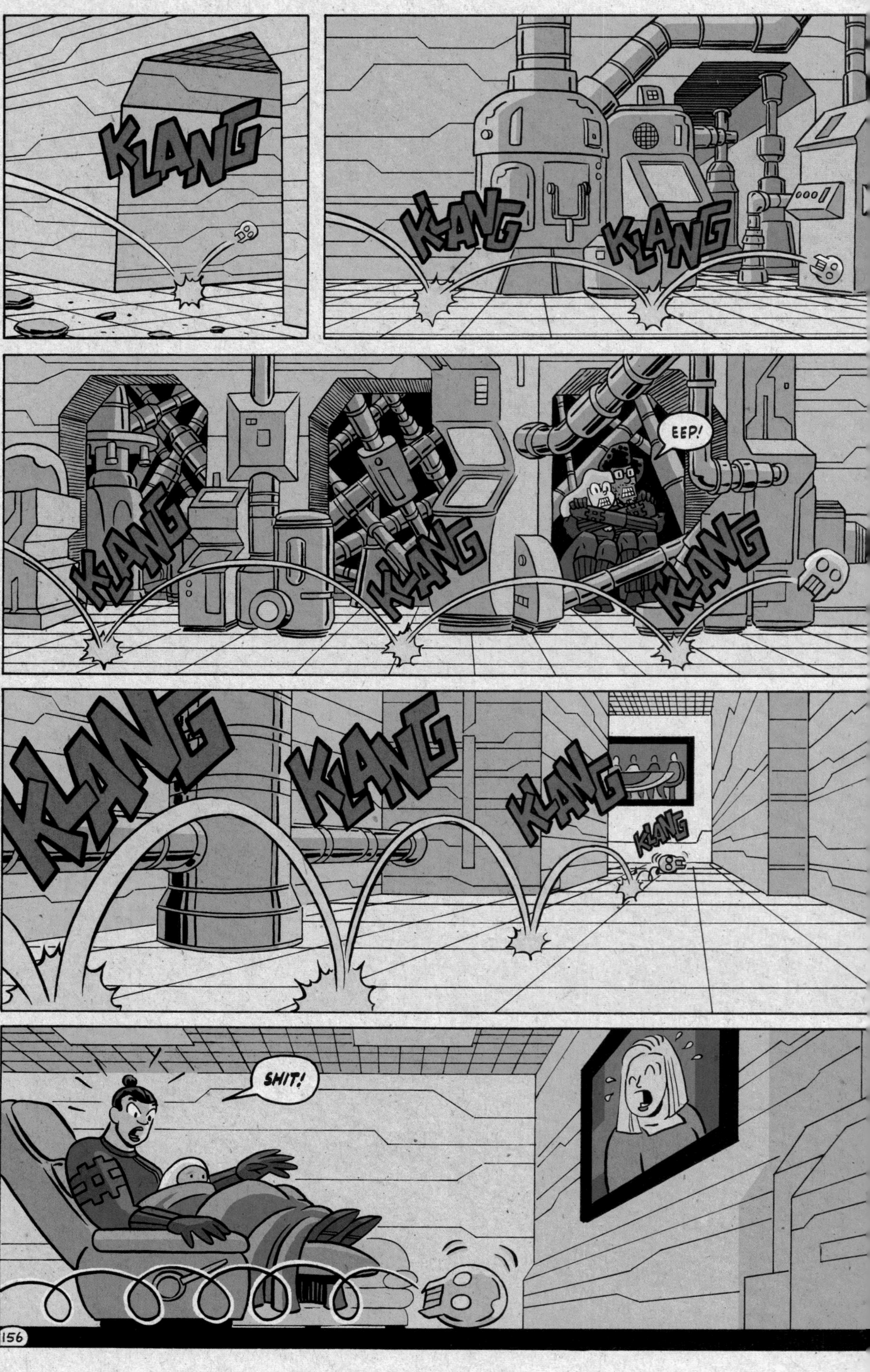
KLANG
KLANG
KLANG
KLANG
KLANG
EEP!
KLANG
KLANG
KLANG
KANG
KLANG
KLANG
SHIT!

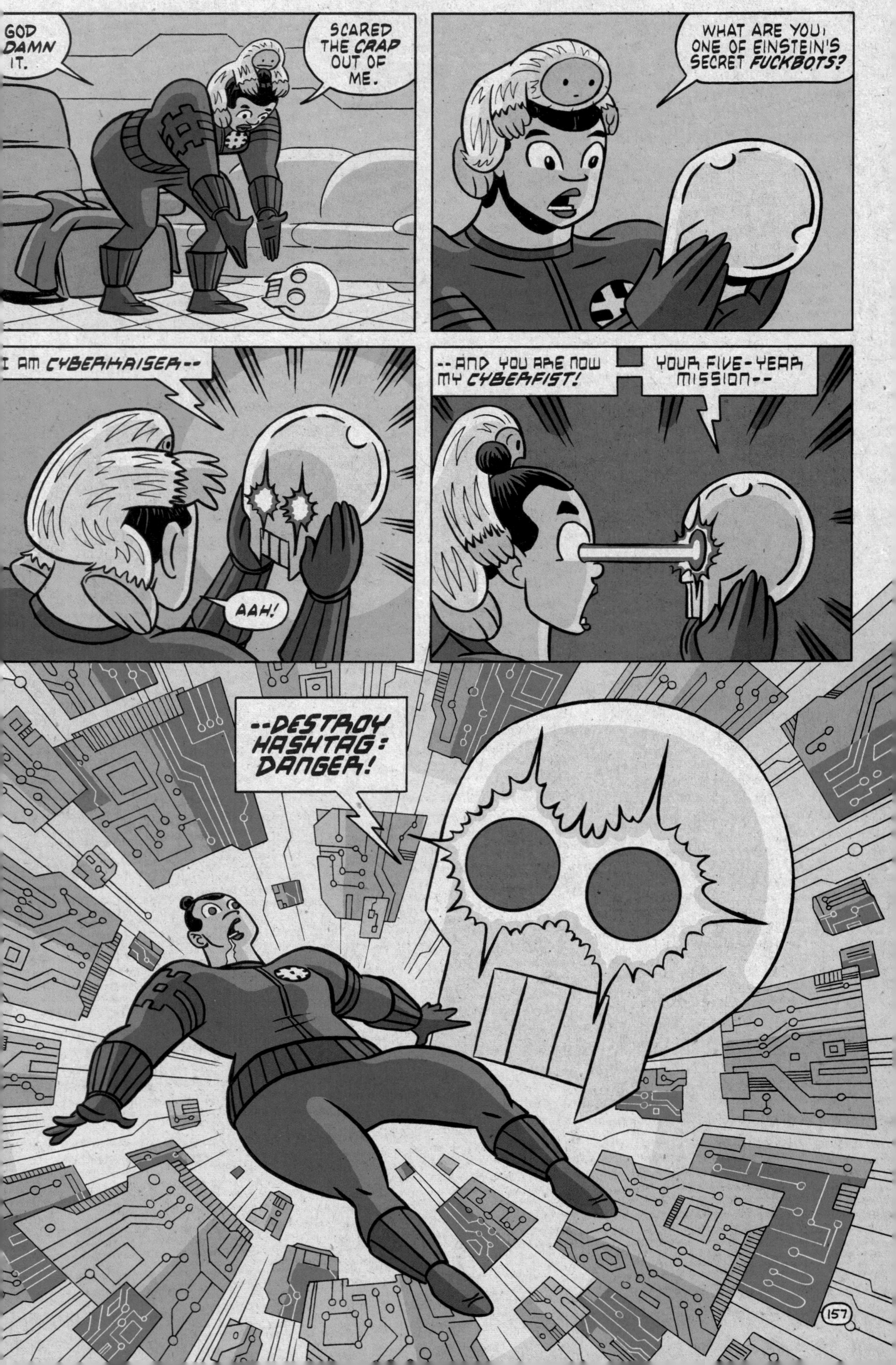
GOD DAMN IT.
SCARED THE CRAP OUT OF ME.
WHAT ARE YOU, ONE OF EINSTEIN'S SECRET FUCKBOTS?
I AM CYBERKAISER--
AAH!
--AND YOU ARE NOW MY CYBERFIST!
YOUR FIVE-YEAR MISSION--
--DESTROY HASHTAG: DANGER!

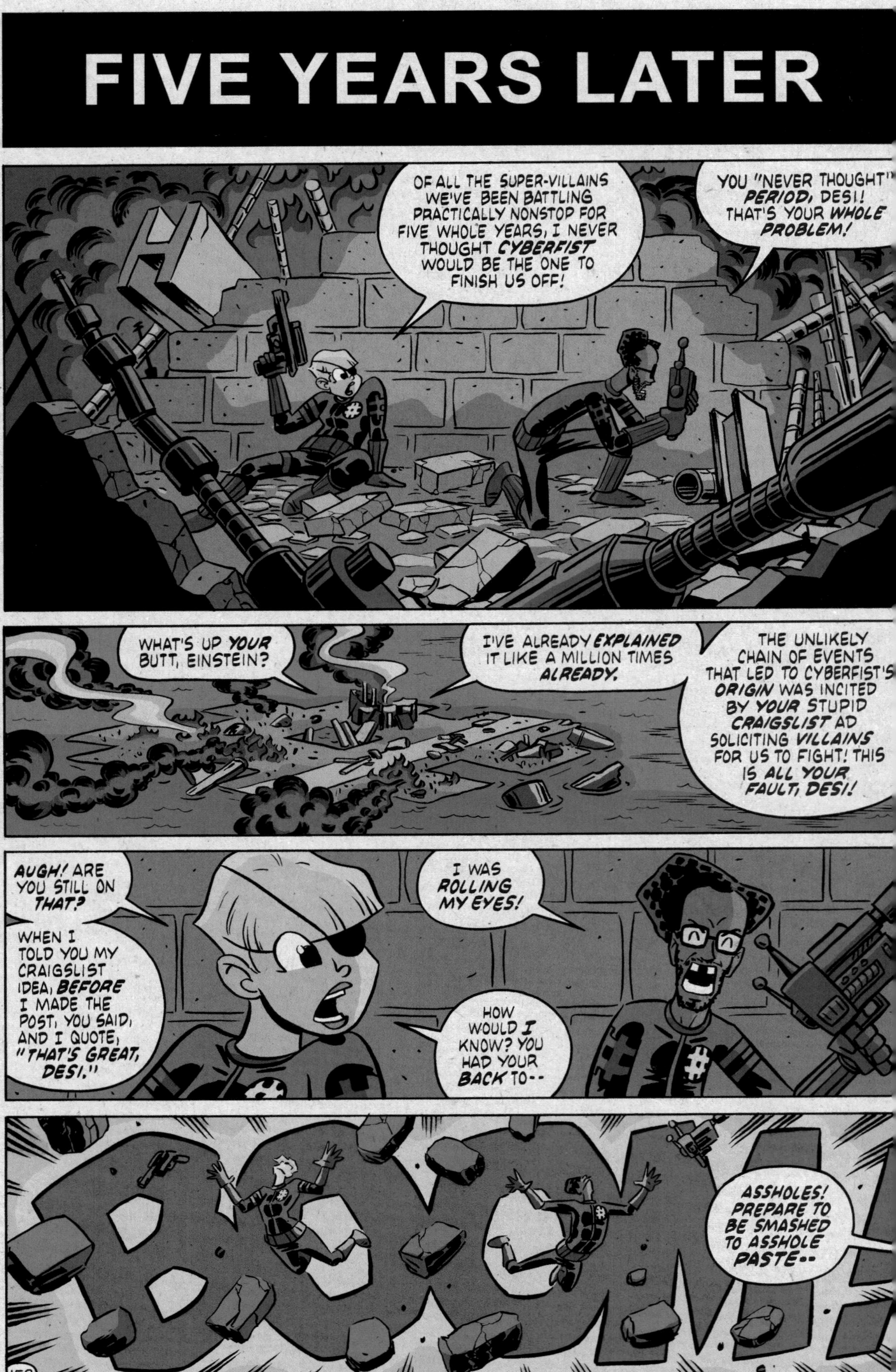
FIVE YEARS LATER
OF ALL THE SUPER-VILLAINS WE'VE BEEN BATTLING PRACTICALLY NONSTOP FOR FIVE WHOLE YEARS, I NEVER THOUGHT CYBERFIST WOULD BE THE ONE TO FINISH US OFF!
YOU "NEVER THOUGHT" PERIOD, DESI! THAT'S YOUR WHOLE PROBLEM!
WHAT'S UP YOUR BUTT, EINSTEIN?
I'VE ALREADY EXPLAINED IT LIKE A MILLION TIMES ALREADY.
THE UNLIKELY CHAIN OF EVENTS THAT LED TO CYBERFIST'S ORIGIN WAS INCITED BY YOUR STUPID CRAIGSLIST AD SOLICITING VILLAINS FOR US TO FIGHT! THIS IS ALL YOUR FAULT, DESI!
AUGH! ARE YOU STILL ON THAT?
WHEN I TOLD YOU MY CRAIGSLIST IDEA, BEFORE I MADE THE POST, YOU SAID, AND I QUOTE, "THAT'S GREAT, DESI."
I WAS ROLLING MY EYES!
HOW WOULD I KNOW? YOU HAD YOUR BACK TO--
BOOM!
ASSHOLES! PREPARE TO BE SMASHED TO ASSHOLE PASTE--

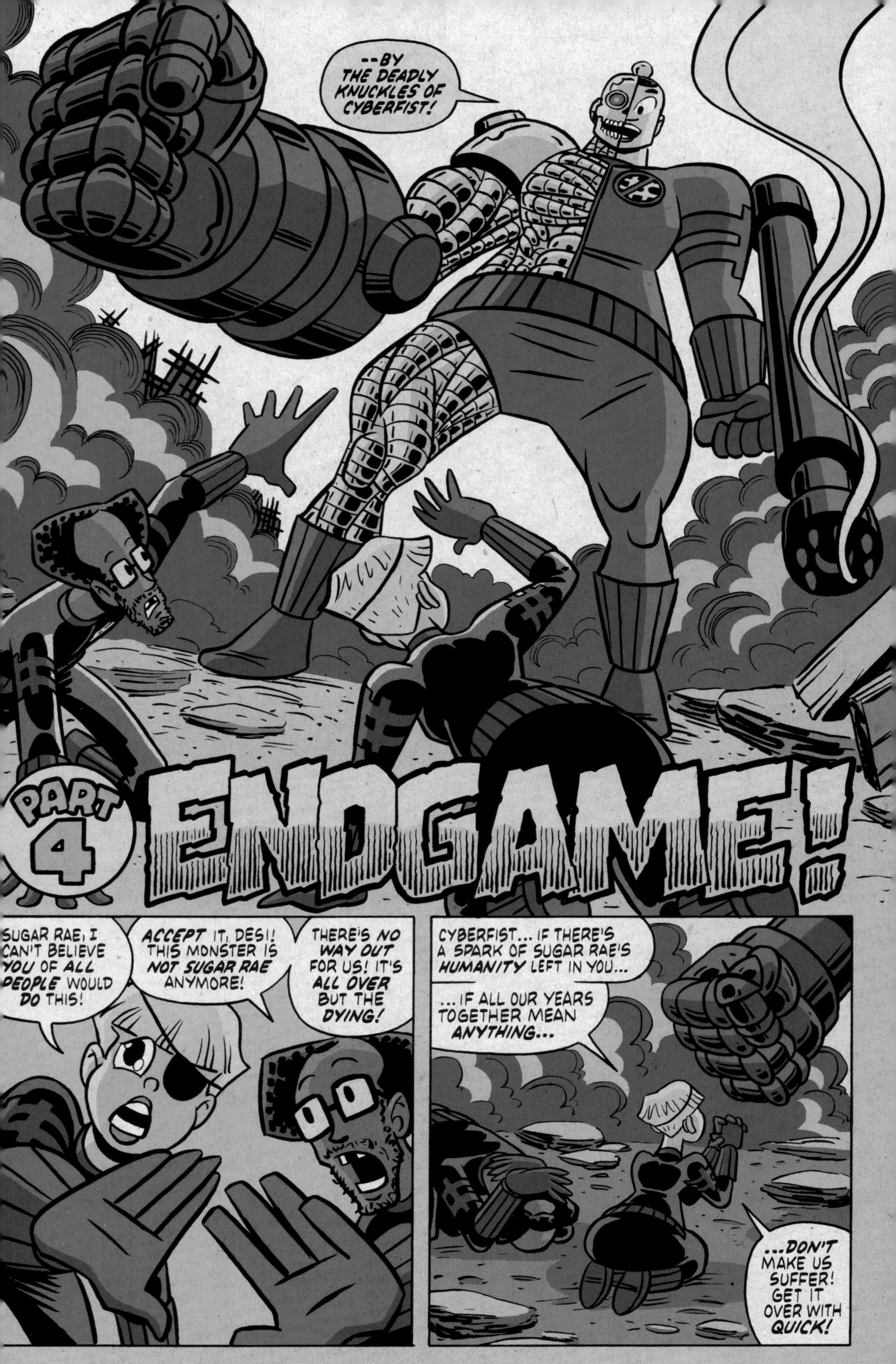
--BY THE DEADLY KNUCKLES OF CYBERFIST!
PART 4
ENDGAME!
SUGAR RAE, I CAN'T BELIEVE YOU OF ALL PEOPLE WOULD DO THIS!
ACCEPT IT, DESI! THIS MONSTER IS NOT SUGAR RAE ANYMORE!
THERE'S NO WAY OUT FOR US! IT'S ALL OVER BUT THE DYING!
CYBERFIST... IF THERE'S A SPARK OF SUGAR RAE'S HUMANITY LEFT IN YOU...
...IF ALL OUR YEARS TOGETHER MEAN ANYTHING...
...DON'T MAKE US SUFFER! GET IT OVER WITH QUICK!

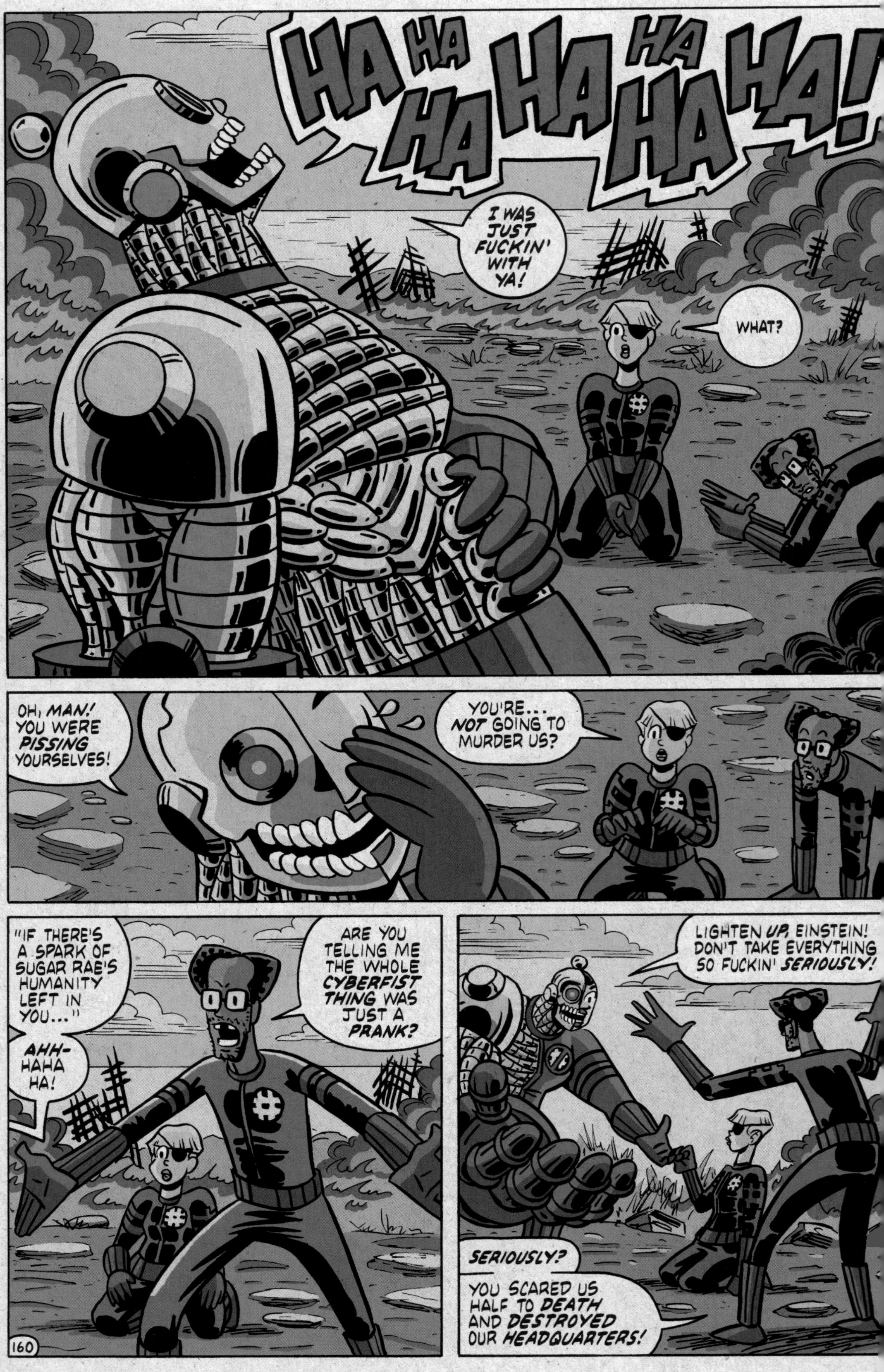
HA HA HA HA HA HA HA HA!
I WAS JUST FUCKIN' WITH YA!
WHAT?
OH, MAN! YOU WERE PISSING YOURSELVES!
YOU'RE... NOT GOING TO MURDER US?
"IF THERE'S A SPARK OF SUGAR RAE'S HUMANITY LEFT IN YOU..."
AHH-HAHA HA!
ARE YOU TELLING ME THE WHOLE CYBERFIST THING WAS JUST A PRANK?
LIGHTEN UP, EINSTEIN! DON'T TAKE EVERYTHING SO FUCKIN' SERIOUSLY!
SERIOUSLY?
YOU SCARED US HALF TO DEATH AND DESTROYED OUR HEADQUARTERS!

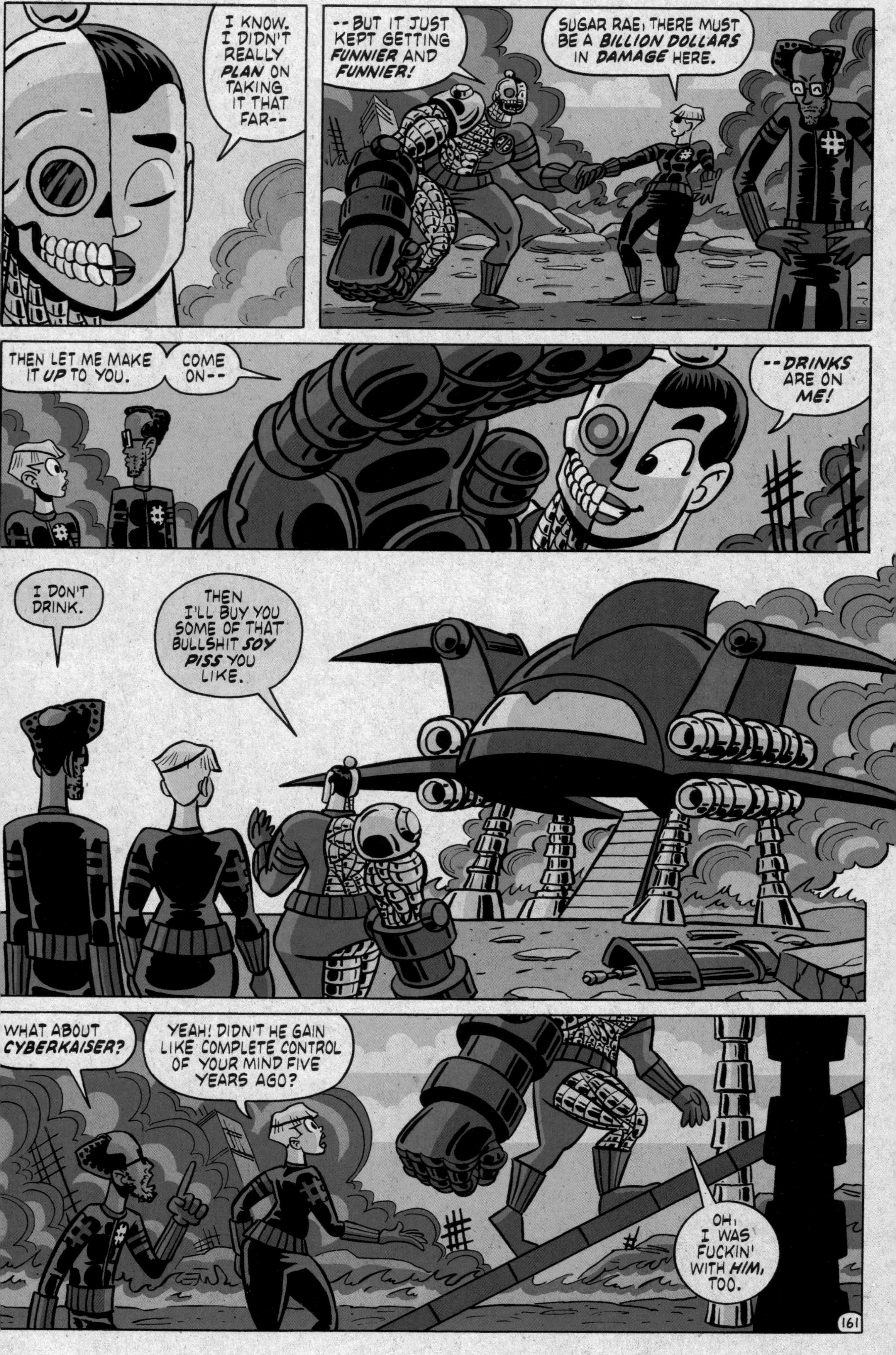

I KNOW. I DIDN'T REALLY PLAN ON TAKING IT THAT FAR--
--BUT IT JUST KEPT GETTING FUNNIER AND FUNNIER!
SUGAR RAE, THERE MUST BE A BILLION DOLLARS IN DAMAGE HERE.
THEN LET ME MAKE IT UP TO YOU.
COME ON--
--DRINKS ARE ON ME!
I DON'T DRINK.
THEN I'LL BUY YOU SOME OF THAT BULLSHIT SOY PISS YOU LIKE.
WHAT ABOUT CYBERKAISER?
YEAH! DIDN'T HE GAIN LIKE COMPLETE CONTROL OF YOUR MIND FIVE YEARS AGO?
OH, I WAS FUCKIN' WITH HIM, TOO.

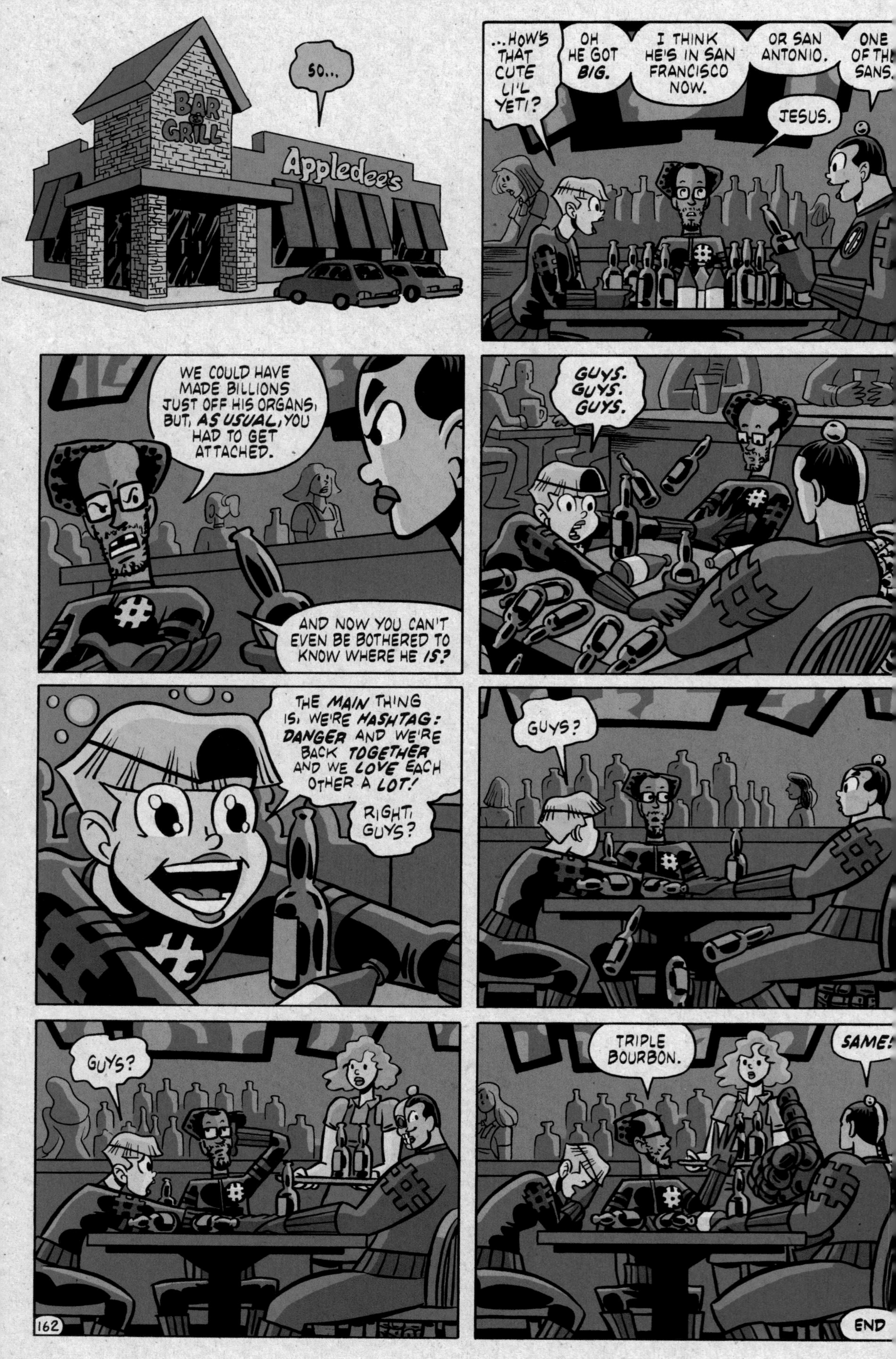
BAR & GRILL
Appledee's
SO...
...HOW'S THAT CUTE LI'L YETI?
OH HE GOT BIG.
I THINK HE'S IN SAN FRANCISCO NOW.
OR SAN ANTONIO.
ONE OF THE SANS.
JESUS.
WE COULD HAVE MADE BILLIONS JUST OFF HIS ORGANS, BUT, AS USUAL, YOU HAD TO GET ATTACHED.
AND NOW YOU CAN'T EVEN BE BOTHERED TO KNOW WHERE HE IS?
GUYS. GUYS. GUYS.
THE MAIN THING IS, WE'RE HASHTAG: DANGER AND WE'RE BACK TOGETHER AND WE LOVE EACH OTHER A LOT!
RIGHT, GUYS?
GUYS?
GUYS?
TRIPLE BOURBON.
SAME!
END

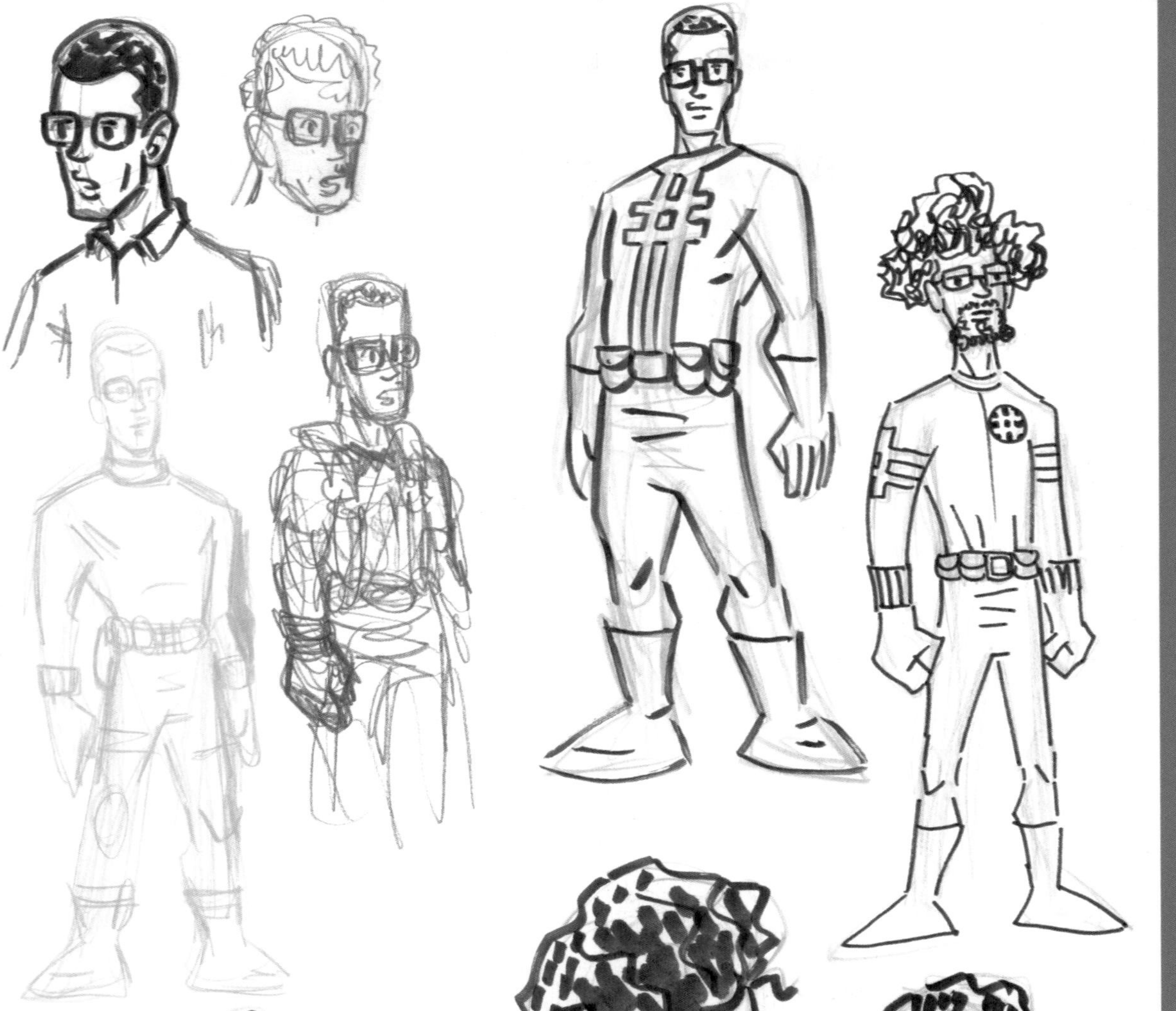

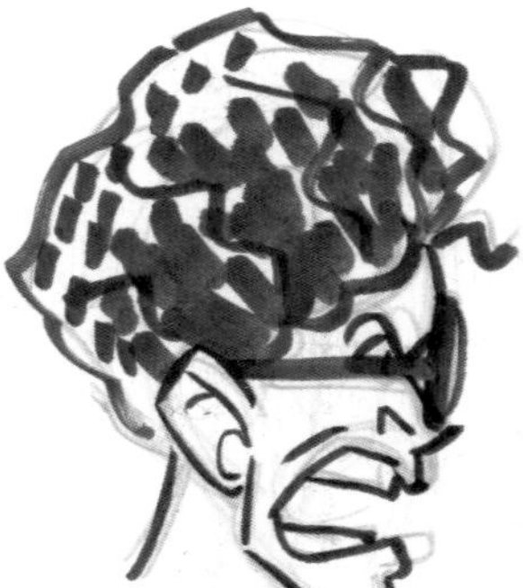

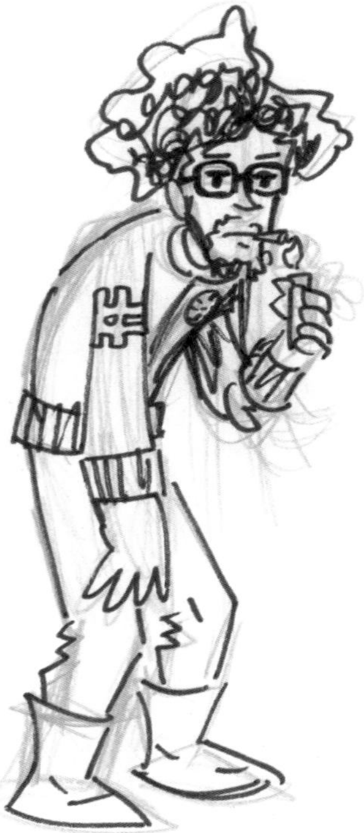

Einstein is the brains of the group. "Scientist. Introverted. Cautious. Thick glasses." I began with a more conservative, stuffy scientist approach. But talking to Tom made me realize I wasn't only "not there" yet, I was 100% backwards. Einstein is a lot more of a locked-in-the-lab, no-time-for-grooming kind of guy. Kind of like a comic book artist in perpetual deadline crunch who doesn't get out much and has forgotten how to be a person.

Einstein is in a perpetually surly mood. It wasn't until I gave him the facial scruff that I felt like he looked properly surly.

— Chris Giarrusso

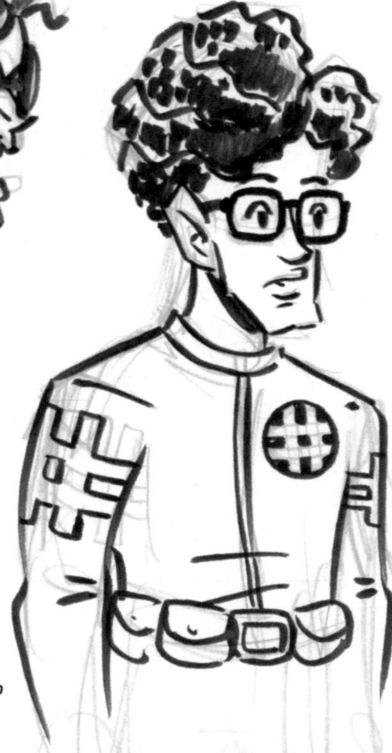

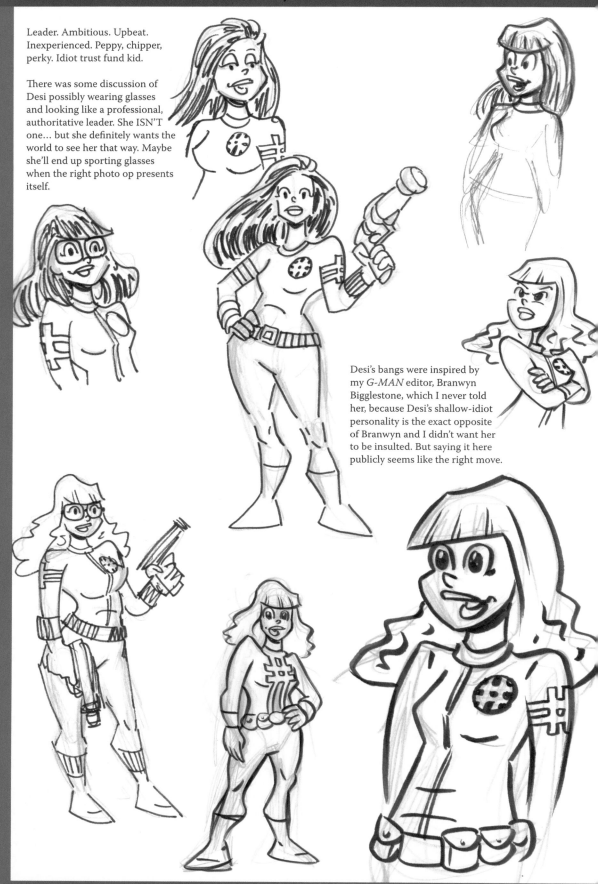

Leader. Ambitious. Upbeat. Inexperienced. Peppy, chipper, perky. Idiot trust fund kid.

There was some discussion of Desi possibly wearing glasses and looking like a professional, authoritative leader. She ISN'T one… but she definitely wants the world to see her that way. Maybe she'll end up sporting glasses when the right photo op presents itself.

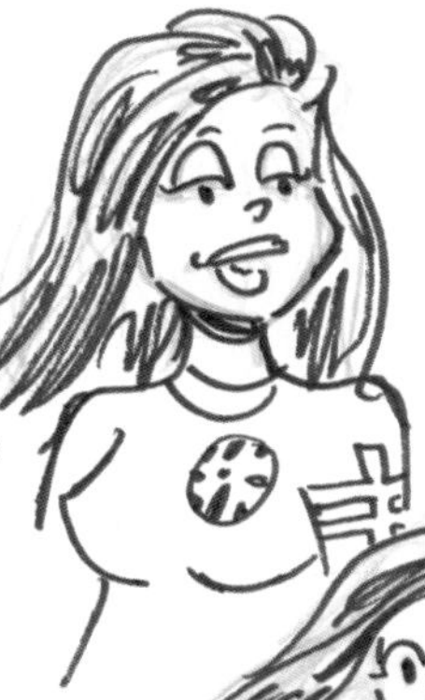

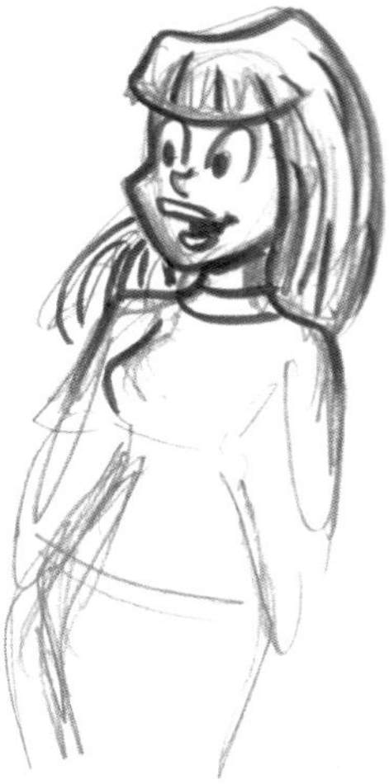

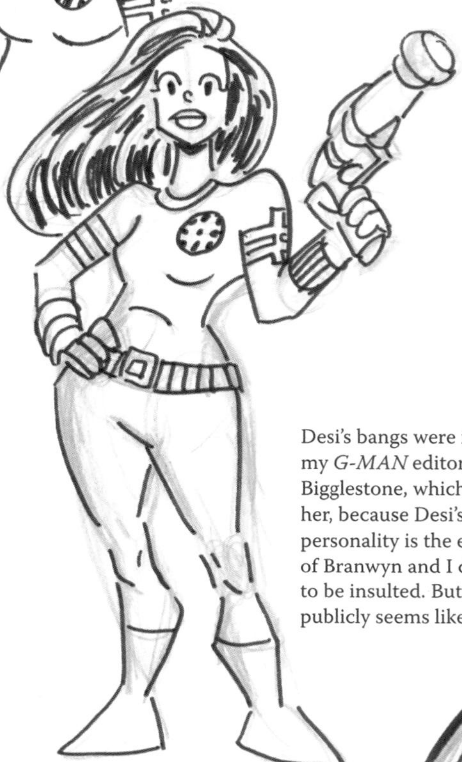

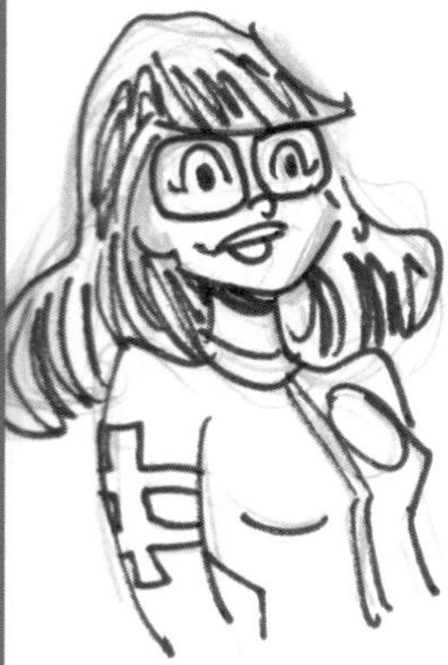

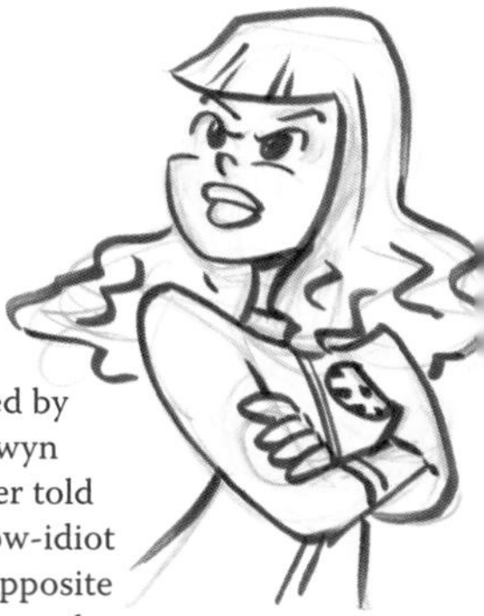

Desi's bangs were inspired by my *G-MAN* editor, Branwyn Bigglestone, which I never told her, because Desi's shallow-idiot personality is the exact opposite of Branwyn and I didn't want her to be insulted. But saying it here publicly seems like the right move.

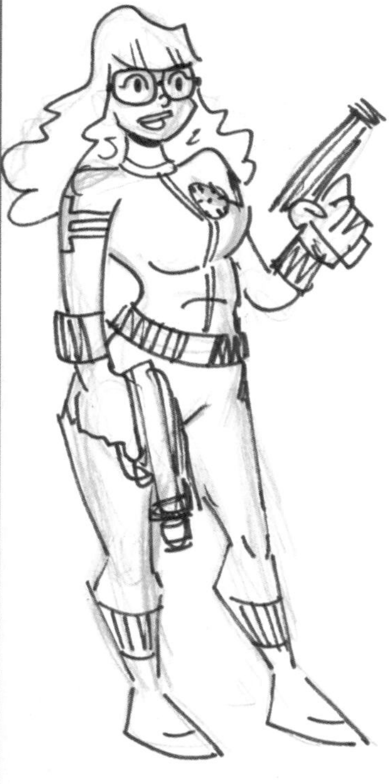

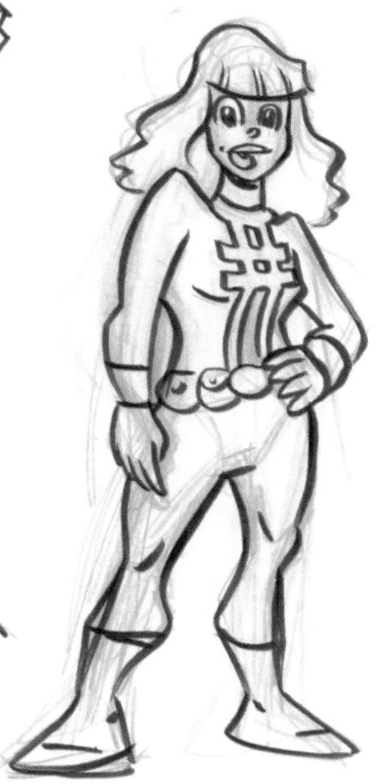

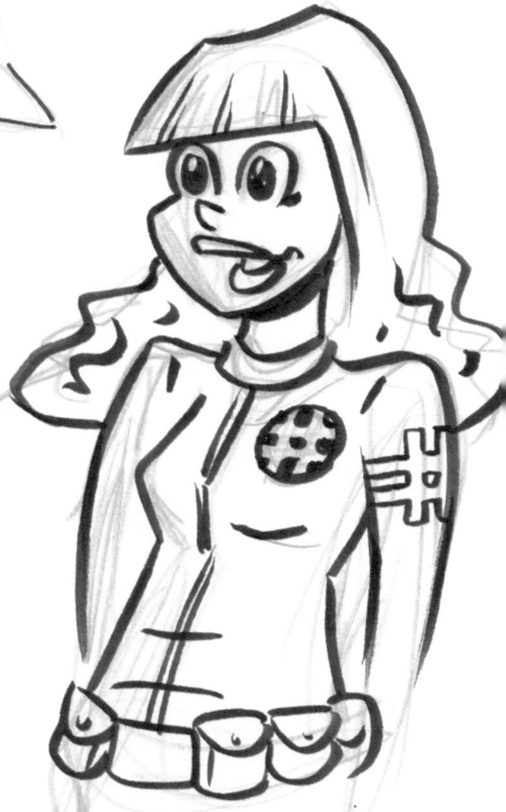

Sugar Rae Huang is the muscle. Stocky and tough, two moods: fun and angry.

My initial sketches for Sugar Rae were rather generic. Frank Cammuso suggested, "Sugar Rae should wear a top knot like Rhonda Rousey," which I liked right away.

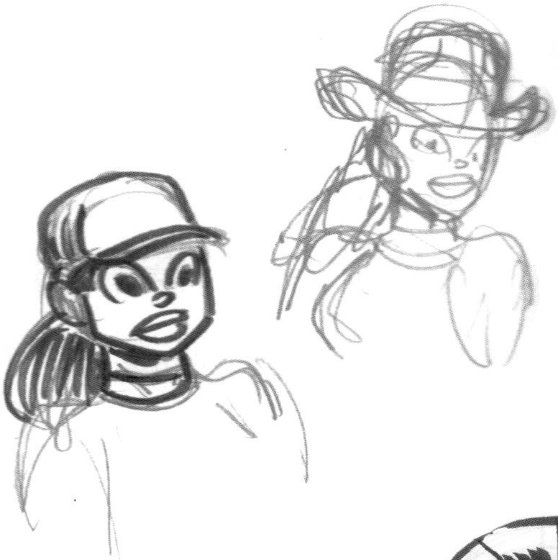

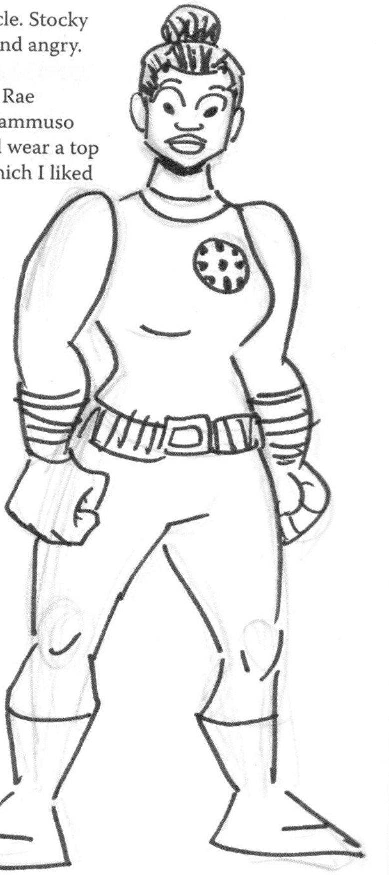

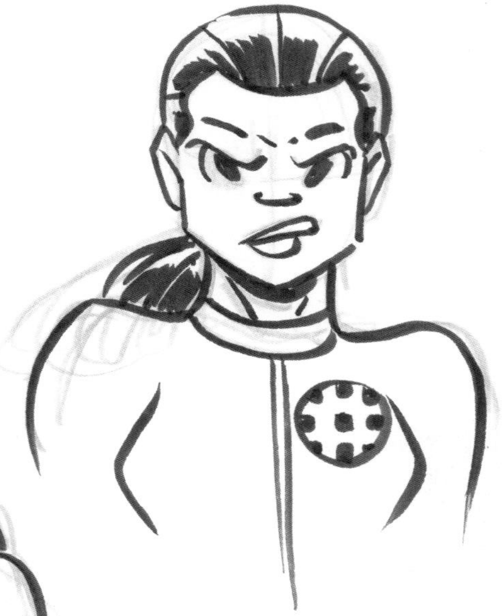

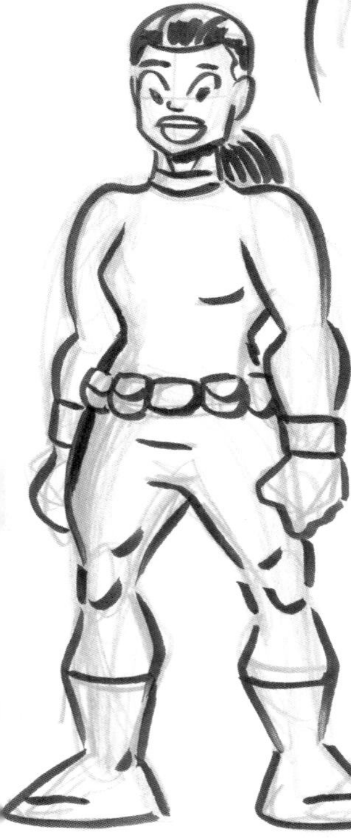

It's ridiculous to me these early sketches were my attempts at drawing "stocky and tough." Sugar Rae should look like she could beat any human or beast in a fight. Her physique came together once I started drawing story pages.

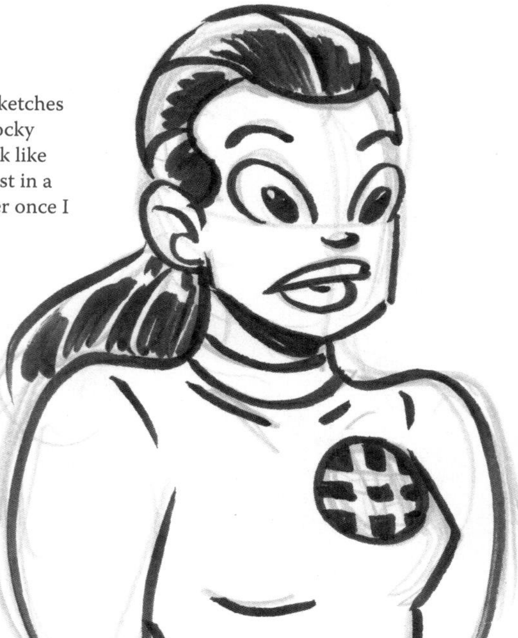

These early costume designs represent a variety of concepts for incorporating the hashtag symbol into the team's jumpsuits. One of the logo concepts (top-right) was kind of a like a hashtag, but also an "H". Because "hashtag" starts with "H"!!! Get it??? VERY CREATIVE.

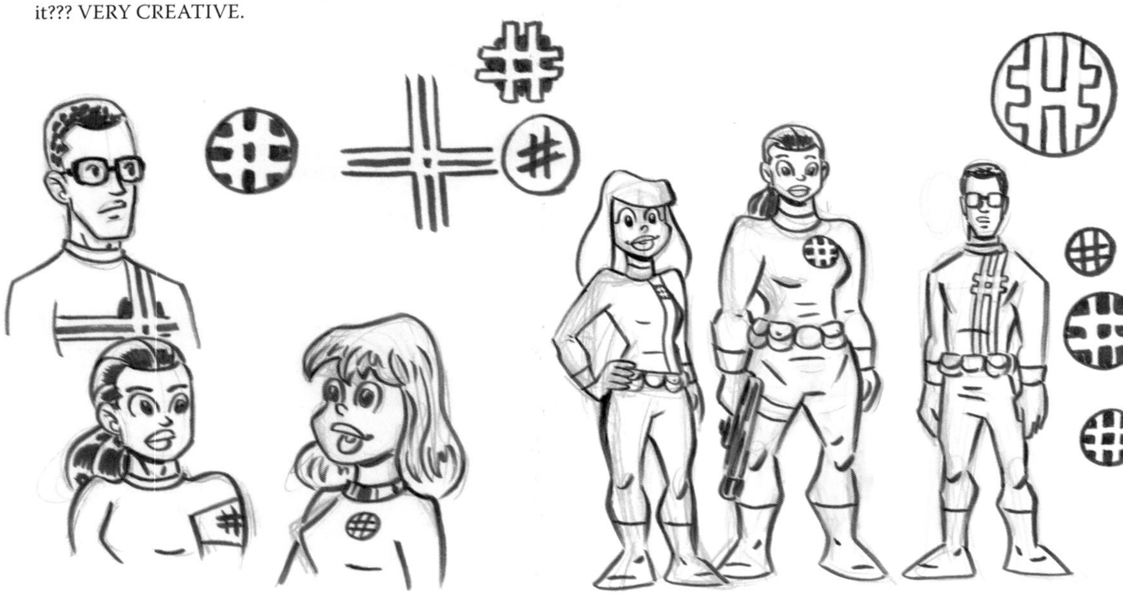

Alternate costume designs and color treatments...

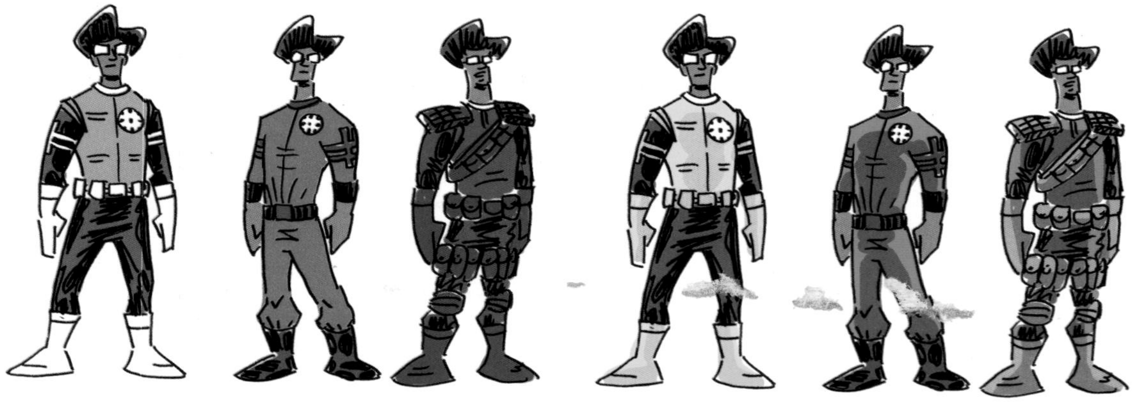

...and the final blue and purple uniforms. Hashtag: Design!

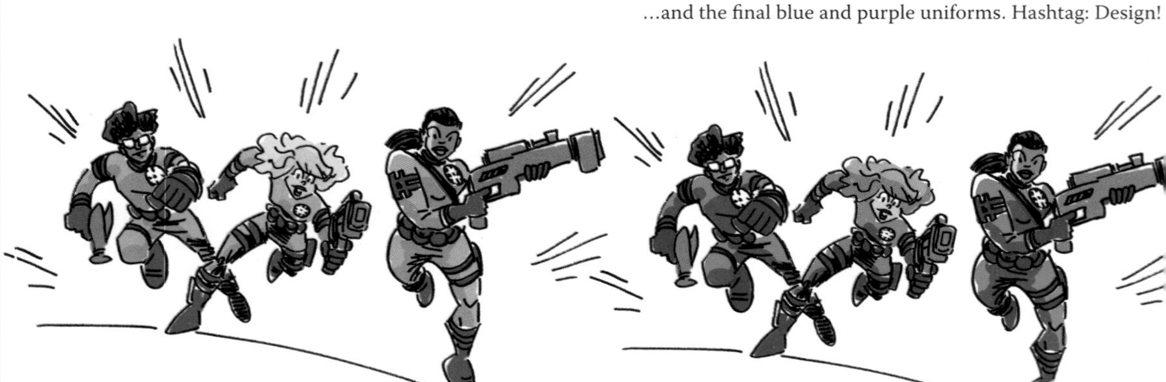